Praise for the Dragos Primeri Series

"This dazzling series starter seizes attention from the start, balancing bravura worldbuilding with compelling characters, urgent storytelling, and a welcome sense of clarity… rewards and upends reader expectations."
—*Publisher's Weekly's BookLife*, Editor's Pick

"Wright presents a setting that is complex and intricate, with layers of worldbuilding details that coalesce into a fictional civilization that's exciting to discover. An engaging beginning to a promising fantasy series.
—*Kirkus Reviews*

"[Readers] looking for titles that open with a bang of psychological and political allure will find that few can equal the force of *Season of the Dragon*."
—*Midwest Book Review*, D. Donovan, Senior Reviewer

"There are some books you wish you could read forever. *Season of the Dragon* is one of them. The author writes with a deft hand, ensnaring us in the mystery that is our great heroine."
—*Independent Book Review*, Alexandria Ducksworth

"If you're looking to get lost in a staggering world filled with magic, folklore, drama, and dragons, *Season of the Dragon* is a perfect escape. [Readers] are welcomed to a visionary new world… Prepare for a fantastical journey of grand proportions helmed by an impressive, female-dominated cast."
—*Indies Today*, Nicky Flowers

"Epic in scale and packed to the brim with action, drama, and romance, *Season of the Dragon* is just the fantasy saga you have all been waiting for."
—*Readers' Favorite*, Pikasho Deka

"With dragons, magical creatures, magic, corrupt kingdoms, and forbidden love, Wright has created an enthralling world."
—**Literary Titan**

"*Season of the Dragon* is a masterpiece in fantasy. Very highly recommended."
—*Readers' Favorite*, Asher Syed

"[A] masterclass in worldbuilding and a triumph for dragon lovers… [T]he story dragon lovers have been waiting for."
—Robyn Dabney, author of *The Ascenditure*

"*Season of the Dragon* is a beautifully woven coming-of-age hero's journey, complete with good and bad players, a bit of romance, and an ending that won't have you cursing over a cliffhanger."
—*Readers' Favorite*, Jamie Michele

•Chosen by BookShop.org and Ingram as a Top 10 Indie Epic Fantasy

•*Season of the Dragon*, Silver Medal in 2023 Readers' Favorite Awards

By Natalie Wright

Dragos Primeri Series

Season of the Dragon (#1)
The Saga of Ilkay & Collected Stories (#1.5)
The Spring Dragon (#2)

H.A.L.F. Series

The Deep Beneath (#1)
The Makers (#2)
ORIGINS (#3)

The Akasha Chronicles (Young Adult)

Emily's House (#1)
Emily's Trial (#2)
Emily's Heart (#3)

Stories Appearing in Anthologies

"Truth Juggler: A Farce," in *Shapers of Worlds*, vol. V

"Sunshine Acres," in *25 Servings of SOOP*, vol. ii

THE SPRING DRAGON

Book Two Of Dragos Primeri

NATALIE WRIGHT

MENARIS
BOOKS

TUCSON

For FF & JRF

CONTENTS

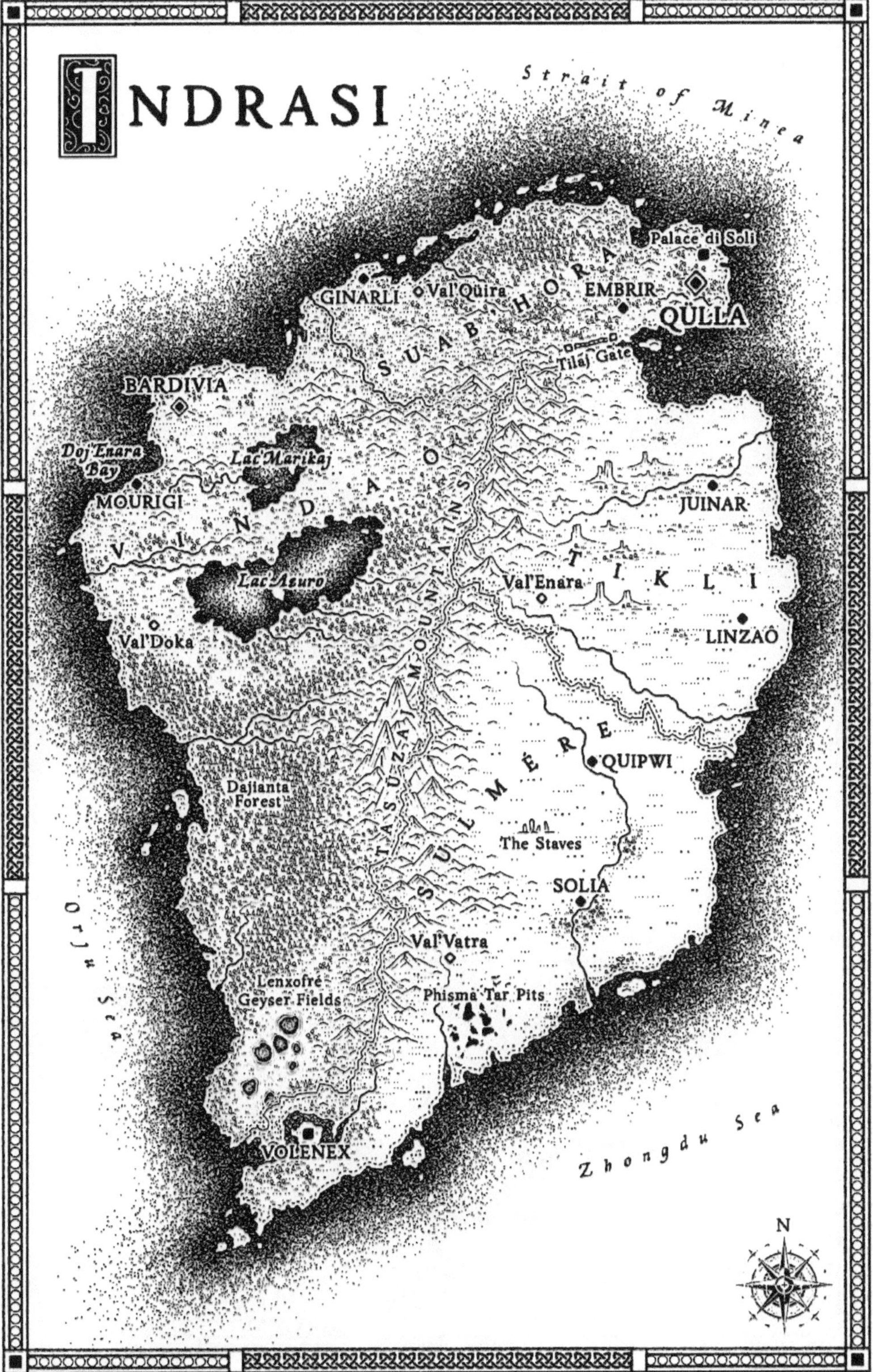
INDRASI
Strait of Minea
Palace di Soli
GINARLI
Val'Quira
SUABHORA
EMBRIR
QULLA
Tilaj Gate
BARDIVIA
Doj'Enara Bay
Lac Marikaj
VINDAO
MOURIGI
JUINAR
TIKLI
Lac'Asuro
Val'Enara
Val'Doka
LINZAO
TASUZAI MOUNTAINS
SUILMÉRE
QUIPWI
Dajianta Forest
Orju Sea
The Staves
SOLIA
Val'Vatra
Lenxofré Geyser Fields
Phisma Tar Pits
VOLENEX
Zhongdu Sea
N

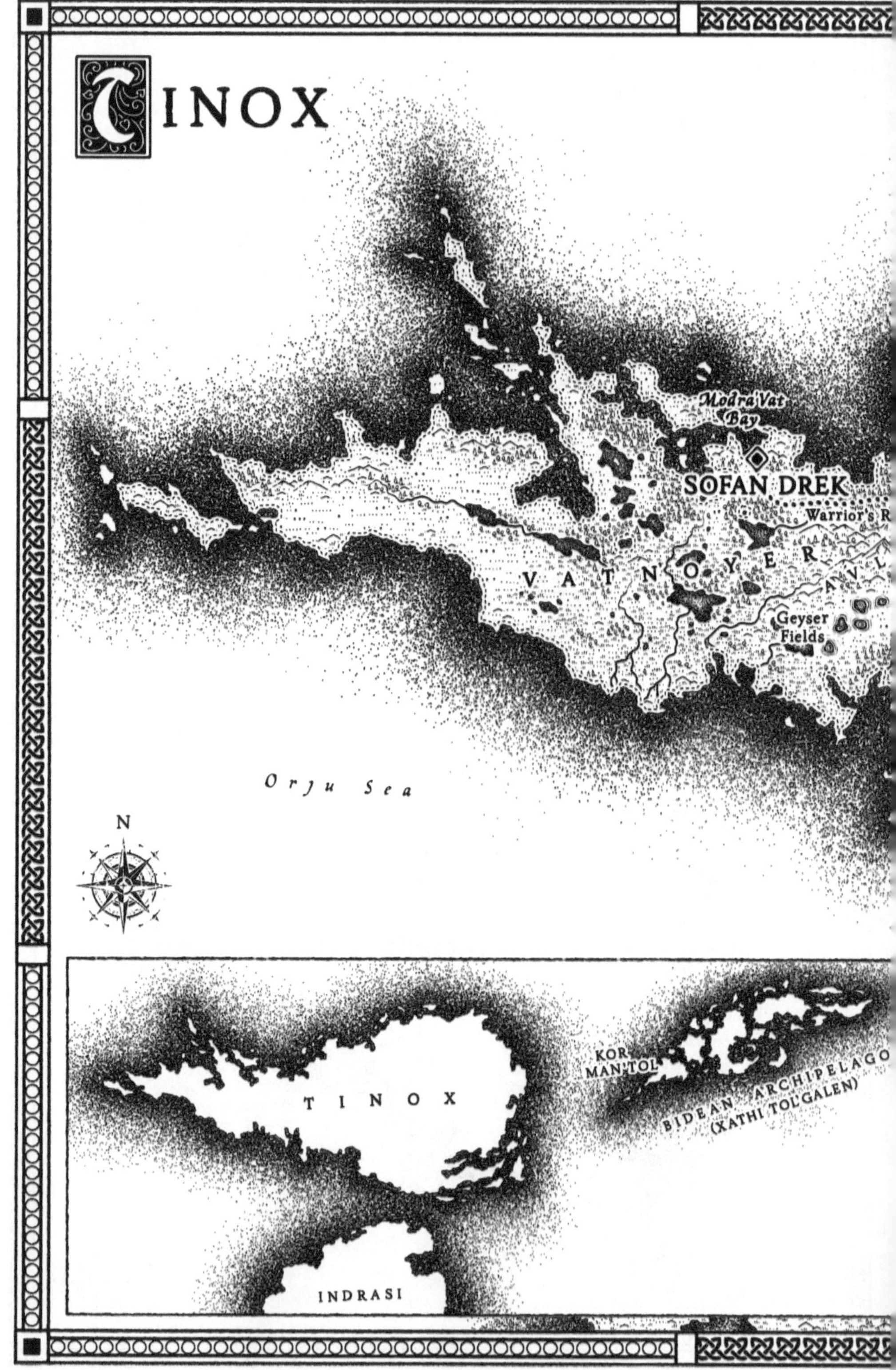
TINOX
Modra Vat Bay
SOFAN DREK
Warrior's R
VATNOYER
AVL
Geyser Fields
Orju Sea
N
TINOX
KOR MAN'TOL
BIDEAN ARCHIPELAGO
(XATHI TOL'GALEN)
INDRASI

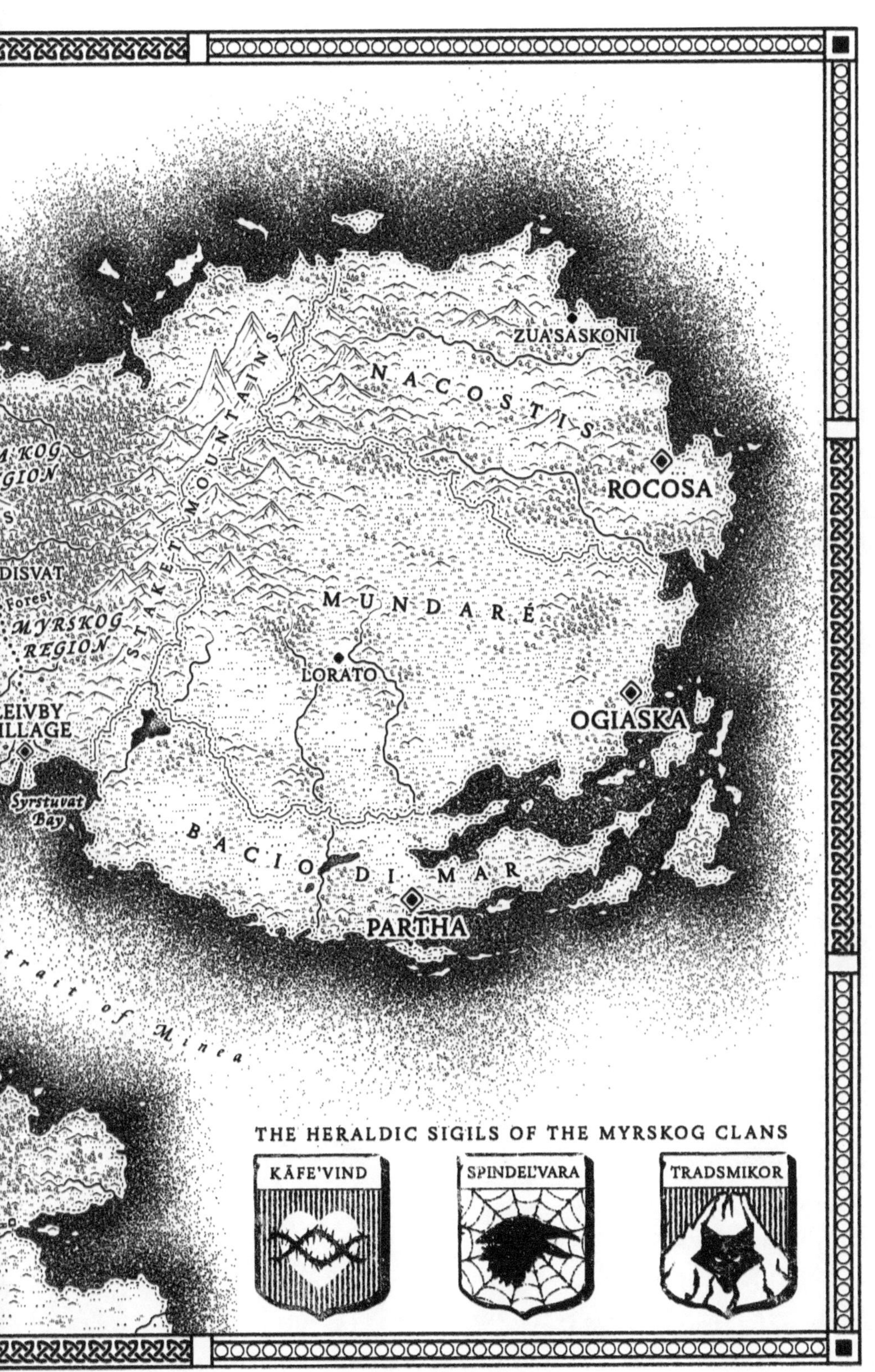

ZUA'SASKONI
NACOSTIS
ROCOSA
KOG
GION
DISVAT
Forest
MYRSKOG
REGION
MUNDARÉ
LORATO
LEIVBY
VILLAGE
OGIASKA
Syrstuvat
Bay
STAKET MOUNTAINS
BACIO DI MAR
PARTHA
Strait of Minca
THE HERALDIC SIGILS OF THE MYRSKOG CLANS
KÄFE'VIND
SPINDEL'VARA
TRADSMIKOR

Dramatis Personae

Humans

Druvna's Pod

Aldewin	Imbica	Shel
Dionus ("Dio)	Nivi	

Sicara's Bane

Captain Ontrosa	Dreni	Linjeera

Kafe'vind Clan

Finn	Ivriga	Jesper
Nalija	Omma	Yngvari

Spindel'vara Clan

Brynjold	Jorfala	Ketla
Thrud		

Tradsmikor Clan

Jikurai	Løpeni

Dragons

Aurixia ("Rixi")	Côzhili	Docar
Ishna	Liejala	Loxen
Moxprai	Naja	Niezhan
Owaanir	Veridia	Vingaska
Zedris		

DRAGON FACTIONS

Cantiva (Spring Dragon)   Iska'van (Winter Dragon)
Ignati (Summer Dragon)   Nao (Autumn Dragon)

GODS & SPIRITS

Fréjoya   Fros'vinspri   Hiyadi
Niyadi   Mara   Sicara
Skogi

PROMINENT CLANS OF THE VATNOYER

Kāfe'vind   Tradsmikor
Spindel'vara   Veidmar

Part I

Skogi's Song

On the undulating waves of Mara's sea,
    We swim.
Over the tender shoots of Skogi's green,
    We stroll.
Under the welcoming canopy of our forest home,
    We dance.

Hush…
Listen.

The yindril's lament joins the cricket's lullaby.
Skogi's song soothes us—
    We sleep.
Beneath sun-warmed skies, two-by-two.
    We march.

Ever onward until we tire,
The Green hails us home.

Fear not the forest's dark, dear ones.
    Skogi's roots await us all.

—Anonymous. A Kāfe'vind Clan song, Myrskog Region, Vatnoyer Province. Era unknown.

CHAPTER 1

ALDEWIN

Aldewin hadn't slit a throat in two days. A record for him, at least since he left Volenex. Since Ishna, the Winter Dragon, erupted from Quen's body. *A sight I cannot unsee*, Aldewin thought.

Ishna had dumped Aldewin and Nivi at the edge of the Damianta Forest. Bound in Vay'Nada for over a thousand years, Ishna couldn't have known feral Nixan shapeshifters had overridden the Damianta. Or that by dropping them where she did, they'd have to survive a gauntlet of wild beasts before making their way toward Bardivia.

Once out of the Damianta, they'd contended with rural folks living at the forest's edge. After witnessing newly reborn dragons circling above, people were on edge and wary of strangers, especially ones traveling with giant tigers. Having sworn to protect the oversized cat, several encounters turned bloody. *I vowed to myself not to kill anymore, yet since leaving Val'Enara, my blade has been bloody.*

Just over a week ago, Aldewin and Nivi arrived exhausted in Mourigi. A dirty backwater coastal town just south of Bardivia, Mourigi smelled of rotten fish, piss, and shattered dreams.

Aldewin had planned to stay only long enough to freshen before facing Rhoji with news about Quen. But a few days had turned into a week. Aldewin found himself again on a barstool at the Purple Peacock Inn, Nivi at his feet. His vow to care for Nivi had supplanted his prior vows, first, to Fen Menir, the house of spies and assassins in Partha. Second, to Kine, Archon of Val'Enara Pillar. *I am nothing without an oath to live for.*

Searching the nearly empty purse at his waist, Aldewin plucked out his last silver Kovar. *Blood money.* He plunked the silver onto the smooth olive-wood counter. The Kovar was the last of the generous allowance Archon Kine had given him to fund his search and retrieval mission—the hunt for the Doj'Anira—the twice blessed. Aldewin had found her, all right. And had fallen in love with her.

For months, Aldewin relived in his mind every moment he'd spent with Quen, as if by remembering, he could bring her back. But as weeks ticked by, memories of their time together became like a dream. *Is it truly love? Or was—am I—ensnared by an intoxicating spell?* Making love with a woman who carried two souls—one a dragon, no less—had been a heady and overwhelming experience. *But by the gods, I cannot stop thinking about her and what could have been.*

Aldewin breathed deeply and pushed thoughts of her away. *Thinking of her brings only pain.* The dragon subsumed Quen and took her from him. *Best to put my time with her behind me.* He flipped the silver coin between his fingers. *If only I could drink away the longing.*

"Treaga," Aldewin called. Once he had the innkeeper's attention, he shoved the Kovar across the bar. "This should be enough to get pished. Add a bowl of whatever Enrio cooked today and a bowl for my friend here." Aldewin pointed down at Nivi.

Nivi glanced up from licking his paw then returned to washing himself.

Treaga's brow furrowed, and he glared at the silver coin. "Damn your silver to Vay'Nada. Take your sorry ass and the fur bag and get yerself out of this shite town while you still got life left in ya. 'Sides, that Kovar ain't 'nough to compensate me for the bloody mess you're likely to make." Treaga grumbled, "Just finished cleaning up the blood spilled from the last time ya was here." As if spying bloody evidence of Aldewin's last altercation to protect Nivi, Treaga glared at Aldewin and wiped the counter.

Aldewin pressed the coin further across the bar. "I'm sorry 'bout the trouble I caused when last I supped here." He flashed a sincere smile. "How can you be cross with a man who always pays his bill and can drink more ale than these Mourigi backwater wine sippers?"

Treaga's expression softened, and he chortled. The barkeep took Aldewin's silver. He grabbed an almost-clean ceramic mug from under the bar and filled it with foamy, northern-style honey ale.

Aldewin downed half a mug of the cold brew and wiped foam from his mustache. Treaga ladled mutton stew into a bowl, and its smell gladdened Aldewin. It was served with crusty brown bread with a side of Vindaô olive oil to dip in. Treaga's husband made the finest food Aldewin had tasted in Mourigi.

Treaga ladled another bowl and shoved it across the counter. "For the bag-o-fur at your feet." He refilled Aldewin's mug. "Whatever pain you're in, lad, you no'a can drink it away."

"Might be true, Treaga. But I'm no quitter," Aldewin said. He stopped shoveling in the food long enough to grace Nivi with a bowl. "Give my compliments to Enrio."

Treaga filled another customer's wine cup, gathered coins from the bar left by a patron, swished a dirty cup in even dirtier dishwater, and then wiped the cup dry for the next person. "Enrio is a fine cook, but that mutton slop ain't Bardivia's finest. What ya been eatin', Northman?"

Aldewin reflected on months of eating what he and Nivi could hunt or forage while avoiding being hunted by the Nixan who roamed the Damianta Forest. He said, "Ah, you know. Greasy fare over at the Olive Branch and sewer sludge at the Vine Master Inn."

A smile on his face now, Treaga stood taller and sauntered back toward Aldewin. "Look, I appreciate your coin and your compliments. But why is a young buck like you spending your last coin getting drunk at old Treaga's? Take your smelly cat and get yourself to Bardivia. The Dynasty is putting its boot on Bardivia's neck, and the merchant guild ain't havin' it. There's lots of merc work for a muscular guy like you who's handy with a blade."

Since finding his way to Mourigi just over a week ago, Aldewin had heard similar news. Bardivia was his intended destination. He had a promise to fulfill there.

Aldewin touched Quen's amber pendant through his shirt. *"If you survive, take this to Rhoji for me,"* she'd said. Aldewin sighed. He knew he'd eventually have to face Rhoji and tell him what happened after Aldewin and Quen parted ways with the rest of the pod. *I haven't yet summoned the courage to put on Rhoji the hurt I feel so keenly.* Aldewin convinced himself that Rhoji was better off not knowing, at least for a while. *Rhoji can imagine her living peacefully at Val'Enara, training in the Way of Water.*

Two men entered the Purple Peacock, speaking too loudly to be sober. *Already drunk and likely to egg on a fight before the night is done.* Aldewin unhooked his belt scabbard and pulled out his Vandu blade. The black onyx-hilted moss-green blade glinted in the candlelight as Aldewin placed it on the bar. For anyone worldly enough, putting a green-bladed Vandu dagger on the counter warned that the person carrying it was not to be messed with.

In a hushed tone, Treaga said, "No violence tonight, Northman. Don't let men with shite for brains rile you, lad."

"I have no intention of spilling blood tonight." Aldewin sipped his ale and smiled up at Treaga. "But I've taken a vow to protect this tiger. As you know from the last time I supped here, it is a promise I'll defend with my life."

Treaga sighed. "For the love of Lumine's teats, man, ignore idle threats of drunk men and stay your blade." As if beset with a flash of genius, Treaga said, "You make it through the night killing no one, and I'll throw in a room with a comfy mattress and fresh straw for your tiger friend. Better yet, leave Mourigi in the morn, and I'll pack a lunch for you to fuel your trek to Bardivia."

Aldewin drained his mug as the two drunk men approached the bar. "You're a generous man, Treaga. And too good a fella for Mourigi."

Treaga dismissed Aldewin's compliment with a wave of his hand. He refilled Aldewin's mug and pulled two wine cups for the newcomers.

"No'a wine for us, you fop." The man slurred his words. "Zhishni water. And leave the bottle." He pulled three dars from a pocket sewn into the waist of his dusty pants.

Treaga glared at him. "You're already quite spirited. Wouldn't you prefer ale? Zhishni spirits will tear a hole in your guts."

The man slammed his meaty fist on the bar. "I'm not payin' ya to nurse me, man. Now grab a bottle of Zhishni water before I take my dars next door."

Having admonished Aldewin about not letting dunderheads get the best of him, Treaga ignored the man's insults. He pulled a clay jar from behind the bar and placed two small cups before the men. "Three dars will cover the bottle. Two more if ya wantin' a meal."

Aldewin choked on the malodorous stink coming from the men. They smelled of rotten fish, briny sea, piss, and body odor. *The stench of trouble.*

Habit pulled his fingers to the Vandu blade. Aldewin traced the symbol inscribed on the metal. He could swear the metal sang as he touched it. *A song only I can hear*, he thought.

The grooves added beauty to the blade and served the dark purpose of being a reservoir for lethal poisons.

The assassin's weapon brought memories of his former life. It was a time that seemed both like it had happened yesterday and as if someone else had lived it. A life in which he served not Archon Kine but Sicara, goddess of death and patron of Fen Menir, the house of spies and assassins serving the Mājas in Partha.

He'd kept the blade hidden from Druvna and the pod. Experienced warriors and battle mages who'd studied at a Pillar would know the blade's significance. Kine's mission had required him to protect his true identity, so he'd kept the Vandu out of sight.

Touching the cool blade, he heard Sicara whisper lovingly in his ear. *All blood flows to Nixaya, the great river that feeds the Well of Souls. Bring them to me, Brother. Show them the comforting arms of the Dread Sister so they will know the loving embrace of Night Everlasting.*

Aldewin took his fingers from the knife and finished his stew. *Think not on Sicara.* He'd heard the phrase and repeated it so often it had become law. The words were Fen Menir's divine scripture. Spoken by its god and intended to quell the shame, guilt, and fear a person should naturally feel from snuffing out a person's candle. *Sicara is an illusion. These whispers are not from a goddess but manipulations by the masters of Fen Menir,* he thought.

The smelly man next to him harrumphed and shifted on his stool. "Your damned cat's in the way, arseling." The man kicked at Nivi and nearly fell off his stool.

Nivi rose and flashed his shredding teeth before the man had righted himself.

His voice raised, Treaga said, "Northman, don't let the beast rip the man apart. Not in here, anyway. I let the cat stay 'cause you a good payin' customer. But I got limits, I do."

The newcomer downed the distilled zhishni in one gulp. His courage fortified, he said in a mocking tone, "You heard him. Don't let your kitty bite me."

A woman's voice called out over the din of the inn's crowded barroom. "I would not do that if I were you."

Both Aldewin and the drunk man turned toward the newcomer.

Two women and a man approached the bar. The diminutive woman who'd given the warning likely came no higher than Aldewin's chest. A pale yellow linen kerchief covered her short brown hair. She wore a simple green linen tunic and yellow apron to match her hair covering. The clothing was customary for vignoisiers—vine workers—in the Vin Gagne grape-growing region surrounding Bardivia and the lower Vindaô Province.

Aldewin squinted and stared at her through drink-bleary eyes. *She looks familiar.*

Before he could respond, the man on the stool beside him said, "Who ya talkin' to, woman?" He poured another shot of the zhishni liquor. "We come here to get away from bosses with their hand up our arse, moving us like puppets." He downed the firewater in one gulp. The man's eyes were shot through with red, his cheeks flushed. Drink had quelled the man's inhibitions, and he was more than just drunk. He was dangerous.

The second woman, considerably younger, her head covered by a cowl, said, "She was talkin' to you, shit stain."

Aldewin sighed and shook his head. *Why did she have to egg him on?* What would happen next felt inevitable. Years of Fen Menir training had honed within him an instinct that made his hand reach for his Vandu blade.

After hearing the young woman's insult, the drunk man rose on wobbly legs. "What the—you two 'ladies' thinkin' ya know what's best for everybody? Then why don't ya know not to come into a man's bar a tellin' him what to do?" He wiped spittle from his lip and swayed as he said, "Now get the hell out before I show ya out."

The young man accompanying the two women pressed forward, perhaps to protect them. *I don't think these women need protecting*, Aldewin thought.

Aldewin grasped his Vandu blade. His voice was low but sure as he said, "Apologize to the ladies, sit your arse down, and shut your trap 'cept to drink that bottle of pisswater you asked for."

The drunk man laughed. "And you, drunk-ass fool, gonna teach me a lesson?"

The older woman again admonished, "I wouldn't—"

Aldewin interrupted her. "I may be a fool. I grant you that. But I've been drinking since I was seven and killing men nearly as long. I can do both at the same time."

The man hooted and laughed so hard that spittle formed in the corners of his mouth. He rolled up his sleeves, revealing dirt-encrusted arms rippled with wiry muscles. "I ain't had a proper fight in a week. Time to teach this dandy Northman with big talk a lesson 'bout how we real men do things in Mourigi."

Aldewin neither rose from his seat nor looked in the drunk man's direction. His eyes never leaving his half-empty mug, he thrust the dagger up into the man's neck, twisted the blade, and gave it a downward stroke as he pulled the knife out. Now covered in blood, the dagger was back on the bar before the drunk man, his neck now gushing warm crimson blood, fell to the floor.

"I warned him," the older woman said. "You heard me, right?" She tsked. "Well, some people have curds for brains, and there's no help for it."

Treaga groaned and called for help with the body. "A dar each for help movin' this shite-eater's corpse from the bar."

The man who'd entered with the now-dead rabble rouser held out his hand for a dar from the barkeep, and another soon came forward to collect drinking money to help rid the bar of the waste.

Pink-tinged foam bubbled at the dead man's mouth. His eyes were wide with surprise. Poison from the Vandu blade ensured he wouldn't survive the encounter. The two men removed anything of value from the corpse as they dragged him from the bar.

The stout older woman sat on the stool next to Aldewin. Nivi nuzzled her shoulder.

Treaga held out his hand to collect whatever Aldewin had left to pay for the mess he'd made. Again.

Aldewin was about to put his last dar into Treaga's hand, but the older woman put silver into the innkeeper's open palm.

"This should cover the mageling's mess." She smoothed her skirts. "And three cups of wine, Ser."

Aldewin rubbed his drink-weary eyes and stared at the three. "Imbica?"

The younger woman stepped up next to Imbica and threw back her cowl. "And Shel." She nodded her head at the young man. "And a new member of our pod. Meet Dionus, but we call him Dio."

The dark-haired man named Dio gave Aldewin a single nod.

"Was that shit stain worth a heart scar?" Shel asked.

Aldewin thought, *My heart is so scarred it barely counts as a heart anymore.* He sighed and gave a wry laugh. "At the risk of repeating the words of the recently deceased, I did no'a come here to have a woman scold me for escapin' my troubles in a cup."

Imbica removed the kerchief and shook out her recently shorn hair. Though still stocky, she'd slimmed down since the last time Aldewin had seen her, and he hadn't recognized her with her short hair. Imbica sipped her wine while Shel and Dio also settled at the bar. Nivi nuzzled into Imbica, clearly enjoying her attention. *He's apparently a ladies' man*, Aldewin thought.

"We did not risk the gauntlet of Kovathas between Bardivia and this rancid armpit of a town just to scold you," Imbica said.

"Good, 'cause I don't fancy a scolding."

"From the look—and smell—of you, it seems you've been punishing yourself plenty," Imbica said.

Shel pinched her nostrils and made a face like she'd smelled someone's stale fart. "For the love of the Three, when did you last bathe?"

"You came all this way to tell me I stink? Mission accomplished. Been nice seeing you." Aldewin took a long draw of his ale. When the three made no move to leave, he added, "If you came to hurl insults or state the obvious, you can go. Before my blade hand twitches again."

Imbica laughed. "You may be Fen Menir, mageling, but it will take more than an assassin's threat to push me from my task. I would love to leave you to your self-flagellation for murders and misdeeds, but the pod needs you. *Rhoji* needs you."

Before Aldewin could inquire what Imbica meant, Shel asked, "Fen Menir? Assassin?"

"How did you know?" Aldewin asked.

Imbica sipped her wine and nodded at Aldewin's bloody blade. "Anyone who studied at Val'Vatra knows how to recognize the blade of a Fen Menir master of the Vandu arts. And understand that the green blade on a table is a warning, not an invitation. Unfortunately, the now-deceased former tenant of this stool did not receive such training."

Shel's brows furrowed. "Fen Menir?" She shook her head. "Months with this woman, yet I rarely know what the shite she's talking about."

Dio chortled and sipped his wine, his dark-brown eyes catching Aldewin's light-blue-grey ones.

Imbica said, "Our friend here trained as an assassin and spy at one of the great Mājas in Partha."

Shel's voice was a whisper. "Assassin?"

"And a skilled one to be honored with a Vandu dagger. Fen Menir only grants such a blade to people who survive the trials."

Aldewin looked away from Dio, uncomfortable with the man's searching gaze. He neither agreed with nor denied Imbica's claims. Remaining silent was a trait literally beaten into him at Fen Menir. *Maybe I've been too silent for too long. Could explain why my only company for the last six months has been a tiger who cannot speak.*

Imbica pulled a dusty linen towel from her waist belt and handed it to Aldewin. "It's caked with road dust, but it will have to do for now."

Aldewin took the cloth and wiped the dead man's blood from the green blade. "Why are you here, Imbica?"

"To find answers."

"I'm fresh out of those."

Shel cut in. "Did Val'Enara accept Quen?" She bit her lower lip. "Or did you…?" Shel eyed the dagger.

Aghast at the insinuation, Aldewin's voice rose. "Kill her? Gods, no." Hot tears stung his eyes. *I cannot speak of it. Not here. Not now*, Aldewin thought.

Imbica resumed the questioning. "Is she at Val'Enara?"

Aldewin shook his head.

The women's faces fell. Shel asked, "Then—"

Aldewin held up a hand. "Not here." He glanced behind. "Too many ears. Some, no doubt, belong to rats that will scurry to trade gossip for coin." In truth, Aldewin didn't know if the Dynasty had spies in Mourigi, but he'd once been a little "rat." Assuming the Dynasty's politics and spy networks worked similarly to Partha's Mājas, it felt right to be cautious.

"Excellent thinking—protecting information, I mean," Dio said.

"Come, then, mageling. Let us leave this place. We have a more discreet space for you to divulge what you know of our friend," Imbica said.

Aldewin shook his head. "I don't have the strength of character to tell that tale more than once. It's for Rhoji's ears. You will learn of the events if he allows others present at the telling."

Silent tears made tracks down Shel's road-dusted face. "No," she whispered.

Seeing her tears, Aldewin's firm gaze softened. He hadn't meant to imply the worst and regretted saying anything.

He coughed lightly and pushed his mug across the bar and away from him. *I've drowned my sorrows long enough. Time to face the morrow, no matter what it brings.* "We should rest the night, and then I will accompany you to Bardivia. Rhoji needs to hear what happened after we parted ways."

"Good to know you're ready to leave the stench of Mourigi behind you, but you cannot saunter into Bardivia right now," Imbica said.

Sobered by the surprising news, Aldewin sat up and gave Imbica his full attention. "Why not?"

"Where have you been?" Shel asked.

"You know nothing of what's happening in Bardivia?" Dio asked.

Been? He'd been fighting off shrieking Nixan bird women in the Damianta Forest. He and Nivi braved the wilding people who live in the borderlands between the forest haunted by Nixan and the civilized wine country of the Vin Gagnon region.

A story to tell another day, he thought. "I have kept to myself, I suppose. Tell me why we cannot go to Bardivia. And what of Rhoji? Is he well?"

"He is well," Dio said. "Safe with Eira, Mishny, and two merc guards when we left them."

Aldewin didn't care for how Dio spoke as though he'd been a brother to the pod for years rather than months. *You were a brother to them for only a few months*, he thought. *And mostly kept to yourself because of your need for secrecy.* Yet

Aldewin's affection for the pod made his time with them seem longer.

Shel pulled a crinkled, coarse paper from an inner pocket in her woolen cloak. She spread the page on the counter.

Printed across the top were the words: WANTED—ALIVE! Below, two faces stared up at him. On the left, drawn in ink, was a woman with long hair. It didn't resemble Quen in the slightest, except the artist inked one eye in blue and the other yellow.

The words below the artist's rendition of Quen were: "Doj'Anira, last seen in Qülla. Wanted by the Kovan Dynasty for high crimes. Battle Mage. Orrokan trained. No reward unless captured alive."

So, the Exalted figured out who Quen was after all. I wonder how? It no longer mattered, though. *If you search for all eternity, you'll never find her.* Though it pained him to think about Quen's demise, it brought a warped satisfaction, knowing that at least the Dynasty couldn't use her to their ends.

Aldewin turned his attention to the other illustration. This drawing depicted a man with shoulder-length wavy hair, a clean-shaven face, a square jaw, and light eyes.

Looking over his shoulder, Dio said, "It's a fair likeness of you. Remarkable what artists can do."

Aldewin ignored him and stared at the Dynasty mandate printed below the illustration of him. "Wanted for high crimes against the Dynasty."

Since when did saving a person from enslavement count as a "high" crime?

The following line made him blanch. "WARNING! Fen Menir trained. Use extreme caution. No reward unless captured alive."

How could the Dynasty possibly know I am Fen Menir trained? No one knew this. The only person he'd left Partha with was—dead. *By my hand.* And since arriving in Indrasi five years ago, he'd told only one person. *Archon Kine.*

But it makes no sense for Kine to reveal I was a Fen Menir assassin. Even before Xa'Vatra ascended to Exalted, Val'Enara Pillar clashed with the Kovans. In Aldewin's presence, Archon Kine revealed her doubt in Xa'Vatra's leadership.

"The Dynasty hung these posters all over Bardivia. The moment you enter the gates, Kovatha will nab you. And if they somehow miss their opportunity, someone will rat you out for the promise of a life of leisure." Imbica pointed to the listed bounties.

The bounty on Aldewin's head? Fifty silver Kovars. Though that was a large sum, the price on Quen's head was enough to make him choke. "One hundred *gold* Kovars?" *Xa'Vatra* really *wants Quen in her grasp. By the gods, that's enough to buy one's way into a Māja.*

A sick feeling roiled in his gut, threatening to make the mutton stew come back up. Aldewin glanced over his shoulder at the inebriated sailors—Engarda, merchant, and Merladro alike—on shore leave. "Why have none of this lot turned me in?"

Shel gathered the page. She quickly folded it and put it back in her pocket. "Probably because these went up in Bardivia yesterday, and we did our best to take them all down." She gave Aldewin a wink.

Aldewin sighed with relief. "Thank you, Shel. That was a very kind thing to do for me. And for Quen."

Shel brightened at the mention of Quen's name, taking the hint that Quen still lived. She smiled and said, "Thank

Dio. It was his idea. 'Sides. We're Druvna's pod. It's what he would want us to do." Shel sniffled. "To look out for each other."

Imbica, too, looked misty-eyed.

Aldewin nodded. "It is indeed." He lifted his mug. "To Druvna, the crusty old bastard."

Imbica and Shel hoisted their cups and said, "To Druvna!"

Dio toasted too, though he looked confused. They all drank and honored Druvna with a moment of silence.

After a few moments, Aldewin asked, "What now? I cannot go to Qülla or Bardivia. I just came from the southern route, and I don't recommend it. That leaves—"

"The Orju Sea," Imbica said.

Aldewin wiped his brow. "I was afraid you were going to say that."

"As soon as we saw these posters, Dio suggested a plan to get you and Quen away from Indrasi. At least for a while," Shel said. Her eyes cast downward. "We all hoped Quen was with you."

He wanted to comfort Shel. To let her know that all was well. *That would be a lie. I cannot give her false hope, nor can I give her the information she craves. Not here.*

"Believe me. I wish Quen was with me." The ale had blunted his ability to squash his emotions. His throat tightened, and tears welled. *One of the first rules of being Fen Menir: "Imbibe neither of the vine nor the still, for it clouds the judgment and makes one ill."* Aldewin drained his cup once more. *I no longer follow your divine laws, Sicara.*

Imbica drank the last of her wine and rose from her stool. "Come, Aldewin. We secured passage on a ship of dubious origin, but it's headed out of Bardivia. Captain

Ontrosa asked no questions and booked us for the journey, but he won't hold in the harbor long. We must make haste. We'll have plenty of time to tell our respective tales on the voyage to your homeland."

The woman couldn't have said anything to put more misgiving into him if she'd tried. Aldewin's palms sweated profusely, and his vision grew dark at the edges.

"What's wrong, Aldewin? You look like you've seen a ghost?" Shel said. She reached across the bar and put a cool hand on his.

A ghost. *Shel knows not how close she has come to naming the truth.* Without thinking, Aldewin grabbed the dusty linen he'd used to clean his blade and wiped his brow. He pulled the waterskin from his waist and drew a drink.

"Come now. You aren't afraid of sailing, are you?" Dio asked.

Aldewin swallowed hard. "Yes, actually." He wiped his brow again. "My boat to Indrasi crashed, you see. And I nearly drowned." It was the truth. At least a partial truth. *I have more to fear than rough seas, but I don't trust our new pod member with the complete story.*

Dio didn't take his eyes off Aldewin. "That's a terrible bit of luck. And were you the only one to survive?"

Imbica tapped her foot impatiently. "And that, Dio, is the sort of story that will make long days at sea more bearable. Now, I need the towering mageling and the rest of you lot to haul ass and get on that boat." She rolled up her sleeves and looked ready to wind her hands and cast a spell.

Not wanting to suffer Imbica's mind-altering spell and the headache and brain fog that followed, Aldewin pushed his cup away and rose. Nivi leaped to his feet as well.

"I will come with you. Away from here, anyway. But you need to fill me in on some things before I venture where I said I'd never return. First—why should we go to Partha, of all places?"

"Oh, we're not going to Partha," Imbica said.

The lesser feeling of mere dread replaced outright terror. Aldewin raised an eyebrow. "I thought you said our destination is my homeland."

"To the Vatnoyer Province. Your people *are* originally from the Vatnoyer, no?" Dio asked.

Do I sense a smugness in his tone? "My father was of the Vatnoyer's Fyrstua people, but I was born and raised in Partha."

Shel donned her hood and said, "Look, I don't know shite about Fir—Fur—"

"Like this. Fear–stew–ah. Fyrstua," Dio said calmly.

Shel rolled her eyes and waved a hand in the air. "Suda, who cares? Point is, Aldewin, you need to disappear. And we must learn why the Dynasty is sending a small army to the Vatnoyer."

She had his attention. "Why would Xa'Vatra do that?" Aldewin asked. "The Fyrstua raid each other, but they care little about political battles between Qülla, Partha, and Bardivia."

"That is correct," Imbica said. "But the Bardivian Merchant Guild spy network reports Xa'Vatra hunts for something the Dynasty calls the Heart of Menaris."

Aldewin scratched his scruffy beard. "Heart of Menaris? Never heard of it."

"You haven't?" Dio asked. "Since your people are Fyrstua, I figured you'd know what it is." He took a sip of wine and regarded Aldewin. "And where it is."

I don't like the way he looks at me. Aldewin shook his head. "I don't know what you're referring to. Menaris—the word for magic. The 'Heart of Magic'? Do you know anything more about this, Imbica?"

Imbica smoothed her hair. "I regret I do not. It was not mentioned in our histories or other teachings at Val'Enara or Val'Vatra."

"It could be a code word for something," Shel added.

"Possibly," Imbica said. "Whatever the nature of this Heart of Menaris, chances are good that Xa'Vatra won't just put it on display in her menagerie like other magical creatures or plants she has plundered from the Vatnoyer. With dragons hunting in the Bídean Archipelago off Tinox's eastern coast—too close for comfort—whatever Xa'Vatra seeks, she likely plans to use as a weapon."

Dragons spotted. Use as a weapon. The meaning behind Imbica's words cleared the inebriation from Aldewin's mind. *Does Xa'Vatra hunt for Ishna?* His heart raced at the ramifications. He whispered, "Quen."

"What was that?" Dio asked.

Aldewin ignored Dio's question. "Sounds like I have little choice but to sail for northern lands. But my unfinished business in Bardivia remains." His hand at his chest, the amber under his shirt reminded him. "A promise I made and intend to keep. I still must speak to Rhoji."

"We have no time for that," Dio said. His voice went pitchy. "You saw the poster. You're a wanted man. If you set foot in Bardivia, you'll end up in a Qülla dungeon."

Imbica narrowed her eyes at Dio then turned her attention back to Aldewin. "Dio speaks true, yet I agree Rhoji must hear the tale you have to tell about Quen. I don't know how we'll get your message to Rhoji, but when the quest is worthy, the gods provide."

Aldewin harrumphed. "Suggesting we put our fate in the hands of the gods? That doesn't sound like you, Imbica."

Imbica adjusted her belt. "My time in the Menagerie dungeon… Well, it changed me." She looked far off momentarily then clapped Aldewin on the back. "There are methods to send messages, and we will find one. You will see."

Aldewin dug in his rucksack for a light wool cloak like Shel's. It wouldn't obscure his Northman height, and there was no way to disguise Nivi, but it was all he had. "Where exactly are we going, then?"

Imbica gave him a small smile and a favorable nod and put her kerchief back on. She spoke in a low, firm voice, attempting to rouse them like Druvna had. "Come on, you moss-brained squibs."

Shel laughed. "Imbica, only you can make that sound like it came out of a Pillar scroll." Adjusting the cloak to shroud her eyes, Shel said, "On the hunt again, hey, Aldewin? At least this time, we're only after Dynasty soldiers, not a dragon."

As they entered the bustling streets of Mourigi and headed to the docks, Aldewin rubbed the dragon scale in his pocket. A gift from Ishna and a reminder of the personal quest, still unfulfilled. Aldewin didn't know what this Heart of Menaris was, but if anything could restore Quen to human form, the Heart of Magic sounded like something that would. *We need to find this Heart before the Dynasty does,* he thought. *And once we secure the Heart, I'll begin my search for the Winter Dragon.*

CHAPTER 2

ISHNA

Their wings, thousands strong, blotted the light of the two suns, casting long shadows on the ground below. Winged silhouettes loomed over the lands now ruled by people known to dragons as the Two-Leggeds or Walkers.

During Dragos Teplo—the Age of Dragons—before Indrasian's rise to power, Ishna never considered how humans viewed dragons. Even during the Dô'bedri—the long sleep—Ishna did not reflect on Two-Leggeds. To her mind, Walkers frightened dragons as much as her dragonkin worried humans. People had hunted and slaughtered dragons, dwindling their numbers to less than a thousand. Walkers even desecrated remains of dragonkin, many her own hatchlings. To Ishna, people were a plague upon her species. *So many of my beautiful children are gone,* she thought.

Yet… she'd lived in an unnatural but tangible co-existence with a human. She and Quen were intertwined. Quen had been a host—albeit unwilling—to Ishna's soul. *And now, I host the essence of Quen.* The strange symbiotic life had softened Ishna's view of humans. *I do not forgive their careless and selfish slaughter of my kin. But I now understand that Two-Leggeds fear dragonkin as they fear anything they do not understand. Or cannot control.*

And Ishna despised admitting, if only to herself, that Vahgrin had been right. Dragons and humans cannot coexist. *Not as it stands now, anyway,* she thought. *And especially not until we make the Dragos family whole again.*

Of the four Primal dragons, Ishna knew her own location and Vahgrin's. Vahgrin, the dragon of Summer and Primal Fire and the founder of the Ignati faction, remained at Volenex. The location of the other two Primal dragons remained unknown. To complete their Dragos family, she needed to find Zedris, the dragon of Autumn and Primal Earth, and Veridia, the dragon of Spring and Primal Wood. *Until all four Primals are together, we can neither mount a proper defense nor stake our claim on this world.*

While Ishna knew Vahgrin's whereabouts, liberating him would have to wait. Veridia—Ishna's sister, oldest friend, and ally—had not answered Ishna's call. The dragon of Primal Wood and Spring was missing, though Ishna did not think she was dead. Veridia's youngest hatchling, Aurixia—the last dragon hatched before the Dô'bedri—claimed she sensed Veridia, her egg-mother. *It may be wishful thinking.*

Aurixia's "feeling" was little to go on but reason enough to mount an expedition to search for Veridia, all of dragonkin's favorite Primal dragon. Such a mission involved significant risk. The search party would likely encounter humans, something Ishna wanted to avoid, both for the sake of dragons and Quen's human family.

For now, Ishna led all dragonkin who answered her call to the farthest northeastern reaches of Xathi Tol'galen, or what humans called the Bídean Archipelago. Like a stone bracelet shrouded in clouds and mist, the sweeping archipelago contained hundreds of small and large islands.

At its western edge, less than a hundred fifty leagues from the human city of Partha, Xathi Tol'galen was soaring basalt, granite spires, and sheer cliff faces. As the chain of islands wound northeast, the islands flattened but grew colder, the northernmost covered in snow and glaciers. Inhospitable to and mostly unexplored by the Two-Leggeds, Xathi Tol'galen was the perfect gathering location for dragonkin.

Being removed from human encroachment was a benefit, but it also had a drawback: lack of food. Home to millions of nesting birds and surrounded by seas teeming with fish and ocean mammals, the islands provided enough food for a small group of dragons to survive long term. *But all dragonkin cannot live by the bounty of these islands alone. Eventually, dragonkin will face our age-old dilemma. How do we survive alongside people?*

That is a problem for another day, Ishna thought. After the thousand-year Dô'bedri, the dragons were in a celebratory mood.

Formed by Veridia, the Spring Dragon, Cantiva was the oldest Dragos faction. Though its founder remained missing, Cantiva had taken over the high ground of the largest island in the western archipelago. The oldest, most social, and largest faction, Cantiva welcomed hatchlings from all four Primals.

Usually looking to their founder, Veridia, for leadership and guidance, they unanimously decided that Owaanir, one of Veridia's oldest hatchlings, should be their shepherd until Veridia's return. Owaanir's bright-green skin and red eyes contrasted with the misty sky and gray rock where he perched. The black scaly ridge on his back was relaxed and flat, his eyes closed as he soaked in what little sun the misty grey day afforded.

From the cliffs below, younger dragons launched and dove into the water, calling and laughing as they plunged into the frigid sea to catch fish and hunt seals. Docar, one of Vahgrin's hatchlings, warmed the rock face with his breath, making it glow orange and yellow. Liejala and Myvishi, the twins, preened on the cliff above and taunted Docar with icy breath, landing a patina of ice on his black scales. Docar shook and flung ice shards that melted in the warmth of his heated stone.

He returned their prank by breathing fire that sizzled on the stone between them. The twins laughed and took wing as Docar's fire sputtered on the icy stone ledge above him. They taunted him to chase them, but Docar remained in the warmth he'd created.

Ishna and Aurixia, the Spring Dragon's youngest hatchling, sat with Docar.

"Why could we have not gathered somewhere warmer? Like the volcanos of the southern Sulmére?" Aurixia asked. She spread her wings, gathering warmth.

Docar harrumphed and thumped his tail twice, a sign he disagreed with her. "Have you not heard? My egg-father is held captive there by dragomancers. That land is no safer for Dragos than we would be in Partha or Qülla."

Her voice was a whisper. "Dragomancers? In Indrasi?"

Docar spit fire against the rock, and it glowed again. "I know my egg-father's betrayal wronged Ishna and all dragonkin. But even Vahgrin does not deserve enslavement, does he?"

Ishna fluffed her wings and scratched her chin with a dewclaw. "I have asked the minds of Nao faction to consider how best to handle Vahgrin and the dragomancer problem. I am certain Niezhan and the Lít council will provide options."

"Yes, of course. But… What do *you* think?"

Ishna rose and flapped her wings a few times as though trying them out. She sidestepped his question. "Come, Docar. Leave thoughts of your egg-father behind for a while. Let us enjoy the air, sea, and fresh fish in our belly."

They took to the sky and circled with several others before flying to a neighboring island to hunt seals.

Dragons gathered in small social cliques and factions on islands scattered like pebbles strewn by a giant across the sea. Though three major factions were missing their beloved founders, they reveled in their reunions just the same. Vahgrin's Ignati faction, true to their isolationist roots, gathered on a small island tucked far to the northeast. Zedris's Nao faction gathered and spent hours speaking the oral histories and debating Dragos ethics and philosophy.

Later in the afternoon, Ishna visited one of her oldest and dearest friends, Niezhan, there. A dragon of earth and one of the largest dragons ever hatched, Niezhan's white scales shimmered in the midday light. He sat on his haunches and stroked his snowy beard. With bright-yellow eyes in a focused gaze, he listened to Côzhili, another Zedris hatchling, and Naja, one of Ishna's hatchlings, discuss Dragos ethics relating to people.

They spoke in Dragosi, and after "listening" for two decades to humans speak, the sound was a sweet relief to Ishna's ears.

"If we exterminate them—" Naja said.

"Assuming we can," Côzhili cut in.

Naja slowly nodded her iridescent blue-grey head and thumped her tail once to acknowledge her point. "That would not be easy. But for this conversation, assume we could rid this world of the human scourge."

The thrumming vibration between Ishna's eyes hammered. *Quen.* Ishna bellowed aloud from the sudden, intense pain.

Naja dipped her chin. "I apologize, egg-mother, if this discussion harms you. It is difficult to remember that you spent time… as one of them."

Murmurs rose among the gathered dragons.

Ishna closed her eyes and breathed deeply of the sea air. She thumped her tail once, a sign for the speaker to continue. "It is I who must apologize, Naja." Ishna then looked at the crowd and raised her voice for everyone to hear. "As you know, I still carry a human soul within me."

The murmurs rose again.

"Hear me and take this to your hearts. I made a solemn Dragos vow and intend to keep it for myself and all dragonkin. There is one human family that must remain unharmed by dragonkin. Quen Tomo Santu di Sulmére's kin are neither food nor foe to dragonkin." Ishna searched their faces and got blank stares in return. The buzzing within her skull pinged, and her forehead throbbed.

This is most unpleasant, Quen. We must find a better way to communicate. One that does not cause such pain that I screech aloud.

Niezhan, acting leader of the Nao faction since its founder, Zedris, was still missing, spoke on behalf of the gathered. "Rest easy, Ishna. Nao is a philosophical lot, not a faction of action."

The dragons of the Nao faction laughed and thumped their tales in assent.

Niezhan continued. "Look to Ignati, Cantiva, and your own faction, Iska'van, to make grand plans and pursue action. We of Nao are content, as we have always been, to stuff our bellies and, with satiated appetites, ponder complexities while doing not a damned thing."

More laughter erupted, and even Ishna laughed, as she knew it was true. The buzzing in her skull lessened. "You just rose from a thousand-year slumber, and this is how you spend your time?" She laughed again. "Only Nao faction finds endless debate entertaining." She gazed at her dragonkin, and a tear gathered in her blue eye. "Zedris would be proud. *Is* proud." *Wherever the dragon of Primal Earth is*, she thought.

Côzhili rose and cheered, "To Zedris!" She thrust her snout to the sky, "Time to take wing, sa'gamlin."

The rest of the Nao cohort let out throaty calls, and several took to the sky. Tails thumped, and the heavens shook from their cries for their founder and beloved leader, Zedris.

Niezhan likely knew Ishna had come to speak to him, but he did not press her, and she did not immediately speak. They did not hasten to fill every silence with sound.

After several moments, Niezhan said, "I know you, sa'gamlin. You would not give up an afternoon of hunting or nuzzling with Docar to seek an afternoon of Dragos history and ethics lessons with Nao. What brings you to our humble pile of rock?"

Ishna smiled and rested her forehead against his. "How I missed you." She remained in that position for what, to Two-Leggeds, would seem an overly long time. Finally, she said, "After a thousand years in Vay'Nada's void, no one desires a rollick more than I, Niezhan. Do not worry your old white head. Docar and I are making up for our lost time."

Niezhan lowered his chin, shook his head, and exhaled a dry puff of dragon breath. "Please, spare me the sordid details of your loving time."

Ishna's laugh, throaty and multitonal, hung in the misty air. "By the gods, Niezhan, we never change, do we?"

He stroked his white beard with digits ending in long black talons as he returned her smile. "To quote one of Zedris's aphorisms: 'To live is to remain.'"

"We remain," Ishna said.

Again, the dragons allowed silence to swell, each considering the full meaning of Zedris's wisdom.

Finally, Ishna said, "To answer your initial question, I seek counsel from my oldest and wisest friends. You, of course, but also Naja and Côzhili."

To that, Niezhan called their names in a slow, low speech that carried a great distance. Before long, Naja's blue-grey scales shimmered as she turned in their direction, still swallowing a harbor seal whole. Côzhili, too, ceased frolicking on the wing with three other dragons and gracefully landed beside Niezhan, belying her great size.

Naja belched, emitting a briny odor to which Côzhili hissed and flapped her wings to rid their area of the foul smell. Naja said, "A gathering of what remains of our small council, the Lít." The gathered thumped. "It has been long since our tiny council of inexpert experts gathered." Naja laughed, and the others joined in her mirth.

Ishna said, "After my time in the Void, aware of all yet unable to interact, and then my time among humans, trust me when I say our Lít is a most adept counsel indeed. Aurixia—"

"Veridia's last hatchling?" Côzhili asked.

"The very same. Rixi, as I call her, claims she senses Veridia," Ishna said.

Niezhan stroked his beard and narrowed his pale yellow eyes. "Have *you* sensed our dragon of Primal Wood?" He asked this of Ishna.

She thumped her tail twice, indicating no.

"Then it is likely hopeful thinking," Niezhan said.

"This is what I fear," Ishna responded.

Niezhan continued. "Aurixia is still a young hatchling. It is natural for her to yearn for Veridia, her egg-mother."

Naja and Côzhili thumped their agreement.

"True, and thoughts I have considered. Yet Rixi is an uncommonly perceptive Dragos. Her egg-mother poured much of her essence into Aurixia."

"You believe, then, that Aurixia truly senses Veridia?" Naja asked.

Ishna thumped. "I do. The young Dragos implores me to take up the search now."

Naja and Côzhili both thumped, but Niezhan remained silent. "Does she sense *where* Veridia is located? This world is vast. Even a dragon can be quite difficult to locate if they choose to remain hidden."

Côzhili thumped and added, "Like my egg-father, Zedris."

All thumped in agreement.

"Aurixia believes we'll find Veridia in the wilds of the continent the Two-Leggeds call Tinox. The region they refer to as the Vatnoyer."

The dragons hissed at the mention of the Vatnoyer.

Naja gave voice to their disapproval. "That land is crawling with Two-Leggeds of the foulest sort. Wildings. They war with each other nonstop and kill anything nonhuman that crosses their path. And they wear the skins of creatures they have killed." Naja shuddered.

Ishna had spent years observing Quen and her family curing animal skins for trade and crafting them into wearable items. It was an odd custom, and Ishna initially struggled to understand it. But the practice made sense to her in the Sulmére, where little grew that humans could use or eat. *I will keep these memories to myself, though,* Ishna thought. *My dragonkin will not understand this as I now do.*

Instead, Ishna said, "The Vatnoyer is a dangerous land, to be sure. I will force no one to come with me."

"You are intent on traveling, I see," Niezhan said. "Then what counsel do you seek of the Lít?"

Ishna had hoped Niezhan would agree more with her idea of mounting a search-and-rescue mission for Veridia. She hadn't desired counsel so much as to gain assent. *He is never one to agree with my every word—perhaps why we have remained friends for over two thousand years. I do not require companions to be easy with me so long as they remain faithful,* Ishna thought.

Ishna said, "In truth? Yes, I plan to find Veridia. She is not only my sister but my oldest friend and ally. Being the dragon of Primal Wood, Veridia carries the essence of life itself. I saw firsthand what the Rajani dragomancers have done to Vahgrin."

The gathered dragons hissed.

Ishna continued. "Using him as a weapon to pursue their own vile ends. Dragos have been free of Two-Legged control since the Jik'Madar when Zedris broke the Drowned World to free us. We cannot allow Two-Leggeds or dragomancers to gain control of Veridia."

They all thumped once and gave a cry of approval for Ishna's words.

Though Ishna still seethed at her brother, Vahgrin, for his role in her first death, that another species shackled any dragon rankled her. "We will, of course, need to mount a mission to liberate Vahgrin. But that must wait. Without the other two Primals, I have no hope of subduing the Rajani dragomancers and Vahgrin. I fear a thousand years has not dimmed his anger with me and lust for vengeance."

Niezhan slowly nodded and thumped once. "Wise words, Ishna, and I fear they are all too true. Nao is pondering the dragomancer problem. We will continue to consider how to sever the Rajani hold on our brother, father, and friend."

All thumped once. Ishna continued, "But for now, I need recommendations on who to take with me on my hunt for Veridia. And counsel on how best to avoid involvement with Two-Leggeds. All dragons on this mission must return. Alive."

Naja let out a throaty call of assent, and Côzhili matched it.

"Come then, settle your lusts, sa'gamlin," Niezhan said. "Let us consider the problems Ishna lays before us." Niezhan's pale eyes glimmered as he spoke, clearly happy to be called upon to think and ponder again.

Ishna smiled, gladdened to see her friends together, cooperating on the problems as only Dragos can. "I leave you to your discussions, my Nao friends. You know where to find me after you have formulated your suggestions."

Niezhan shook his head. "Do not begin speaking of your lusty cavorting with Docar again."

They all laughed, and Ishna took wing. She twirled as she soared, icy wind rippling her snowy hair. Ishna shook and sent twinkling iridescent scales raining onto her friends. She flew west toward the glowing rocks of dragon-heated spires. To the open wings of her lover, Docar.

Chapter 3

QUEN

Above. Screeching. Soaring.

Birds?

No, I am the one who takes wing.

Icy wind. Clouds enshroud a ragged, rocky coastline.

They're speaking.

Tongue clicks and drawn-out vowels.

Somehow, I know what they say.

Jubilation! So many years in caves and graves. Buried beneath mud and water. "To wing! To wing!" they call.

Higher. Higher.

We're in the clouds now. I hate heights. I should be dizzy, but I'm not.

Beneath, a land of mottled grey-brown hugging a grey-green coast. A cacophony of shrieking calls.

They sound like Rajani Nixan.

No, not Rajani. Bird rookeries. Sea birds gather on a desolate coast.

Something else. A heartbeat?

The ponderous beat of one heart. A rhythm so slow it became barely perceptible.

One heartbeat. Such a strange, lonely feeling.

The beat—not her own.

I am the tenant now. I don't see the sky with my eyes or hear dragonkin with my ears.

Ishna owned the eyes, ears, and heart. Quen? The silent observer.

As Ishna had been within me. Did she feel as alone as I do now?

Even years as a pariah hadn't prepared Quen for this exile.

Do I still exist?

Only months after making the pact with Ishna—to "fill the void"—Quen knew she was slipping away. Pure consciousness, she had only memories and thoughts to occupy her.

A cave. Frigid and dark, even when both suns shone bright.

Even I had trouble breathing in that lofty place. I slowed my system to survive.

No. Wait. That was—not Quen. Not me. I didn't live in that cave. That was the Winter Dragon.

Ishna lived the end of her first life sequestered atop the TasūZaj's tallest peaks. It was Ishna who hibernated away from humans. She had planned to sleep until humans outgrew the need to destroy anything they perceived as a threat.

Quen. I was… Quen. I lived not in an icy cave but in warm sands. Two suns. There were… the Brothers. And I was… a woman.

Quen. I was—am—Quen. A woman. A person. And there were—others. People I cared about. People I loved.

Quen focused herself, whatever that self now was.

Memories. Remember my life as Quen.

I had a man… Santu. A father. I called him… Pahpi.

Two other men. Brothers? Lio and… Rhoji.

Humans rarely stop to consider the miracle of a beating heart in their chest. Quen never had.

I cursed my two heartbeats but I now long for the double thump.

She yearned to feel the steady rhythm of her own heartbeat. Quen, though, felt like the lingering sensation of an amputated appendage. She was now a phantom quiver within the cage of the magnificent beast's body.

Remember. Think on being Quen. It's all I can do.

Quen recalled blowing sand and a shrieking raven.

I wanted to speak with that bird, but the sands almost claimed me.

Rhoji. My brother. He saved me.

She meditated on the name.

Rhoji.

He had been important to her, but Quen's feelings about him were confusing.

I loved him. At least, I think I did. But I disliked him too? Is it possible to love someone for whom you also have ill feelings?

Rhoji.

My brother.

Does he still exist?

Do I?

Quen concentrated again.

I am… Quen.

Quen, the other voice within said.

A woman. A person.

I am Quen, and I had friends.

Fano. A blacksmith. My friend who gifted me a beautiful blade and taught me how to use it.

Fano.

My friend. Killed. By a … dragon. Vahgrin.

Vahgrin incinerated Fano.

Why didn't you kill Vahgrin? Why didn't you bring that dragon to justice for Fano? For Pahpi?

Settle your turbulent mind, Quen. I have explained this. I need Vahgrin alive.

My impatient human companion, you live on dragon time now. We measure our lives in eons, not decades. Vahgrin will get what he deserves. In time.

Pahpi. My father.

Yes, you had a father named Santu. Who else do you love?

Liodhan. My brother. Eldest brother.

Yes. And?

Lio… and his herdwife. Zarate. She gifted me a kopek. Nabu. He wasn't afraid of me. At least not as much as others.

Who else? Name them, Quen. Keep the memories alive. I need you to stay with me. Do not lose yourself. Remember.

A baby. Zarate watches as Lio holds the babe in his arms.

No, I cannot remember this. If I think about Lio's family, whatever is left of me will shatter. I want… to cry.

Tears are falling, Quen. Do you feel them? I cry for you. My tears are our tears. For all the loved ones we have lost.

I do… feel them. For… Lumina. Her name was—

Is.

Lumina. And she was—is—my niece. And I love her.

Yes. And who else do you love?

I had friends. Shel. Eira. And a man. An older man. Smoke rings and power, but I was not afraid. He was… Druvna. May the Sister greet him at River Nixaya and usher him to his Corner, where the Three will wrap him in their arms.

Humans have many strange thoughts about death.

Druvna… died?

Yes.

Killed by a dragon?

No.

The Dynasty killed him?

Yes.

Took him from me.

Yes.

They, too, deserve justice they've not yet received.

All in due time, Quen.

Quen. I am Quen.

Yes.

A human.

Yes. And who else do you love, Quen?

Whiskers tickle my cheek.

Whose whiskers?

Hands, warm and strong. Calloused yet gentle. His fingers on my spine. My insides quiver, and I am afraid, but not of him. I wish… we were alone. Warm breath on my cheek. He smells of sweet tobacco. "You have friends in the capital," he said.

Who is he?

He wipes wine from my lip. Pale-blue eyes grow dark. He wants me. And I want to know him. If it's the last human thing I do, I must know him.

Who is he? Name him.

It pains me to think about him. Don't make me remember this. It was the greatest happiness Quen— I—ever knew. And it was the last. Don't make me suffer, reliving what I'll never know again.

You must. I need you to remain. To stay whole. To be Quen, you must remember. To *want* to exist. Pleasure and pain. Love and hate. Purity and evil. All of it makes the whole of you. Name him. Who is he?

Aldewin. My friend. My love.

Aldewin.

Aldewin.

Your soul radiates when you think of him. Stronger. Yes. There. Keep thinking about him, Quen. Think on Aldewin and fill the void.

Aldewin. We made love in the meadow. I wanted to stay with him forever. The way he looked at me. He saw me, Ishna. All of me. Yet he was not afraid. He… loved me.

Yes.

Were you there? That day in the meadow?

Yes.

Did I love him? Truly? Or was it only my need that drove me into his arms?

You loved him. You *do*.

How can I know it was… real? We hardly knew each other. And he was on… a mission. He admitted— things. Yes, there was a lie. How could I truly love a man who lied?

You did. You do.

How do you know?

I was there. I am here.

Perhaps it was you who loved Aldewin. He accused me of seducing him with my Nixan ways. Did you? Did we?

Aldewin loved you, Quen. And you loved him. Human love. So quick. Short. Sweet. Dragons court for centuries, dear Quen. Our love lasts eons, but so do our hurts.

You didn't answer my question. Did you seduce Aldewin?

I have no interest in your human affairs. I simply want you to remember. Keep his memory—his love—alive. That will keep you alive.

Me.

Quen.

Quen. I am Quen Tomo Santu di Sulmére.

Yes.

And I loved—love—Aldewin.

Aldewin di Partha.

A Northman. From Enara Pillar. And… a spy?

And an assassin.

Assassin?

I'll leave you to your memories now, Quen. Remember…

Aldewin…

Who are you, Aldewin?

CHAPTER 4

ALDEWIN

The sky glowed brilliant purple and orange as Aldewin and the pod headed to the docks of Indrasi's western shore. Shel pulled her cloak over her head, and Aldewin did the same.

Shel nodded her approval. "At least it will cover your pale hair and eyes."

"The wanted posters really capture his essence, don't they?" Dio observed.

Shel laughed and gave Dio a gentle elbow to the side. "Shut it, or you'll make him paranoid."

Again, Aldewin was uneasy with Dio's over-familiarity with his friends. *Or perhaps I am jealous that he seems closer to them than I am.*

Aldewin had wanted to be friendlier. He genuinely liked the company of Druvna's pod. But duty had required him to keep his distance. *I've nearly drowned in duty my whole life. And where has it left me?* Yet without an institution to place his faith in, Aldewin swam in open water without a shore in sight.

"No wonder Mourigi is awash in blood. There are no Kovathas here," Imbica said.

Shel laughed. "Suda. You haven't been a Kovatha for months now, Imbica. Yet you still believe the world is lost without them? People don't need the Dynasty to tell them right from wrong."

Imbica tsked. "Maybe someone should. Look around. There isn't a moral code or Dynasty law that isn't being broken somewhere in this fetid burg."

Old habits die hard, Aldewin thought. Concerned as she was with ensuring people obeyed rules, Imbica had been well suited to life as a Kovatha, the Dynasty's roaming law enforcers. *Do our life paths naturally draw us to what we're best at, whether or not we choose it?* If so, Aldewin was destined to be a killer. *Not a comforting thought.*

Unlike Bardivia, where people retreated to their homes as darkness drew near, Mourigi's streets came alive. The throng of night-loving people was a blessing. The four blended into the throngs, wading through the winding alleys and ever downhill toward the still-active docks.

They arrived at Doj'Enara Bay—"Blessed Waters"—as Hiyadi's last light kissed the water. A natural cove of calm water in a crescent bay made Doj'Enara Bay the perfect place for ships to dock.

Fishing boats were heading out for the night, their square sails of many colors catching Hiyadi's vibrant last rays. The boats headed south in search of plentiful night fishing.

Aldewin recognized the large single-masted merchant ships. Their square sails with stripes or sigils were common at the docks in the Shills area of Partha. The bulky ships ferried large loads of goods between Partha and Bardivia.

But Aldewin didn't recognize a third type of ship in the harbor. Smaller and double-masted with triangular sails, the vessels bore stripes of deep aubergine on white, some with a peacock crest. An armored top tier with slits for archers set these boats apart from the others.

Aldewin pointed to the nearest one and asked, "Who mans those? They don't look like merchant-class ships."

"Good eye," Dio said. "They're Bardivia's Engarda fleet. The only seafaring soldiers in Indrasi. Their sails are triangular for speed."

"Engarda? Bardivia has its own navy?" Aldewin hadn't been aware of any city-state or country in the known world having a full-time military force on the seas.

"That." Dio pointed to one of the stately docked Engarda ships. It sported a fore sail of crisp white with deep purple stripes and an aft sail emblazoned with a royal-looking purple peacock. "That's why the Dynasty is stirring the pot with Bardivia."

"Over ships?" Aldewin asked.

"The Dynasty doesn't have a sea force. That makes them dependent on Bardivia to protect merchant ships crossing the Straits of Minea headed to Partha and back," Dio said.

Shel spit out a bit of kabu stalk she'd been sucking on. "Protect 'em from what?"

"The Merladro. Sea bandits." Dio pulled his cloak tighter about his face as they approached the far southern end of the docks. "Some also claim sea Nixan and other fearsome creatures infest these waters." He laughed. "Stories told by men who've had too much firewater and sun."

Imbica glanced behind and picked up speed. "I think we might have company. Let us make haste."

Looking back toward the direction they'd come, Aldewin saw nothing of concern. But then, lumbering at the top of the hill, he saw it. *A yindril.* The creature stood out like green grass in Sulmére sands.

He didn't need to be warned twice. Aldewin opened his stride and quickly caught up to Imbica. "How did you know? You couldn't have seen the creature. I could only barely, and I have the height advantage."

Imbica gave him a sideways look. "Really? You need to ask? I didn't *see* it." She harrumphed. "I *felt* it."

"Said it before, and I'll say it again. Glad I'm on your side, Imbica," Aldewin said.

The crowds thinned as they neared the far southwestern end of the bay. The stately beauty of Engarda ships and brightly colored fishing boats gave way to weathered wood docks and ships with faded emblems and tatty sails. This side of the bay weathered choppier waters and took the brunt of storms. The farther they walked, the more motley the boats became. Some looked like a strong wind would shatter them into splinters. Imbica led them to one of the harbor's ugliest, most unkempt boats.

The ship they approached was a midsized, two-masted merchant ship with both an aft castle and forecastle. Its largest mast bore a square sail with a crimson splotch. Now too faded to discern, the smear might have once been a sigil.

Aldewin's palms were clammy, and he said, "Please tell me this is not the vessel you hired."

Imbica didn't answer but stepped onto the rickety gangplank. She marched up purposefully and neared the gangway while the others stood on the dock. Her face red from the exertion of the walk from the inn, she called down, "Are you coming? Or am I to sail alone?"

Shel shrugged and scampered up the gangplank. "I've never been on a ship before," she called over her shoulder.

Shel will lose her last meal and enthusiasm for sea travel when the first massive wave rolls this floating coffin, Aldewin thought.

Dio bowed slightly and nodded toward the ship. "After you." His lips curled into a smile that didn't reach his eyes.

Aldewin sighed and took a breath to calm his racing heart. He knew the Kovathas were behind them, likely catching up, but he couldn't get his feet to step onto the gangplank. Memories of nearly drowning six years prior made him break out in a cold sweat.

Ahead, Shel called to Nivi, but the giant tiger remained at Aldewin's side. His tail was down, and his ears were back. *Nivi wants to board this ship no more than I*, Aldewin thought.

"If it helps, know I'm a strong swimmer," Dio said. "If you should find yourself in the water, I promise to pull you and your pet out."

There was no sarcasm in Dio's tone. But there wasn't a man in Indrasi strong enough to drag a sodden Northman clinging to a giant snow tiger from the high seas.

Kovathas roamed the docks behind, but the promise of finding Ishna and Quen lay ahead. With renewed purpose, Aldewin said, "Come, Nivi."

But Nivi danced away from the gangplank. *Perhaps he recalls being hauled from his homeland against his will.* Aldewin pulled a bit of dried meat from the provisions pouch at his waist.

"We are going to your homeland, my friend." Aldewin held out the snack, hoping Nivi's stomach would overpower his fear.

Nivi sniffed the meat, and as he was about to snatch it from Aldewin's fingers, Aldewin took a step backward and up the walkway. "If you want this, you must come with me."

Behind him, already on the ship, Imbica called down. "Do you need my help?"

Aldewin knew the sort of help she spoke of. The kind that involved her befuddling spells that wreaked havoc on the mind. "Let me try my way first."

Over the months with Nivi, Aldewin discovered the tiger understood more of what Aldewin said than a kopek or horse. And Nivi had a powerful instinct for danger.

When even the treat didn't impel Nivi onto the gangplank, Aldewin kneeled and whispered into the tiger's gold-banded ear. "Kovatha mages are coming for us, Nivi. They will take us back to Qülla. To a cage. Trust me, friend. I have killed to protect you, haven't I? Come with me, and together, we will search for Quen."

Aldewin rose and began again to walk backward, holding out the meat. This time, Nivi took a tenuous step onto the narrow wood walkway. It swayed beneath his copious weight but did not break.

"That's it. Come with me. Together, we will hunt." *For Ishna,* he thought. Aldewin imagined Ishna soaring above as she left them and flew toward the TasūZaj mountains. *Somewhere within that great dragon, Quen still lives.*

Nivi followed Aldewin then, with Dio on his heels.

Once both of Nivi's feet hit the deck, Aldewin gave him the meat treat and ruffled his head. "You are so brave, Nivi." *Lend me courage, friend, for I loathe ships.*

On deck, young people scurried up rigging to the crow's nests atop each mast. Other crew members wound ropes, lashed sails, and prepared to draw anchors. A bald man standing atop the raised deck of the aft castle barked orders.

The man, presumably Captain Ontrosa, held a spyglass to his eye, scanning the northern harbor then shifting his gaze to the docks. He lowered the glass and yelled, "Pull the gangplank and anchors away, you cockwaddles. And with speed. I spied two Kovathas. Time to set sail out of this bilgewater town."

Imbica waved up to the bald man. "Captain Ontrosa," she called.

Ontrosa hurried down the worn steps, his swiftness belying his apparent age. "Show me your pouch of coin, woman. Or I'll order the crew to throw you over the side. The sharks and Kovatha take ya for all I care."

Imbica pulled a sturdy woolen sack from her tooled leather belt purse. She held it in the air for the captain but pulled it back as he reached for it.

Captain Ontrosa's fuzzy black eyebrows furrowed, and his face flushed red with anger. "Don't be playin' games or so help me—" He pulled back a hand like he'd strike her.

Dio and Aldewin stepped forward, inserting themselves between Imbica and the captain.

"Stand down, young fools." Imbica's voice was a low growl. She flashed a look that said she was not to be tested. Turning a more congenial gaze on the captain, she said,

"Captain Ontrosa, this purse contains the agreed-upon fee. But first, you must assure me you have the Enar'atori aboard as you promised."

Shel had been giving a hangnail a good chew but chimed in, "Enar'atori?"

Ontrosa and Imbica ignored her question, but Aldewin whispered to her, "Sea Singer."

Shel's face scrunched into a puzzled look.

Aldewin rolled his eyes and put a shushing finger to his lips. He mouthed, "I'll tell you later."

"I've got one aboard, as I told ya I would. This is the last sail of Yngvari's contract. She's got a mighty good 'centive to get ya to the Vats."

Ontrosa pointed to a tall, lithe woman with white-blond hair and pale-blue eyes. *She bears an unsettling resemblance to Pelagia.* The woman wore a pale-blue shirt and form-fitting pants that nearly matched the color of her eyes. Over the underclothing, the Enar'atori wore a striking white leather tunic armor quilted in blue thread with a vertical wave pattern. She wore an elaborate mass of braids atop her head. Yngvari stood near the wheel on the high aft deck, her white skin reddened by the sun, her nose splotched with freckles. The Enar'atori wore a gold band on each ear. *Like Nivi wears—and Quen wore.*

Aldewin's voice was low and seething. "An indentured." *Seems indenturing themselves is the only way Fyrstua folks leave the Vatnoyer.* He thought of the Enar'atori but also himself. The effort to restrain himself from cutting the captain down and freeing the woman made his jaw twitch. *This is not your battle—yet. Once harbored on Tinox's shores, if the captain doesn't free her, I will.*

Imbica's glare warned Aldewin not to do what she seemed to know he wanted to do. She dropped the woolen money purse into Captain Ontrosa's hand. "Best get the sails unfurled. If you spotted Kovatha, they're probably on our tail."

The captain stowed the bag at his belt. He grunted at Imbica, bowed slightly, and said, "Welcome to my ship, *Sicara's Bane*. Respect her, and she'll respect you."

Already uneasy about the sea journey, the mention of the ship's name nearly brought up Aldewin's dinner. *Sicara*. The goddess of death that Fen Menir worshipped. *If I was still a praying sort, I'd pray it's not an ill omen.*

Captain Ontrosa paid them no further attention and resumed yelling orders as he hurried to his position at the wheel beside the Enar'atori. He yelled down into the rower's pit. "Row like you be escapin' a giant sea serpent. As soon as we clear the harbor, sails up." He turned to the Enar'atori. "Best hatch the waters behind us, Yngvari."

"What should we do?" Shel called after him.

"Stay the fuck out of the way. Dreni will show you to the foredeck passenger quarters. She put down fresh straw and buckets for your sick. You should stay there 'cause when Yngvari gets a-going, the waters of the Orju Sea gonna pitch and roll. And if ya fall overboard while puking, we ain't gonna stop and scoop up your sorry hides."

A young woman sailor, probably only sixteen, put two fingers between her teeth and whistled. Tightly woven braids down her back swished as she motioned with her head to follow her. Dreni stopped and waited for them by the narrow stairs leading to the forecastle's deck.

Aldewin headed toward Dreni first. A storm had once swept him overboard. He wasn't keen on repeating the experience. But Aldewin also recalled the stench of ship quarters. *I'd give anything for huson pine oil and a keffla.*

As if reading his thoughts, Dio tapped his arm and held out a vial. "You'll need this."

Aldewin took the oil and rubbed some into his mustache and around the collar of his shirt so it would waft to his nostrils. "Thanks," he said as he handed it back. *You'd only know about the need for huson pine in cramped ship berths if you'd sailed before,* he thought. *Was Dio a sailor before casting his lot with the pod in Bardivia?*

"You three go ahead," Imbica said. "I'll wait on the captain's deck in case the Enar'atori needs my assistance."

"Are you a Sea Singer too?" Dio asked.

Imbica smoothed her apron and brushed her fingers through her shorn hair. "No. But I have other skills which may become of use." She said no more and mounted the stairs to the aft captain's deck.

Shel stood on the deck and didn't follow Aldewin and Dio to the forecastle. She fixed her gaze on Yngvari, the ship's Sea Singer.

Aldewin called over the din of the creaking oars, winding ropes, and sails unfurling. "Come to our quarters, Shel."

She cupped her hands around her mouth, trying to get her voice to carry. "I've never been on a boat. I'm not giving up the sweet sea air to smother in the stench of you two kopek turds and Nivi's wet fur."

Or of getting to know a beautiful woman she hopes to spend time with, Aldewin thought.

A youth in the mainmast's crow's nest called down, "Fire! Kovatha fire incoming!"

Imbica had already begun winding her hands and gathering Menaris energy. Yngvari lifted her face to the skies and started singing. It wasn't a high, lilting song, as one might expect from a woman. Instead, the song was tenor and throaty, resembling the low rumbling of a yindril. If she sang words, they weren't discernable to Aldewin.

Behind the *Sicara's Bane*, the waters churned as if bandied by a storm. But the sky was cloudless, and no winds whipped the sails.

From this churning ocean cauldron, Imbica raised a shield of water. Her brows were tightly knit, and her face was red and sweaty. Imbica's arms shook with the effort of her concentration.

"It's too large, m'lady mage," Captain Ontrosa hollered. "When you drop that shield, it will rock us too hard."

Yngvari didn't take her eyes from the skies or cease her song. She placed a thin hand on the captain's as if to soothe his fears.

On shore, a lone yindril keened and flailed its overly long arms. Kovatha stood on either side of the bark-covered man-beast. Both Kovathas hurled tight balls of fire toward the ship's sails.

Seeing the incoming magefire, or perhaps sensing it, Imbica raised her arms higher and drove the water shield upward even more. Whirling fire smacked into Imbica's water shield. The fire sputtered and sizzled but didn't make it through.

The crew clapped and whooped, and Shel joined in their cheer. But Captain Ontrosa didn't join the celebration.

"It no'a time for celebratin.' Ya think the damned mage-rots gonna let us go dat easy? Battle stations, you squib. We still gotta get past the Engarda."

The cheers died immediately, and Dreni flushed white. She ran to the mainmast, opened a door built into the deck, and pulled out buckets that she and a few others filled with bits of broken glass.

While one group took these buckets to the raised aft deck, another group swept by Aldewin and Dio as they ran belowdecks with their odd cargo.

The *Sicara's Bane's* sails were now fully unfurled. Juka, the chaotic goddess of æther, blew powerful winds. The *Bane* plowed the waves, speeding out of the harbor.

Belowdecks, the oars captain shouted encouragement. "Kovathas spotted on shore, lads. Let's show those wood wankers how we outrun Engarda."

Drums beat a steady rhythm to keep time for the oarspeople. Without help from gods or drawing on Menaris abilities, the oarspeople pulled the ship's massive weight using only muscle and teamwork.

Between fair winds at their back and a strong rowing crew below, *Sicara's Bane* quickly cleared Doj'Enara Bay. The captain headed the ship northwest, toward the open waters of the Orju Sea. *Shouldn't we go northeast toward the Minea Straits?*

While Aldewin had less than zero desire to remain on deck, the ship's direction caused him concern. *What if he intends to dump us in the deep sea like bootleg cargo?*

Aldewin left the comfort of the door to their assigned quarters and headed toward the captain's deck. Nivi followed, hunkered down, his ears flat against his head.

Dio called to him, "I thought you wanted to ride out this voyage inside."

"Imbica may need help." *I haven't one-tenth the Menaris ability that Imbica possesses, but I can lend strength where needed,* Aldewin thought.

Perhaps not wanting to be the only one of their party to stow himself away in their quarters, Dio made his way to Shel. She stood at the railing amidship on the port side. Dio said something and took her arm to pull her back from the rail. Shel jerked away and held her ground. Dio relented to Shel's stubborn insistence on being doused with sea spray. He pulled a rope from the rigging and lashed Shel and himself to the boat.

Captain Ontrosa ignored Aldewin and Nivi as they approached. He was busy shouting back and forth with the lad perched in the mainmast's crow's nest, scanning the aft waters for Engarda.

"I can hold the shield no longer," Imbica said. Her arms trembled, and the neckline of her tunic was dark with perspiration.

Yngvari stopped singing long enough to say, "Release your hold, Lady Mage. I will return the waters to Mara, Mother of the sea." The Enar'atori then resumed her song but modulated her tone discordantly.

As Imbica released her spell, Yngvari's song gently lowered the massive water shield. With Yngvari's help, the wall of displaced water returned slowly and gently to the sea. It rocked the ship but didn't cause a thunderous ship-busting wave.

Imbica rested on a barrel and wiped her face. "It has been a long time since I communed with Enara to that degree."

Aldewin handed her his water sac. "Even Val'Enara Masters couldn't hold such a massive spell that long, Imbica. Even though you left Val'Enara, the water spirits still favor you."

With still-shaky arms, Imbica welcomed Aldewin's water offer and drank deeply. "Perhaps. But there was a tension there, Aldewin. One I have not encountered before."

"You think the gods of Enara are angry with you for leaving Val'Enara and working as a Kovatha?" Aldewin asked.

Imbica shook her head and handed Aldewin his water sac. "No. It was not a tension between me and the spirits. Not exactly." She wiped her forehead and took a deep breath. "More like a tension within Enara itself."

Aldewin frowned. "That's not encouraging, especially when sailing." *And fearing the damned boat will meet the same awful fate as the last ship on which I sailed.*

Seeing his expression, Imbica relaxed her face and sighed. "It is likely only my lack of practice weaving such an intricate spell on such a grand scale. Think on it no more."

Yngvari remained at Captain Ontrosa's side, and without changing her position, she cast her gaze on Aldewin. Perhaps noticing his height and pale eyes and hair for the first time, her eyes grew wide. Yngvari smiled, but only briefly. "A Northman." Her speaking voice was as smooth as polished sea glass and lilted with a Fyrstua accent.

Aldewin gave her a courteous nod, but he doubted she noticed. Her eyes returned to scanning the horizon, focusing solely on the sea.

Belowdecks, a young woman seated between two drummers called out to the oarsmen in a sing-song call and return.

"We row away from beds and bay—" the oars coach called.

"Goodbye, sweet love, goodbye," the oarsmen responded.
"We row today to treasure and pay—"
"To take what's ours by right."
"Row, men, row. Don't disobey—"
"Or Cap Ontrosa will have our hide."
"Stroke your oars and row all day—
"Give us honey-ale, and we'll conquer the tide!"

With the help of their coach's urging, the oarsmen pulled the ship at great speed past the last land outcropping of the crescent-shaped bay. Their job became more difficult as the intensity of waves grew in the open waters of the Orju Sea.

Ahead lay blue skies and favorable winds. Her sails full, *Sicara's Bane* was now out of reach of the Kovatha mages.

Captain Ontrosa's gnarled fingers gripped the wheel as his wiry arms strained to keep the rudder going in his intended direction. The back-and-forth calling with the crew died down, but Ontrosa's eyes remained fixed on the sea ahead.

Aldewin called to him. "I thought we were going to the Vatnoyer."

Ontrosa didn't look back at him or answer. The captain's silence made Aldewin's unease grow.

He tried to hide the panic from his voice. "Why are we then going west rather than east?"

The question made Imbica rise from the barrel she'd rested on. The query also pulled Yngvari's steady gaze away from the water and to Aldewin.

Captain Ontrosa glanced back at him with a look that conveyed his impatience with the question. "Ya know what's in the Straits of Minea just off the Indrasi coast?"

Aldewin imagined many things lurking in the murky water but just shrugged.

"Trouble, lad. Lots of it. Do you want to face an Engarda flotilla? Or a crew of vicious Merladro too lazy to pilfer their own bounty, so's looking to pillage ours?"

Aldewin shook his head.

The captain returned his attention to the water. He yanked the wheel hard to the right. The ship keened as it slammed into a wave during Captain Ontrosa's course correction.

"Now see here, if ya gonna keep botherin' and takin' my eyes from blessed Mara's waters, then ya gotta leave. We're headed to the Tinoxian coast, all right. But we'll hug the Fyrst Shoals to avoid the jammed-up lane of the Straits."

Satisfied with the answer and not wanting to distract Captain Ontrosa from his task, Aldewin turned to make his way back to the main deck.

Behind him, Imbica said, "If you need my aid, Yngvari, I will be in our quarters with the others in my party."

She'd no sooner spoken when the boy in the aft crow's nest called down, "Engarda! Coming fast."

Ontrosa mumbled curses and called up, "How many?"

The boy stared through his small spyglass. "Counting."

"Count faster!" Ontrosa hollered.

The boy wiped his face and resumed looking through the glass. "Four. No. Five single-masted boats, Cap. Wait. Another. Behind the smaller boats. A three-masted warship, Cap! And her oarsmen are hauling ass."

The *Sicara's Bane* rowing crew didn't need to be asked. The drummers pounded faster and more vigorously, and the coach barked to the men, "Pull, you ham-fisted bilge-wench fuckers. Don't make Yngvari do all the work." The oar coach glanced up through the wooden grate and winked at Yngvari.

But Yngvari likely didn't notice the appreciative gaze of the oars coach. The Sea Singer swept her arms upward in a graceful arch. Niyadi's pale light glinted on Yngvari's gold earcuffs as she raised her face to the sky.

From her mouth came a low, throaty sound. Yngvari spoke to the sea and sky in part song and part speech.

Only moments before, the sky had been clear as could be. Now, ominous clouds gathered between the approaching flotilla and the *Sicara's Bane.*

Juka's breezes had been a welcome boon that filled the ship's sails. Now, the tricky goddess of winds, weather, and æther favored Yngvari's plea and blew a gale that whipped the waves until foamy whitecaps roiled.

A sailor busy lashing himself into the rigging called to them. "Ya should get into the forecastle or belowdecks to wait this out. Yngvari's raisin' a powerful storm."

Aldewin wanted to do as the young sailor had suggested. *To crawl into a bedroll until this infernal rocking ship stops in port.* But he couldn't rest idly while a flotilla of warships gave them chase.

He glanced up at the captain's deck. Yngvari stood still as a statue, her mouth open as her eerie song churned the sea. Imbica stood at her side but faced the aft deck, her arms twirling gently as she gathered Menaris energy.

Aldewin was handier with plunging steel into squishy, vulnerable flesh than with the finesse of mediating magic through gods and spirits. *I can't help Yngvari and Imbica sing the waters, but I can defend should they board.*

Behind *Sicara's Bane*, Yngvari's isolated storm slowed the Engarda advance. While the smaller ships fell behind, the triple-masted warship ate Yngvari's waves and plunged ahead. And it was bearing straight for them.

The boy in the crow's nest called down, "He aims to broadside, Captain!"

Ontrosa grumbled, "I knows what 'e aims ta do. But he'll no'a be takin' the *Sicara's Bane*. Brace!"

Before anyone could steady themselves, Captain Ontrosa cranked the ship's wheel hard to the right. Yngvari's song created unnaturally gigantic waves. The enormous swell buffeted the ship as it grudgingly turned one hundred eighty degrees.

"Ontrosa's heading straight for them!" Dio screamed.

"Full stop, on my mark," Ontrosa bellowed. He cranked the wheel and glared at the approaching warship. After a pause, he called, "Full stop!"

The drumming ceased, and the oars coach yelled, "Stop oars!"

Silence followed, making the hairs on Aldewin's neck stand on end.

The Engarda warship, nearly a third again as large as the *Sicara's Bane*, could not match the *Sicara's* ability to turn. While the warship's crew worked to swing it around to face the *Sicara's Bane*, Captain Ontrosa wasted no time.

"Glass shot, now. Aim for the sails. Shred the fucker's fancy crest and make it into pretty ribbons for his lice-infested hair."

The Enar'atori's eerie song ceased, and the seas calmed.

Captain Ontrosa shouted, "Fire!"

Below, the crew lit fires in mage cannons they'd loaded. The fires ignited an alchemical concoction, and the three cannons boomed in unison. The air whistled as thousands of glass shards whizzed toward the warship's sails.

A ripping sound filled the air as the *Sicara's Bane's* ammo ripped into the warship's sails. The warship's mainsail, though, remained unperturbed.

The Engarda ship continued its effort to turn so it could once again point its mage cannons at the *Sicara's Bane*. Though they'd done minimal damage to the mainsail, the tears in the smaller sails hampered the warship's efforts.

"Archers to the ready and stoke your coals," Ontrosa called.

Shel's eyes lit up at the call. Before anyone could dissuade her, Shel untied the rope Dio had knotted her in and pulled the bow from her back. "I'm going up top." She scurried to the foredeck while nocking an arrow. Following the lead of the other archers, Shel dipped her arrow into the steel barrel of coals smoldering on the forecastle deck. When they pulled the arrows out, the steel tips were red-hot.

The archers lined up along the side of the raised foredeck. One archer, a young man in his teens, called out, "Pull!" After they readied their arrows, he yelled, "Loose!"

A half dozen arrows flew toward the warship. A few wobbled and fizzled just after clearing the deck of the *Sicara's Bane*. Aldewin sized up the archers. The two closest to the prow were teens, their arms still lean and thin.

Two arrows, though, flew true and with power. One hit the deck, and its fire-hot tip ignited the age-dried wood. A small fire erupted, though the warship's crew quickly doused it with water.

The other arrow, though, struck the Engarda ship's mainsail. Yngvari's storm had soaked the sail, but the arrow tore a large gash.

Not to be outdone by the archers, Imbica hurled a tight ball of Vatra's fire at the mainsail. It, too, sputtered as it met the soggy sail. Not deterred, Imbica hurled volley after volley at the exact location until, finally, fire erupted and created a large hole in the warship's mainsail.

While the captain and crew had been busy fending off a broadside by the Engarda warship, the small flotilla of single-masted Engarda boats gained ground on *Sicara's Bane*. The crew aboard these smaller ships loaded their mage cannons while angling to surround the *Bane*.

"If they get close enough, those cannons will shred the *Sicara's Bane*," Dio said. His eyes were wide and searching as if looking for a way out of being sunk.

Ontrosa demanded power from below deck, and the drums pounded anew. The oars coach, sweat gleaming on her brow, called, "Pull, you whoresons. We got a flotilla of sail shredders chomping at our ass, and unless you wanna be food for the darmanitong, stroke hard like ya do when you're…"

Cannon fire swallowed the coach's last words. An explosive boom pierced the air. Shrapnel whistled as it launched toward the *Sicara*. The smaller ship was still too far from the *Sicara* to hit the sails, but the ballistics grazed the edge of its aft side.

"These little bastards are gonna sink us 'less we sink them first. We need a wave, Yngvari. One big 'nough to swallow these Engarda fuckers," Captain Ontrosa said.

Imbica smoothed her sweat-soaked hair back from her face and asked, "Can I lend you power, Yngvari?"

The Enar'atori gave Imbica a nod. "Together, we'll sing the sea," Yngvari said. She turned her attention to the captain. "Brace the crew and passengers. Ride this wave well, Captain, or it will devour us too."

Ontrosa's jaw set, and he scowled at the watery horizon. "Anyone not manning a rigging get your ass belowdecks. Cretius—where'd that bilge rat go? I need his help to man the wheel."

A rogue wave off Indrasi's coast had demolished the ship that sailed from Partha with a seventeen-year-old Aldewin aboard. He'd survived but wasn't keen on riding out another boat-crushing wave.

But when Cretius didn't appear to help the captain, Aldewin's feet defied his will. He marched up to the captain's deck. "I've got strong arms, Captain. Tell me what to do."

While the captain shouted commands and showed Aldewin how to manage the wheel, Yngvari's mouth opened wide in song. Imbica gathered Menaris into herself, her eyes closed, her face serene but focused.

"We have the advantage 'cause we know it's coming," Captain Ontrosa said. "Help me aim into the wave, lad, and we got half a chance."

Yngvari sang a wave ahead of them. It was already large enough to clear the deck and still hadn't crested.

Aldewin called down to Dio. "Get Shel and Nivi belowdecks. And stay with them. It will be the safest place to ride out this wave."

With his hands on the wheel, the semblance of control eased Aldewin's fear. *We can do this,* he told himself. Like the captain, he focused his entire mind, body, and soul on meeting the oncoming wave head-on. It felt like the last thing they should do. *Shouldn't we aim away from a ship-swallowing wave?* But Ontrosa seemed like a man who'd spent more time at sea than ashore, so Aldewin trusted the seasoned captain.

Behind them, the water was still and unnaturally calm. Ahead, Yngvari and Imbica pulled the ocean into a massive surge. It was the sort of wave sailors called boat breakers.

Aldewin stared ahead and into a wall of water rising from the sea. The monster wave was three times the height of the mainmast of *Sicara's Bane.*

"Do no'a look at the top of that wave, ya bilge fucker. Stare straight ahead and keep your hands on this wheel. Do no'a let go for nothin.' We gotta broadside that wave and kiss it like it's the most beautiful wench in all Indrasi."

Aldewin moved his gaze downward and found it helped settle the flip-floppy feeling in his gut. He focused on gripping the wheel.

The captain moved his foot and screamed over the wind. "Put your foot in the hold. Here."

Aldewin glanced down and saw steel foothold straps on the deck to help hold a captain in place. He jammed his right foot in the left-most strap while Ontrosa put his left foot in the right-most strap.

Dreni ran up the aft castle steps and lashed Yngvari and Imbica to the railing of the raised deck. Both women, deep into spell-casting, seemed unaware of Dreni.

With the help of Aldewin's strength, together, he and Captain Ontrosa kept *Sicara's Bane* moving straight ahead and into the oncoming water.

"Brace!" Captain Ontrosa hollered.

"Brace!" the oars coach screamed.

Yngvari ceased calling the winds, and Juka's breath stopped blowing. The oarsmen ceased rowing. Another eerie silence enveloped *Sicara's Bane*.

Aldewin had expected the ship to plow nose first into the ship-swallowing wave. Instead, the suction of the wave pulled the ship upward as if heavenly gods held the boat on a string.

The boat rose, the prow now at nearly forty-five degrees to the sea's surface. Anything or anyone not strapped to the deck rolled downward. The waves slammed untethered crew into the aft castle or swept them overboard.

A wall of water swallowed the crew's screams.

Not yet over the crest, *Sicara's Bane* tipped even further. Soaked through with bone-chilling water from an angry sea, Aldewin tried to focus on holding the wheel steady. It fought against them. The churning seawater yanked on the rudder.

The ship now standing nearly on end, several bodies fell from the deck. Aldewin watched as unfortunate crew members tumbled past him. *A watery grave awaits. Sicara welcome them.* His legs burned from the effort of keeping himself on deck. And as he ducked in the nick of time to avoid a barrel from smashing into him, Aldewin realized they were at dire risk of capsizing. *If this wave does not set us down soon, we will slam keel into the Orju Sea.*

Then… falling. Like a baby bird shoved from its nest atop a stately pine, *Sicara's Bane* dropped back to the Orju Sea.

Falling from such a great height, the previously soft and easily parted ocean became like a hard, sunbaked road. The keel of *Sicara's Bane* slammed into the water. Wood cracked and splintered. *Has the ship split in two?*

Ears once filled with water popped as *Sicara's Bane* bobbed above the smaller wave behind the boat crusher wave. The ship crested and now hugged the sea.

Beside him, Ontrosa still held firm to the wheel. His skin, ordinarily ruddy red, was pale, his face drawn. *Even the sea-hardened captain saw his death.*

Behind them, bits of wood, crates, and other detritus floated to the surface of the Orju Sea. Swallowed by the boat-crusher wave, the small Engarda flotilla had disappeared.

The three-masted warship remained afloat, but the killer wave had ripped off its bowsprit. A splintered gash marred the prow. The wave had snapped the mainmast like a twig and shredded the ship's sails. Listing, it was taking on water as crew jumped overboard, clinging to bits of timber. The massive ship was dead in the water.

"They'll bother us no more," Captain Ontrosa said. He wiped briny water from his face and looked to his side, where Yngvari remained lashed to the railing.

The Enar'atori hung like a limp doll, her head lolling.

Ontrosa's face went ashen. "Man the wheel, lad, and keep it straight." Without further warning, the captain let go of the wheel and began working the ropes that held

Yngvari tied to the ship. Under his breath, the captain mumbled salty invocations to the gods.

Imbica hurriedly undid the last knot in the rope that had kept her tethered to the *Bane*. Soaked to the bone and shivering, she otherwise appeared none the worse for wear. Once free of the ropes, Imbica rushed to Yngvari's aid.

Captain Ontrosa scooped Yngvari into his arms. His eyes were red and bleary. The captain asked Imbica, "Do ya know healing spells, Lady Mage?"

With three fingers pressing lightly on Yngvari's throat, Imbica focused on an invisible spot ahead. After a few moments, she said, "She lives. But barely."

Imbica pressed her palms to Yngvari's chest and again focused intently. "Lungs full of water." Without a moment's hesitation, Imbica wound her arms. She whispered a spell Aldewin couldn't hear and thrust her hands toward Yngvari's chest.

Yngvari's limp body convulsed.

"What vile magic is this?" the captain yelled. "Mage, if ya kill her, I'll burn ya, then hang ya."

Imbica ignored his threats. She remained focused as she repeated her spell and convulsed Yngvari's body again.

This time, the Sea Singer spewed water. Yngvari coughed and gagged as Imbica's spell drew water from her drowning lungs.

Captain Ontrosa's eyes grew wide, and relief flooded his face. "By the Three…" he whispered.

Imbica teetered. Aldewin hadn't seen Dio approach, but the man was there to catch Imbica.

With an arm around her, Dio said, "She's exhausted. I'll get her to our quarters and settled."

While it unnerved Aldewin that the man kept popping up unnoticed, Aldewin was grateful to have a second pair of muscular hands aboard. He gave Dio a curt nod and returned his attention to the endless sea ahead.

With Yngvari still in his arms, Captain Ontrosa said, "Ya did well at the wheel, lad. Do ya think ya can keep us afloat a while longer? I need to get Yngvari to her quarters to rest then take stock of my crew. I fear we lost more'n a few."

Aldewin gave Captain Ontrosa a nod. *Truth is, I fear if I let go of this wheel now, I'll fall into a jellied heap and go nattered, thinking about what we just did.*

The captain gave him a wan smile. "That's a good lad."

Before Ontrosa hit the stairs, Aldewin asked, "What should I steer toward?"

Though Hiyadi, the large sun, had set, Niyadi, the little brother sun, was still just past zenith. There would be few stars for several hours, and Lumine had not yet risen. Ahead lay endless blue-black waves under Niyadi's pale light.

The captain gazed upward, squinting into the dusky light of Niyadi's daily solo journey without his big brother's light overpowering him. "Point it just east of Niyadi. That'll keep us on course 'nough 'til I get back to the wheel."

Ontrosa left Aldewin alone to worry if Nivi and Shel survived the killer wave. Soaked through, the stinging cold numbed his arms. His legs were like mushy tubers. Aldewin called on his training. Fen Menir and Val'Enara had honed his ability to focus on a task rather than listen to his body's complaints. *Fear, hunger, thirst, and fatigue. All can wait.* Another mantra pounded into him. He called on the mantra now to stay awake and keep *Sicara's Bane* headed toward Tinox's southern coast.

Chapter 5

Aldewin

ldewin steered as the captain had said, keeping the prow of *Sicara's Bane* pointed just east of the little brother sun. He'd nodded off briefly, but Nivi's wet nose nuzzled his shoulder and roused him from sleep.

"Nivi, old boy." Aldewin removed his hand from the wheel long enough to scratch the giant snow tiger's head. "Thank the gods you made it through storm and wave."

Nivi kept his giant head nuzzled against Aldewin.

"I'm sorry you had to ride out the horrid wave alone."

"He wasn't alone." Shel ambled up the steps, walking like she was saddle-sore.

Relieved to see her, Aldewin's shoulders relaxed. "And thank the Three you made it too. Are you okay? You walk as though you're injured."

Shel stretched backward, her hands pressing into the small of her back. "Tossed around but nothing broken." She rested a hand on Nivi's shoulders while she pulled a bit of damp kabu stalk from her pocket. Shel offered the sweet bark to Aldewin.

He shook his head. Kabu would revive his energy, but Aldewin detested the overly sweet taste of the stuff and how it kept him from restful sleep.

Shel sucked the bark. "Yngvari sure gave us an exciting ride, huh?" Her eyes shone brightly.

Aldewin nearly choked. "Exciting?" He harrumphed. "Not exactly how I'd describe it. People died, Shel. Yngvari was nearly one of them."

A dark shadow washed over Shel's face. "I—didn't know."

Uncomfortable silence swelled between them.

Breaking the quiet, Shel said, "Looks like we're going to need to stay in the Vatnoyer Province of Tinox longer than we expected."

"Why's that?"

Shel glanced behind them. "After destroying an entire Engarda flotilla? Can you imagine the bounty they'll put on our heads? If we want to return to Indrasi, we'll need to raise an army to conquer the Dynasty. Not likely, huh?" She wiped a tear from her glistening eyes.

Aldewin put an arm around her shoulders. "We'll figure it out."

Her body relaxed a bit, and she nodded.

Aldewin took Shel's hand and placed it on the ship's wheel. "Steer with me. Feels good, doesn't it?"

Shel grasped the wheel and smiled when the ship obeyed her command. She put her other hand on the wheel and moved closer, her attention now entirely on steering.

"Captain Ontrosa said to steer just east of Niyadi. That's it."

Shel pushed against Aldewin, giving a gentle shove to both him and Nivi so she could be at the helm. She sucked the kabu stalk between her back teeth and smiled widely. "I could get used to this."

Aldewin laughed. "You'd have to kill Ontrosa before he'd let you take his wheel from him."

From behind them, Ontrosa bellowed, "Been on my ship less than a day, and ya already plottin' mutiny?" There was mirth in his tone.

Aldewin stepped aside to allow the captain his helm, and Nivi followed suit. But Shel looked positively unyielding, her hands remaining on the wheel.

"Looks like I found a new first mate in training," Ontrosa said.

Shel's eyes grew wide. "Really? I'm hardly qualified."

Ontrosa shoved her aside and took the wheel. "You're not. But thems without curds or turds for brains is dead, see. So, ya want to train or not?"

Shel didn't hesitate and nodded her acceptance.

Ontrosa gave her a wink then issued his first order. "Go below and wake up day crew. The lazy ratlings will sleep all day 'less you put a fire under their arse."

"And then what?" Shel asked.

"Watch. Learn. And do whatever the crew tells you."

Shel switched the kabu stalk to her other side, her brows scrunched. "I thought you said I was training to be your first mate?"

Ontrosa gave her a side-eye. "I am. Now, get going before I change my mind and pick someone with more gumption."

Shel pestered him no further. She took the stairs to the deck by twos.

After she'd cleared the deck, Aldewin said, "You made her day. Shel gets antsy when idle, so thank you for giving her something to do."

The captain narrowed his eyes at Aldewin. "Oh, I was no'a lyin.' Lost half of my crew in that blasted wave. The fat purse your lady mage paid me don't mean shite when I got good crew now at the bottom of goddess Mara's sea." Ontrosa's eyes watered, and he wiped his face with a filthy handkerchief he pulled from his belt.

Aldewin spent the morning helping Ontrosa and the *Bane's* crew clean up after encountering the ship-eating wave. Imbica lent her healing abilities, and Shel did as the captain requested. Dio stayed in their quarters, for which Aldewin was grateful. Aldewin couldn't put his finger on why Dio rankled him, but he'd have preferred the trip without the newest member of Druvna's old pod.

By midday, the captain told Aldewin, "Go get some shut-eye while ya can. I'll need your strength when we hit Fyrstua Shoals."

Aldewin brooked no argument. Truth be told, he was exhausted, and his aching limbs longed for rest. He left Captain Ontrosa alone on the captain's deck and went to their fetid quarters in the forecastle.

Despite bone-aching fatigue, rest did not come quickly. The *Bane* sailed to Tinox, where Aldewin had been Timonay—"Little Mouse." A young boy pledged body and soul to Sicara, the Dread Sister and goddess of death. And they made this trip aboard a boat named *Sicara's Bane. An ill omen if ever there was one.*

When he arrived at their assigned quarters, Aldewin found the others sleeping or at least trying to. For a small fortune paid in advance, Ontrosa provided their pod with what amounted to a large closet with only two hammocks. *At least there's a small porthole for fresh air.*

Aldewin settled his back against the wall and stretched his aching legs. His feet nearly touched the opposite side.

Rest. Sleep. Aldewin could do neither when, with every oarsman's stroke, the *Sicara's Bane* reeled him back to a life drenched in death. A vocation and life he'd vowed never to live again.

His eyes closed, Aldewin wrapped one hand around the amber pendant and rested the other on Nivi. The amber warmed beneath his touch, as Quen once had. The small blob of hardened resin had become his touchstone, a tether to his promise.

By the Three and all gods and spirits who hear me. Guide this ship to Tinox's shore and aid us in finding the Heart of Menaris before the Dynasty does.

The prayer didn't bring comfort or sleep. Hell, Aldewin no longer knew what—if any—gods he had faith in. These last months, he'd been unmoored. Tripping through his days without purpose since his encounter with Hooxaura.

But the amber reminded him of Quen and of what they'd had, if only briefly. It revealed his new purpose, encased in the yellow rock just as the hair of Quen's mother was bound within. "My promise," he whispered.

He'd thought Shel was asleep in a hammock, but she whispered down to him, "We're out of danger—"

From her hammock, Imbica said, "For now."

Shel continued. "You can't make us wait any longer. We're out of danger, and you're out of excuses. You've gotta tell us what happened to Quen."

Aldewin's jaw tightened. The pitch and roll of the ship matched the roiling of his gut. "I told you before. I'll only relive this once. And Rhoji needs to be the one to hear the story first."

"You may never see Rhoji again," Imbica said.

Dio rested against the wall with his eyes closed. He opened them and said, "That's a fatalist attitude, even for you, Imbica."

In a short time, he knows Imbica well, Aldewin thought.

Shel glared over at Imbica. "Yeah, it's not like we're all going to prison or being exiled on some island to die alone." She uncrossed her arms and leaned forward, her eyes suddenly wide. "Are we?"

Imbica softened her gaze and tried to smile, but it came across as gas pains. "We will not die. Well, we will. Someday." Exasperated, she sighed. "What I mean to convey is that unless the merchant faction that Rhoji has aligned with throws Dynasty control off Bardivia, it is *he* who is effectively a prisoner. And unless the Exalted cancels the bounty on Aldewin's head, our two brothers cannot see each other."

Imbica usually finds the right of it. The idea brought tightness to Aldewin's chest.

"I still think my news about Quen is for Rhoji to hear." Aldewin pondered the water-speaking he'd once shown Quen. The ancient Tinoxian magic was related to Yngvari's Enar'atori water spells. *Perhaps I can send a message to Rhoji as I'd once sent updates to Archon Kine.*

But now, knowing that the Archon was a Nixan—a darmanitong beast tied to a water spirit no less—Aldewin realized the water-speak with Archon Kine likely worked so well because of Kine's magic, not his.

Yngvari. Maybe she possesses the ability I lack.

Aldewin rose. Stiff and sore from gripping during the wave ride earlier, his legs were unsteady.

"Where are you going?" Shel asked.

"To speak to Yngvari."

Dio and Shel moved to come with him, but Aldewin said, "I want to speak with her alone." Aldewin put out a halting hand to Nivi too. "You stay here too, old boy. And rest while you can."

Nivi didn't need further encouragement to resume napping. Shel gave Aldewin a sideways glare. Dio closed his eyes and pretended he didn't care why Aldewin wanted to speak to the Enar'atori.

Aldewin made his way down the narrow stairs to the main deck. His burning leg muscles protested as he climbed to the top of the aft castle again.

He'd last seen Yngvari wan and exhausted after their battle with the ship-eating wave. That she now stood by the captain's side surprised Aldewin. Yngvari looked none the worse for wear. She wore fresh, dry garments of the same style she'd worn before, but her braids had come undone, and her white-gold hair fell to her back.

Before Aldewin could speak, Yngvari said, "Yes. I am from Tinox too. And no, I am not available to bed you."

Her first statement was no surprise, but the second threw him off task. Aldewin coughed lightly. "I do not seek a bedmate. I had—have?" He coughed again.

Yngvari gave him a sideways stare. "Which is it? Had? Or have?"

I wish I knew, Aldewin thought.

Captain Ontrosa interrupted. "Whatever ya seekin', Northman, sniff somewhere else. Yngvari here is workin.' And in her free time, she don't need no cockwaddles like you and your contraband pod sniffin' at her tail. So off with ya."

Though Aldewin hadn't passed for nonthreatening since puberty, he tried on the smile Fen Menir masters had taught him as a child. The one that conveyed reassurance. He took a step back to put space between them. "Look, Captain Ontrosa, I assure you I have no intentions of that sort toward Yngvari or any of your crew. I seek only to ask her for help with water-speaking. I have an urgent message that needs to be carried on the winds."

Ontrosa scrunched his face and didn't seem convinced. Yngvari turned a withering gaze on Aldewin.

The captain asked, "Do ya know what the fuck this lad's talking about?"

Yngvari's look grew distant as she moved her gaze from Aldewin to the captain. But the look was gone quickly, replaced with a practiced stare of cool nonchalance.

Yngvari's voice was steady and indifferent as she stared at the sea. "Water-speaking? It's a silly legend that old ladies of the Fyrstua clans tell. A story meant to instill awe about the time of legends."

Captain Ontrosa didn't look convinced and turned his attention to Aldewin. "You have a method to send messages on the wind? Using water magic?"

Behind the captain, Yngvari's eyes grew wide. Her hands gripped each other as she silently implored Aldewin to lie.

Aldewin didn't know Yngvari. He owed her nothing and desperately needed her help to get word to Rhoji. But though they owed one another nothing, the gold bands on her ears reminded him of Quen. And Yngvari's status as indentured was something Aldewin knew well. *Technically, I am still indentured too.* He decided to trust Yngvari and do as she pled. *I'll have to find another way to send Rhoji my message.*

"Me? Use water magic?" Aldewin chuckled. "Nah. I have no Menaris skills at all. I wasn't raised in the Vatnoyer or with the Fyrstua people." *One truth within the lie to make it more believable.* "I just figured it was worth a shot, seeing as how Yngvari is so obviously gifted with water magic."

Captain Ontrosa rolled his eyes. "Gods preserve me." The veins in his neck pulsed, and his face grew red. "We got important business here. It's called keeping this tub afloat. I told ya to be restin' 'cause I'll need your muscle later. Get the fuck off my deck and leave Yngvari be. Ya bring your nonsense up here again? I'll throw ya to the darmanitongs."

Aldewin had barely survived his last meeting with a darmanitong, and that was only because Quen channeled the Dragos power surging within her to pull him from Hooxaura's icy grip. "I don't fancy a swim today," he said.

Before he left, Yngvari gave him a smile and a barely perceptible nod. She turned back to watching the sea and dimmed her attention to all else.

❖   ❖   ❖

A week passed with fair weather and calm seas. Shel spent most of her days doing whatever Ontrosa ordered of her while chatting with Yngvari whenever the Sea Singer wasn't on deck. Imbica passed the time staring toward the vast horizon ahead, arms resting on the railing as though waiting for something to happen. Aldewin and Dio assisted the captain and crew as best they could, lending aid where needed.

The warm shores of Indrasi were now well behind them, and *Sicara's Bane* entered the cooler waters of the northern lands. Though the skies remained clear, the winds picked up and brought strength-sapping cold. Aldewin wished for woolen breeches instead of linen.

Hiyadi had set, and twilight brought a chill. Aldewin pulled the wool cloak from his rucksack as he tried to bed down for the night. Sleeping in their cramped quarters made Aldewin feel like a barrel of ale rolling down a Bardivian hill.

Apparently made for water travel, Shel slept peacefully in one of the two hammocks. In the other hammock, Imbica also slept soundly. She stirred only when her own snoring jolted her awake.

Like Aldewin, Dio tried to sleep leaning against the wood wall of their quarters. Aldewin's legs were outstretched, and his feet touched the wall opposite where Dio rested.

Growing up under the harsh tutelage of Fen Menir masters, Aldewin had grown up sleeping curled into a tight ball on a hard floor with no blanket. The masters said it was to teach them to sleep in any conditions. *"You may have to rest standing if your duties require it of you,"* Master Mordranis had said.

Under normal conditions, his childhood training would kick in, and Aldewin could sleep anywhere, even standing. But the rolling waves made his stomach uneasy, and the gnawing feeling that he was back in a fate weaver's plot didn't help.

Dio, perhaps sensing that Aldewin was awake, opened his eyes. "Can't sleep either?"

Aldewin quickly looked away, his face growing hot from being caught staring. "As I told you, I *hate* sea travel."

"I do not love it either." Dio cocked his head to stretch his neck. "Yet it is a necessary means to an end."

"You seem familiar with boats. For a Bardivian merc, I mean," Aldewin said.

Dio smiled. "You know many Bardivian mercenaries, do you, Northman?"

Before Aldewin could answer, Dio said, "Oh, but Imbica established you are—what did she say? A Vandu assassin from house Fen Menir in Partha? That sounds— important." Dio glanced at Aldewin's Vandu dagger, sheathed, as always, at his right hip.

Aldewin kept his gaze calm, his features as empty of emotion as possible. "I'm not now, nor have I ever been, important. I am a tiny insect, finding my way from web to web, trying not to get eaten." The words reminded him of his conversation with Quen in the meadow.

"*I could become a giant snake,*" she'd said.

"*Then I will love a snake,*" Aldewin had replied.

"*Or an eight-legged hairy beast that spins one of those webs you're so fond of.*"

"*I'm already caught in webs,*" he'd said. "*They might as well be yours.*"

Aldewin closed his eyes and breathed deeply to quell his emotion. *When I said I'd love you no matter what you became, I spoke the truth. You became a nightmarish creature, yet I cannot wrest you from my heart and mind.* Aldewin quickly dashed the thoughts lest he show Dio something he didn't care to share.

Dio pulled a wine sac from his pack and drank. He held it out to Aldewin. "No offense, mate, but I don't buy your humble insect story."

Aldewin waved off the offer of wine. "I don't give a fuck what you 'buy.' And while we're speaking openly, I don't believe you're a merc."

Dio took another sip and wiped his mouth. "Then we're two guys stuck on a boat, not believing the shite coming from the other's mouth, huh?"

Aldewin nodded. "'Bout sums it up."

Dio laughed. "Okay, then. Watching our backs. Got it." His mirth gone, he leaned forward and lowered his voice. "Just know this, Northman. I took an oath to watch these two." He indicated Shel and Imbica with a nod of his head. "My past is not your concern. My job is all I've got. And my reputation? All that matters. I gotta do my job and do it well, see? So if you cross me or put them in harm's way, I'll take you out."

Aldewin wanted to laugh and say something like, "Yeah? You and what Kovatha battle mage army?" He also wanted to set Dio straight about Imbica and Shel. They didn't need his protection. The pod had escaped the Dynasty Kovathas in Qülla only because of Shel's skill with the bow and Imbica's prodigious mastery of Menaris.

Aldewin's hand twitched from the effort of remaining at his side. He wanted to grasp his Vandu blade and teach the curds-for-brains how incapable he was of taking Aldewin out. But Aldewin stayed his hand. *Keep things civil. Dio needs to feel important? Fine. I'll ignore how he grates me. For now, anyway.*

Aldewin held up his hands in a "You win" gesture. "Whatever you say, Dionus. I'm just a bug, remember? Currently trapped in a Kovan Dynasty web, trying not to get killed. Or vomit my guts out."

Dio's gaze softened. Aldewin sipped from his water sac. The two men resumed staring at each other until Aldewin finally found sleep.

◆   ◆   ◆

Her fingers twirled the hair on his naked chest. Aldewin's hand tangled in her long, wavy hair. He stared up into her golden eye. Being with Quen was like being enveloped in a Sulmére sunset.

"Aldewin," she whispered.

"I'm here, sol'dishi," he replied. "I'm always by your side."

Cupping her head in his large hand, he gently pulled her closer and reached for her lips. The passion of their kiss exploded into pain as she dug into the flesh on his chest. Her gentle fingers now talons, she scratched and tore at him.

"No!" he screamed. Or he tried to, but his words lodged in his throat. "Quen! No, my love. Do not become… Do not leave me."

Quen's face morphed before his eyes as she became Ishna. The Winter Dragon.

"Shh," the dragon hissed.

"Quen!"

Something shook him. Hard. Someone whispered into his ear. "Be calm, Aldewin. You are dreaming. Wake and come with me."

Aldewin blinked. Pale hair reflected Niyadi's dim light. *Yngvari.*

"It will be full dark soon. Captain Ontrosa takes his rest now. Come. We will send your message." She gave him a weak smile.

Aldewin raked a hand through his hair and scratched his scruffy beard, trying to bring himself to waking. The dream, one he'd had frequently since Volenex, was the kind to linger. Aldewin was glad to have a focus to take his mind from memories of Quen.

Yngvari lent him a hand up, and he took it. She passed him mizan bark to chew to freshen his breath.

For her sake, Aldewin took the mizan. "We should wake Shel and Imbica. They need to hear what I have to say," he whispered.

"I'm already awake, mageling," Imbica said. She rolled out of the hammock and wobbled, her legs unsteady. Aldewin lent her an arm, and she quickly righted herself. "Let Shel sleep. She's exhausted from assisting the crew. Besides, she has zero volume control and will probably cause unwanted attention. I will repeat your tale to her when she rises."

The two followed Yngvari around the forecastle to the prow. Barely large enough for them, the space was the farthest from the captain's quarters.

With Lumine in crescent behind them, the forecastle created a dark shadow at the prow. Briny spray from the ship's wake quickly covered Aldewin's beard.

Standing between Imbica and Aldewin, Yngvari said, "You both have the understanding, don't you?"

Imbica nodded, but Aldewin wasn't sure he understood what she was asking.

Seeing his apparent puzzlement, Imbica said, "Menaris. We both understand Menaris."

He nodded then. "We both studied at Val'Enara. For a time, anyway. But Val'Enara doesn't teach old magic like Sea Singing or water-speaking."

Yngvari turned her gaze on Aldewin. "If this is true, how do *you* know of water-speaking? Did you learn of it at your ma's knee when you were a pup?"

The image of Aldewin sitting at his ma's knee, learning anything of value, made him chortle. "No. My mother wasn't Fyrstua."

Yngvari raised an eyebrow, clearly unable to believe he had no Fyrstua blood, given how he towered over Indrasian people and had such fair hair and pale eyes.

Aldewin quickly said, "My father was Fyrstua. Or so my mother told me. I never met him."

"She must have told it true," Imbica said. "You don't grow legs that long unless you've got blood from the Fyrstua clans in you."

"I learned about water-speaking from Archon Kine." Aldewin's expression grew dark, his voice tinged with bitter acid. "Archon Kine. To whom I took special vows. Not the standard Val'Enara vows." That was for Imbica's information. "Vows to serve *her*. A woman who turned out to be a Nixan." For Imbica's sake, Aldewin gave that statement time to breathe and sink in.

Imbica's face turned ashen. "Nixan?" She gulped as though trying to hold herself back from vomiting. "How? Are you sure?"

"Quite certain. Kine's beast form is a darmanitong."

While that news made Imbica reach for the railing to keep herself upright, Yngvari's face lit up. "A darmanitong. What a gift your Archon has!"

Imbica pulled her linen cloth from her waist belt, unfazed by the now-dried blood that caked it. She wiped her forehead and dabbed her face. "Gift? Darmanitong are vile creatures." Watery tears twinkled in the corners of her eyes. "To think I revered her."

Aldewin took her hand in his. "As did I."

Yngvari gave Imbica a disapproving glare. "The Fyrstua treasure changelings. Anyone gifted with the skin-changing ability *and* blessed with water-speaking? Doubly blessed, they are. Being afraid of such creatures is— immature. That's what it is. Do all people in Indrasi feel this way?"

Both Imbica and Aldewin nodded.

Yngvari shook her head. "Shows that Indrasi people can't handle the bounty of Menaris-gifted creatures your leaders plunder from our lands."

"Like yindrils?" Aldewin asked.

Yngvari nodded. "They were the first to be 'discovered.' Your Exalted? She sends Dynasty soldiers to tame the marshlands and forests of my homeland, the Myrskog." Her voice took on a bitter edge. "They're plundering more than creatures."

"They took—you?" Aldewin asked.

Yngvari sighed. "Not the Dynasty. Not exactly."

Imbica asked, "So Captain Ontrosa was there—"

Yngvari shook her head and put up a hand. "It is complicated. Ontrosa has never set foot in the Myrskog region of the Vatnoyer Province. Never been to my village."

Yngvari sighed. "We can speak of this another time. If you know water-speaking, why do you need my help?"

"Because my ability to send messages over long distance was tied to my connection to Kine. She performed a binding spell between us, you see, so my water-speak reached her ears only."

Yngvari nodded. "Ah, now I see. You could send the message, but having it reach your intended recipient is the challenge."

"Exactly. Can you assist me with that part?"

"I can certainly try. Let us make haste. I want to send your message before Captain Ontrosa wakes. While I have come to trust Ontrosa in most things, there are some Fyrstua magics I do not share. To begin, who am I sending the messages to?"

"Rhoji Tomo Santu di Bardivia," Aldewin said.

"Since I've never met Rhoji and have no connection to him, it will help if you have an object that was his. Or something that holds special meaning for him."

Imbica shook her head. "I didn't think to bring Rhoji's trinkets aboard. Not that he has many now. We left everything behind in Qülla before our escape."

Aldewin pulled the amber pendant over his head. "Rhoji's father was wearing this when he died in a dragon attack. The amber encases a lock of Rhoji and Quen's mother's hair. If I understand it correctly, this is the most treasured object of the Tomo Santu clan."

Yngvari took the pendant and held it up by the singed cord. She closed her eyes briefly then opened them slightly in a soft, blank gaze. "This object," she whispered. "Such…" Her voice cracked, and her lips contorted in pain as tears sprang to her eyes. "The anguish—it's nearly unbearable. Dragos. The last person who wore this pendant was—touched. No, more than touched. Was… a dragon."

Imbica's eyes widened. "I knew it. Something about her—"

Aldewin cut in. "Can you sense Rhoji? He's the one I need to speak to."

Imbica dug into the purse at her waist. From the pouch, she pulled a folded bit of coarse paper. She quickly unfolded it to reveal a drawing of Rhoji with his arms around Eira. Though crudely drawn, it still captured Rhoji's essence. He had a straight, prominent nose and one feather earring dangling from his right ear. And a look about him that said, "I think I'm better than you."

Yngvari took the paper and pendant. She closed her eyes and pulled the items to her chest. Though the boat swayed beneath them, Yngvari's body remained still as stone, her focus intense. She nodded and whispered, "I feel him. Yes, this pendant calls to him."

Before them, a fine mist gathered and swirled. At first, barely noticeable, it soon formed into a swirling water ball.

Yngvari whispered, "There, Aldewin. The waters are ready to serve you. Speak your words for Rhoji's ears."

Aldewin understood what to do. He'd used such magic many times to send messages to Archon Kine. "It will take several speakings."

Yngvari's eyes were barely open slits. Her gaze remained focused on the swirling water sphere. "Make haste. The Big Brother sun will soon rise."

Aldewin said a quick silent prayer to Lumine. *Habit.* He leaned toward the orb and spoke his story.

He left out the time he'd spent with Quen in the meadow. *A brother should not hear such things about his sister.* And he glossed over details such as traveling through the Void. *That would make Quen seem like a shadow spawn, which I suppose she is. But I don't want Rhoji to remember her—think of her—that way.*

Yngvari maintained the deep concentration required to send nearly a dozen spheres of spoken message. After each, she whispered words to seal the story and a spell of instruction telling the waters to deliver the message to Rhoji.

Aldewin ended his story at the point when Ishna dropped him and Nivi at the edge of the Damianta Forest. His last message told of Ishna's promise and her pledge to discover how to restore Quen to human form and separate their souls. *Best to leave it on a hopeful note,* he thought.

Her hands flying into the air, Yngvari sent the last sphere to the winds. The orb dissipated into a fine mist and finally disappeared south to make its way—hopefully—to Rhoji's waiting ears.

Fatigued from the intense focus, Yngvari leaned back against the ship. Wet tears made tracks down her smooth, pale cheeks. "May the goddess Juka favor us with kind winds. Quen's loving brother needs to hear the fate of his dear sister." Yngvari put a thin hand on Aldewin's arm. "I'm sorry, Aldewin. I know the ache of losing one you love."

Telling the story aloud had lifted a weight from Aldewin's heavy heart. He appreciated Yngvari's caring

but did not consider Quen gone. "She's not dead, Yngvari."
Not human, but hey, she's not dead. It was little comfort, but
all he had.

With brows furrowed deep, Imbica's small eyes
narrowed, her lips set in a thin line.

Imbica looks angrier than a bee without a hive.

"What say you, Imbica?" Aldewin asked.

She stroked her chin. "The Exalted." Imbica stared at
the vast sea, stretching across the horizon as if it had
answers.

"What about her?" Aldewin asked.

"That Edict 42 business. Doj'Anira. The thing that
brought me into this mess." She let out a long breath.
"That's what she was looking for. Xa'Vatra knew.
Somehow, she knew there was a Nixan—a 'Doj'Anira'—
that would become… a dragon."

Aldewin hadn't given thought to Edict 42 and why
Xa'Vatra wanted Doj'Anira. Once they'd escaped Qülla, he
preferred not to think about how close he'd been to
spending the rest of his life in a Dynasty prison. "How
could she know? Suda—even Quen didn't know exactly
what dwelled inside her until… well, until near the end."

"This woman—Quen. A twice blessed? And with a
dragon soul?" Yngvari's voice was an awed whisper. She
handed the amber necklace back to Aldewin. "Imagine.
Being the vessel for a living god."

"Vessel?" Aldewin's voice held an edge. "I hardly
think Quen was happy to be used that way, against her
will." Hot tears stung his eyes. Unlike Yngvari, Aldewin
hadn't grown up in the Vatnoyer with the Fyrstua people.
He didn't share her awe for skin changers or reverence for

being used by dragon-cult zealots to raise one of their gods from the dead.

"I don't think Quen felt blessed when she was—" He swallowed. "When she was—destroyed."

Yngvari got his meaning. "I am sorry. I did not mean to… The magic is extraordinary. Perhaps terrible, too, but wondrous. I wasn't thinking about your loss or what you're going through having witnessed… that."

Aldewin wiped his eye and gave her a reassuring nod. *I wonder if all Fyrstua people are like Yngvari. Maybe, when this quest is done, I'll make a home for myself in the Vatnoyer. Away from the Dynasty, Pillars, Mājas, and Fen Menir. And away from the scorching sands that remind me of her.*

Imbica didn't let her ruminations on the Dynasty go. "We might never know how Xa'Vatra knew about Quen's—condition." Imbica's eyes grew wide. "Perhaps Xa'Vatra did not know Quen would become a dragon. Maybe, like me, she thought Quen was a Rajani dragomancer. Like the one I witnessed on Vahgrin's back when he attacked Quen and me on the Trinity Road. If she thought Quen was a Rajani, then if Xa'Vatra controlled Quen, she'd have a dragomancer at her beck and call."

Imbica smoothed her hair, satisfied with the answer she'd given herself. "We saw Xa'Vatra has—had—possession of dragons. But those fool Kovatha clearly had little ability to control the beasts." She snickered. "Using prods." Imbica tsked. "Like a pathetic pulse of skyfire on their rumps could bend a dragon's will."

"Dragomancers?" Yngvari asked.

Pale violet lit the eastern horizon. "Hiyadi rises," Aldewin said. "We should separate before Captain Ontrosa takes his post. I hope to speak with you again,

Yngvari. I would like to learn more about you and your clan. And I will answer questions you have about my sol'dishi."

Yngvari nodded and smiled. Without further words, she slipped quietly from their company without squeaking a single board.

Imbica gripped the railing and scowled as she surveyed the pink-tinged sky.

"What troubles you, Imbica?"

Without glancing in his direction, she said, "I fear the turbulent waters behind us are like a still pond compared to the frothy waves ahead." She reached out and drew water up from the sea below. With a flick of her wrist, the water became icy shards that she shot back to the waiting ocean.

A gale slapped the riggings as if in answer to her angry magic outburst. The mid-mast swayed and sounded like it would splinter.

From the foremast crow's nest, a young girl called down. "Ring the alarm. All hands. Captain to the deck."

Shouts of alarm rose, and someone clanged the large bell that hung at center deck. It took only a few moments for Captain Ontrosa to storm onto the deck from his quarters, tucking his shirt into his breeches and barking orders and questions.

Captain Ontrosa called up to the crow's nest. "What do ya see, Linjeera?"

"Leeward. Ships on the horizon."

An unnatural wave rocked *Sicara's Bane*. It was the sort of wave Yngvari had sent toward the Engarda ships.

Imbica nearly toppled over as the ship rocked. Aldewin caught her, gripped the rail, and planted his feet to keep them from being carried overboard.

"Gods, but I hate sea travel," he said.

"Let us hope they are Merladro, not Engarda," Imbica said.

"You're wishing for bandits?"

"No. But between the two, I would rather not face my former comrades before I've had the *Bane's* bitter brew to prevent throwing up."

The captain bellowed, "Mind your stations and tits up. Linjeera, what sails do ya see?"

She put a small spyglass to her eye. Linjeera sounded alarmed and called, "Fyrstua ships, Captain. Two of 'em. No, make that three."

Ontrosa shouted back, "For fuck's sake, what's the colors, girl? Do they bear sigils?"

Linjeera squinted into the glass and shouted, "Vines twisted 'round a heart. Kāfe'vind Clan. And they've got a Sea Singer aboard, Captain."

"Ready the coals," Captain Ontrosa shouted. "I'm no'a fuckin' with this lot." He spit out tobacco juice. "Damned choke-vine clan. Archers—ready on my mark."

On the horizon, still a barely visible speck between waves, three sets of sails. The boats were smaller than the *Sicara's Bane* and the Engarda single-masted boats they'd sunk earlier.

Captain Ontrosa looked down and caught sight of Aldewin and Imbica gripping the rail. "By all the gods, who *are* you fuckin' lot? And why is every ship in the Straits and Shoals lookin' to get a piece of ya'?"

Chapter 6

Aldewin

Dark clouds gathered between *Sicara's Bane* and the approaching ships. The Kāfe'vind clan's Enar'atori sang the sea into choppy waves.

Awakened by the commotion of the *Sicara's Bane*'s now-bustling crew, Shel and Dio joined Aldewin and Imbica on deck. Dio arrived with tousled hair and bloodshot eyes. Shel had slept so soundly a hammock ring left an indented print on her cheek.

Shel stretched her arms overhead. "You two are up early. What did we miss?"

Aldewin pointed to the darkening sky. "Besides a small flotilla approaching with a pissed-off Sea Singer?" He chuckled and added, "We were up because Yngvari helped me send water messages to Rhoji."

Shel smacked him on the shoulder. "Suda, Aldewin! I can't believe you told Yngvari what's happening with Quen but not me." Her typically nonchalant expression gave way to a sneer and knitted brows.

Imbica interjected. "Don't be angry at him. Aldewin wanted to wake you, but I insisted we let you sleep."

Arms crossed, Shel shot Imbica an indignant glare.

"I promise to divulge every detail, but later," Imbica said. "Perhaps you noticed the storm their Enar'atori brewed? I must help Captain Ontrosa and Yngvari. I suggest you three make yourselves useful."

Shel looked only slightly mollified, but churning waves rocked the ship. Encroaching danger forced Shel to let it go for the time being.

Shading his eyes, Dio squinted at the boats. "Looks like they stole those ships from Engarda." He pointed at the sails. "Painted their crest right over the Engarda stripes."

The sails of the approaching mini flotilla bore crudely painted emblems of a thorny vine choking a heart.

Rubbing sleep from her eyes, Shel said, "These waters are full of complications." Shel nimbly braided her long, unruly hair into a single braid and tied it with a leather wrap. "So, what am I lookin' at here? Friend or foe?"

"Unclear," Imbica said.

"Really?" Aldewin harrumphed. "Their Enar'atori is building a storm. Seems clear they see *Sicara's Bane* as a foe."

"I agree with Aldewin," Dio said.

With hands on hips and fresh kabu stalk between her teeth, Shel looked ready to kick ass. "Do I need to get my gear and nock an arrow or not?"

Without taking her eyes from the darkening skies, Imbica said, "Gear up, Shel. And bring whatever weapons we have for these two."

Shel scurried off to their quarters to gather weapons.

"I thought you said it was unclear what Kāfe'vind's intentions were?" Aldewin asked.

"I did. But Shel must stay busy, or her nattered energy will fray my wits."

Upon her return, Shel handed Dio a sword, Aldewin his staff, broadsword, and scabbard. She adjusted her quiver onto her back. "What did I miss?"

Imbica sighed. "Only us staring at these ships, trying to divine their intent."

"And?"

Aldewin chuckled. "How should we know? You've got the same sight we have. What do you think?"

Shel didn't look at the ships hugging the horizon. Instead, she gazed at the *Bane's* Sea Singer. "Yngvari looks… relaxed. Is she smiling?"

The other three shifted focus to the captain's deck. Yngvari stood at Ontrosa's side, her eyes gleaming. With furrowed brows and his face in a tight grimace, Captain Ontrosa stared through the spyglass and muttered.

Yngvari must have felt their stare. She glanced down and quickly changed her expression back to a mask of cool indifference.

Dio asked, "Aldewin, are you certain Yngvari sent your messages to Rhoji? Or did she send them to the Leid of a Fyrstua clan?"

It hadn't occurred to Aldewin that Yngvari didn't send his messages to Rhoji. *Is Yngvari capable of such betrayal?* But Yngvari owed them nothing. Yngvari could deliver

Aldewin to the Dynasty and amass a fortune. *The captain said this was her last sail. Collecting the bounty would help her establish a new life.*

But Imbica had an alternate opinion. "Don't assume betrayal at every turn. Cynicism will not serve us." She lifted her skirt to step over Nivi's outstretched paws and made her way to the captain's deck.

Hypocrite, telling Dio *not to be cynical,* Aldewin thought. *Imbica has spouted cynicism the entire time I've known her.* Aldewin asked Imbica, "Where are you going?"

"To get answers," she said.

Aldewin didn't need to wait for Imbica to return with news. No sooner had Imbica left than a powerful jolt of magical energy passed through him and prickled his skin. Though not unpleasant, the phenomenon carried powerful emotion. Intuitively, Aldewin knew the sensation was a message but not intended for him.

He moved his gaze toward Yngvari and witnessed the moment the energy wave hit her. Eyes closed, her face lit up with a wide smile as her body subtly swayed.

It is *a message. Dammit, did Yngvari send my messages to Rhoji? Or is Dio right? Did she instead send my pained words to her allies on shore looking to profit?*

Ontrosa bellowed, "Damn your hide to the Void and back, Yngvari. My nerves are like the frayed ropes of my riggings. Tell me, woman. Are these Kāfe'vind going to play nice or not?"

Yngvari pulled her arms toward her chest. With palms toward the heavens, Yngvari released the Menaris energy she'd gathered. "They aren't foe, Captain. At least, not to me."

"Dammit, are they goin' ta sink my *Bane* or no'a? 'Cause I do no'a have the crew to man all the oars and sails. If they attack, saving the *Bane* is up to you."

The roiling waters between the ships calmed. The gathered clouds dissipated. Hiyadi's growing light revealed a marshy coastline beyond the approaching Kāfe'vind ships.

"See, Captain. Their Sea Singer has released her storm clouds. She recognizes me."

"How?"

Yngvari smiled broadly. "Because the Sea Singer aboard their ship is my sister, Nalija." Yngvari waved a hand toward the approaching ships. "Kāfe'vind is my clan."

Captain Ontrosa wiped his brow and shook his head. "By the gods, woman, ya coulda told me that afore and saved stress on my old heart." Ontrosa called out, "Weapons down, and archers relax. This here is Yngvari's clan."

Yngvari's smile didn't wane, but she said, "I had to be certain. It has been two years since…" Her skin paled, and her eyes drifted away. Yngvari sighed, and her smile returned. "Two years since raiders nabbed me from my home. Much has changed, but my sister lives."

Ontrosa's face softened. "Then, at last, I bringin' ya home. I promised I would." Tears shone in the crow's feet of the captain's eyes.

Yngvari placed a thin, pale hand on the captain's beefy sun- and sea-weathered forearm. "That you did, Captain. I will ensure Kāfe'vind knows you are a friend to the Fyrstua, not a foe. Have the crow's nesters wave the green flags. I will sing the waters into a dance so they understand we do not intend to fight or pillage."

The captain called orders to the crow's nests as Yngvari asked. While the young people in the crow's nests waved emerald-green flags, Yngvari stood facing the side of the *Bane* from which the Kāfe'vind ships approached.

Yngvari tilted her head back, and her white-gold hair fell to nearly her buttocks. She raised her white-leather-clad arms to the heavens and opened her mouth in a large oval. Her song began soft and slow, like a sweet lullaby. A long, low, rippling wave rose in the sea between *Sicara's Bane* and the Kāfe'vind fleet.

Yngvari modulated her voice in an odd but harmonious song, and the waters responded. The wave rippled sideways. Under Yngvari's command, the ocean danced.

After a few moments, the drummer on the large Kāfe'vind ship pounded a beat. The drumbeat matched the rhythm of Yngvari's dancing waters.

From the smaller ships, cheers erupted, and a chant rose. At first, it was difficult to discern what they called. But after a few moments, the chanters synced their voices to the drum, and their collective song became clear.

They shouted, "Yng—var—ee! Yng—var—ee!" Over and over, they sang the word.

Yngvari didn't lower her arms or cease her song. Tears soaked her face, but joy made her eyes bright. Even Captain Ontrosa wiped a tear.

The captain placed a beefy hand on Yngvari's slim shoulder. "I told ya they would no'a shun ya, Sea Singer."

Yngvari slowly lowered her arms and allowed her song to fade. The dancing wave returned to the ocean, and the chanting faded. Save for one ship, the entire Kāfe'vind flotilla turned west and headed to shore. The remaining vessel veered east.

"Follow that guide boat, Captain," Yngvari said. "It will lead us to a safe place for the *Bane* to drop anchor."

Sicara's Bane followed the guide ship to a wide channel through shallow rocky islets. Unlike Doj'Enara Bay's protected cradle of calm waters and sandy shores, the Vatnoyer Province's coast didn't offer a ship effortless docking. To land, a boat must contend with rocky shoals likely to splinter a hull and reedy, weed-laden marshlands to tangle a rudder and render it useless. Unlike the smaller, single-masted Kāfe'vind boats, the much larger *Bane* had to weigh its anchors offshore.

Once they'd safely reached a small cove, Ontrosa ordered the crew to drop anchors. He then hollered, "Ready the ship's boat!" Ontrosa turned to Imbica and said, "I'll take your pod and 'nough crew to get ashore."

"I'll not miss this ship," Dio said.

Shel adjusted her quiver and chased after the crew, where they readied the dinghy. "I will. But hey, we get another boat ride to shore."

Imbica chortled. "Perhaps Shel has found her calling at sea."

Shel got to the small boat first. Ever gallant, Shel lent Yngvari a hand into the boat. Yngvari smiled, her eyes coyly downcast, and a blush bloomed.

"Maybe a new calling, but perhaps a new love interest too," Aldewin whispered to Imbica.

Dio asked, "What did you say? You mean, Shel is—"

"Never going to join you in your bed," Aldewin said.

Dio halted and stared at the back of Shel's head. *Maybe he doesn't know the pod as well as he pretends to, Aldewin* thought. Dio quickly dashed the look of surprise from his face and replaced it with cool nonchalance. Aldewin stifled a smug chortle.

Seeing that the rowers Ontrosa brought were youth, Aldewin volunteered to row. "I'm not an experienced oarsman, but my strength may lend speed."

Ontrosa took him up on the offer. Apparently, not wanting to look like a lazy pile of kopek dung, Dio offered to row too. Dio and Aldewin took seats across the aisle from each other. Each sat on a bench with a more experienced crew member.

Locked in an unspoken competition, the pair rowed as if being chased by a blood-frenzied shark. Swinging around on the bench, Shel faced them and assumed the rowing coach role. She spurred them to keep time by singing a few rounds of "Dance Wee Niyadi" but saved the lustiest lyrics for another time.

"The sooner we get ashore, the faster we'll get fresh ale in our bellies." Shel turned to Yngvari and asked, "Your kin drink ale, no?"

Yngvari laughed. "Ale? Sure, if drinking musky pisswater is your thing."

Shel laughed and moved closer. "What is your thing?"

Yngvari's cheeks colored again. "I like many things. But if you're asking about drink, I prefer our sweet goshi berry wine." She leaned closer to Shel, her voice low. "Perhaps we can drink some together later."

Shel nodded. "I would like that." She then returned to egging on the rowers. "Aldewin, you row like my gran. Stroke like ya got somewhere to be."

While Dio laughed, Aldewin picked up his pace. His satisfaction came when he noticed Dio's face was red as an apple and sweat poured down his temples. "If I row like your gran, Dio must row like your dead gran."

The entire boat erupted in laughter. Dio did not laugh.

While on the sailing ship, they'd welcomed Juka's winds. Now in a rowboat, Aldewin thanked Juka for fair skies and calm waters. After nearly a half hour of rowing, Yngvari pointed to a small wooden dock to tie the boat.

"Where did the Kāfe'vind ships come ashore?" Dio asked.

"They docked farther up the coast, closer inland. We'll have a bit of a walk to Leivby Village." Yngvari's expression turned wistful. "My home."

"It will be good to stretch my legs," Aldewin said.

Being ashore was a relative term. The Myrskog coastline was more like a marshy lake. Yngvari led them through thigh-deep waters filled with sea-loving reeds. Finally, she found a half-sunken wooden walkway.

Yngvari sounded relieved to have found it. "The waters are high today."

They were all soaked from the thigh down. Yngvari, though, had it especially bad. Because she was clad entirely in leather, the boggy water drenched her clothes.

Her animal skins have grown soggy and heavy, Aldewin thought.

Yngvari rested for a moment to catch her breath. "The walking will get easier as we go farther inland."

As Yngvari predicted, the waters soon receded. The sodden wooden walkway became drier and the path less rutted the farther they went.

Soon, reeds and low-growing water shrubs gave way to stubby trees with legs raising their trunks above the water. The inland water was so clear that Aldewin spied silvery fish darting under the raised trees.

"By the Three," Shel said, her voice filled with awe.

"You are no longer in the Sulmére sands," Imbica said.

"The Sulmére?" Yngvari asked. "Are you from the great Sea of Sands?"

"Not originally," Shel said. "But my brother and I ranged there. First with my da. And then later with the Jagaru."

Yngvari smiled at Shel. "I would love to hear your stories about the Sulmére. And the Jagaru are legendary."

Marshy terrain gave way to a temperate coastal forest. The squatty trees grew until the wooden walkway meandered through a copse of trees with trunks as large as a Sulmére house. Despite their enormous size, these trees, too, thrust "legs" into the soggy ground to raise themselves above the marshy soil. Pink water lilies on lean stalks jutted fifteen to twenty feet high, their gigantic flowers upturned, seeking Hiyadi's light among the dense canopy. Verdant ferns covered the ground like a vibrant green rug.

Before long, the land dried even more, and the trees grew higher. Beneath the lush canopy, vines tendrilled onto anything that gave them purchase, and mushrooms of red, orange, pale blue, creamy white, and dusky brown sprouted from the ground and tree trunks alike. The farther they walked, the larger the mushrooms became, some big enough that a person could sit upon the cap.

From the corner of his eye, Aldewin noticed movement. Instinctively, he pulled the broadsword from his back and spun, ready to defend. He met not a man or even predatory beast but a yindril meandering through the muck.

When it noticed him with a weapon drawn, the barky man-beast began keening and flailed its arms. The yindril pulled its woody leg from the mire, and it made a sucking sound as it tried to scurry away.

"Put your weapon away. They are peaceful," Yngvari said.

Aldewin quickly stowed his sword. "I know. I… I saw movement and thought—" He watched as the yindril met up with another, smaller one farther away from the road. "Is that—a baby yindril?"

"Yindrils don't have babies. Not like people or animals, anyway. They spread runners along the ground, and sometimes, if they stay planted in one spot long enough, it grows."

"That's the strangest damned thing I've ever heard," Shel said.

Yngvari shrugged. "Not so strange, really. At least not for the Myrskog."

They watched the yindrils slowly make their way deeper into the forest, where they planted themselves among other yindrils. From a distance, the gathered yindrils looked like a grove of trees. Only when one raised its arms or began moaning its mournful lament did they reveal themselves as something other than mere plants.

Humidity soaked the air, and the lush forest thrummed with life. Bees buzzed, and dragonflies zinged as they darted by. *Thank the Three it is not also hot*, Aldewin thought. The Myrskog was chilly compared to Indrasi or Partha to the east.

Evidence of civilization appeared as Aldewin noticed some trees sported bulbous swellings just above the wide-spreading roots. People had built wooden stairways or ramps up to these swellings. Many had wooden doors or thick tapestries covering the openings.

"Are those houses?" Shel asked.

Yngvari nodded. "It is good to be home." She spread her arms and breathed deeply. "That smell. The trees." She smiled. "There is nothing more comforting than sleeping in the wood."

Throaty bird calls filled the air. Aldewin breathed deeply, noticing the odor of damp wood and unfamiliar herbaceous smells. Ahead, human voices added to the sounds of insects, birds, and distant animal calls. The group passed through a thicker congregation of tree homes, some two stories with winding wood staircases on the outside leading to a second floor.

They approached an area from which all trees and brush had been cleared. A large cookfire crackled at its center, and stools and benches circled it. At the clearing's eastern edge, smoke tendrilled from the chimneys of two large clay ovens. Merchant tents covered in colorful tapestries dotted the edges of the clearing to the west. Eating tables and benches filled the rest of the clearing.

After surviving the sea voyage on dried meat and stale bread, the odor of freshly cooked food made Aldewin's stomach growl. Shel hung by Yngvari's right side as Yngvari led them toward an enormous central cookfire.

A young man dug a packet of glossy green leaves from the fire. He took a large wooden platter from a young woman and placed the packet on it. She opened the smoking leaf packet, and steam rose, wafting the delicious scent of spicy fish into the air. Another cook scooped nutty rice onto plates, and yet another ladled a thick vegetable stew while a small boy placed flatbread on each plate.

Having beaten the *Bane's* small land crew back to Leivby Village, the Kāfe'vind crews already sipped from mugs and ate from plates heaped with food. When they heard the newcomers approach, someone called Yngvari's name.

A woman dressed also in white leather but with green vine stitching called out, "Sister!"

Yngvari ran toward a woman who could have been her twin. Nalija scooped Yngvari into her arms, her tears wetting Yngvari's shoulder. The women embraced, oblivious to the world around them.

Interrupting the sisters' reunion, a tall man with long silver hair, a sun-weathered face, and broad shoulders approached. "Welcome home, Sea Singer." His deep voice carried an air of authority, and he put out an arm.

Aldewin glanced around the clearing. *This man is in his middle years yet the eldest in this clan.*

Yngvari still held her sister's hand but took the man's forearm as he clasped hers with her other hand. "Jesper." Her ordinarily serene voice quavered. "This is new." She touched his face, tracing a long, slashing scar that created a pink stripe from Jesper's right eyebrow to his left cheek. Her fingers trailed to his neckline, where a tattoo was visible through the upper lacings of his shirt. It appeared to be the same emblem Aldewin had seen crudely painted on the sails of their ships—a thorny vine choking a heart. "This is new too. You are Leid of Kāfe'vind now?"

"First came the scar, courtesy of Tradsmikor Clan." He rubbed the scar. "The vine mark of Leidship followed."

Yngvari's eyes glistened, and she shook her head. "Those damned clan traitors. What of the Eldurskir?"

Jesper released her arm. His jaw twitched. "Tradsmikor and the Dynasty savages they teamed with slaughtered all the Eldurskir except for Omma. I suppose killing our Modra was too cruel, even for them."

"The entire elder council? Gone?" Yngvari asked.

Tears glistening, Nalija nodded. "And Omma, though spared, hasn't been the same since. She blames herself, you see. Wonders why she didn't see the raid coming during her time in the Dreaming."

Yngvari shook her head. "A terrible burden for Omma."

Jesper eyed Captain Ontrosa then surveyed the rest of the *Bane*'s crew and the pod. He noted Aldewin, but when his gaze landed on Nivi, his eyes grew dark, and his jaw set. Jesper drew his sword, a timeworn and dull-looking silver straight blade. "Come no closer." Jesper pointed to Aldewin. "You're not of the Myrskog."

As soon as Jesper's sword left its scabbard, the crews of the Kāfe'vind ships were on their feet, weapons drawn. They circled the pod and Captain Ontrosa's land crew.

The Kāfe'vind grossly outnumbered Ontrosa's small crew. They circled Ontrosa and Yngvari, weapons drawn, ready for a fight.

Aldewin's Fen Menir training urged him to draw steel and meet any attack with a death blow. But he'd spent enough time with Master Hrabke at Val'Enara to know he should call upon Still Waters and assess the situation before cutting people down. He could practically hear Master Hrabke's voice, still ringing in his ears. "Be the still pond, which reflects all." With great effort and restraint, Aldewin remained calm, his hands at his sides, not reaching for a weapon.

Jesper pointed the tip of his steel blade at Nivi. "The last time I saw that beast, he walked beside that vile Iska'kog woman. The one who flounced in here like she owned the place and helped your Dynasty raid and decimate our clan."

Can he be talking about Pelagia? Aldewin wondered.

Out of the corner of Aldewin's eye, he noticed Dio's hand go to his belt scabbard. Imbica noticed it, too, and put a calming hand on Dio's as she shook her head at him. *No need to be jumpy,* Aldewin told himself. *Imbica and I could destroy this youthful group in minutes if we had to.* It was not a pleasant thought, and he hoped the young Kāfe'vind clan didn't force him to show how deadly he could be.

Aldewin held up his hands. "By all the gods, I swear we did not come to raid. I may look like a Northman, but I've never been to Vatnoyer Province." Aldewin put a hand on Nivi's neck, hoping to calm him. "This tiger, rescued from the Dynasty's menagerie, is under my protection. Like Yngvari, they took Nivi from his homeland against his will and held him captive. We return Yngvari and Nivi to their ancestral lands." *In truth, I don't know if someone took Nivi against his will. But I saw Pelagia torture him into obedience. Nivi wears the same gold bands as Yngvari and Quen. Pelagia's hand shows in all of this.*

Yngvari stepped forward and pushed Aldewin behind her. "He may appear Iska'kog, but his modir raised him in Partha. Aldewin says he never knew his bodir, and I believe him."

The Kāfe'vind still had their weapons drawn but nervously looked to Jesper, awaiting his commands. Jesper took a step toward Aldewin, his sword still drawn. "What is your bodir's name?"

Aldewin looked to Yngvari. "Bodir? Is that the same as father?"

"Yes, but no." She thought for a moment, trying perhaps to find the words. "It is the man whose seed you spring from. Any man of a clan could be your father, but only one can be your bodir."

"I see." Aldewin turned to Jesper and told him the truth. "I don't know my bodir's true name. My mother only referred to him as 'the lout that filled me with his giant's seed and left me to birth a babe who nearly broke me in half.'" Aldewin hadn't intended bitterness to fill his words. The sour feelings came from memories Aldewin had locked away. *I'd forgotten her words and have never spoken of it before. Why did this come bubbling forth now?*

Perhaps sensing the pain of Aldewin's admission, Jesper's facial muscles ceased twitching, and his brow relaxed. "So, like Yngvari and the tiger, you are Fyrstua and returning to your ancestral lands. And you truly never knew your bodir?"

Aldewin shook his head. "I don't know my father's origins. Growing up in Partha, I knew nothing of the Vats—I mean Vatnoyer Province—except what people told me. Because folks recognized my Fyrstua blood, I assumed all people of the Vatnoyer looked like me."

The Kāfe'vind people surrounding him were a varied group. Even though most were teens or in their early twenties, all were taller than adults in the Sulmére. But their eyes were brown, green, golden, and even pale blue. Hair colors ranged from black to pale white-yellow like Yngvari's, and some had red hair like Aldewin's mother. *Could my mother's people have originally been from the Myrskog?* But none were as tall, broad-shouldered, and fair of hair and eyes as Aldewin.

It wasn't something he'd wondered about. He grew up in the Shills area of Partha, as smelly and seedy as Mourigi or even more. Shills people didn't ask where they were from because it didn't matter. Partha's poorest were born in the Shills and were likely to die there. Shills people didn't have time to ponder things like their heritage.

"I see now that I was wrong about the Vatnoyer people," Aldewin said.

Jesper nodded. "The Iska'kog people of the northern Vatnoyer differ from Myrskog folks, as much as Parthinians differ from people at the sandy southern tip of the world."

"The Sulmére," Imbica said. She pressed forward, adjusted her belt, and smoothed her hair. "I am Imbica, Pillar Mage and most senior of our pod." She held out a hand to shake.

Jesper turned his attention to Imbica. Being at least a head taller than her, he had to crane his neck downward to meet her gaze. His demeanor shifted from wary to warm. Jesper took Imbica's forearm in his, as he had Yngvari's. "Imbica, you said?"

She grasped his forearm, too, and nodded. Her face flushed as she gazed up at Jesper.

Their eyes locked as they held each other's arms. "I welcome you, Imbica, to Leivby Village." He coughed and released her arm. "Forgive my stare, but it has been long since I had the pleasure of speaking with a peer." He smiled warmly. "I am happy to meet you, Lady Mage."

Imbica blushed an even darker crimson and continued to lock his eyes with hers. Usually quick with retorts and never at a loss for words, Imbica stood like a mute pillar of stone.

Yngvari coughed lightly, and Jesper released Imbica's arm. "Shall we share a meal then, Leid Jesper? The fresh food will be welcome after a week at sea."

The tension-filled moment passed, and the Kāfe'vind stowed their weapons.

Jesper pulled his eyes from Imbica's. "Come, travelers. Partake in a meal as we thank you for returning our dear sister, Yngvari, to our shores." Jesper put a weathered hand on Yngvari's shoulder while Nalija squeezed Yngvari's hand. The youthful villagers whooped and cheered for Yngvari.

Jesper's smile faded. He said, "We will discuss what venture brings the captain and you others to our Myrskog shores."

With Jesper's blessing, the youthful villagers resumed their boisterous chatter and preparing the meal. The pod and Captain Ontrosa followed Yngvari and settled onto benches and stools around a large, central cooking fire. A villager led Ontrosa's crew to gather at tables and benches spread throughout the clearing.

As they ate, several conversations happened simultaneously. Jesper spoke with Captain Ontrosa about happenings beyond Myrskog shores. Yngvari and Nalija listened with rapt attention as Shel regaled them with tales of the Sulmére.

"Sand, as far as you can see? And no trees?" Nalija spoke in an awed whisper. "A world without the skog?"

Dio asked, "Skog? I'm not familiar with that word."

Nalija cast a gaze upward, thinking. "Hmm, how to describe it? The trees, the woods."

"I think I understand," Aldewin said. "In Indrasi, we call it Doka—the wood element."

"But it is more than just the wood," Yngvari said. "The skog is every living thing in the forest and marsh. Ruled by Skogi, our goddess of the Green."

Nalija nodded and smiled. "Yes, that's it." She turned back to Shel. "How do you survive in this Sea of Sand without the skog?"

Shel threw her head back, laughed, and held her mug of wine aloft. "Lots of this, I 'spose."

Nalija raised her mug as well, and both women drank. *I wish Quen was here to join in their fun*, Aldewin thought. *She would enjoy experiencing this new place with her friend.*

The thought threatened to sour his mood. He didn't know Quen's location or even if she still experienced the world. For all he knew, Ishna had flown herself and Quen to Menauld's farthest reaches. Perhaps across the Zhongdu Sea to the land from which no travelers returned.

Jesper called to Aldewin, rescuing him from descending into a foul mood. "Aldewin. Not a Parthinian name."

Aldewin felt like he was being accused. Again. He forced his body to remain calm and worked his face into a nonchalant mask. "It is not my given name but one assigned to me by Archon Kine when she accepted me to study at Val'Enara Pillar." He casually scooped the stewed vegetables with his bread, appreciating the peppery flavor. *I hope his interrogation ends soon. All I truly want is to stuff my belly, get pished, and sleep.*

Jesper's forehead muscles relaxed a bit. "I apologize if I question. After Tradsmikor Clan's deadly raid—helping your Dynasty plunder—we Kāfe'vind are a small clan. We Myrskog folks are peaceful, you see. For generations unending, content to follow the ways of the Green."

"Is that why you have a flotilla of small but powerful warships, clearly stolen from Bardivia's Engarda?" Dio asked. Despite the accusatory question, Dio's voice held no malice.

Jesper's eyes grew dark, and his jaw twitched. He sighed and drank a sip of wine. "Difficult, perhaps, for people from conquest-hungry Indrasi to understand, but we believe Skogi provides. Those are Merladro ships. They floundered off our coast in a violent storm. In the past, we'd allow the sea to reclaim sunken ships. But circumstances force us to marshal our resources. We must defend ourselves. Or would you have us surrender our lands? Our people? And all we hold dear?" Jesper's voice rose with each question.

Imbica glared at Dio, her look imploring him to stop his inquisition.

"I meant no offense, Leid. I was merely curious about the apparent contradiction." Dio sipped his wine and proffered a smile. "I stand corrected."

Jesper's eyes narrowed at Dio, but he soon released Dio from his gaze and turned to Aldewin and Imbica instead. "We Myrskog clans are content to follow the ways of the Green. We listen to our Modra—our Moth Mother—and her wise counsel. She interprets the signs our goddess, Skogi, gifts us through vine and wood."

"Like a Sulmére Bruxia," Aldewin said.

Yngvari said, "Something like that. But our Modra are more..." She rubbed her chin, pondering. "Mysterious. Yes, I think that is the word."

Jesper continued. "Myrskog people protect and revere Skogi's naturfrandi. What is the word in the common tongue?"

"Nature friends," Yngvari said.

Jesper nodded. "To us, whether human or yindril, tree or flygesroom—all are our kin, you see."

"Not a philosophy shared by the Dynasty's ruler," Aldewin said.

Dio's piercing stare bore into Aldewin. "And not one commanded by worship of the Three," Dio said.

Aldewin wanted to retort that he didn't need Dio's sanctimonious reminder about proper prayer to the Three, but he held his tongue. *By Sicara's bloody blade, that man gets under my skin.*

Jesper's face was dour, and his tone turned bitter. "Tradsmikor Clan has forgotten the ways of the Green. They led outsiders here—and killed anyone who stood against the Dynasty. Watched as the Dynasty uprooted yindrils, taking them from their families." His face was now red with emotion, and Jesper wiped his brow. "They did nothing as the Dynasty killed folks and even took people captive." His gaze landed on Yngvari.

The Kāfe'vind hissed their disapproval of the Dynasty and Tradsmikor's actions.

Jesper's eyes were wet, and he coughed and sipped wine. "After losing our Eldurskir, the duty of Leid fell onto my unworthy shoulders. Not a job I trained for or wanted."

I know about living a life I didn't choose. A memory came to Aldewin of Master Mordranis handing Aldewin's mother a purse filled with silver.

Imbica looked at Jesper with admiration. "We don't always get to choose our path, do we?" she asked.

Jesper smiled and shook his head. "No, we do not."

Imbica returned his smile. "There is little more admirable than accepting one's duty." Imbica gestured around them with a sweeping movement of her arm. "By the gods, Jesper. They broke your clan, but you stepped up and put them back together."

Cries of "Helja!" erupted around them.

Jesper blushed, clearly uncomfortable with her praise. But he didn't look away from Imbica either.

Aldewin had never seen this softer side of Imbica. *Perhaps time with Jesper will burnish the sharp edges of her heart.*

Jesper motioned for the clan to quiet down. "I may not have asked for the title, but once I accepted it, I took responsibility for the well-being of the Kāfe'vind clan and the skog we inhabit. And as Skogi is my witness, I will never allow Kāfe'vind to suffer another reaping."

With at least one cup of wine down the gullet, the gathering took Jesper's impassioned oath as an invitation for more cheers and whoops.

Jesper continued, "I protect the clan, and Kāfe'vind protects the naturfrandi our goddess gifted us. It's our sacred duty."

The crowd cheered again and drank.

Aldewin locked eyes with Jesper, his gaze unwavering. "I cannot speak for Captain Ontrosa or others. But I have no interest in bartering humans or plundering your naturfrandi." He'd never spoken of his past, even at Val'Enara, let alone to strangers. Being among people who'd suffered similarly made him feel welcome to share. "My mother bartered me away for a small purse when I was still a lad." Aldewin ruffled the hair of the young boy who'd become his silent shadow during the meal. "No older than this turf muffin here."

The boy laughed. Eyed by his idol, the boy ran for cover in the crowd.

Jesper rapped his chest lightly with his left fist then held it in the air. Others of Kāfe'vind did likewise. "We will speak words of prayer to Skogi on your behalf. May the root and vine absorb your suffering so you may walk anew in the world."

With their fists in the air, as Jesper had done, the rest of the Kāfe'vind repeated the words in hushed voices.

Though he wasn't cold, chills ran through Aldewin. It was the same sensation he'd had earlier when Nalija's energetic message reached Yngvari. *This is a different sort of magic than they teach at the Pillars.* Though new to him, it also felt oddly familiar. And welcome. Besides his brief time with Quen, Aldewin had never felt so... loved. *But I only just met them.*

As if sensing his reaction, Yngvari caught his eye and gave him a reassuring nod.

"Your father likely hailed from the Iska'kog. The Northmen, judging by your height and breadth of build. You should meet with our Modra—Omma—when she returns from meeting with the other Myrskog clan Modras," Jesper said.

"Omma is wise. In the Dreaming, she sees what others cannot," Yngvari said.

Shel whispered to Yngvari, "Modra?"

"Moth Mother," Yngvari said.

Shel's face crinkled, and she shook her head, then her eyes widened. "Do not tell me you're referring to a giant moth." Her lip curled in distaste.

Nalija laughed, as did others gathered around.

Yngvari said, "Of course not. Modras are friends with moths, you see. A clan's Modra carries the clan's history and wisdom. They're also seers, and once a year, all the

Modra in the Myrskog gather and enter the Dreaming. Omma always returns from the Dreaming understanding what comes next for the clan."

"Like an oracle?" Dio asked.

Both Yngvari and Nalija nodded.

Aldewin's heartbeat hastened. "Then it sounds like I should speak with your Modra upon her return. I have many questions. Perhaps she has answers."

"Your eyes speak of the Vatnoyer, Aldewin, and we feel it. Your blood runs with the skog, Brother. We welcome you and your pod to stay with the Kāfe'vind for a time, anyway." Jesper raised his mug to Aldewin and sent a warm glance Imbica's way as he drank.

Does he welcome me or Imbica? Aldewin wondered. *I suppose it doesn't matter so long as no one spills blood.* Aldewin raised his cup and drank.

Captain Ontrosa had been uncharacteristically quiet. On his second plate of food and with his mouth full, he said, "You omittin' me and my crew, Leid Jesper. Are ya givin' us the boot, then?" Ontrosa chortled. "Why, we've been on our best behavior. And we're not even ass-up drunk yet."

"Your visit to our village has been more pleasant than most of our encounters with ship crews from Indrasi." Jesper eyed the captain over his mug. "So far."

Imbica gave the captain a withering glare as if willing him to speak carefully.

Captain Ontrosa wiped crumbs from his beard and put his plate down. "My crew and I have no interest in raiding you." Ontrosa fanned a bug away and said, "We prefer sea breezes and Bardivian honey ale." Realizing he'd just potentially given offense, he quickly backtracked, "Not that this wine isn't fine, 'cause the Three know it is." He took a sip.

"I believe you did not come here with pillaging on your mind, Captain." Jesper's jaw muscles twitched again. "But for reasons I've already stated, we do not trust outsiders. People like you have arrived on our shores for nearly a decade and taken whatever they please."

The air crackled with tension. Dio set his food aside, his hand on his scabbard. The captain sat up straighter.

Yngvari cleared her throat, her voice calm but loud enough for all to hear. "You all know my story. At least until the Dynasty arrived. With Tradsmikor's help, they bound and kidnapped me." She paused as if collecting herself.

Captain Ontrosa gave her a reassuring nod.

"You don't know what happened after," she said.

Murmurs rose.

Yngvari held up a hand. "I will not speak of most of it. Not now or ever."

I respect her silence about the past. Speaking of it only peels off the scab, and the wound bleeds anew.

Yngvari's sister, Nalija, wiped tears from her pale cheeks.

"But know this," Yngvari said. "Captain Ontrosa rescued me from a life of servitude. He and I struck a bargain, one I freely made. And he fulfilled his promise." Yngvari wiped a tear and raised her mug in the air. Her tone brighter now, Yngvari said, "So I say Helja! To Captain Ontrosa and his crew. Loyal friends of the Myrskog peoples."

The gathered Kāfe'vind looked to Jesper to see what he would say. He eyed Yngvari then the captain and finally raised his mug. Though he gave a rather unenthusiastic 'Helja,' the rest of the clan's greeting was more boisterous.

Captain Ontrosa raised his mug and nodded to the gathered. "I thank ya for the warm Kāfe'vind welcome. And I hope not to wear it out while we wait for Mage Imbica's group to return from their mission." Ontrosa scratched his beard. "I have a trade proposal that might interest ya, Leid Jesper."

Jesper eyed the captain. "We have no need for Dynasty Kovars or Parthinian Soldats here."

"I was no'a offerin' coin." He caught Yngvari's eye, and a dour look overcame him. "I'm offering ya something more valuable than money."

Yngvari seemed to realize what Ontrosa would offer before he said it. "No, Captain. You can't barter that away."

Ontrosa gave Yngvari a wan smile. "The *Bane*'s no use to me now, Sea Singer. After what we did to the Engarda fleet? Suda, the bounty they'll put on my head… As soon as I enter the Straits of Minea, Merladro will attack. They'll be keen to capture me and my crew for the reward."

I had not considered that, but there is truth to his words. Aldewin recalled the Wanted poster Shel had shown him and the exorbitant bounty Xa'Vatra had placed on his head and Quen's.

Jesper gave the captain an indignant laugh. "You want to unload a worthless ship onto us, then?" His voice dripped with sarcasm. "And what do you ask of the Kāfe'vind in exchange for such a generous offer?"

"You can put new sails on the *Bane* and paint your mark. Carve a new bowsprit. You can make the *Bane* anew with some elbow grease and imagination."

Jesper's expression changed from skepticism to interest.

Seeing that he still had Leid Jesper's attention, Captain Ontrosa continued. "I will gift *Sicara's Bane* to the

Kāfe'vind Clan. A warship, even one as old as the *Bane*, will make a fine addition to your growing fleet."

Dio asked, "How will you sail us back, then, Captain? That was part of the deal when Imbica handed you the fat purse, right?" He looked to Imbica to join his inquiry.

Imbica nodded but said, "Patience. Let us hear what the captain has to say. I cannot imagine he would consider reneging on his obligation." Imbica's dark-brown eyes bore into Captain Ontrosa's.

The captain, perhaps feeling the heat of multiple questioning gazes at once, wiped the back of his neck with a filthy cloth. "I'll give Kāfe'vind my three-masted warship. In exchange, you give me one of your single-masted ships. The fastest one in the best condition."

The Leid rubbed his chin and narrowed his eyes at Ontrosa. "That is not a fair trade, captain. Not for you. What else will you be wanting?"

The captain held out his arms. "There are no tricks up my sleeve. One of your ships for mine. I lost half my crew getting here, so I need a smaller ship anyhows. And while I wait for my passengers to return, my crew will rotate, taking shore leave here in Leivby. Your crews are young. Sailing is new to the Kāfe'vind. While here, I can train your sailors. Ready 'em to face what's comin'."

Jesper's eyes widened, and he let out a whistle. Yngvari said, "That's very generous of you, Captain"

"Least I can do for your clan, Sea Singer. After all ya done for me o'er the years," Ontrosa said.

"You mentioned the *Bane* will help us face what's coming. What did you mean?" Leid Jesper asked.

The captain looked him in the eye. "Dragons out of their barrows. A war looming between Bardivia and the

Dynasty. The Exalted sent a small army to comb the Vatnoyer for anything to give her an edge. Xa'Vatra already sent a raid upon you once. She thirsts for battle and appears to crave war. The Dynasty has already pulled the Vatnoyer into her schemes. Do you really think you can hide from the coming war?"

Can any of us? Aldewin wondered.

Jesper's jaw set. He didn't answer Captain Ontrosa's queries. Instead, he said, "Your proposal is intriguing, Captain. I will discuss it with our Modra upon her return. In the meantime, you and your crew are welcome guests of the Kāfe'vind."

Murmurs rose, and people raised their cups again to cheer for Ontrosa and his crew. As the din of cheer waned, a woman's voice entered the clearing.

"You're feasting and didn't invite old Omma?"

The gathering turned their attention to a newcomer entering the cooking center of Leivby Village. Her silvery-grey hair fell in abundant waves below her shoulders, her leathery skin deeply lined and weathered by sun and age. Though her face told a story of a long life, her body was neither stooped nor bent but fit and trim. She had a large, timeworn wooden walking stick in one hand and a pack strapped to her back. A massive moth with green, orange, and brown wings in a pattern like stained glass sat on the shoulder of her brown leather jerkin.

A young man cleared off his wide stool and offered it to Omma. Two others quickly filled a plate for her. Yet another person poured her a mug of chilled wine. A young woman trailing Omma took her staff and pack and sauntered off. Omma stowed her leather gloves at her waist belt and accepted the plate of food while she whispered a prayer of thanksgiving to Skogi. She deftly used the flatbread to scoop the vegetable stew and fish.

No one spoke, apparently waiting for her to begin the conversation when she was ready. The woman cleared nearly half a plate without uttering a word, devouring food like she hadn't eaten in days. Dark circles under her eyes showed fatigue, but from what, Aldewin didn't know.

After a time, she paused, sighed, and smiled. "Kāfe'vind food. Nothing in the Myrskog quite like it. I thank Skogi for the blessings of this feast and the makers in the kitchen for this fine meal."

The youthful cooks who had dished out the food smiled, proud they'd pleased Omma, their clan's Modra. Though Aldewin had known Dini only briefly, Omma reminded him of her. *A grandmother to the entire clan.*

Omma's eyes were vibrant green, nearly unnaturally so. Sun and age hadn't ravaged her blind like many elders in the Sulmére.

Having received their Modra's blessings for the food, the rest of the clan resumed their chatter, though more quietly than before.

Jesper said, "It is an even more fit day for a feast now that our Modra has returned. I am eager to learn what you and the other Moth Mothers saw in your yearly vision time. And I have much to discuss with you, including an offer of barter by Captain Ontrosa here."

Omma smiled at Jesper. "Skogi's blessings to you, Leid. Yes, we have much to discuss." She turned her gaze on the captain and took in the newcomers. Omma raised her mug and bid them welcome. She then focused entirely on Aldewin. "But first, I must welcome the Varskog to our humble village."

Dio, Shel, and Imbica joined the captain and the Kāfe'vind as they looked around, puzzled about what Omma referred to.

Aldewin felt her eyes pierce him, and he knew she referred to him.

Jesper asked, "Varskog? That means 'Wolf in the Wood.'" He said this to Imbica, perhaps sensing she'd appreciate a translation.

Imbica nodded in gratitude as she repeated the words to herself softly.

Jesper's tone was respectful. "Of whom do you speak, revered Modra?

Omma pointed a knotted finger at Aldewin. "The Northman that belongs to no clan." She lowered her finger, and her gaze landed on Nivi. "The one who travels with the white beast, both touched by the Dragos."

Aldewin's heart raced, and his chest grew tight. Murmurs rose. Nivi, perhaps sensing Aldewin's tension, stood and bared his teeth.

Aldewin touched Nivi's back and whispered, "Calm, my friend. I do not believe she means us harm." Yet Aldewin remained unsure.

"Revered Modra, do you speak of me and my friend Nivi?" Aldewin asked. *If this woman can see past or future, like the Zeniths at Val'Enara, I'm not sure I want to know what she saw. Or is she just another weaver pulling me into a web?* The last time Aldewin had trusted a revered woman, he ended up soul-pledged to a darmanitong who tried to kill him.

Omma's intense gaze and knowing smile disarmed Aldewin.

"Rignar Nyanja di Shills, also known as Timonay. Little mouse?" She laughed. "That was long ago, though, wasn't it? Not so little anymore."

Aldewin swallowed hard, trying not to choke on his own spit. *She used names I have never spoken since crawling onto Indrasi's shores six years ago. And a name known only by my masters and brothers at Fen Menir.* Her use of his prior names upended him, and his voice revealed a tension he didn't intend to share. "You have me at quite a disadvantage, Omma. You somehow know much of me, but I know nothing of you." He sipped his wine and stared at her over his cup. "Or your intentions."

Omma threw her head back and laughed again, her mirth deep and throaty. "Calm yourself, Aldewin." She glanced at his belt scabbard, her eyes landing on the ebony hilt of his Vandu blade. Omma's smile waned, and for a passing moment, her calm demeanor vanished, replaced with wariness. But like Aldewin, she'd been trained to put aside feelings when necessary. The look of fear was fleeting, and with a smile again, she said, "I am glad you have finally arrived, Varskog."

"No one has called me that name." *At least, not yet. Has this woman seen my future?* He drank a long draw of wine to steady himself.

"I admit I have you at a disadvantage," Omma said. "From my recent time in the Dreaming, I feel I know you. In the vision time, we know you as Varskog—the Wolf in the Wood." Omma stared at him over her mug as she drank. "We have much to discuss, you and me. Much we must learn from one another. But for now, eat. Rest. I need you at your best for our journey north. To Iska'kog lands."

Aldewin laughed nervously. "We only just arrived."

"Took you long enough," Omma muttered.

Imbica laughed indignantly and rolled up her sleeves. "I am Imbica, Vatra Master and Dynasty Battle Mage."

Shel put in, "*Former* Dynasty Battle Mage."

Imbica's face turned red. "Yes. *Former.* But I am the elder member of our small Jagaru pod. Thus, I decide where the pod goes and when."

Omma asked, "You range beyond your jurisdiction, don't you, Jagaru?" A smile lit Omma's eyes.

Imbica harrumphed. "Our quest takes us beyond Indrasi, yet our Jagaru precepts remain. I lead our pod for this mission, anyway. And I say we remain uncertain where our quest leads. We have not yet gathered the relevant information."

Omma stared at Imbica evenly, her eyes glazing over as if seeing something beyond typical seeing. After a few moments, her eyes refocused. She said, "Lucky for you, the Dreaming will save you much time. *You* don't even know what you search for—or who." She laughed. "At least not yet. But with my help, you will."

Imbica, Aldewin, Dio, and Shel sat up straighter, their full attention focused on the elderly woman. The crowd, lively and full of conversation only moments before, was now so quiet they heard dragonfly wings buzzing. The air crackled with tension.

Aldewin asked, "Who do we search for?"

Omma pointed a flatbread at him. "Don't ask questions you know the answer to. Waste of time." She bit the bread and returned to eating.

Dio shook his head, his brows furrowed. "I'm confused. I thought we came here to follow the Dynasty's trail. To head them off—" He looked around, unsure if he should be forthright about their ultimate intention of finding the Heart of Menaris. "We want to meet our aim before the Dynasty beats us to it." He turned his attention to Aldewin. "If you know where—"

Aldewin cut him off. "I don't."

Omma narrowed her gaze at him. "No, you do not know, do you?" She tsked. "Not yet, but you will. You will enter the Dreaming. There, you will find the answers you seek."

Aldewin laughed nervously. "I'm not sure I want to be part of anything like that. The Zeniths at Val'Enara who spend time in the dreamworld are half nattered. Walking about, muttering to themselves."

Omma smiled, her eyes alight. "Do I look nattered?"

Aldewin shook his head. "Not particularly. But I just met you."

Omma laughed and shrugged her shoulders. "Good answer, Varskog." Her look grew intense, and she directed her words to Aldewin. "What if I told you *she* was in the Dreaming?"

CHAPTER 7

ISHNA

Curled into the tightest ball he could make of himself, Docar slept on the wide basalt ledge he'd claimed. Ishna landed softly, but the click of her talons woke him. Docar blinked, his orange eyes warm and welcoming like the two suns on a wintry day.

Docar smiled when he saw her, and Ishna placed her forehead on his. Though not as massive as his egg-father, Vahgrin, Docar was a third again as large as Ishna. *I long for my first body. It was larger and more robust than this one,* Ishna thought.

They sat in silence for many moments, with only their foreheads touching. Docar opened his wings and welcomed Ishna to curl into him.

She did not hesitate to accept his offer of intimacy. Alone in Vay'Nada for over a thousand years, Ishna had only memories of Docar for company. Remembering his wings' warmth and his fiery heart's rapid beat. Yearning to interlock with him. Docar kindled her passion not only for him but for life. *Docar will never understand how he kept my spirit alive.*

They locked necks now, breathing in each other's scent, and remained in that position until Docar's skin grew cold. Ishna's voice was low and husky. "You sweet fire boy. I fear this icy clime will freeze your beautiful heart if you remain here long."

Docar spewed fire against the rock wall behind them until it again glowed orange. He pressed his forehead to hers and said, "Your affections melt the frozen wastes of my lonely Dragos heart."

She chuckled, low and melodious. "How I wish it were true." Ishna pulled her head away and caught his eye. "We must speak, Docar."

He looked away. "No pleasurable words ever began thus."

Ishna crooked a claw under his chin and gently returned his gaze to her. "Docar, you know you are the sole sun in my sky. My vôsh'lavi."

Docar snuggled closer, enveloping Ishna in his wings. "Vôsh'lavi," he repeated and placed his head again against hers.

After a long pause, Ishna said, "I wish to remain wing-to-wing with you on this frozen rock you've made warm, but I must leave soon. Veridia… I worry about my sister."

Docar remained touching Ishna but nodded and thumped his tail once. "Veridia is a beloved egg-mother to many of our dragonkin, sorely missed by all."

Ishna thumped. "And I fear…" She wasn't sure how to put it into words. *I miss speaking with you, dear sister. Between us, we need no words.*

Docar cuddled her neck. "What do you fear, vôsh'lavi?"

It was even more challenging to consider her words when Docar made heat rise in her chest, threatening to turn her icy breath to steam. Ishna forced herself to pull away from him. "I fear the worst, Docar."

His languid gaze vanished. "Death?"

She thumped twice. "Worse. It is… a vague unease. This new body and mind… Thoughts are my own, yet I feel… off. I am uncertain if I can rely on my senses or intuitions."

Docar nuzzled and playfully nibbled at her neck. "You taste the same to me." He inhaled her aroma. "And smell the same as well."

She slapped him with her tail. "I am quite serious, Docar. This is an earnest problem."

"I know," Docar said. "I was being serious too. In the process of your rebirth, there were changes. That much is true. But I *know* you, vôsh'lavi. Trust yourself as I trust in you. Or do you question me as well?"

Ishna sensed only sincerity in his voice and demeanor. His words eased her worries. "Aurixia senses Veridia is somewhere on the land mass west of here. In the wilding Two-Legged lands."

Docar let out a smoky breath. "I know these lands. The least civilized Walkers we know populate the region. Unless they changed during our Dô'bedri."

"*You* spent time there? I thought you never ranged north of the Sulmére sands."

"Oh, it was early in the second era, after the breaking. There are splendid hot springs there. They smell damned unpleasant and make your wings rimy. But the large prey on the tundra makes for easy hunting."

"Truly?"

Docar spread his wings to warm them again. "Truly. Except for the wilding creatures who threw spears and stones at us. That got tiresome. And you can't eat *all* of them. They are too prolifically productive."

Ishna rose and fluffed her wings. The frigid air did not bother her as it did Docar, but she enjoyed moving. "How you speak of these Walkers does not set my mind at ease, Docar. But Veridia is a Primal. Surely, these primitive creatures could not harm a Primal dragon. The vile Rajani creatures can subdue your egg-father only because they are not human." She shuddered at the recollection of their horrendous screeching as they sang the song of their Rend spell. Time was melting her resolve to remain angry at her brother. *Melting like Nevara turned to jelly on the black stones of Volenex.*

"Your point contains wisdom, vôsh'lavi," Docar said. "Those spear-chucking wildings cannot best our Veridia. I've seen her raise choke vines in the desert. No doubt, Veridia could ensnare a horde of wilding people before they harmed a scale on her back."

Ishna envisioned the picture he painted, and it was easy to imagine. She'd seen Veridia do that very thing so many eons ago in a land now buried beneath waves.

Docar's words comforted as much as his mere presence grounded her. In Ishna's thousands of years alive, she'd had close and intimate relationships with many dragons. Some remained, but many no longer lived. No other Dragos had both ignited her passion yet provided calm reassurance as Docar did. *It is selfish to ask this of him.*

"You know the wilding lands—"

Before she could ask, Docar said, "Of course I will go with you." He enfolded her in his wings again.

"We will face these wildings, Docar. And the more advanced humans of Indrasi and Partha. Rumors on the wing say humans have more formidable weapons than when last we faced them. We could lose dragonkin in this quest, vôsh'lavi."

Docar snuggled her neck and placed his forehead on hers. "You must try harder to rid yourself of my presence. I am like sticky amber stubbornly clinging to your wing."

Ishna laughed and butted her head against his.

"Open a portal, and we can begin our search immediately. I am happy to leave these frozen cliffs behind," Docar said.

Ishna hesitated but said, "We will not travel by portal."

Docar pulled away so he could see her face. "Traveling overland. That is risky, vôsh'lavi. It puts us in more danger. Why would we not…" His eyes widened, and he released a smoky breath. "You cannot open a portal. Am I right?"

Ishna thumped her tail.

Docar's furry brows furrowed. "I do not understand. You opened a portal at Volenex, did you not?"

Ishna thought on his words and recalled the last moments at Volenex. A portal had opened, and she used it to rescue Quen's lover, Aldewin, and her tiger friend, Nivi. "This troubles me. A portal opened. Of that, I am certain. But did *I* create the gateway, or was it—someone else?"

"Who else could have? Only Primal dragons can create gateways through the Void." But no sooner had Docar spoken than a dawning realization came over him. "Could it have been Vahgrin?"

"Maybe? Though it seems unlikely. Even after a thousand years apart, his extreme distaste for me has not abated."

Docar chuckled. "I think you overestimate his ill feeling toward you."

Ishna bellowed. "Overestimate? He had me killed, Docar. In a cowardly and most disgusting manner." Thinking about losing her head at the hands of Indrasians made her breath grow frosty, icicles hanging in the air after each word.

Nuzzling her neck, Docar said, "Think on it no more. That is history, vôsh'lavi. Now, we focus on Veridia."

Ishna returned his affection. Their embrace calmed her racing hearts, both the dragon heart and the phantom quiver of Quen's heart.

Docar said, "Remember, my egg-father may be a petty and vengeful Dragos, but he is also shrewd. Vahgrin knows that to free himself of the yoke of those dragomancers, he needs you."

"Perhaps." Ishna had not considered this. She and Vahgrin had been rivals since they hatched. She could not remember a time of ease between them. *Yet I remain his only hope for liberation from being used by those Rajani as a living weapon. I know he keenly longs for freedom.*

Though a sound reason for Vahgrin to have assisted Ishna by opening a portal, another alternative had occurred to her. *Perhaps it was the human within me who opened the portal? Quen created a portal through the Void on several occasions. She possesses a command of interstitial ways between realms even though she does not fully comprehend it. And she adds an element I do not have. In her first encounter with Vahgrin and again at the Menagerie, Quen altered time. Temporal gateways were not within reach, even for the Primal dragons. Is it possible that together, we are stronger than either of us alone?*

For now, Ishna would ponder these ideas on her own. She wasn't ready to speak about the possibility that Quen, a Two-Legged, possessed a skill even the mightiest dragon lacked. *I will talk privately with Niezhan about this.*

Ishna said, "Whatever the source of the portal created in Volenex, the important fact remains. I have tried many times but can no longer create a gateway. We will thus have to journey on the wing."

Docar moved closer. He gently nibbled her neck. "Flying side by side, as we are meant to be." He playfully slapped his tail against her haunches. "Put worry behind you, vôsh. Let us hunt." Docar flapped his mighty black wings and took to the sky.

Ishna did not require a second invitation. She had sorely missed flight while Quen was her host. Her body lithe, Ishna undulated upward and snaked herself around Docar. His wings around her, their flight fueled by her Primal magic, they twirled and rose, higher and higher. Intertwined and with foreheads locked, Ishna and Docar were oblivious to the world around them as they stared into each other's eyes.

After a time, they parted but flew wingtip to wingtip and dove toward the water, wind flattening their hair and ears against their heads, icy hoarfrost slicking their bodies. Just before meeting the water with a painful slap, both thrust their heads upward and soared into the twilight.

The western sky now painted hues of salmon, Ishna and Docar flew along the coast of Xathi Tol'galen and called to their dragonkin to join them. Ishna rejoiced in the loving kinship of her Dragos family. Soon, though, she and Docar would leave them again. She only hoped they returned with her sister, the Spring Dragon.

❖   ❖   ❖

Niezhan had not exaggerated when he said the Nao faction preferred inaction. It had been weeks since the Lít Council began deliberating the optimal strategy for locating Veridia, the dragon of Primal Wood.

At long last, Ishna felt Niezhan's summons. Emitting a sound only dragons heard, Niezhan's call rumbled through Ishna's chest and vibrated her teeth. "Eee-sh-naaaaa," he called.

When the summons arrived, Ishna and Docar were hunting seals off the coast of an island at the eastern edge of the Xathi Tol'galen archipelago. "I must cut our morning hunt short, Docar. Niezhan calls, and I am eager to receive recommendations from the Lít."

Docar twirled around her and nuzzled her neck. "Why must you leave? We both know you are unlikely to follow the Lít's recommendations, vôsh'lavi."

"That's not—*entirely* true." Ishna's laugh, low and multitonal, echoed off the basalt wall of the mountainous island they circled. "Niezhan asked Côzhili, Owaanir, and Myvishi to scout west. I am eager to hear their reports."

"Old Owaanir woke from napping long enough to fly, did he?" Docar's laugh rumbled. "Let us hope they report nothing more of the Two-Leggeds in the western isles than farming and fisherfolk."

Ishna veered west and ascended higher. "We will see. Humans grow ever more clever. While in the Two-Legged capital, Quen and I saw flying boats."

"Walkers flying?" Docar blew a puff of steam. "That does not seem possible. Also, it does not bode well."

"Fear it not, vôsh. Two-legged ability to fly is limited and confined to a single location. They harvest poisonous vapors there and use them to ascend," Ishna said.

Docar laughed. "Leave it to the Two-Leggeds to harness deadly gas." He paused momentarily then added, "After a second thought, perhaps that is not odd. They have ample history of turning nearly anything dangerous into a weapon."

From Ishna's time in the capital and after observing Xa'Vatra, she could not disagree with Docar's point. *And it is a disturbing idea*, she thought. "I look forward to Côzhili's scouting report about what Two-Legged are doing in the western isles."

They flew in silence, icy winds sleeking Ishna's snowy white mane. After a time, she said, "I asked Naja to spend time with Aurixia. The hatchling begs me to take her with us, but I am concerned with Aurixia's lack of experience."

Docar flew now at her side as they headed west. "Will the Lít Council welcome me at this meeting? Or shall I wait for you on my lonely island?"

Ishna flew closer until their wingtips touched. "Of course, I welcome you to come with me, vôsh'lavi. Why would you think otherwise?"

"Oh, I know *you* welcome me. But Niezhan is another story."

"Old hurts and wounded pride." Ishna let out a puff of icy breath. "Unlike your egg-father, Vahgrin, Niezhan does not allow hurts to overwhelm his reason."

"Should I be more like Niezhan, then?" Docar flew under Ishna, their bellies nearly touching. "Shall I become a ponderous Dragos, spending my days in endless debate with Nao faction?" He moved even closer until their sensitive undersides skimmed each other. "Should I quell my Vatra passions?"

Ishna flicked him with her wing and spun upward. "You think I care for you only because you ignite my passions? I am a Primal Dragos, Docar, yet even I express more than one elemental side. You are more than simply the fire that warms my nights."

Docar flew upward, touching her wingtip again. "And you are more than the icy queen that freezes mine."

They both laughed as they twirled together. Their necks intertwined, foreheads touching, they spun in an embrace. Docar's red-tipped black scales blurred with her iridescent white scales until the two dragons appeared as one.

◆　　◆　　◆

As Docar predicted, his presence did not thrill Niezhan. But as Ishna foresaw, the old Dragos dropped his dissent when Ishna asked why Niezhan protested. *He does not want to reveal to others that he, too, is not always in control of his emotions*, Ishna thought.

While several Nao faction dragons weighed in on Ishna's quest to find Veridia, only the Lít was present for this small council discussion.

Niezhan began. "First, the Lít clarifies that we do not unanimously agree an overland journey into the heart of Two-Legged territory is a good idea."

Naja said, "We can dispense with our first recommendation since my egg-mother will disregard our advice and pursue her journey anyway." There was mirth in her tone, and all present chuckled.

Ishna joined the laughter and said, "You are correct, Naja."

After their laughter died down, Niezhan continued. "The Lít recommends a small coterie rather than a full shock of Dragos."

"Why a small group?" Docar asked. "A full shock, say twenty or thirty, can combat a small human army. Especially if we take mostly Vatra and Enara Dragos."

Niezhan sent Docar an icy glare. "Ishna, we suggest you and Docar take two, perhaps three additional dragons on this expedition. A Zedris hatchling—earth element— and a Veridia hatchling to add the wood element. If you want additional Dragos in your party, we recommend an additional Vahgrin hatchling."

All members of the Lít Council thumped once.

"Keep your group small and agile," Niezhan said. "We will provide more information on why we recommend this when Côzhili gives her scouting report."

Docar thumped his tail once to show his assent and agreement.

Niezhan gave Docar a languid nod.

"The number I take depends on the individuals in the party," Ishna said. "But continue. I will add my thoughts once I hear you out."

Thumping his tail once, Niezhan continued. "Precisely that. Representing the earth element, we recommend Nao faction's own, Côzhili. As you know, Côzhili is the primary scout. She knows more about the potential dangers and routes than any other Dragos."

Being part of the Lít, Côzhili was present and gave her tail a decisive thump. All the others present thumped as well, and Ishna added, "I am gladdened you will join me, Côzhili. Your counsel will be welcome on this journey." The two dragons briefly touched foreheads.

"Of all the elements, humans seem to fear one more than the others. Unwise, of course, but there it is." All but Docar thumped. "Docar is the obvious choice for a Vahgrin hatchling to accompany you."

Côzhili laughed. "Docar brings Ishna the fire, all right."

The mirth did not reach Niezhan. "Shall I continue? I believe that brings us to the question of who will represent the wood element. On this journey, perhaps the most important element."

All thumped once.

"What say the Lít? Is Aurixia ready for this mission?" Ishna asked.

Naja answered. "At your request, honored egg-mother, Nao faction explored this question from several angles. We conclude that her desire to assist is genuine. She harbors no hidden agendas. There is no evidence of the potential for sabotage."

Ishna interrupted. "A saboteur?" She laughed. "You were not genuinely considering such a thing, were you?" Her demeanor shifted from jovial to earnest. "I asked the Lít to consider if she truly senses her egg-mother or only wishes she does and her readiness for a long overland journey. I did not suggest you waste time searching for shadows at night."

Niezhan rumbled the stone, calling for all to quiet themselves. "Nao does not waste time pondering shadows. Need I remind you that when last you lived, your own Primal brother acted against you in a way most vile?"

"But that was Vahgrin. Aurixia is—"

Niezhan held up a wing and rumbled the stone again. "Aurixia is no less corruptible than any Dragos."

Ishna and Docar spoke simultaneously, arguing that Vahgrin was an exception to the norm. "In our thousands of years, one sour old Dragos acting on petty jealousies does not mean that all Dragos will behave similarly," Ishna said.

All spoke at once, arguing over each other until Niezhan bellowed, "Huuush!" and trembled the ground making chunks of basalt fall into the sea below. "Vahgrin is not the only Dragos to harbor hidden hurts, Ishna." He paused a moment to allow his words to bloom. After a while, he continued. "While in our Dragos history, Vahgrin's actions are singular, we note that his treachery came at a time of increased interaction with Two-Leggeds."

Niezhan paused for several moments, allowing his audience to consider his words. Finally, he said, "During our Dô'bedri, the Walker population grew. They spread across the land like summer mosquito storms on the tundra. Unless we intend to live forever cramped on this small bit of rock, Dragos interaction with Two-Leggeds is inevitable. The Lít, therefore, counsels increased caution when choosing who to accompany you on any overland journey."

The Lít all thumped once, and even Docar agreed. "Your reasoning is sound, I give you that," Ishna said. "And I hear your arguments, Niezhan. But I refuse to allow Vahgrin's despicable action to poison my well of trust for dragonkin."

Naja and Côzhili both thumped once.

"The Lít recognizes your point," Niezhan said. "We will continue to consider issues of trust amongst the Dragos."

Ishna thumped.

"What say the Lít about Aurixia's claims of sensing Veridia?" Docar asked.

Naja said, "The hatchling insists her egg-mother's Primal energy calls to her. No other Dragos—not even you, Ishna—have felt the same vibration. But we cannot disregard Aurixia's claim, for she could have an experience that no other Dragos has. The Lít, therefore, concludes that we must investigate Aurixia's claim, as the ramifications are too important to ignore."

All thumped once, and Ishna's thump was firm and enthusiastic.

"Then we have settled upon our traveling. Aurixia will represent the wood element and lend healing energy. Côzhili will represent the earth element with wise counsel and grounding. Docar will bring the fire and me the water and ice," Ishna said.

"Why do I feel like the Lít has put me on hatchling sitting duty?" Docar asked.

Finally, Niezhan's face loosened, and he laughed with the others.

"Docar, please go find Aurixia. Advise her she will join our search mission," Ishna said. "I will receive Côzhili's scouting reports and route recommendations."

Readying to take wing, Docar halted when Ishna called to him. "Make haste, Docar. If Aurixia truly senses Veridia's Primal energy, Two-Leggeds with magic near Veridia's hidden location may sense her too. We must reach Veridia before Walkers find her."

Docar took off and headed east again to search for Aurixia, the youngest dragon.

Niezhan continued their council. "While I agree with your plans to make haste, I do not agree Walkers threaten Veridia's safety. She is more than capable of defending herself."

"Oh, I agree," Ishna said. "But after seeing what those dragomancers have done to Vahgrin…" She shuddered, and all of them grew quiet. "You urged me caution regarding our own dragonkin, Niezhan. I urge you—all Dragos—to be wary of Two-Leggeds. Our interactions with them never end well." *Except perhaps for one.*

All thumped once.

"That leads me to reports of concerns regarding the westernmost islands in Xathi Tol'galen," Côzhili said. "When we entered our Dô'bedri, Walker magic was rudimentary. They conjured fire for their hearths, mixed herbs for poultices and tonics."

"No battle mages flinging Vatra weapons or singing seas into tsunamis," Ishna said.

"Precisely," Côzhili said. "The Lít recognizes that Two-Legged magics advanced during the Dô'bedri. But we believe their magical abilities do not significantly threaten dragonkin."

"Unless Walkers sprout wings, dragonkin still have a substantial magical advantage," Naja said.

Ishna recalled the flying boats the Two-Leggeds called jib-rigs but decided not to bring it up. *That flying feat is confined to a limited area. No need to add unnecessary concern.* She said, "That is good news."

The Lít all thumped once, but Côzhili continued. "They have, however, developed new and more powerful weapons than before the Dô'bedri. Our scouts report Two-Leggeds are moving new weapons onto the western islands of Xathi Tol'galen."

"Then we should avoid the western islands. We could circumvent the Two-Leggeds by going north," Ishna said.

Thumping twice, the Lít disagreed. "Only *you* can survive such temperatures," Niezhan said. "Poor Aurixia and Docar—even Côzhili—will have trouble with their wings icing if they range too high or too far north."

"I see." Primal Water and Ice energy comprised Ishna's very nature. Able to survive the deepest freeze, she had never experienced freezing or icing wings. *Besides, Primal magic fuels my flight.* Ishna asked, "What do you suggest?"

"Since Walkers appear intent on engaging in battle, the Lít unanimously agrees on this recommendation," Niezhan said.

"And what is that?" Ishna asked.

"Show them no mercy," Niezhan said.

The other two dragons thumped once, their demeanors earnest. Côzhili and Naja continued with discussions of the route. Ishna listened, but an unpleasant thrum throbbed in her head and distracted her.

Not now, Quen, Ishna thought to her.

"Promise," Quen thought back. "Your promise."

I know the vow I made and intend to keep it.

Keep your promise. No harm to my family.

We are not going to Indrasi, Quen. Fear not for your loved ones.

Dreaming… pale morning light… a meadow. His powerful arms surround me. Frigid air, I see my breath. But in his arms. I'm… warm. Loved.

It was not a dream.

I loved him, but he is not blood kin. True or dreaming?

True.

Does your vow include him?

Ishna did not answer.

Promise?

Finally, Ishna thought to Quen, **I will do my best.**

CHAPTER 8

ALDEWIN

Omma said *"she"* is in the Dreaming. Aldewin's heart now felt like a thukna herd thundering, and hope made his throat tight. Aldewin thought, *Is it possible that Omma speaks of Quen? How could she know about my sol'dishi?*

Omma continued eating, oblivious to the tsunami of emotions she'd unleashed within Aldewin. All eyes still on Omma, she finished her food, washed it down with wine, and finally spoke. "The currents quicken now. Our time grows short. Ready yourself, Varskog. You enter the Dreaming tonight." Omma spoke to the young assistant who'd helped her into camp. "Go, Ivriga. Prepare my home for the Dreaming." She eyed Yngvari. "And take the Sea Singer with you."

"With respect, Modra Omma, I do not need help to prepare the tea for the Dreaming," Ivriga said.

Omma gave her a warm smile. "I know you don't, but Yngvari needs to learn the process."

Ivriga argued against it, but one withering look from Omma rendered her silent. Frowning at Yngvari, Ivriga said, "Well. Come on, then."

Yngvari rose but didn't immediately follow Ivriga. "Modra Omma, I am a Sea Singer. I'm unfamiliar with the Dreaming, or how to brew the Dream Tea."

Omma's eyes narrowed into slits. She cocked her head and stared in Yngvari's direction. Finally, she nodded. "Yes, you must learn the ways of the Dreaming. Now go."

Yngvari hunched her shoulders at Shel but didn't question her clan's Modra. She followed Ivriga, and the two disappeared into the maze of hustaig tree houses.

Each time Aldewin believed himself free of snares, a new spider spun a sticky web. *That's the way it feels, anyway,* he thought. Omma, this Moth Mother of a clan he didn't belong to, had decided his next move before she'd met him. *She draws me into her web by promising what I most desire.* Somehow, the elder knew Aldewin would trade his last breath for a chance to repeat the singular day when he knew he was loved.

Without another word, Omma drained her cup and disappeared into the thick copse of hustaig tree houses and giant mushrooms. Still sitting in a large group, Aldewin nevertheless felt alone.

Aldewin withdrew, as he often did, to his thoughts. Fen Menir and Val'Enara both trained him for a life of solitude. He'd grown accustomed to spending more time alone with his mind than with other people. *My best friend and worst enemy*, he thought.

Now, several cups into the evening, Shel regaled Nalija and other young Kāfe'vind with her exploits in the Sulmére with the Jagaru. As she told the story of their escape from the Dynasty's Kovathas and dragons, they were rapt with attention.

Wobbling, she stood and continued her tale. "I was backward on the kopek now while Eira rode hard toward the chasm. And I nocked an arrow—like this—and yelled up to that damned mage on a dragon's back, 'This is for hitting Nivi with your fire!'" Shel pantomimed shooting an arrow. Hearing his name, Nivi lifted his head, but only for a drowsy moment, before returning to his nap. Shel sat back down and drained her wine cup.

"What happened next?" Nalija asked. Her eyes were wide with wonder.

"My arrow shot true, of course, and knocked that vile mage off the dragon."

The Kāfe'vind listening to her story clapped and cheered. Shel stood and took a bow.

Aldewin chuckled to himself. *She embellishes a fair bit, but I suppose she captures the essence of what happened.* Shel omitted the part about Druvna dying. For that, Aldewin was glad. He didn't want to enter the Dreaming with a heavier heart than he already had.

Imbica had become glue at Jesper's side. She'd recounted recent happenings in Indrasi and listened as Jesper answered questions about the Fyrstua people and their magics. "You have no schools or seats of learning for mages?" she asked.

Jesper smiled warmly, his grey-blue eyes alight. "We don't lock our magic folk away in lonely stone buildings."

Imbica's smile faded. "They are quite lonely," she said.

I hadn't realized how alone I felt at Val'Enara until I joined with the Jagaru, Aldewin thought.

Jesper nodded. "Magic is a gift of the Green. It's meant to be celebrated and shared."

Imbica's smile returned, and she lifted her wine cup. "I toast to that," she said.

Perhaps unaccustomed to the concept of a toast, Jesper looked at her quizzically.

"In Indrasi, we raise our cups and clink them together. That's called a toast," Imbica said.

Jesper crashed his cup into hers, and wine splashed out. They laughed, and Imbica said, "Gently tap them together." They toasted again then sipped wine, their gazes never wandering from each other.

By my Vandu blade, I would never have guessed Imbica had a romantic bone in her body. Aldewin sipped his wine and couldn't help but smile as he saw love blossom for Imbica. It made him long for Quen, but he pushed the idea aside. *Don't dwell in the memories of a life you cannot have.*

Aldewin looked around the gathering for Dio. He finally spied the newest member of their pod at the far northern edge of the central communal area. In his usual fashion, Dio hung at the periphery, apart from everything. *Yet somehow aware of everything,* Aldewin thought. *It reminds me of… how I was with the pod. When I was Aldewin of Val'Enara, not a true part of the group.* The idea supplanted reminiscing about Quen but brought a new level of concern about their companion. *I must be vigilant and watch out for this one,* he thought.

Aldewin tried to relax, but Omma's cryptic words nattered him. To onlookers, Aldewin appeared calm. Inside, though, memories and thoughts churned like sand in a haboob. *Can I really contact Quen in the Dreaming?* This question led to an idea that troubled him more than any other. *If I find Quen in the dream realm, will she still feel for me as I do for her? Or worse, what if I discover she never did? What if our love was an illusion? A spell cast by the dragon soul within her.*

The roiling worries made the few hours waiting for the Dreaming seem like days. Finally, Ivriga quietly appeared at Aldewin's side, Yngvari behind her. "The Modra is ready for you," she said.

Aldewin hopped up and began gathering his pack and weapons.

Ivriga placed a pale, thin hand on his arm. "You don't need those things. Sea Singer and Aldewin, bid good night to your companions. You will likely be in the Dreaming 'til dawn."

Her eyes unfocused, and her movements languid from drink, Shel said, "Good night, Beerskoog..." She laughed, and Yngvari joined in the laughter. "Beerspoo..." Laughing so hard she could barely speak, Shel pointed to Aldewin and said, "Good night, you."

Aldewin helped Shel up and laughed as she nearly fell over. "That's your new name. Beerspoo!" she said.

Gods, I hope she forgets this when she wakes tomorrow. I can't go through life being called Beerspoo.

She swung a hand at his shoulder, missed by a league, but allowed him to bolster her. Shel looked up at him, eyes bleary as she tried to focus but failed. "You don't look like a wolf to me." She poked his shoulder. "Or a tree. Neither bark nor fur."

Perhaps emboldened by drink, Shel kissed Yngvari's cheek softly. "Good night, Sea Singer."

Yngvari blushed but brushed her lips against Shel's briefly before turning to catch up to Ivriga. She turned back, her voice pleading, "Don't leave without me, Shel. Promise?"

Shel touched two fingers to her lips where Yngvari kissed her. Her tone was suddenly stone-cold sober. "I promise, Sea Singer. I will wait for you."

Ivriga led them through the village center and to the northwest. Though Niyadi was still just past his zenith, the dense forest canopy in this area made the little brother sun's light pale. Fireflies rose from the damp soil, and oil lamps lit the path.

Omma dwelled in a giant hustaig tree rising far above the lower canopy. An enormous, blue-capped mushroom sprouted from the side of the rounded bulge of her house, and mushrooms of many varieties sprang up around the tree. Moths spread their colorful wings on the mushrooms and flitted around Modra Omma's house.

Ivriga led them up rickety wooden stairs to a thick tapestry of purple and blue woven in a spiral design. Several moths clung to the weaving and did not move when Ivriga pushed the tapestry aside to enter.

Aldewin had to duck, and once inside, he still couldn't rise to his full height. "Hustaig houses weren't built for Iska'kog men, were they?"

Omma, seated on the ground by what looked like a steel box with a wide, shallow bowl on top, simply tapped the ground next to her. A light green and black moth perched on her shoulder. "Sit here, Varskog." She patted on her other side. "And you, Yngvari, sit here."

They did as she asked and settled onto thick cushions. The steel box was hot, and steam rose from the bowl atop it.

"To enter the Dreaming, we will inhale the vapors of the sacred flygesroom," Omma said.

Yngvari's eyes grew wide, and she shifted on her cushion. "Flygesroom mushrooms are poisonous, aren't they?"

Aldewin wasn't concerned about inhaling poisonous vapors. He thought of his Vandu blade and its grooves and sigils etched into the metal, intended to carry poisons to ensure his attacks were lethal. *I did more than merely inhale poisonous vapors to earn that blade.* He'd endured a six-month-long vigil of ingesting poisons, little by little adding more each day until he either succumbed and died or emerged virtually impervious to death from ingesting toxic substances.

Omma put a calming hand on Yngvari's knee. "Would I ask you, our Clan's beloved Sea Singer, to ingest poison?"

Yngvari's look of fear faded.

"Yes, eating a flygesroom will kill you. Nearly instantly. But we Modras know the secret of the flying mushroom."

Ivriga came over and opened her closed hand. Inside was a pale golden mushroom with a cap like a floppy hat melding into a thin stem. "The flygesroom," she said, showing it to Aldewin.

"Looks tasty. Too bad it's poisonous," he said.

The mushroom took to the air, flying of its own accord. It flew from the fire's heat and toward the window behind them.

"Did that mushroom just—fly?" *These vapors already make me see things.*

Omma nodded, and Ivriga said, "Not all flygesroom fly, but some can. And it is these special ones that the Modras distill into a powerful tea that we pour into the Dreaming kettle. Relax now, Varskog. Allow the flygesroom vapors to take you to the Dreaming. There, Modra Omma will guide you. Together, you will find the answers you seek."

Fen Menir introduced Aldewin to substances for heightening alertness in battle. At Val'Enara, Rising and Ascended enjoyed experimenting with herbs they'd learned about in alchemy lessons. The Masters encouraged them to create alchemical concoctions to deepen their meditations. Their students took it further, though, and produced mind-bending tinctures and potions.

Aldewin took part in the experiments with fellow acolytes. Ultimately, he'd decided he preferred the mellowing effects of smoking heja to the odd and surreal experiences of more experimental potions.

Aldewin shouldn't have had reason to feel ill at ease with the flygesroom Dreaming ritual. *By the gods, I've taken part in experiments far riskier.* Yet he squirmed on his cushion and wanted to flee. Aldewin fought against the creeping sensation of being pulled into an alternate reality.

"Stay with me, Timonay," Luatha cried. His friend lay on the bare floor on his stomach, Luatha's upturned back seeping blood from lashes he'd taken for disobedience.

I'm already losing control of my mind, Aldewin thought. *This might help me find Ishna and Quen faster, but I cannot lose myself.*

Try as he might to rise, though, the flygesroom vapors had taken effect. Aldewin felt as though weights pressed his legs down. His mind urged him to flee the situation, but the flygesroom robbed his body of ambition.

Omma spoke aloud. Her voice, clear and unwavering, beckoned his mind back to her hustaig hut. "The Dreaming has guided Modra for countless generations. It is a gift from the Green, and the Green will protect you. Fear not, Varskog. You will not lose yourself."

Aldewin's mind drifted. He felt as though tender new-growth vine tendrils wrapped around his arms and encircled his waist. The vines didn't choke or constrict but were like a caress.

Omma's voice intoned, "Now, as it has always been. In the Dreaming, your spirit shows what you need to see. The collective will guide us as we weave the story together. Past, present, and future—all are one. The Dreaming will show the way."

Through drooping eyelids, Aldewin glanced across the steaming pot to Yngvari. Her eyes looked heavy too, and her head bobbed.

Omma's voice sounded warbly, as if she were sitting in a boat on the surface and speaking through deep water. "In the Dreaming, we do not care about the mortal realm. Ivriga will wipe your sweat and bring you sips of cool water. Curl into a ball and sleep, or sit wide-eyed and staring. It matters not. The Dreaming will find you either way."

Aldewin barely heard the last of what Omma said. His mind had already returned to wandering. Though his body remained seated next to Omma, his mind had left the cramped room smelling of simmering mushroom tea and earthy, damp wood.

In one instant, Aldewin noticed that the flygesroom vapors tasted bitter. The next moment, he was in Partha, in the Fen Menir compound.

He still sat cross-legged, as he did in Omma's tree cottage, but now, his legs were thin and much shorter. He was not Aldewin, the Varskog, or even the name his mother gave him.

Known as Timonay, the "Little Mouse," the lad sat in a Fen Menir courtyard, surrounded by fifteen-foot-tall walls of black stone.

A chicken with sleek brown feathers sat on his lap. Timonay's pale hand stroked the young rooster's feathers. *Kizmet.* He hadn't thought about his pet chicken for years. *Not since… this day that I'm apparently going to relive.*

Behind him, his master approached. As silent as new-fallen snow, little Timonay knew Master Mordranis was there only because he felt a slight waft of air across his cheek. And because of the sudden dread that drained his warmth and made him shiver.

Mordranis's voice was deep, steady, and low, with a Parthinian accent. "Do you enjoy caring for your pet? Kizmet, I believe you call him?"

Aldewin nodded and instinctively pulled the young chicken closer, happy for its warmth.

Master Mordranis put out a long, thin hand and patted Kizmet's head. It was the same hand that Mordranis had put on Aldewin's shoulder a year ago when he'd led a young lad then known as Rignar away from his mother and home. Mordranis purchased Rignar in a transaction not unlike merchants buying sacks of wool or barrels of wine on the docks. And Mordranis had brought little

Rignar to a house dedicated to Sicara, the Dread Sister and patron of Fen Menir, a Māja dedicated to spying and death.

Young Timonay, barely eight in the Dreaming vision, had the urge to smack Mordranis's hand away. *"Do not touch him. He is mine,"* Timonay wanted to say.

Aldewin, reliving the memory in this Dreaming, was little eight-year-old Timonay and an adult observer. He was present but also unable to act on Timonay's behalf.

Aldewin screamed at Mordranis, "Leave him be." But Mordranis did not hear him, and neither did Timonay. Wet tears on his cheeks, Aldewin tried to scoop up Timonay and Kizmet. To carry them from that place, never to return.

But his arms encircled air, and Timonay continued clinging to little Kizmet. Aldewin could not stop the inevitable.

Omma was a hazy vision, more felt than heard or seen. Her lips moved, but Aldewin couldn't hear what she said. He concentrated on perceiving her, and his thoughts on Kizmet faded. Aldewin left behind the agonizingly painful memories and ever-present heart scar of his first kill.

Aldewin followed Omma as she led him away from Fen Menir. Away from his shame. He had to run to catch up to her.

When he did, Omma said, "You could not have saved Kizmet, you know. That chicken was bound for the stew pot, one way or another. And if you had not wrung its neck to prove you deserved to remain in Mordranis's cold shadow, he would have killed you."

"I know." And Aldewin did know that. By then, he'd been in Fen Menir for a year. He'd seen boys go to their trial but not return. Or, like his friend Luatha, come back broken and scarred only to die later from the injury inflicted by the sadistic masters of death. The silver scars across Aldewin's back tingled at the memory of how he'd received them.

"It was Kizmet or me," Aldewin said. "I knew that then. I know that now. But after all I've done—all the lives I've taken—none was more innocent than Kizmet. Should I not weep for the life I took? Should I not suffer for it?"

Yngvari took his hand in hers. He hadn't realized she was there, observing his memory as well. "Do not let it weigh heavy in your heart, Varskog. Even the gods have done regrettable things."

Omma nodded. "I couldn't have said it better. Come. Let us leave the lifeless walls of your shadowy past, Varskog."

Aldewin and Yngvari followed Omma as she led them through a dense, fog-covered, marshy land. "The flygesroom love to wander. It is their nature to float and flit this way and that. Usually, we allow ourselves to meander where the vapors take us. But not in this Dreaming. Not today."

She took their hands and asked them to join hands, too. "Let us focus our energies—our minds. Aldewin, you must guide us. Reach out to Quen, Varskog. Be the wolf. Use your keen senses to prowl the Dreaming. Remember her scent, her taste. The feel of her."

As Omma spoke, Aldewin took them to the meadow. The place where he and Quen had lain intertwined. Her fingers traced lines on his chest, his hands entangled in her hair.

Omma's eyes slits, she nodded. "Good, you have the idea of her. Now, consider the dragon. Draw on the senses of your inner wolf, Varskog. Show us the dragon."

Aldewin didn't want to leave the meadow. If flygesroom could take him there, he'd be content to sit in a musty hustaig hut and inhale the vapors daily and forever.

Quen moved subtly but positioned over him until he was inside her. She undulated her hips and pulled him deeper inside. He was part of her, as she was of him. Melded into one. Each flawed and aching on their own, but together, perfect and whole. *All I wanted or needed*, he thought.

Yngvari said, "I… this is private, Moth Mother. I do hope you will lead him away from here soon."

A thump between his eyes. Searing heat, like the sting of frozen rain. *Nothing burns like the cold.* Hooxaura spun icicles at him, Quen grabbing him and pulling him into the barren darkness of Vay'Nada. Ice raining from above. An unnatural breeze and a shower of shimmering scales.

Ishna.

Gripping Ishna's upper shoulders with his thighs, grabbing handfuls of her white hair to keep from falling off. Pressed into her snowy beard, the lingering scent of Quen but also of a frosty morning when the cold cleanses life's odors from the world.

"Very good, Wolf in the Wood. You have the scent. Now, become the Wood. You are the roots of life. Your threads are everywhere and all at once. Life pulses through you as through the roots. Do you feel it?" Omma asked.

Beneath them, worms wriggled through the soil, and insects tended eggs in burrows. Subtle at first, like the gentle ripple in a still pond. Aldewin was in the earth and of it. Stone yielded to him as he sped through the soil of Menauld.

The roots throbbed, and their beat matched his own life's heartbeat.

"That is right, Varskog. Be the Wood. Use the roots to find Ishna," Omma said.

He shouldn't have known what Omma meant or what to do. But somehow, he did. The roots made him feel welcome. *Home, at last.*

"You are of the Wood, Aldewin," Yngvari said in the Dreaming. *"You are life, not death."*

Doka. The Skog.

"Allow Skogi to guide you, Aldewin," Yngvari said.

The thrum of the Wood, alive with promise, enveloped him. Within it, he allowed his essence to course along the roots, ranging far and wide in search of the familiar scent and feeling of his sol'dishi.

"Think about the dragon aspect," Omma said. "Allow the roots to draw you to the Dragos."

"Relax into the Dreaming," Yngvari said. *"Allow the roots to take you. Do not be afraid."* Yngvari took his hand in hers. She was familiar in this unknown place, and her touch soothed his lingering worries. Whether Yngvari held onto him only in the Dreaming or also in the waking world, Aldewin didn't know.

His last resistance abated, and Aldewin forgot to fear what he would discover. Aldewin wrapped his fingers around the amber resting on his chest. Warming beneath his touch, the resin now throbbed in the same rhythm as the roots.

Speeding through the ground now, the roots led him north. How he recognized it was north, Aldewin didn't know. The roots led him deep into Iska'kog territory. Instead of the Myrskog's soggy warmth, now, the ground felt constricted and icy. Roots still tendrilled throughout, but the travel was slower. Not as slippery.

"That's it," Omma said. *"Keep going."*

A burrow. Deep. Buried where humans could not find her.

Above, sensing the power but unaware of its source, a clan built their settlement over her. A thriving clan of tall, fair-skinned people with pale eyes and white-gold hair.

People who looked a lot like Pelagia.

And like me.

Omma said, "It is the Spindel'vara Clan."

Yngvari, still holding Aldewin's hand, shuddered. "That horrid woman. The one who put these on me." She tugged at the gold cuff on her ear. "She is from that clan."

Aldewin's stomach roiled, and nausea rose in his gullet. The room spun, and the roots felt as though they tangled him.

Omma said, "Release your memories from this Dreaming, Sea Singer. The past is not our journey in this Dreaming. Breathe deeply, Varskog. Don't dwell on the implications of what you see in the Dreaming. You can sift through it later."

Cool on his forehead. Ivriga said, "Sip this." Water at his lips.

Yngvari, her Sea Singer voice soft and lilting, sang a calming song of tranquil waters. It brought Aldewin immediately to the feeling of the Still Waters mantra. The nausea ceased.

Are these my father's people? My *people?*

He didn't need Omma to answer. Aldewin knew it was true.

Out loud, Aldewin said, "They take what is not theirs. They… weaken her."

Omma said, "Ishna? How did Spindel'vara get their hands on the Winter Dragon?"

Aldewin relaxed back into the ground, becoming the roots again. The dragon's ancient skin and scales caked in soil.

He listened. Aldewin waited with the patience of a seed, awaiting the perfect conditions to sprout.

There. *Tharump.* Nearly imperceptible, and what seemed like an eternity between beats. A dragon's heart.

"No, not the Winter Dragon."

A long pause, then… *Tharump.*

"It is the Spring Dragon. She lives."

The instant he perceived the slow beat of a dragon's heart, other beats joined. This time, a double beat.

I have heard that before. I know this beat.

His head to her chest, waiting and listening. *"Sometimes, it's not there at all. But other times, I feel like that second heart is going to rip me apart,"* Quen had said.

Thump… Tharump.

"Roots do not exist in the sky," Aldewin said. *"I cannot follow you there."*

"I know you," Quen thought to him. "You are other. Not of the Dragos."

Thump… Tharump.

Quen?

But no sooner had he sensed her than she was gone. Dashed away as if someone yanked her from the Dreaming.

"Quen!" he screamed out loud.

A damp cloth on his forehead and cool water at his lips. Sweat poured, and his bones ached. *Quen*, he thought. *Come back to me.*

Yngvari hummed a lullaby-like song. Omma's warm, soft hand on his cheek. "Your Dragos-touched friend remains," she said. "And through your connection with her, you are a conduit, Varskog. A connection between the Primal dragons of Winter and Spring."

Now lying on the ground, Aldewin panted. He wanted to leave the Dreaming, but the flygesroom vapors held him still in their grasp.

"Sing us back into deep layers of the Dreaming, Sea Singer," Omma said.

Now modulating her voice into a deep, throaty song, Yngvari pulled them back down to the deep waters of the dream world. Back to the thrum carried through the roots and dirt, passed from worm to tree and back again.

Thump… Tharump… Tharump.

Once again, Aldewin felt her. The Dragon of Spring. The embodiment of Primal Wood, stirring for the first time in over a thousand years. She didn't move, and her inhalations were so slow and long, a human couldn't perceive them. But the Spring Dragon's heartbeat, slower than any human could survive, quickened and beat stronger.

"*She lives,*" Aldewin said again.

Yngvari squeezed his hand. "*She is—beautiful.*"

"*And the Spindel'vara… vile magic here, Varskog. Something they are doing… it weakens the Dragos of the Wood,*" Omma said.

Aldewin agreed, though how he couldn't have explained. *"Their magicks. That is why the Spring Dragon does not answer Ishna's call."*

Yngvari said, *"We must rescue this dragon from the Spindel'vara."*

Omma's voice, low and sure, said, *"This explains much. They siphon from an unnatural well of Primal magic. But how?"*

As Omma had guided Aldewin away from dwelling on questions during the Dreaming, he now admonished Omma. *"Seek answers once out of the Dreaming, Modra. For now, we focus on what the roots show us."*

"And what is that, Varskog?" Yngvari asked.

Aloud, Aldewin said, "To find the Winter Dragon—to recover my sol'dishi—I must first seek the Spring."

Chapter 9

Quen and Ishna

uen remembered a saying of the great Vas O'Nai. "Dwell not in the remembrance of bygone days, for in memories we become lost. Memories are not life."

But Vas never lived inside a dragon, Quen thought.
Memories are all I have.
I've got a new saying for you, Vas.
To remember is to live.

Remember…

Rocks pelting, I put my hands over my head and ran.
"Vay'Nada spawn," they yelled.

I can't let them see me cry. Speeding away faster than any of them. No one can catch me.

Maybe I am Vay'Nada spawn.

Behind the hide tanning shed, making myself small. I didn't mean to be stronger than them. I tried Still Water, Pahpi, but it didn't help.

A hand on my shoulder. I flinch it off.

"You've got work to do. If Pahpi sees you being lazy—" Rhoji had said.

I turn. Rhoji sees my red, puffy eyes.

On the floor next to me now, Rhoji puts an arm around my shoulder. He says nothing because he doesn't have to.

Rhoji…

"Remember, I love you, little sister, and always will," Rhoji said.

"No matter what—I become?" I asked.

"You are Quen Tomo Santu di Sulmére, daughter of Santu Inzo Dakon di Sulmére. Never forget that."

It's beginning to slip away, Rhoji. Bit by bit…

Remember…

Pahpi…

His eyes glistened. "Name you?" Pahpi's lower lip quivered. "You are Quen Tomo Santu. My daughter. You walk in Lumine's light."

If only I'd taken his hand. Why did I run?
Pahpi…

He is no longer in this world.
But then again, neither am I.

Remember…

If I slip away, will I meet Pahpi at Nixaya River? Will Lumine welcome me? Or will I spend eternity in Vay'Nada's icy realm with other shadow spawn?
Or am I lower than even a shadow spawn? Not entitled to eternal existence, even on Vay'Nada's frigid shores?

Dreaming…

My back against the Staves, resting. Sands whistling. Juka's winds rage.
Two hearts. Thump… tharump. Thump… tharump.
My two hearts. I've known them my whole life.

Thump… tharump… tharump.

A third beat? Who…?

Thump… tharump… tharump.

Listen. Feel.
Familiar.
Follow the vibration. Listen to the roots.

Dreaming…

Floating above a pond still as glass. Roots buoy him, and vines wrap their arms around him. Was he always that peaceful?
The roots say he's a wolf in the wood. He looks like neither wood nor wolf.
A green glow surrounds him.
I hadn't noticed it before.
I know this man—knew him.
Aldewin?

His eyes open.

He sees me. How?

"Quen…" he says.

Thump… tharump… tharump.

He feels it too.

She lives, Ishna says.

We both ask, "Who?"

My sister, Ishna answers. **The dragon of Spring and of Primal Wood. Go to her, Varskog. Go north. We will find you there.**

PART II

No Sorrow for the Breaking

Waste no tears for the Breaking, sa'gamlin.
For the Breaking brings death to our Two-Legged foes.
    Death to the Old World.

We shattered the chains that once bound us.
Wings dance!
    A new day dawns for dragon kind.

Rise, Fire faction! Gather Heart of the Dragon!
Leave the drowned place behind.
    Wisdom of the Wise Ones guides us.

Behold, under western skies,
Blue ocean falls, and towering rocks rise.

On wings of ice.
Under breath of fog.
    Soar, dragon kind, take wing!

Ishna of the Icy-Water faction,
Friend to all dragon kind,
    Leads us.

Follow her trail of glistening scales,
To the spine of the world,
    Freedom for all dragon kind.
    Our Urixos* awaits.

    —Translated from Dragosi in the 3rd Era by Rajani
    of the Dragos Sol'iberi, Volenex.

*Translates as "Golden Time."

CHAPTER 10

ISHNA

Being dragged into human visions, her mind momentarily not within her control, unnerved Ishna. *My deeply interwoven connection to Quen yanked me with her into that vision state,* Ishna thought. *To resist dragomancer control, I require my link to Quen. Yet I long for our connection to end.*

Though Ishna disliked experiencing the human Dreaming, it confirmed Aurixia's report. Rixi *did* sense Veridia, her egg-mother. *My sister lives, and we must travel into Two-Legged lands to retrieve her.*

Ishna called to Côzhili, Aurixia, and Docar. All had been hunting but came quickly when they heard Ishna's call.

"It is time," Ishna said.

Aurixia's golden-yellow eyes, like Bardivian sunflower petals, brightened. "You felt her, didn't you? The pulsing of my egg-mother's life force?"

Aurixia's perceptiveness should not have surprised Ishna. Rixi was, after all, Veridia's hatchling. *So like her egg-mother.*

Ishna did not reveal that the human within her had seized control of her mind, if only briefly. She said only, "Côzhili has completed her scouting."

"Conditions will not improve," Côzhili said. "If we plant to mount a retrieval mission into Two-Legged lands, we should go now." Like many Dragos, Côzhili had grown tired of being confined to the dreary grey rock of Xathi Tol'galen. Hearing that Ishna was ready to proceed, Côzhili's mood brightened.

Perhaps no dragon was more eager to leave Xathi Tol'galen than Docar. Like many of Vahgrin's hatchlings, before the Dô'bedri, he had enjoyed a primarily solitary nomadic life and warm Sulmére sands to frigid basalt. "Please tell us we leave soon," Docar said.

"We leave today. But I must alter our prior plans," Ishna said.

Docar raised his brows and blew a puff of hot air. "And do Niezhan and the Lít know of your shifting plan?"

Ishna huffed, acting indignant. In truth, she had discussed her idea only with Côzhili. She had not had the opportunity to speak with the Lít. *But we have no time for Nao faction's lengthy debate. We must act now,* she thought.

"Loxen of Ignati faction will be the fifth in our search party," Ishna said.

Docar's eyes swept between Ishna and Côzhili, perhaps trying to discern which had hatched the idea. "Interesting choice," he said at last.

"I will retrieve Loxen," Côzhili said. Her tail thumped excitedly when she spoke his name.

After Côzhili took wing, Docar said, "An earth-dragon playing with fire." He exhaled a scorching breath that turned into a steamy fog. "I would not have thought Loxen would interest Côzhili."

Aurixia blew a loose whistling sound. "Ooh, a new Dragos pair? Is Loxen her vôsh'lavi?"

Ishna thumped Aurixia with her tail. "Do not gossip." She quickly added, "And don't refer to him as her vôsh'lavi. I do not think Loxen knows the warmth for him building in Côzhili's heart."

Before long, Côzhili returned with a dragon twice her size. Loxen's scales were black like Côzhili's, but his eyes were fiery red, while her eyes were mossy pools of green. When he spread his wings, they shone deep purple near his body but flamed to orange like a Sulmére sunset at the tips.

Loxen, a member of the Ignati faction, was used to hierarchy and formality. He bent his head low before Ishna, his neck almost touching the ground. "It is an honor to be summoned by our esteemed Winter Dragon. I am your humble servant."

Docar snorted while Aurixia looked flustered and knelt as well.

Ishna gave the two a short head bow then said, "Rise. There is no need for ceremony among us on this journey, Loxen. We will travel in a small search party, not a war battalion or shock. And please, call me Ishna."

Loxen raised his head and said her name as if trying it out for the first time. "As you are my esteemed elder, I cannot help but show you deference. That is the Ignati way."

Docar caught Ishna's eye and smiled. *Docar knows how I detest such formality*, Ishna thought. *And calling me an elder? It wins Loxen no points.*

"We are not of Ignati, Cantiva, Nao, or Iska'van factions on this journey. We represent all Dragos."

Loxen stood tall, his magnificent wings spread wide, his head high. "Côzhili briefed me on the mission. I am ready to serve. When do we depart?"

"We leave now." Ishna paused to receive any protests. When none voiced complaint, she continued. "Since Côzhili has scouted our route, she will take point." Ishna turned to Aurixia. "You, Rixi, will fly directly behind her. Loxen, you will guard Aurixia's right wing. I will take the left. That leaves Docar. He will guard the rear."

Aurixia considered the announced formation and said, "But that will hem me in. I won't be able to see a thing."

Côzhili playfully whipped her tail into Aurixia's rear. "Do not pout."

Docar said, "Aurixia, you have many years ahead to explore this world. But the Winter Dragon and Lít council have chosen you for this vital mission. Your connection to Veridia will guide us. Thus, your safety is paramount. If we lose you, our mission will fail. It is not a punishment, sa'gamlin, but an honor."

All thumped their tails once, and each dragon gave Aurixia a gentle head nuzzle for encouragement. Côzhili took flight first. She flapped her wings in steady, powerful strokes and caught the wind. The others followed, content to leave the misty, grey eastern islands of Xathi Tol'galen behind.

They flew past the towering basalt cliffs Nao faction had claimed. Ishna called to her old friend, Niezhan.

"We are on the wing! Our search for Veridia begins."

Niezhan's deep voice rumbled, calling out well wishes to Ishna's small rescue party. Though Niezhan remained resting on the rocky outcropping that had become his home, other dragonkin soared beside and behind Ishna's small group.

They screeched, whooped, and called well wishes and pleas to bring their egg-mother and friend home. Many of Veridia's hatchlings flew nearby, their wings a flurry of green and gold, purple and black.

As they reached the western cliffs of the swell of islands dragonkin had claimed as their own, most of the farewell entourage turned back. Some were reluctant, though, hanging on until Docar admonished them to follow no more.

Before the Dô'bedri, Dragos roamed Menauld freely. Most dragons preferred the nomadic life and ranged great distances. Their mood took them where it willed, like dandelion seeds on the wind.

Since the Awakening, most dragonkin heeded Ishna's advice—she preferred not to think of it as a command— that dragons confine themselves to the isles of eastern Xathi Tol'galen. Excited to see one another after the sleep of the Dô'bedri, they gladly frolicked, hunted, and reveled in the company of their brethren.

But old feuds, fractures, and reignited faction quarrels had shown frayed nerves. Ishna knew she couldn't keep her kin safe much longer by confining them to the relatively limited space of Xathi Tol'galen. It was in the Dragos nature to roam, and confinement was as unnatural as not shedding scales. *We need to spread out, or I fear infighting will divide us again as it once did before Jik'Madar—the Breaking.*

But that is a worry for another day, Ishna thought. *Once we bring Veridia back, things will calm for a time. Her elemental Wood energy soothes the Dragos soul.*

As they flew, Côzhili advised the coterie of their plan for the day. "We will press hard today. I want to clear the western isles of Xathi Tol'galen, cross the sea, and make landfall on the northern shores of Tinox."

"Two-Leggeds dig and make craters in that region. Why do they do that, I wonder?" Loxen asked.

"They call it mining," Ishna said. "Pulling vital mineral energies from the ground."

Côzhili hissed. "Scarring and scouring. And for what?"

"I understand little that Two-Leggeds do. But I know they create weapons from ores they mine," Ishna said.

She recalled watching Fano, the blacksmith, pound a dagger into shape then finally dip it into what he called the quench. *Quen loved that dagger. I wonder what happened to it after she struck Vahgrin in the eye with it.*

"Human weapons are of no concern to Dragos," Loxen said. He sounded sure of himself.

"Did you just rise from your barrow yesterday?" Docar asked. "We slept long, brother. The Two-Leggeds have advanced beyond sharpened sticks."

"Until they discover a way to send fire to the sky, I do not fear their ground-based weapons," Loxen said.

Typical of Vahgrin hatchlings. Most of them assume fire is a superior weapon, Ishna thought.

Aurixia said, "Loxen has a good point. We can fly. Two-Leggeds do not."

Côzhili let out a low, deep rumble. "Hush, Dragos. We near the isle of Kor Man'tol. Two-Leggeds have been busy here, digging and erecting structures atop the western cliffs."

Ishna said, "A reminder. Côzhili is our battle commander. Understood?"

All gave their assent.

"Aurixia, do exactly as Côzhili commands. Docar is your second, so if Côzhili is occupied, stay with Docar," Ishna said.

"Do you truly think Two-Leggeds will attack us?" Aurixia asked.

Ishna snorted a puff of icy breath, a signal to be quiet. Though humans did not comprehend the Dragosi language, dragon speak carried long distances, and humans heard them before they saw them. If humans stood watch for dragons on this atoll, Ishna did not want to reveal their approach any sooner than necessary.

Côzhili led the coterie higher and veered north. Below, Ishna spied the evidence of Two-Leggeds digging that Côzhili had reported. *Why would they do that?* She saw no buildings or encampments, only recently overturned soil along a long stretch of land at the edge of the white cliffs facing the ocean.

Now soaring high enough that landforms appeared flattened, Aurixia struggled to keep up. *She is not strong enough to handle the thin air and icy wings.*

"We need to descend," Docar called. "Aurixia is flagging."

"I'm not—"

An icing wing cut Aurixia's protest short. The freezing temperature numbed her wings and rendered them useless.

"I thought you prepared her for high flight and icy wings," Ishna bellowed. Ishna levied the accusation at Côzhili.

Côzhili said, "Naja said she trained Rixi, but—"

Aurixia tumbled and flapped her left wing wildly, trying to right herself. Panicked, Rixi forgot the command for silence and screeched as she plummeted.

Loxen descended, but Ishna ordered him back. "Stay with the coterie, Loxen. I will retrieve Aurixia. Côzhili, fly lower, as Docar suggested."

Fueled by her Primal magic, Ishna's wings, while convenient to aid in steering, were not strictly necessary for flight. She dove, driving herself downward with preternatural speed.

Still flailing, Aurixia remained airborne but wobbled, struggling with an iced wing. Ishna wound herself around Aurixia and said, "Trust me, Rixi. Allow my magic to do the flying for both of us."

But Aurixia continued flapping in a jerky, panicked manner. Her wings beat against Ishna, making it difficult to maintain the close contact required to buoy them both in the air.

"Stop trying to fly, Aurixia!" Docar shouted down from above. "Trust Ishna. She can carry you."

Now flying lower, Ishna discerned more detail of what the Two-Leggeds had been working on. The Two-Leggeds had turned up the soil, not by digging holes or trenches but by wheeling giant wooden devices along a newly trenched path.

The contraptions were as large as a small dragon but looked like a giant crossbow. Below, Walkers shouted and called to one another as they scurried to their weapons.

Ishna spotted a Dynasty battle mage with a yindril following close behind her. The poor uprooted creature flailed its long, woody arms. Its sinewy mouth open, the yindril keened its lament. The deep, sorrowful sound made even the dragons uneasy. *Côzhili did not report Dynasty mages and their yindrils to contend with.*

From the ground, a Two-Legged called what sounded like a command.

Walkers on either side of the contraption pulled ropes. As the ropes tightened, they wound a wide wooden lever. *They intend to fling that giant arrow-tipped bolt at us.* A fifth person maneuvered the machine, aiming it at the approaching dragons.

Ishna twirled around Aurixia. She attempted to place herself underneath the young Dragos and between Aurixia and the projectiles.

Docar shouted, "Upward, Ishna. Pull up!"

"I'm trying!" she yelled back. To Aurixia, she said, "Do you feel that pull?"

Aurixia thumped her tail once.

"That is my Primal magic, Rixi. It is strong enough to carry us both, but you must not fight it. Cease struggling, young Dragos. Trust me." Ishna realized it was a big ask. Unless a dragon had experienced being carried by a Primal dragon's magic flight before, it was an unnatural experience that required total trust. *I should have practiced this with her.*

Eyes wide and searching the ground below, Aurixia let out a screech as a giant wood bolt with a steel tip whistled through the air and right for them. Instead of relaxing into Ishna, Aurixia resumed flapping. Though Aurixia's wings had thawed, the young dragon was exhausted. She wobbled like a lopsided leaf bandied in the wind.

Ishna pulled with every ounce of intention and lifted Aurixia. But a second bolt ripped clean through the base of Aurixia's left wing. The young dragon's pained cry echoed off the cliffs below.

Injured and fatigued, Aurixia finally calmed enough for Ishna to pull her upward and back into formation.

"We need to get Aurixia to a safe place where we can assess the damage." Ishna placed Aurixia on Docar's back. "Côzhili, lead Docar and Aurixia to the cave you scouted north of here. Docar, stay tight on Côzhili's right wing and fly steady."

"As soon as they are safe within the cave, I will return to assist you," Côzhili said.

But Docar said, "No, you will stay with Aurixia. *I* will return."

In a tone that invited no argument, Ishna said, "You *both* will stay with Aurixia. Loxen and I will deal with the Two-Leggeds. Let us get to work, Loxen."

Ishna did not wait for counterarguments. Instead, she turned on her left wing and flew toward the human battlements. Loxen flew to her right and slightly behind. A low rumble began in Loxen's belly as he primed the fuel of his fiery breath.

Behind them, Docar let out a Dragos battle cry unheard for over a thousand years. "Nox'Kili!" Docar yelled.

Ishna and Loxen returned the call. "Nox'Kili!"

Soon, Ishna spotted the large wooden weapons armed with giant flying arrow-tipped bolts. Dipping lower, Ishna spewed icy shards onto the people scurrying below, careful not to freeze the yindril. "Avoid burning the hapless yindril if you can, Loxen. It did not ask to be used by the Two-Leggeds to attack us."

"Understood," Loxen called.

From the height they flew, Ishna's attack was a scattershot of icy rain. It did not freeze the Two-Leggeds solid but slowed them as they raced to load their weapon.

Even though the dragons had shown no hostility toward them, the Walkers sought battle. *And have pulled an innocent yindril into their warring ways,* Ishna thought.

Before Ishna lost her first life to Indrasian's blade, yindrils had been stationary plants without bestial traits. Ishna did not know if the creatures understood language, either Dragosi or the languages spoken by Two-Leggeds. She called to the yindril anyway, hoping it could take her meaning. Even from a distance, she sensed the creature's fear.

Ishna called to it in Dragosi. "The Dragos mean you no harm, gentle creature. Run inland and leave the mage behind. You will find safety away from the battlefield the Two-Leggeds created."

At first, the yindril did nothing but stand, flail, and keen. Ishna repeated her plea aloud then thought to the yindril using the mind-speak she used with Primal dragons. To her surprise, the yindril seemed to understand her mind-speak. It ceased thrashing and wailing and lumbered away from the cliff side.

Behind the yindril, the mage screeched and yelled, "Come back, you towering fool!" The mage wound her hands, gathering magical energy. She hurled a tight fireball at the yindril.

Ishna spewed frosty breath and extinguished the mage's fire attack. The yindril continued ambling away from the field of battle.

Ishna spat a frozen shard at the mage. The icy projectile hurtled downward and speared the mage through her skull. She toppled like a felled tree, her dead eyes wide with shock.

You will harm yindrils no more, mage.

The yindril glanced back but wasted no lament on its former handler. It topped the crest at the western edge of the bluff and continued moving away from the danger zone.

Several men shot handheld crossbows. Their small bolts fell to the ground before reaching the dragons. Even if the dragons flew lower, a crossbow bolt was not large enough to significantly damage Ishna or Loxen.

"If it's war the Two-Leggeds want, then war we shall give them," Ishna said. "Bring them the bloody battle they crave, Loxen."

Quen buzzed in Ishna's skull. The intense throbbing made Quen's disapproval of Ishna's thoughts and actions painfully obvious.

Now is not the time, Quen. Your survival depends on mine. Do not forget that.

Loxen soared past Ishna and dipped downward. He opened his massive jaw and rained white-hot fire upon the line of wooden projectile weapons the Two-Leggeds had hauled to the cliff side. The wood burst into flames, and several Two-Leggeds burned too. Their screams met with crackling fire and waves crashing onto the rocky shore. Though Loxen's first attack decimated the arsenal, a few ballistic machines remained.

"Pull up, Loxen. We'll reform and attack again."

They swooped away from the sheer white cliffs and headed toward the ocean. Sea spray covered Ishna's whiskers.

Quen vibrated Ishna's head. The pain was nearly unendurable.

Stop, Quen. I must concentrate and protect Loxen. If anything happens to him...

Not only had her sa'gamlin, Côzhili, taken an interest in the fire dragon, but Loxen was one of Vahgrin's favorite hatchlings. *If I lose another of Vahgrin's favored children in a firefight with Two-Leggeds...*

Despite Ishna's internal pleading with the human soul she shared consciousness with, Quen did not quiet herself. The incessant thrum in Ishna's skull made her feel as though someone had thrust a giant sword through her head. *This is as bad as the horrid Rajani Rend.*

Dangerously distracted, Ishna continued flying west. She headed out to sea rather than returning to the coast for another volley.

Still close on her tail, Loxen called, "Ishna? Have you changed the plan?"

Though she had not commanded a battle in centuries, Ishna knew better than to change a plan during a fight and not advise her attack party. *But I do not want Loxen to see how I struggle to maintain focus.* Ishna had told no one, not even Docar, about the epic battle she fought to keep Quen's soul alive but also to protect her own identity from becoming lost. *I did not appreciate how difficult it had been for Quen all those years.*

During the Dô'bedri and before this life as a dragon reborn, Ishna's consciousness lived in Vay'Nada's realm, the Void. Though she had been lonely beyond measure, she had also found infinite peace on Vay'Nada's shadowy shores. Though it was risky, Ishna was desperate to quiet Quen's insistent protests. *I must seek the stillness of the Void. If I allow my consciousness to dip into the Shadow Realm briefly, perhaps it will pull Quen into the Void as well. Maybe that will quiet this parasitic soul who destroys my peace.*

Though no portal opened, and Ishna did not travel bodily into the Void, Ishna's mind slipped into the dark realm. For a fleeting moment, she no longer smelled smoke or heard human cries, waves crashing, or the flapping of her own wings.

Peace.

The feeling of languid existence tempted her to remain in the icy shadow realm. *No, I cannot linger. My dragon family needs me. And Quen's family needs me too, though Quen does not yet comprehend the role I will play in their future.*

The irritating buzzing ceased. Ishna's mind again became clear, and she returned her consciousness fully to the present and Menauld. Like the world spinning backward, sensation returned.

Ishna turned back toward the coast. Her brief mental journey to Vay'Nada had lasted mere seconds. *Not long enough for Loxen to sense anything amiss.* "Ready yourself, Loxen. We will finish what these Two-Leggeds began."

"Nox'Kili!" Loxen cried.

Loxen's battle cry thrummed in Ishna's broad chest and rumbled the ground below. *I can only imagine how that dragon war cry frightens these Walkers.*

Her mind once again clear and focused, Ishna dove toward the cliff. Below, people shouted and scurried. Two people pulled back on the levers on either side of the giant crossbow machine, winding the machine to let loose its giant bolt. A barrel-chested man at the rear of the weapon aimed, trying to keep his sights on the approaching dragons.

"I'll take out the Two-Leggeds," Ishna said. "Turn their machine to ash, Loxen."

Ishna flew lower this time. She got near enough that she smelled the odor of their fear. Ishna twirled and drove downward, moving so fast she became a blur of flickering white, icy blue, and turquoise. Maintaining her downward spiral, Ishna aimed her icy barrage with precision this time. She froze the Walkers on the left side of the machine solid.

With one side of the ballistic machine unmanned, the Two-Leggeds no longer had the power to pull the lever to unleash the giant arrow-tipped bolt. Before pulling up, Ishna laid down a swath of sharp icicles before ascending. She dodged several handheld crossbow bolts fired at her.

Behind, Loxen targeted his fiery attack on the remaining siege weapons the Two-Leggeds had built. Several groups of people aimed their handheld crossbows at Loxen, but with deadly accurate aim, he set them ablaze. The Walkers who aimed to attack Loxen were soon only sooty cinders.

Once Loxen was again at her wing, Ishna returned to inspect the battlefield. Loxen's fires burned in a line along the coastal cliffs as the siege weapons smoldered.

Most of the Two-Leggeds manning the weapons were frozen lumps of flesh or piles of cinder and ash. Yet nearly a dozen still lived. The living Two-Leggeds would remain alive if Ishna allowed it.

You do not need to kill them.

The thought was not Ishna's but came from the human consciousness inside her.

Remember what I once told you, Quen. Dragon loves lasts eons, but so do their hurts.

The sight of the Walkers below, still aiming impotent weapons despite their injuries, brought recollection of similar scenes played out across centuries. *Still trying to crush what they cannot control*, Ishna thought.

Since the siege weapons were now destroyed, Ishna had no fear of the remaining Two-Leggeds below. She again wound herself like a spinning cylinder and drove downward.

The Two-Leggeds who still lived limped and crawled, trying to escape the Dragos counter-attack. Some, legs frozen solid, crawled on their bellies like snakes, pulling themselves by their arms. Ishna watched with aloof disregard as a man shattered his own frozen legs so he could crawl to what he hoped would be safety.

None of the living Walkers could run. *And none will survive*, Ishna thought.

She called, "Nox'Kili!" Ishna swooped so low she could count the hairs on their heads. She spewed frozen shards like icy daggers, and soon, the battlefield was quiet and still.

They will attack us no more.

Ishna expected the horrendous thrum of Quen asserting herself through the only means available to her. To express her moral outrage at what Ishna had done to the Walkers. But the reproach did not come, and Ishna was glad for it. *The Two-Legged soul within me does not understand—she does not know—the ancient hurts inflicted on dragonkin by her kind.*

As a Primal dragon, Ishna did not require nourishment to survive. The same was not true for other dragonkin. "Eat your fill, Loxen," she said. "We will take food to the others. Aurixia will need the nourishment to heal."

Loxen gobbled a few frozen Walkers then helped Ishna gather more to take to the others. Relying on her ability to sense her dragonkin across short distances, Ishna led Loxen to the hidden cave that Côzhili had scouted.

A short distance from the human battlement, the sea had carved a cave into the soft cliff-side stone. The opening, large enough for only one dragon to fly into at a time, belied the size of the cave inside. Once the tide rose, the cave would be nearly impossible to see, even for sailing Two-Leggeds.

Docar welcomed Ishna with a forehead rub and a neck nuzzle. "I assume your raid of their battlements was successful?" Docar asked.

Loxen dropped the thawing human carcasses to the ground. "Those Two-Leggeds will trouble dragonkin no more," he said.

"How fares Rixi?" Ishna asked.

Aurixia's wing still seeped purply blue blood where the wooden bolt had pierced her. Docar had removed the bloody bolt, snapped it in half, and thrown it to the side.

Rixi rose swiftly when they entered. She pranced excitedly and, without thinking, flapped her wings before yowling in pain.

Côzhili wrapped a wing around her. "Settle, young one. You need to rest your wing for a few days."

Loxen nudged the carcass of a dead Two-Legged toward her. "Eat, Rixi. You need nourishment to heal."

Aurixia tore into the midsection flesh of a half-frozen Walker and devoured the nutritious vital organs. She spoke with her mouth full. "Tell us of the battle, Loxen. Did you set their weapons ablaze? I was so worried about you both."

Docar laughed. "Worry not for those two. They fought in many battles against humans before Jik'Madar. Before the breaking of the old world."

The youngest dragon again pranced excitedly and blurted out, "Tell me. I want to hear stories about the old world. Tell me of the drowning time. Of Jik'Madar."

Docar and Côzhili joined Aurixia in eating. Loxen said, "Another time, Rixi. We have long travel ahead and time aplenty for stories. Now, you must rest."

Ishna put her forehead to Aurixia's, which calmed the young Dragos. "Rest, child. The sooner you recover, the faster we can set out again to find your egg-mother."

After filling her belly, the young dragon washed then folded herself into a ball. She lay between Loxen and Côzhili, their massive bodies lending warmth.

Ishna wished she could speak with Docar silently, mind to mind, as she could with Veridia and the other two Primal dragons. *I do not want to stir Aurixia up again,* Ishna thought.

Though she did not need sleep like her dragonkin, Ishna curled into Docar's wings and rested anyway. *They all need to recharge, and I need them strong for this journey. I fear the worst lies ahead.*

Even though he could not hear her thoughts, Docar echoed her concern. He whispered, "I hope Aurixia's injury heals fully. I did not expect we would meet with this level of resistance by the Two-Leggeds. Or that we would suffer such a setback on our first day out."

Ishna nuzzled his neck and wound herself tighter into his body. "Settle your worried Dragos mind, vôsh'lavi.

Aurixia is a Veridia hatchling. Even as we speak, she enters a healing trance. Her histrionics are the stuff of youth, not indicative of a deep wound."

Docar sighed. "You are right, as always, vôsh. But what of the Walkers? How concerned should we be about what we face in the weeks ahead?"

Ishna wanted to reassure Docar that all would be well. In truth, though, she had never been more concerned about facing Two-Leggeds. Instead of voicing her fears, she gently nibbled Docar's neck and pressed her chest to his. "Worry not, vôsh'lavi. Our coterie may be small, but we can still act like a shock of Dragos. We will show no mercy to any Walkers that stand between us and our dear Veridia."

CHAPTER 11

ALDEWIN

As the flygesroom vapors dissipated, the hazy sensation of embracing Quen faded. Aldewin slowly regained full awareness of Modra Omma's cramped, humid cottage.

Aldewin's hand curled around the amber pendant, and he still sensed two heartbeats. Like a typical dream, the experience quickly ebbed. The double thump of Quen and Ishna's hearts gone, Aldewin felt more alone than ever.

Quen…

Though the flygesroom vapors didn't upset his stomach or make his head throb, they brought fatigue. Aldewin preferred sleeping outside, the forest's night song of nocturnal insects and creatures his lullaby. But the flygesroom robbed him of ambition. Aldewin curled into a ball and drifted into a dreamless sleep. He woke once to the sound of Yngvari retching, but seeing that Ivriga aided her, he fell back asleep.

Aldewin rose with Hiyadi's first light. Thanks to his ability to weather poisons and toxins, he was neither nauseous nor hampered by an aching head. *The only blessing of my Vandu training at Fen Menir.* Though he'd slept only a few hours, the nap energized him.

And the Dreaming had given him renewed purpose.

Aldewin grasped the amber pendant. *Quen lives*, he thought. He'd felt her presence. Even somehow heard her thoughts.

"She has a beautiful soul, Aldewin," Yngvari said. Judging by the dark circles under her eyes and her face wan, Yngvari's body hadn't handled the flygesroom vapors as easily as Aldewin.

"How are you feeling?" he asked.

Yngvari sipped from an earthen mug. "Better." She reached for his hand, and he took hers. A well of tears in her eyes reflected the pale morning light. "I don't know Omma's reasons for bringing me into the Dreaming, but I know this. I will help you find Quen. And I will lend any aid I can to restore her to human form."

"What if Quen doesn't want that? What if…?"

Yngvari laughed. "Men." She shook her head. "How can you see yet be so blind?"

Aldewin took his hand back and crossed his arms. "Blind?" He scoffed. "Fen Menir masters trained me to be a silent observer. I am a lot of things. Blind is not one of them."

Yngvari tsked. "A person can see with their eyes yet be blind, Varskog. See with your heart. Quen's love for you drew her to you. If she didn't care for you, you couldn't have found her in the Dreaming."

"How can you know that?" he asked.

"Because Skogi blessed her with ample Menaris gifts. And Yngvari pays attention," Omma said. She had left the cottage but returned with a steaming mug. "Drink this, Varskog." She handed him the cup. "This tea will clear your head and settle your stomach."

Aldewin expected a bitter brew, but it was pleasantly tart with a hint of sweetness. "Is that—?"

"An herbal tea steeped with blackberry and goshi berry." Omma settled onto her cushion, her legs crossed, her eyes bright and deep emerald green from the flygesroom.

I wonder if my eyes, too, are green now?

"All my years—so many Dreamings. None prepared me to share my mind with a dragon, if only fleeting."

Yngvari sipped her tea. "Thank you, Modra Omma, for allowing me to experience the Dreaming. It was more than I imagined."

Omma chuckled. "You thank me now, but you might curse me on the 'morrow next."

"Why is that?" Aldewin asked.

The Modra sighed and readjusted herself. "What we experience in the Dreaming blends with our waking world. Dreaming rattles the mind. It makes you wonder what is real and what is the Dream."

Aldewin had already lived three distinct lives, each feeling like dreams occasionally bleeding into his current reality. *Where does Timonay end and Aldewin begin? And now to be named Varskog. Does it usher in yet another life?*

Omma said, "Yngvari might also wish she had not joined us, as I now want to invite her to train to be my replacement."

Yngvari gasped. Ivriga, standing quietly in the shadows sipping tea, dropped her cup. Ivriga left the toppled mug on the smooth wood floor and pushed through the tapestry into the morning.

Modra Omma looked down at her cup. "I should have broken that more gently." She sighed. "I will always welcome Ivriga at my side, but despite her efforts and mine, Skogi has not blessed her with the deep knowledge and rapport with the Green required of a Modra."

"And you think I have that?" Yngvari asked.

Aldewin and Omma answered simultaneously. "Yes."

They laughed, and Omma slapped Aldewin on the knee. "Even the Varskog, who can't see love when it slaps him in the face, recognizes that Skogi and Fréjoya have blessed you mightily."

Aldewin wanted to protest her comment about him but couldn't. *Omma speaks the unwelcome truth. For all my training, neither Fen Menir nor Val'Enara prepared me to understand love and friendship as well as I'd like.*

Yngvari beamed. "I am honored, Modra. When does my work with you begin?"

Omma rested a warm hand on Yngvari's knee as well. "After we return from our journey to the Iska'kog."

This was news to Aldewin. If the captain allowed, he intended to journey with only the pod and a half dozen of Ontrosa's crew.

"I welcome your company, of course, Modra Omma." He nodded to Yngvari. "And you too, Sea Singer. But this journey we undertake..." A fleeting vision passed across his mind. Of flames raining from above, a city ablaze, people running and screaming while others were burnt to ash. *I'm unsure if this is a memory or prophecy from the Dreaming.*

Modra Omma seemed to know a vision ensnared him. "Do not dwell on visions from the Dreaming, Aldewin. Filter it into feeling. What does the vision make you feel?"

Without hesitation, he quickly said, "Fear. Though for others more than for myself. Worry for the two of you. Perhaps it's unwise to follow my path. It will probably lead to danger and things you wish you hadn't seen."

Yngvari reached for his hand again. "I told you, Varskog. I will help you restore Quen if I can." She glanced out the window and smiled. "Besides, I'd like to spend more time with Shel."

"And I've been walking these lands since long before you were born, pup," Omma said. "You'll need a guide. Even Jesper doesn't know Iska'kog lands like old Omma."

Aldewin couldn't argue against having a capable guide. He also couldn't deny the power he'd sensed in Yngvari. Her rapport with the spirit of Enara was not only equal to or greater than Imbica's, but she also augmented others' abilities. *I don't know how to restore Quen to human form. But if we find a way, we'll need tremendous magical power. I would be a fool to refuse Yngvari's offer of aid.*

Besides, he couldn't separate Yngvari and Shel. He'd seen how smitten they were and their tender kiss. *If I refuse to bring the Sea Singer, Shel will never forgive me,* Aldewin thought. *She might even tell me to shove it and abandon the pod and this damned quest altogether.*

"Welcome to the pod, then," Aldewin said. "But I'd like to take skilled warriors for protection." He considered

Ontrosa's remaining bare-bones crew. *They are as green as tender pea shoots in spring.* "I'd planned to ask Ontrosa to lend perhaps a half dozen of his crew—"

"Fah." Omma shook her head. "Nothing against the captain's people, but they are sea folk, not born of the skog. For this, you need people used to thrashing through vine, brush, and muck. Allow me to pick a crew from the Kāfe'vind, Varskog."

Aldewin nodded. "I welcome the help. But what of Ontrosa and his crew?"

"I will advise Leid Jesper to accept Ontrosa's offer. Our people could use additional sailing and sea combat training, and Ontrosa can teach them much," Omma said.

"Will Leid Jesper allow us to pull warriors away from Leivby? Especially with the Dynasty like a poisonous creeping vapor, spreading across the Vatnoyer," Yngvari said.

A churlish smile came to Omma's face. "Do you really think Leid Jesper will deny a request from the clan's Modra?"

Yngvari laughed. "Forgive me for even asking. I have been away too long." She sipped her tea then breathed deeply, taking in the humid, wood-scented air. "It's good to be home again."

"Finish your tea, both of you, then we will seek Leid Jesper and discuss our plans," Omma said.

They silently finished their tea, each deep in their own thoughts. The quiet contemplation reminded Aldewin of mornings at Val'Enara when he'd meditated with more than a dozen others. The Dreaming had been more intense than mere meditation. Aldewin felt closer to Omma and Yngvari than he had to other Val'Enara acolytes. *They know*

things about me now. Things I've told no one, not even Quen.
The thought should have made him wary. Instead, he felt
glad. *They know my darkest secret yet neither judge me harshly
nor run from me.* Aldewin wasn't sure all people could
accept his grim truths.

The larger sun was now well above the horizon, and
they ventured into Leivby Village to search for Leid Jesper.
"We will speak to the Leid first then regroup with your
pod," Omma said.

They trod across the village square, now virtually
empty. After celebrating all night, few were up early.

Omma led them to the southeast and down a wide
path paved with large stones. On either side rose giant
mushrooms and towering pink and yellow lilies.
Previously blending unseen into their surroundings,
moths flocked to Modra Omma. They hovered over her
and now covered her leather vest and hair.

The path wove through a hustaig grove. The paving
ended at a magnificent hustaig tree. Instead of a simple
tapestry covering the door, this hustaig house had a large,
rounded door carved with tendrilled vines and leaves
intermixed with moths, dragonflies, and other creatures.
With a spiral ladder on the outside, the house carved
within this tree was three stories high.

Omma rapped loudly on the door with her walking
stick. When no one immediately came to the door, she
knocked again and called, "Leid Jesper—Modra Omma
here to speak with you." Her voice echoed around the quiet
glen, and several moths flew away.

From within, Aldewin heard scurrying and whispers.
Finally, the door opened.

Leid Jesper smoothed his hair and finished lacing his pants. His shirt was untucked and the laces still open, revealing the tattoo of Kāfe'vind's sigil on his chest. His eyes were red and his clothes rumpled. "Modra, it's an honor to welcome you to the Leid's home." He swept his arm out, beckoning them in.

Though the doorway was taller than the door to Modra Omma's modest tree cottage, Aldewin still had to duck to enter. But once inside, he could stand at full height.

This hustaig tree house was considerably larger than Omma's. They'd built the house for larger gatherings with a long wooden table and eight carved chairs for the Leid and Eldurskir. A grouping of seat cushions by the window allowed for onlookers as well.

A narrow staircase wound from above, and Imbica ambled down, smoothing her hair and clothes. Yngvari smiled and shot Aldewin a glance, mischief in her eyes.

"Modra Omma, I believe you have already met Mage Imbica, a member of the late Druvna's Jagaru pod from Indrasi," Jesper said. Jesper poured clear water from an earthenware jug into an iron kettle nestled in a box of glowing coals as he talked.

"Honored to see you again," Imbica said. She gave Omma a deferential bow but shot Aldewin a narrow-eyed glare that warned him to hold his quips.

He smiled at her and held his tongue. *She has been with the pod long enough to know we don't judge one another for falling into a stranger's bed, but we'll tease mercilessly until we find something else to wag our tongues about.*

"Ah, Imbica. I am glad you are here too. Saves me having to track you down," Omma said. Omma indicated the seat to her left. "Sea Singer—come sit here at my side."

Omma chose the largest, most ornately carved seat at the end of the table intended for the Leid. Jesper didn't object, though, and continued making his morning brew.

"What brings you to the Leid residence so early? Was the Dreaming of import?" Jesper asked.

Omma tilted her head to Aldewin. "Ask the Varskog."

Details of the Dreaming were already fading, but the essence remained fresh in his mind. "We discovered…" Aldewin glanced behind. Habit made him cautious, unsure who he could trust with sensitive information.

Modra Omma seemed to understand his hesitancy. "There are no Dynasty ears here."

"And Kāfe'vind doesn't trade secrets or work in the shadows," Yngvari added.

Jesper handed each guest a steaming mug and sat on Omma's right side. "If the Varskog hesitates to speak of it, the Dreaming must have been momentous."

Aldewin sipped the bitter and bracing brew. "I apologize for my caution. It's a habit born of being too often ensnared in the machinations of the Mājas and Pillars."

The Kāfe'vind may have been patient, but Imbica wasn't. "Spit it out, mageling."

Jesper raised an eyebrow but wore a bemused smile.

He's a smitten man, Aldewin thought.

"I made contact with Quen," Aldewin said.

Imbica's eyes grew wide, her mouth agape. She shook her head. "How? I thought she—"

"Quen was," Aldewin said. "*Is*." He said the awful truth aloud for the benefit of Leid Jesper. "My sol'dishi's soul is… currently imprisoned in the body of a dragon."

"And not just any dragon," Yngvari said. "Quen is soul-entwined with the Winter Dragon."

Jesper held up a hand. "Wait. I'm confused. Who is Quen? How did she get inside a dragon?" He shook his head. "I don't even know what that means. And how does this relate to your mission to find the Heart of Menaris?"

Imbica put a hand on Jesper's arm and smiled at him. "It is a long, strange story. I will fill you in on the details later."

Aldewin nodded. "Through Quen and the Winter Dragon, we discovered the general location of another dragon."

"Another *Primal* dragon," Yngvari said. The Sea Singer sounded gleeful, and her eyes twinkled. "Tell them, Aldewin."

"The Primal dragon of the Wood element is somewhere in the Vatnoyer," Aldewin said.

"She lives!" Yngvari said. "She is somewhere to the north. I sensed her, Leid Jesper. It was like touching the Green."

I've seen that look before, Aldewin thought. *It's the look of a true believer. I hope Yngvari does not become a dragon zealot like those Dragos Sol'iberi women at Volenex.*

Omma's voice and demeanor were more restrained. "The dragon of Primal Wood remains hidden, but something weakens the dragon. We all felt her heartbeat, though, so we know the dragon lives."

Leid Jesper put his cup down and leaned forward, his look stern. "Spindel'vara I bet. I wish their possible involvement shocked me."

"Why is that?" asked Imbica.

"Long ago, Spindel'vara ceased holding reverence for Skogi and the ways of the Green. Their clan's current matriarch, Thrud, has led Spindel'vara to engage in war with other clans of the Iska'kog."

"She longs to see herself as ruler of all the northern lands," Omma said.

Jesper's jaw clenched, his lips thin. "Thrud won't be content to stop there."

"I see," Imbica said. She eyed Aldewin. "This Thrud sounds like a copy of the gold-eyed, power-hungry woman who sits on the throne on Mt. Néru."

"Not a welcome notion," Aldewin said.

All of them nodded.

"You must go north, then," Jesper said.

"Exactly right," Modra Omma said. "I will go with the Varskog. Be his guide."

Jesper's face took on a grave expression. "With respect, Modra, our clan cannot risk losing you on this journey. You'll have to cross Tradsmikor lands to get to the heart of Spindel'vara territory."

Omma's determination didn't waver. "I appreciate your concern, but something more important than a clan's Modra is at stake."

"And what is that?" Imbica asked.

Omma looked Imbica square in the eye. "We of the Myrskog pledge ourselves to protecting the naturfrandi. To the survival of the Green. To life itself."

Yngvari nodded and added, "From the pesky biting fly to the majestic hustaig, Skogi blesses all living things. All deserve to live."

Imbica adjusted her belt and smoothed her tunic. *Imbica's patience wears thin*, Aldewin thought.

"I think what they're driving at, Imbica, is that it's Kāfe'vind's duty to help living things held against their will or subjugated," Aldewin said.

"Not just a duty," Omma said. "Protecting the naturfrandi is the essence of being Kāfe'vind." She directed her words at Leid Jesper.

He put up his hands. "I concede your point, Modra. And I can see that I won't be able to deter you from this path you're committed to, even if I tried. But I cannot allow you to journey into the heart of Spindel'vara lands without protection. I will choose eight of our best warriors to go with you."

Omma smiled and gave him an appreciative nod. "You do our fallen Eldurskir proud, Leid Jesper."

"I would go with you myself, but…" He touched the tattoo on his chest, his badge of office. "Someone has to stay here and lead the remains of our once-flourishing clan."

"Kāfe'vind has merely experienced a winter, Jesper." Omma placed her hand on his and caught his eye. "Our vines have deep roots. Like the choke vine that is our namesake, even when we lose our leaves and look like a dead stalk, we return with the spring, virile and flourishing."

Jesper smiled and gave her a nod. "Thank you for reminding me." He then turned to Aldewin. "Since I cannot make this journey with you, protection of our Modra and the Kāfe'vind that accompany you falls to you, Varskog."

"Of course," Aldewin said.

Imbica thrust her chin out. "I, too, will ensure their safety."

His brown eyes crinkling at the corners, Jesper said, "I wish we did not need to part company, Lady Mage. But it eases the worry for my clan to know that you will watch over them."

Imbica blushed crimson. "Entrusting me with care for your clan honors me," she said.

The uncomfortable tension of witnessing a couple's passion settled over them, but only briefly. Omma seemed oblivious to what was transpiring between Imbica and Jesper.

"Now, on the business of Captain Ontrosa and his crew…"

Jesper coughed and sipped from his mug, breaking eye contact with Imbica. "Yes, well, he has offered to stay in Leivby and provide training to our sailors."

"You should allow that," Omma said. "And accept his offer of trade. Bitter winds will blow up from the south sooner rather than later, Leid. Kāfe'vind—all the Myrskog clans—will need help to protect our lands."

The grave look returned to Jesper's face. "I know that sound in your voice. It is the wisdom of prophecy."

Omma merely nodded. "The captain's large ship will be a welcome addition to our small sea force."

"When can your warriors be ready to leave?" Aldewin asked. Though the specifics of the Dreaming were hazy, the flygesroom trance gave him a sense of urgency. "I'd like to begin our journey north as soon as possible."

"Agreed," Omma said.

"Even if you meet no resistance and the path is smooth, walking to the northern edge of the Vatnoyer and back…" Leid Jesper stroked his beard, thinking. "You'll need supplies for at least a month's journey, possibly two."

"Two months?" Imbica harrumphed.

"And that's if you maintain a brisk pace the whole way," Jesper said.

Imbica laughed. "Oh, you are making a joke with us. I have seen maps of Tinox. The northern edge of the Vatnoyer cannot possibly take that long to reach."

Omma grinned but didn't join Imbica's laughter. "I, too, have seen maps created by your Dynasty, Lady Mage. They draw their territory larger to match the importance they place on themselves. As you will soon understand, the scale is quite out of balance."

Imbica's face fell.

"I look forward to seeing more of the Vatnoyer," Aldewin said. Bringing their conversation back to the topic of timing, he added, "Can we be ready in three days?"

Jesper shook his head. "Three? That's not long to gather—"

Omma interrupted. "We will be ready to leave at Hiyadi's first light three days hence."

Rising from the table, Jesper said, "Then I best get busy gathering the crew and assigning jobs."

"May I accompany you?" Imbica asked.

Jesper's face lit up, and he nodded. "I welcome your company. Your presence is like Skogi's gentle breeze on a warm summer day." He took Imbica's hand and helped her from her chair.

Imbica headed to the door, but Jesper held onto her hand and gently reeled her back. Jesper wrapped an arm around her waist, pulled her close, and kissed her deeply. "My thorny heart will cease beating until you return from your journey north."

Aldewin expected Imbica to give a snappy retort, as she often did when a person expressed flowery sentiments. But she instead blushed, even deeper red this time, and stared up at Jesper like a love-smitten young lass, not an experienced woman in her middle years.

The two left together, oblivious to everything except their budding affection for each other.

Once they left the Leid's house, Yngvari said, "I haven't seen Jesper that happy since… Well, since…"

Omma nodded and turned to Aldewin. "He had a companion, you see. But Tradsmikor took her from him in the raid."

"That's awful," Aldewin said. He knew what it was like to have someone he loved violently ripped from him.

"Jesper buried the loss beneath the burden of the Leidship." Omma drained her mug and rose. "'Tis good for the lad to have company again."

Aldewin smiled at the notion that Jesper, likely in his fourth decade, was a "lad" to Omma.

"Come, let us clean our mess here and begin preparations," Omma said.

"We need to tell Shel the good news," Aldewin said.

Yngvari asked, "What good news?"

"That you are coming with us." Aldewin smiled.

Yngvari smiled back and said, "Knowing you contacted her friend will gladden her. Oh, please let me tell Shel."

"Of course," Aldewin said.

Yngvari rushed out into the warm spring day in search of Shel.

Aldewin was about to leave, too, when Omma caught his arm. "Varskog, a moment."

Aldewin glanced down at her.

"The company you keep…" Omma said.

He frowned and crossed his arms. Aldewin wasn't used to having friends. He didn't always know how best to interact. But he understood the Jagaru bonds and informal oaths. *"You protect the ass of your pod mates," Mishny had said.*

"What of them?" Aldewin asked.

Seeing that she'd raised his hackles, her expression softened. "I did not mean offense. They are a fine lot. Mostly."

Aldewin didn't change his stance. "Mostly? Go on. Speak your mind. We have a long journey ahead, and I do not want foul air between us."

She nodded. "Agreed and well said. It is just that in the Dreaming… We Modras sensed a shadow swirling around you. I cannot say whence it originates. Someone in your group, perhaps?"

Or the shadow represents my own dark past, he thought. But a cold foreboding overcame him.

Sensing the change in his demeanor, Omma patted his arm. "I am sure that in time, you'll uncover the shadow presence. Do not forget. You are the Varskog. I am certain you will be fine."

With that, she swept by him and left Aldewin alone to consider the ramifications of her words.

Only three pod members are with me, and I can eliminate Shel from my suspicions. That left only Imbica and Dio.

He recalled how they made acquaintance with Imbica. *Working for the Dynasty, she took Quen from us and set this horrid series of events into motion.* The former Dynasty battle mage had pledged herself to serve Quen, but that was only after being stripped of her office by Xa'Vatra. *Is she still loyal to the Dynasty?*

But he had disliked Dio from the start. *Dio is like sand in my crack on a long ride. Itchy, damned uncomfortable, and always present.*

"Keep your wolf senses sharp," Omma had said.

Aldewin pulled his Vandu dagger from its scabbard. The metal glinted mossy green, and the poison reservoir was the color of dried blood, darkened by many applications of asperatu poison over the years. Two possible "shadow" people were accompanying him, and he hoped it wouldn't be Imbica because he'd grown fond of her.

Aldewin knew one thing, though. "If either crosses me or attempts sabotage, I will not hesitate to end them."

CHAPTER 12

ISHNA

Aurixia healed more quickly than Ishna expected. The youngest dragon slept for nearly a full day, resting in a deep, restorative state. When she woke, a pale white scar marred the base of her wing. *Her first battle scar,* Ishna thought.

Though eager to continue their journey, Ishna decided the coterie would remain in the secluded area on Kor Man'tol a while rather than press forward immediately. Now that they had destroyed the human battlements, the area was safe for their group.

Ishna chided herself for not fully considering how young Aurixia was. Rixi hatched less than a decade before the Dô'bedri. Still a child before the long sleep, Aurixia had spent her time frolicking and hunting rather than learning about battle. *I should have assessed Aurixia's readiness for myself. We have not fought Walkers that were a genuine threat to dragonkin since the Old-World battles. Not since Jik'Madar. And Aurixia was born after Jik'Madar. She has no memory of the Old World or its wars.*

Ishna's coterie had remained in the secluded reaches of Kor Man'tol for a week now. Côzhili, the level-headed tactician, regaled Rixi with tales of battles fought during the Alpinean Conquest wars. Côzhili's war stories riveted the young dragon. With the patience only a Nao faction dragon could possess, Côzhili tolerated Rixi's virtually endless questions.

Tales of the old wars did more than entertain the battle-anxious young dragon, though. From these ancient struggles, Côzhili taught Rixi tactical maneuvers and winning strategies against Walkers.

Loxen provided a respite to Côzhili between her lessons. Known for his excellent flying skills, Loxen was second only to Ishna's magic-fueled flight. He and Docar took Aurixia on training exercises and simulated battle situations.

Sitting on the windswept seaside cliffs, Ishna and Côzhili spread their wings, absorbing warmth from the morning suns. They watched the three fly in formation. Docar broke away from the group on purpose.

"Will she follow?" Côzhili asked.

"After how much you and Docar have drummed into her to stay with the lead unless ordered otherwise? I should hope not," Ishna said.

They watched, and Aurixia remained behind Loxen. The two dragons on the ground let out a cheer, gladdened to see the lessons finally sinking into the young dragon's mind.

"That took too many lectures for her to learn," Ishna said. "Even if we remain on this atoll for years, Rixi is not cut out for defensive flight, let alone battle."

"Remember, she's of the Wood element. If a dragonkin is injured, Rixi's instinct is to heal. You cannot blame her for staying true to her nature," Côzhili said.

"Your wisdom is welcome to my heart, sa'gamlin." Ishna touched her tail to Côzhili's, and the two continued gazing at the sky as the three flying regrouped for another formation.

Loxen led the dragons higher. Soon, the three dragons were flat silhouettes in the sky.

"What is Loxen doing? Rixi's wings will ice again." Ishna rose, ready to take to the sky.

"He's testing her on his icing wings–prevention lessons. See, she dips lower at the first sign of stiffening."

Aurixia tucked her wings, dove lower, and called to Loxen and Docar. Rixi flapped with full, smooth strokes, pumping to keep body heat flowing to her wings. From above, Docar flew in a circle as he spewed fire, creating a pocket of heated air. Rixi flew into the warm air and momentarily hovered. Aurixia called gleefully, affirming she had warded off wing freezing.

Again, Ishna and Côzhili whooped and called cheers of encouragement. Aurixia twirled as she rejoined the other two in a V formation.

Ishna breathed a sigh of relief. "I suppose she has made progress." The Winter Dragon caught her friend's gaze. "Of course, young Rixi has had the best teachers from the Old World while here."

Côzhili did not meet Ishna's gaze. Instead, her eyes remained fixed on the increasingly grey skies over the westernmost seaside cliffs of Kor Man'tol. "I only hope our Old World knowledge serves us in navigating this new time."

Ishna thumped once to show her agreement. The two sat in silence, observing the skillful dance of dragons in the skies above.

The coterie spent two more days training, hunting, and resting on Kor Man'tol before returning to the sky. They soared in the same formation as before, with Côzhili in the lead and Docar at the rear. With no Two-Legged ships in sight, they dared travel lower. Ishna allowed Aurixia to fly with Docar and skim the water, dipping her tail and splashing.

Ishna couldn't help but laugh at the sight. *Young dragons so enjoy their play. Was I ever that young?* If she was, Ishna could not recall it.

Docar was like a new hatchling within his old Dragos heart. He reveled in the misty sea air nearly as much as Rixi.

With the eastern coast of Tinox now a thin line on the horizon, Côzhili called them back into formation. She then banked right and steered the coterie north but remained over the water.

The larger sun was now low in the dusky bronze southwestern sky. Côzhili turned west and flew toward the setting sun and the vast land mass Two-Leggeds called Tinox.

As they neared land, Côzhili took them higher until shapes below melded into large, variegated blots. "We fly toward those mountains ahead," Côzhili said. "Stay in tight formation. And remain alert."

"Aurixia, remember your training," Ishna advised. "At the first sign of wing freezing, do exactly as Docar and

Loxen taught you. Worry not about Two-Leggeds catching sight of you. I will handle them."

Rixi crooned her assent. She flew with her head high and her wing strokes more confident than at the beginning of their journey.

Purple- and pink-tinged mountains rose from the land. The basalt and granite mountain peaks did not look as tall and mighty from the sky as from the ground. Though not as high as the great TasūZaj range of Indrasi, the Staket Mountains of Tinox still cut a rocky demarcation separating east from west.

Before the Dô'bedri, Ishna had flown the entire length of this formation of uplifted stone and earth that began at Volenex, existed beneath the sea, and continued to the northern edges of the land mass Two-Leggeds called Tinox. *Walkers, limited to the ground, cannot see this,* she thought. *From their Menauld-bound view, they cannot see their true circumstances.*

East of the mountains, they flew over vast prairies dotted with occasional Two-Legged farms. Walkers tended herds of beasts that looked much like the drey of the Sulmére, only larger and woolier.

At the sight of dragons overhead, fearful farmers yelled to each other to take cover. They scattered from the open fields, sheltering under trees or behind rocks.

From the height at which the coterie cruised, the Two-Leggeds looked to Ishna like rats scurrying. *Not to worry, Walkers. We will not eat you. At least not today.*

"My stomach churns with hunger," Rixi said. "When can we hunt? Those animals look like easy prey."

Loxen lashed Rixi with his tail, a signal to stay in formation.

"What did I tell you, Rixi?" Docar asked. "Use your mind to subdue your hunger and hurts. Your leader will not let you starve. She will begin a hunt when it is safe."

"But they look plump and tasty. And the Walkers run and abandon them," Rixi said. "Why should we not fill our bellies with these prey if the Two-Leggeds care so little they leave their prey unattended?"

This time, both Ishna and Loxen sent a tail lash Rixi's way, hitting her from both sides.

"Where there are kept animals, there are Walkers," Côzhili said. "And where there are Two-Leggeds, there is trouble. Our goal lies ahead, not in that field."

The large sun was now below the horizon, and they flew over the Staket mountains under the pale light of the smaller sun. Côzhili led them over a narrow pass between the two highest peaks. Still, Rixi struggled in the mountain air. Docar created heated air pockets several times to keep the young dragon's wings from freezing.

Having to repeatedly deice Rixi's wings slowed their progress west. Finally, they cleared the highest peaks as the small sun set. They descended into the western foothills of the Staket mountain chain as full night cloaked the world below in darkness.

The sunless time was no hindrance to the dragons, though. They saw nearly as well in murky conditions as Two-Leggeds could see in the midday light of both suns.

The craggy granite peaks of the mountains above the tree line gave way to thick forests. Though spring was waking up the world at lower elevations, snow still clung to tree branches at the higher reaches of the forest. Because she felt most at home in the cold, the snow-covered pines were a welcome sight to Ishna's Primal winter heart.

Côzhili had pressed them hard, as she had said she would. Since departing Kor Man'tol, the coterie had flown for nearly a full day. Ishna did not experience hunger or fatigue like the other dragons, but she recognized signs that Rixi tired. Rixi's wingbeats became jerky and her flying erratic as her strength flagged.

"We should rest soon," Ishna said.

"Agreed," Côzhili called back. "We will descend to that ridge."

Just ahead, the gently rolling forest-covered foothills ended at an abrupt limestone rim. Below, the forest became a mix of pine and leaf-covered trees. The rim provided a natural vantage point to view the valley below.

Côzhili brought the coterie down, but Docar remained in the air. He swung wide and took a few laps around the perimeter to scope out their area before he, too, landed.

"What did you see?" Côzhili asked. She scooped snow and swallowed it to slake her thirst.

"No smoke or fires in the woods," Docar said. "And no other signs of Walkers either. But Rixi will be happy to know I spotted large game west of here."

Exhausted from the intensely long flight, Rixi had been uncharacteristically quiet after they landed. Upon hearing about fresh game, she flapped her wings excitedly and said, "Are we to hunt, then?" She hopped toward Docar.

His laughter rumbled the ground and shook snow from the pines. "Stay with Loxen and Côzhili," Docar said. "Ishna and I will bring fresh meat to fill your belly."

Rixi protested, but Ishna ended Rixi's argument with a swift tail slap and a frosty breath. "Do as your rear-wing commander orders, hatchling. Rest and recuperate while we hunt. You will need your strength on the morrow. Soon, we enter Two-Legged territory."

Revealing just how exhausted she was, Rixi gave up her fight readily. Loxen warmed the granite of their cliff-top camp, and Aurixia enfolded her wings and lay down to rest.

Ishna took to the sky again, Docar at her side. "Are you not tired, vôsh'lavi?"

Docar shot upward, dove, flew under and then over Ishna, showing off his acrobatic flying maneuvers. "After a thousand years dreaming of flying with you?" His laughter trembled the surrounding air. "Sleep can wait."

Ishna's magic allowed her to fly faster, farther, and with more acrobatic skill than other dragons. Many eons ago, when she was a much younger Dragos, she had enjoyed strutting her aerial skills for all to see. But Ishna was no longer compelled to prove her expertise to others. She laughed with Docar and enjoyed watching him show off for her.

After several circles around the nearby forest, Ishna spotted a small herd of prey animals with curling horns and wooly fur in a small clearing. "There," she called and turned back toward the herd.

Docar's belly rumbled as he primed his fire breath.

Ishna halted him. "No need to burn this forest to the ground, vôsh." She dove, picking up speed as she plummeted. Spewing icy breath, Ishna froze a half dozen of the animals solid in one fly-by. The herd bolted, scattering and disappearing into the thick woods.

"That should be enough to sate appetites, at least for the night." Ishna and Docar landed in the clearing. Docar ripped one animal apart and devoured it entirely, including fur, bone, and horn.

Over the sound of Docar's bone crunching, twigs snapped. Docar showed no sign that he heard it and continued gorging himself.

Ishna sniffed the air and caught an unmistakable odor. "Two-Leggeds," she said.

The blood of the fallen prey covering his lips and beard, Docar snorted his derision. "Damnable creatures. Two-Leggeds truly are everywhere now, are they not?"

"Finish your meal, vôsh. I will take care of these Two-Leggeds so you can eat in peace," Ishna said.

Ishna didn't bother flapping her wings and shot to the sky. She flew silently in a tight circle as she scanned the ground, searching for the Walkers she'd smelled.

Below, movement caught her eye. Staying low and weaving between the trees, human hunters snuck toward the clearing.

I will wait for them to enter the glade then ice-burn them all, Ishna thought.

As soon as she formed the plan, Quen made her presence known. Quen's consciousness rattled the dragon like a giant beehive exploding in Ishna's skull. Pounding pain like a searing spear stabbing made her lose focus. It was like it had been that first day of their journey when they faced Two-Leggeds on Kor Man'tol. Only this time, it was worse.

The stabbing agony affected Ishna's ability to fly, and she lost height. Falling uncontrollably, Ishna flapped madly, trying to regain speed and control.

Stop this instant, Quen. You risk us both with your outbursts.

You promised to protect my human family.

These people are not *your* family, but they threaten mine.

Quen did not cease vibrating Ishna's skull. Searing pain behind Ishna's eyes made her vision bleary. To stave off crashing, Ishna had no choice but to land.

As Ishna returned to the clearing on foot, screams pierced the night. Burning trees crackled, and the odor of charred wood filled the air.

Her head still pounding, Ishna galloped through the dense forest, felling sapling trees and trampling bushes. As she neared where she'd left Docar, Ishna expected to see the burning bodies of Two-Leggeds Docar had set aflame.

Two downed Walkers lay lifeless at the edge of the clearing, but a dozen more surrounded Docar. Three mages had created magical shields that wavered the surrounding air. They glowed white-gold in the blue-black night.

From the trees above, mages flung magical spears of Primal ice at Docar while archers shot steel-tipped bolts. Flinging his head side to side, Docar spewed fire into the trees, trying to hit as many Two-Leggeds as possible.

As Docar spat fire to his left, a mage in the trees to his right sent a spear of elemental ice soaring through the air. Ishna ran even harder and froze everything in her path to Docar. But the mage's icy spear caught Docar in the neck, and he yowled with pain.

Speaking in Dragosi and undecipherable to the Two-Leggeds, Ishna called out anyway. "Damn all of you to Vay'Nada's shores. Bring your icy taunts to me. Nox'Kili!"

The mages in the trees turned their attention to Ishna and sent spear after spear of Primal ice in her direction. The frozen attacks, of course, did not affect her.

Still in agony from Quen trying to Rend her from within and angry at the Walkers for injuring her vôsh'lavi, Ishna bellowed so loudly it trembled the ground. The sound shook several of the Two-Leggeds from their perches in the trees.

Fighting through the pain, Ishna reared her head back and covered the ground in icy shards. Her attack froze everything that dared move or breathe. She did not let up until every Walker who had entered the glen lay frozen, their corpses like newly made statues.

Docar's eyes rolled, and his breathing was labored. His spilled blood had colored the snowy ground beneath him dark purplish-blue. Ishna bolted to Docar as he crashed to the ground.

Ishna bellowed again, "Docar!"

Copious blood poured from the wound in his neck. Ishna spat ice at the gash, hoping to close it.

From the ridge above, Côzhili called to her.

So much for our attempts at stealth. Even when we do our best to avoid confrontations with Two-Leggeds, they bring the fight to us.

Ishna wrapped a wing around her vôsh'lavi and called back to her dragonkin as loudly as she could. "Docar is down!"

Chapter 13

Aldewin

At dawn of the third day, the pod and a small group of Kāfe'vind gathered in a staging area at Leivby's northern end. Aldewin, Shel, and Yngvari helped members of the Kāfe'vind organize supplies and rework their own packs for the long journey into the northern Iska'kog territory.

Finn, the young boy who'd taken to Aldewin the first day, had followed him around like a puppy since. He ran up to Aldewin and handed him a present. "My sis says they took this from one of the bad men who killed our kin."

Finn spoke matter-of-factly and without a hint of rancor. Likely only seven or eight, the boy perhaps had no memory of the deadly raid that orphaned nearly every child in the clan.

Aldewin accepted the neatly folded gift. Aldewin unfolded a freshly cleaned, undyed, creamy-white woolen coat trimmed in the fur of a white mountain fox. "It is a very fine gift, Finn," Aldewin said.

Seeing that Aldewin liked the present, Finn's face lit up in a wide smile. He pulled out a matching pair of pale leather gloves and handed them to Aldewin. "Sis says you lot are gonna fight the skishaturs who killed our folks. She says you gonna get justice for our kin. Dat true?"

Honestly, Aldewin hoped his path didn't lead to a confrontation with the clans of the north. He didn't want to burst the boy's hope, though. Aldewin ruffled Finn's hair and said, "Justice always serves the just."

It was the sort of circular aphorism spoken often at Val'Enara. Although he had lost faith in institutions, such sayings now rang hollow for Aldewin. But young Finn smiled at him and seemed to accept Aldewin's words as an affirmation of Finn's hopes.

"You'll be coming back though, right? After you teach that bad clan a lesson?"

Aldewin assumed they would return to the Myrskog, but in the Dreaming, he hadn't seen their return. And their journey would likely be perilous. He kept these thoughts, too, to himself.

Aldewin wanted to give Finn something to thank him for the much-appreciated gift. But Aldewin's possessions had dwindled to a paltry few. He couldn't part with his weapons or the amber pendant.

Rifling through his rucksack, he pulled his flute from the bottom. Without Eira to play with and Rhoji's smooth voice to sing, Aldewin hadn't played since he'd parted with them in the mountain pass.

Aldewin handed the old wooden flute to the boy. "Here, this is for you."

Finn held out his hand. "What is it?"

Before Aldewin handed him the instrument, he put it to his lips and blew a quick tune.

The child's eyes grew wide, and he clapped. "Teach me. Teach me to play!"

Aldewin gave Finn the flute. "I will teach you when I get back. For now, practice on your own. Maybe your sis can help you."

Finn eagerly snatched the flute from Aldewin's hands and skipped toward a grove of tree homes to the east.

Aldewin refolded the coat and stuffed it into his pack along with the gloves.

"You were kind to give Finn a gift," Yngvari said. She and Shel busied themselves with organizing food stores for the journey.

"Gift to the boy?" Shel said. "Hah! It's a gift to us." She pantomimed playing the flute and said, "Trust me. Giving away that thing—Aldewin did us a kindness."

The three laughed and continued packing. Imbica, typically eager to oversee and ensure they packed to her liking, had been absent all morning.

"There is a shadow among your party," Omma had said.

Imbica's absence might have made Aldewin suspicious, but he'd seen her saunter off with Leid Jesper the night before. *She is likely saying her last sloppy-kiss goodbyes to the Leid. Whatever warmth he provides will have to last her months.*

That left Dio unaccounted for. "Where is Mr. Always-absent-when-there's-work-to-be-done?" Aldewin asked.

Shel shrugged and swallowed the last of her bitter tanxia tea. She tossed the dregs before wiping her cup and fastening it with a leather thong to the outside of her pack. "He always shows up when we need him most. That's all I really care about."

If Shel wasn't bothered, Aldewin figured he could let it go too.

Soon, Imbica sauntered to their gathering area, her eyes bright, her lips upturned in a rare smile. Someone had found woolen leggings, a short tunic, and a finely worked leather belt for her. With her short-cut hair and having lost the ankle-length embroidered tunic, she no longer resembled a Dynasty battle mage.

Imbica hummed a jaunty tune as she packed her own rucksack.

"Something sure has lit a fire in your heart," Yngvari said.

"And a fire somewhere else, I'd wager," Shel said.

Imbica ignored them and continued merrily humming and packing.

Yngvari elbowed Shel. "Don't tease. We should be glad when love touches the hearts of clan or kin."

"True," Aldewin said. "But teasing is our pod's way of saying we care."

Shel gave him a nod and stuck a kabu stalk between her teeth. She hoisted her pack onto her back. "Take Aldewin there. The Varskog, as you call him. I pick at him plenty, but it's 'cause he's like kin to me. And he knows that even though I jab at him, I'll have his back in a fight."

"Right back at ya," Aldewin said and gave her a smile.

"And if he double-crosses me, I'll use the blade I'd protected him with to stab him in the back." Shel stared at Aldewin pointedly.

He gave her a nod. "I'd expect nothing less," he said.

Yngvari considered this for a few moments. She said, "But, Shel, you don't tease me. Does that mean you won't have my back?"

Shel took the kabu from her lips and helped Yngvari up. She gazed up into Yngvari's pale-blue eyes and said, "Sea Singer, I promise I will always have your back."

Shel kissed her gently, and Yngvari's pale hair fell across her eyes as she bent her head to receive Shel's kiss.

"You promise, huh? Protect me from anyone?" Yngvari asked.

Shel hooked an arm around her waist and pulled closer. "Anyone," she whispered as she planted another kiss. "Even if the Varskog goes barking mad and howls at the moon, I'd put an arrow between his eyes before I'd let him harm you."

Yngvari smiled and pulled Shel even closer. "Let us hope that does not happen. I'm rather fond of him." She kissed Shel again, this time more deeply. "But not nearly so fond as I am of you."

"Oh, for the love of the Three. Are you going to slobber on each other the entire journey?" Imbica asked.

They all laughed, and Aldewin was frankly glad a bit of the rancid Imbica shone through. *Sometimes, her grumpiness is a welcome respite from too much sunshiny happiness.*

Dio emerged just as they finished packing supplies, and Omma sauntered into the area with Ivriga at her side. The Kāfe'vind gathered to wish them well on their journey and handed out more gifts of dried fish, fruits, and other foodstuffs.

Captain Ontrosa and his land crew came to their send-off as well. Sleeves rolled up and hair neatly tied, Captain Ontrosa looked ready for work.

"Don't get lost in the vines, Lady Mage," he said as he bowed to Imbica. The captain shook Aldewin's hand. "And you—what are they callin' ya now? Wolf Boy or some such?"

Aldewin laughed. "Aldewin," he said. "You can just call me Aldewin. Take care, Captain."

"And you stay out of trouble, lad." The captain eyed the onyx hilt of Aldewin's Vandu blade. "Try not to soil your blade too much. Leave some of those Dynasty shite eaters for the rest of us."

"And you don't leave without us," Shel said. "You made me first-mate-in-training, remember? I'll take you up on that when we return."

Captain Ontrosa gave Shel a bushy-eye-browed wink and said, "You can count on it."

Omma finally cut off the last goodbyes, and Jesper snuck one last kiss with Imbica. Waving and shouting so-longs and goodbyes, they finally set off on the narrow Kinswood Road north.

Aldewin thought it generous to call the wide trail hacked through the dense forest a "road." Unlike roads in Partha and Qülla, the Kinswood Road was unpaved. Omma led the group and used her walking stick to ferret out ruts deep enough to swallow a person's leg.

Sticky humidity made the march through Kāfe'vind territory slow and miserable. Aldewin's fascination with the giant hustaig trees, towering mushrooms, and lilies faded with each painful insect bite.

He slapped at a mosquito. Already fat with blood, it left a nasty blood splatter on his neck. "Is it awful that I prefer the dehydrating heat of the Sulmére?" he whispered to Shel.

Shel fanned herself with a cloth, slapping it against her shoulders and neck. "Not awful. Sane," she said.

Yngvari asked, "How does the Myrskog's beauty not awe you?" She threw open her arms. "The naturfrandi. It's so alive." Her eyes twinkled, and her lips curved in a wide smile. "Can't you feel it?"

Shel beat her neck with the cloth again. "Oh, I feel it, all right. How do you stand the biting insects?"

In a matter-of-fact tone, Yngvari said, "I ask them not to snack on me."

Ivriga rolled her eyes and said, "Skogi, preserve us." She dug into the large bag hanging from her waist belt and pulled out a well-oiled leather pouch. Tossing it to Shel, she said, "For those of us mere mortals who cannot converse with mosquitos, try this. Rub it on your neck and upper chest. It smells awful, but it will help to keep the bugs from feasting on you."

Shel hastily rubbed a large dab across the back of her neck, undid the upper laces of her shirt, and rubbed like she was trying to peel off a layer of skin. "Gods, you were right. This smells like my brother Eira's feet dunked in drey shit."

Aldewin laughed. "You've smelled that, have you?"

She tossed the bag to him. "Yes." Shel held up a hand. "Don't ask."

After one whiff, Aldewin had to agree. "I'm not so sure the bug bites are worse." He rubbed it on anyway, figuring if they were all wearing it, he'd eventually get used to it.

They trudged for hours, Omma as much a taskmaster at keeping them on pace as Druvna used to be. They kept talk to a minimum since they were likely to swallow a small swarm of bugs every time a person opened their mouth. Besides, there wasn't much to remark on. The terrain continued unchanged for many leagues. There were no settlements along the path, let alone an inn with fresh beds and a meal for weary travelers. *What I wouldn't give for a cup of ale and some greasy stew at Treaga's inn.*

Though they saw no houses, huts, or tents, a small group of young hunters appeared every few hours along the path. They gave Omma offerings of small game or packets of herbs or fruits.

"Why do they do that?" Imbica asked.

Ivriga said, "Though the thick forest conceals them, the Myrskog folks see us. And word has spread that a Modra is walking the Kinswood Road. It is customary to offer honorariums to pay respect. To thank the Modra for the work done for all clans."

Omma added nothing to the explanation. She handed the most recent offering to Ivriga, who tucked it into the pack on her back, now considerably heavier than when they began the journey.

At the beginning of the trip, Aldewin had offered for Omma to ride atop Nivi. "He is gentle," Aldewin said. "To gentle people, anyway."

Omma gave the tiger a side-eye glance and refused the offer. "No offense to you or your tiger companion. But Omma gets where she needs to go on her own. I suppose my feet know the Kinswood Road better than nearly anyone and I trust them to guide us."

"No offense intended. I trust in you, too," Aldewin said.

Omma waved it off. "No offense taken."

"I just thought that if Nivi or I can unload some of your burden—"

Imbica placed a staying hand on Aldewin's arm. "The Modra has stated her preferences, Aldewin. Respect her wishes."

He dropped the topic and didn't offer it again. Aldewin walked rather than riding on Nivi. *If our group's eldest carries her own weight, how can I rely on another to carry me?*

Omma pushed them hard the first day, walking from Hiyadi's first light to his last. Though she let them sleep in later the following days, the trip still pushed all to their limits. The Kinswood Road was a muddy, rutted, narrow path that took them through a dense temperate rainforest. The only saving grace was that the path wasn't uphill.

Aldewin's feet were perpetually soaked, his hair constantly filthy and wet, and his body aching. He'd made his way further than this, from the Damianta Forest to Bardivia. But his pace had been more leisurely, and he'd ridden on Nivi. *I've gotten soft.*

Over two weeks into the journey, the leggy hustaig trees, vines, and soggy air changed to pine with fringy needles, immense ferns, and drier air.

"We are at the northernmost edge of the Myrskog territories now," Omma announced. "In the borderland forest known as the Ghost Woods. That means we're entering Iska'kog lands."

"No more offerings to our Modra," Yngvari said.

"The Iska'kog clans don't have Modra?" Dio asked.

"They have wise women, but they aren't quite like our Modra. But really, it's because they respect nothing from the Myrskog," Yngvari said.

Omma sighed. "To be fair, our people aren't likely to pay homage to Iska'kog wise women, the Crowskir, either. Peoples perpetually warring with one another do not pay respects to each other's elders, leaders, or gods."

"True," Yngvari said.

Shel said, "So you're saying we should be on our guard."

"Just as we didn't see Myrskog people, but they saw us, the same is true in the Iska'kog. And especially in this Ghost Wood," Ivriga said.

Dio shifted his pack. "I like this not. We are easy prey. An enemy could sit in the trees and pick us off, one by one." He subtly moved toward the center of the group.

Content to allow Shel and Imbica to be his human shields. By the Three, I grow less fond of him by the day.

Imbica's voice held a tinge of concern. "Dio makes a fair point. I can counteract battle spells but not shield our entire crew from arrows or spears."

Omma didn't slow her pace or alter her path. "I have no comforts to offer other than this. They know that if they kill a Modra or her traveling party, they offend not only our clan and all Myrskog people but Skogi herself. It's why the Tradsmikor Clan spared me two years ago during their despicable raid. Even they are not brazen enough to ignite the ire of the Wood gods and spirits."

Superstition is a thin barrier against the threat of interclan violence, Aldewin thought. He remained vigilant.

Though no one approached, occasionally, he noticed a flash of pale skin among the evergreens or heard twigs break. By the time Aldewin turned his head to focus, they were gone.

In the dense, northern forest lit only by Niyadi, the nights were long and dark. After slogging through the dense Ghost Forest for days, they were relieved to reach a wide clearing and happy for a fire and rest.

But misgivings replaced relief as soon as they neared the campsite. Those pale faces that disappeared into the forest had left a haunting effigy.

Using sticks and twigs, they'd made a crude human figure dressed in a tattered jerkin with a weathered deer skull for a head. The stick person was not harrowing on its own, but a still-bloody animal heart pinned to the effigy with a dull blade made a chill run up Aldewin's spine.

Dio circled the figure and examined it. "Looks like someone is sending us a message."

Nivi bared his teeth and growled at the thing. Aldewin patted Nivi's head and urged him to remain calm. "Steady, Nivi. Sticks and skulls are no threat." *At least, I hope it's not. Vatnoyer magic differs from Pillar magic.*

Omma strolled by the totem without a second glance at it. She proceeded to the center of the clearing and plopped herself on a rock. It was a clear signal she was not concerned about the effigy, so the others began unburdening themselves of their packs and readied to make camp.

At the beginning of their journey, Omma's eyes had been clear and her gait nimble. For weeks now, the Modra maintained a brisk pace for the group. But dark circles appeared under her eyes over the past few days, and her pace had slowed.

She is fatigued. Perhaps it's the journey's length or wariness of being in Iska'kog territory.

Sensing that Aldewin stared, Omma called him over with a nod. She smiled up at him and said, "Sit with me for a moment, Varskog."

The long trek fatigued everyone, and tempers had flared. Aldewin didn't want to be accused by the others of shirking his duties. "I should help the others build camp." *And elders calling me to their side usually ends in me being sent on a death mission.*

Omma wiped her neck with a cloth, and Ivriga took Omma's waist belt and handed her a water sac. "You will be on after-dinner cleanup duty," Omma said. "Now, come. Sit with this old woman a while."

There were no other large rocks on which to sit, so Aldewin sat cross-legged, facing Omma. She drank deeply from the water and offered it to Aldewin when she was done. He waved it off, and Omma handed the water flask back to Ivriga, who left them alone to speak.

"Ivriga efficiently tends to your needs. It reminds me of the Acolytes at the Pillar. Masters choose some to become apprentices. It's a great honor but also requires devoted attention to a master's every need besides tending one's studies."

"But you weren't an apprentice, were you?"

Aldewin shook his head. "Honestly, I was glad not to have the burden." He'd never envied those chosen by master's to be their apprentices.

Omma eyed him. "Ivriga is a capable assistant. But she will never be a Modra."

Aldewin watched Ivriga help Shel and Dio build a fire ring. Imbica called on Vatra and lit the fire, building it to a roaring blaze within seconds. Nivi wasn't much help at building camp. He sat by the fire, licking his paws.

"Ivriga is as obedient as a well-trained hound and every bit as loyal. But she hasn't a magical bone in her body," Omma said.

"Truly? I thought everyone in the Vatnoyer had at least some understanding of Menaris."

Omma rustled in the pack Ivriga had placed at her feet. She pulled out a bundle of dried fruits, the last of the honorariums she'd received during their time in the Myrskog forest. She offered fruit to Aldewin. This time, he took some. The goshi berries popped with sweetness. *The taste of the Myrskog.* It made him long for some sweet goshi berry wine.

Sucking on the berries, Omma's lips puckered. "Ooh, a sour one." She laughed. "Always among the sweets, there is sour, no?"

Aldewin nodded. *True for fruit and people.*

"Menaris flows from the heart of Menauld. Did they teach you that at the Pillar?"

Aldewin shook his head.

"I suspected as much. And I bet they also didn't tell you that magic is abundant in the Vatnoyer because it is the fountain from which all magic flows."

"The Val'Enara Masters taught us that magic comes from the æther—from the gods, goddesses, and elemental spirits."

Omma chuckled. "They've never been to the Myrskog, have they?"

Aldewin pondered what she said. Finally, he said, "No, I suppose they haven't."

Omma pointed a gnarled finger at Ivriga. "I suspect she was not born in the Vatnoyer. You see, her parents came to us when she was a wee one. By the way, she doesn't know this. So please do not be the one to enlighten her about it."

"It's not mine to tell," he said.

Omma gave him a satisfied nod. "Like most of the young people in Kāfe'vind, Ivriga lost her parents in the Tradsmikor raid. I took her on as an apprentice."

"Even though you know she has no Menaris understanding? How can she fulfill the role of Modra? I mean someday, when..." Though not a superstitious person, Aldewin held with the custom of not speaking about an elder's future death for fear that merely speaking of it would bring it about.

"To put it simply, Ivriga will not be the next Modra of the Kāfe'vind Clan." Omma tied her fruit bundle and stowed it. "But that is a worry for another day." She stretched her legs. "I rarely need healing hands. I call upon the Green's life-giving energies when I have illness or injury."

"So that's how you maintain such a brisk pace."

"That's part of it. Also, I'm blessed with a powerful body." She winked. "But today, I must ask you to lend me healing. Will you please use your vine magic to revive an old woman's aching bones?"

The request took Aldewin by surprise. He rubbed a hand through his dirty hair. "I'm not sure what help I can be, revered Modra."

"Please stop with the 'revered' stuff. It grates me something awful."

Noted. "Look, I learned much about alchemical healing at the Pillar. You know, poultices, herbal remedies, teas, and tinctures. That sort of thing. But I didn't study at Doka Pillar. I never learned how to weave spells to knit bones or speed healing. I'm skilled at killing people, not healing them."

"Death is merely night's twin to life. If you are master of one, you likely possess great skill at the other." Omma sighed. "If you didn't learn that at your Pillar, then what in Skogi's name do they teach there? Are all Val'Enara Masters magic blind?"

Though Val'Enara recently shunned Aldewin, he had studied there. Omma's words stung and made him defensive. "They are quite skilled, I assure you. And wonderful teachers. It's not their fault I'm not overly blessed with water magic, a problem when studying the Way of Water."

She shook her head. "They could have used the sight. Why, any mage worth a damn can see you're radiating the energy of the Green, young Varskog. You're practically swimming in Skogi's light."

His brows furrowed. "I don't take your meaning. Archon Kine, a Zenith of Enara, admitted me to study and live—perhaps all my days—in the walls of Val'Enara, the Pillar of Water. Hooxaura, the Guardian spirit of Val'Enara, bade me enter Val'Enara." *Before she tried to kill me, but that came later. Much later.*

"Come, Aldewin. You think people hold the spirit of only one Corner within them? Look at your friend Imbica there." She nodded toward Imbica, who was resting by the fire, waiting to help cook the evening meal once Shel and Dio returned from hunting. "Equally blessed with both

Enara and Vatra. And she also has threads binding her to Qüira, though she ignores how it tugs at her."

Omma turned her attention back to Aldewin. "They didn't create your Pillars to empower mages of great magical skill. You know Indrasian, the first Exalted of the Kovan Dynasty, founded the Pillars."

Aldewin nodded. The Pillars taught first-year Rising students the history of the founding of the Pillars.

"So who ultimately holds the leash of mages in Indrasi?" Omma asked. "Perhaps the Dynasty created the Pillars to contain magic, not promote it."

Aldewin hadn't thought about it before. His heart raced with the implications. *Her words contain truth I have been reluctant to admit.* Omma's words recalled the brief conversation he'd had months ago with Imbica at camp after the pod helped Quen escape Qülla.

"It is okay to speak your feelings aloud. There are no Dynasty spies here."

"The Dynasty holds the mages in check," Aldewin said. The words rang true to him and led to his next thought, which he gave voice to. "And Xa'Vatra now holds the leash."

Her eyes alight, Omma nodded. "And how does she choose to use the great magical power of her mages? From what I hear, the Dynasty shunts Doka Pillar healers away with the fewest resources and allows that Pillar to rot. They could be a positive force in Indrasi. They could heal the sick and aid farmers and vintners during droughts. The good mages could do for Indrasi… well, I think it outweighs the bad."

Aldewin wanted to agree with Omma, but he'd seen the inner workings of powerful elites while working on their behalf in Fen Menir. "I wish that were true—that mages could be used for good purpose. But how do powerful people handle power? They abuse it like how Xa'Vatra pairs mages with yindrils. With yindrils at their sides, these mages terrorize with their hand out for bribes, promising not to burn a market stall or scorch a field. For the right price." *And I saw plenty of scorched fields in the Vindaô Province while traveling to Bardivia.*

They were quiet for a moment, each pondering the other's words. Omma said, "Like most mages, the gods blessed you with the ability to touch all four Corners, Aldewin. Yes, you have natural inclinations toward one or two of the four. Your training at Val'Enara opened your mind to the Way of Water. But the vines…" She squinted at him, seeing him without seeing him. "The roots and vines are yours to command, Varskog. Do you not sense it?"

Aldewin closed his eyes, seeking the calm of Still Waters. He hadn't meditated for months, and since the incident with Hooxaura and shunning by Master Hrabke, he'd avoided reaching for his Enara training. And the implications of Omma's words made his mind race. Not only did she suggest the Dynasty had a mage-control scheme he hadn't considered, but she also suggested a new direction for him. *Something I sorely need, for I am unmoored without purpose.*

He continued to breathe and center himself, seeking the still point. In his mind's eye, he imagined himself in the place he always used to find Still Waters. He sat cross-legged and floated above a pond so calm it was a perfectly smooth mirror.

In his mind, he'd been to this place thousands of times. Countless hours at Val'Enara floating weightless in a peaceful glen above a glass-like pond.

Once he recalled the image, it was like coming home. He quickly escaped his nattered mind chatter. But today, he felt something new. Beneath the water's surface, arising from the fathomless depths, vines rose.

At first, they merely tickled at his bare feet. But soon, they encircled and buoyed him. Aldewin felt like hundreds of woody arms ensnared him, though they did not constrict or cause discomfort. Instead, it was like a warm hug.

Modra Omma's voice, low and soft, interrupted his trance but did not break it. "Skogi's loving embrace has always been with you, Varskog, even if you did not realize it. You are a friend of the skog and naturfrandi. They will come to your aid when you need them."

Though a new idea, he also felt he'd known it his whole life. *I am aligned with Doka—with the wood element.* Fear and uncertainty faded.

He stretched his arms and spread his fingers. Vines wound between his fingers while roots built a nest below him. In his mind's eye, Aldewin was at one with the Green. Roots spreading underground in all directions grounded him to Menauld.

Still in a trance state, Aldewin encircled Omma in his vines. Careful not to constrict, he urged the wood to instill life-giving healing energy into the Modra.

As he'd experienced in the Dreaming, his heartbeat synched with the life force pulsing through the roots and vines. Aldewin focused his attention on that beat then sought Omma's heartbeat. Her heart beat slower than Aldewin's, so he slowed his own and the Green pulsing through them to match Omma's heartbeat.

But as he sensed her heartbeat growing more robust, he slowly picked up the speed for all of them. Soon, her rhythm was hardy and steady. He sensed no blockages to the flow of her life force. He then pulled his vines and roots back to himself.

Usually, when he performed an Enara spell or incantation, such as water-speaking, he felt drained afterward. But conferring with the Green energized him. Aldewin felt like he could defeat a small army. He didn't want the sensation to end.

"You can release the vine and root now. And do not fear. You can reach out to them anytime. You are a friend of Skogi now, Varskog. She will not abandon you."

With reluctance, Aldewin released his hold on the roots and vines. Aldewin floated above the still pond a few moments then gently returned to the world. His eyes still closed, he heard the crackling fire and Shel and Yngvari chattering, felt the chilly evening air, and smelled the hunger-inducing odor of charred meat cooking.

Aldewin blinked, his eyes bleary and his cheeks wet with tears. *I hadn't realized I'd cried.*

Omma's cheeks were wet, too.

"Why do you cry?" Aldewin asked.

She wiped tears with a bent finger. "The beauty of Skogi's loving embrace always moves me."

Aldewin smiled and took her weathered hand in his. The dark circles were gone from under her eyes, and she looked refreshed. *At last, I've done one decent thing in this life.* As there were no words in the common tongue to name what passed between them, they sat in contented silence for several moments.

Finally, Aldewin squeezed her hand and said, "Thank you." A sentiment wholly inadequate to acknowledge the unmeasurable gift she'd given him, but it was all he had.

Bending her knee a few times, Omma said, "Ah, much better. I feel seventy again." She laughed and added, "Come, friend. Let us see what the others are up to." Her stomach growled loudly. "I hope they found fresh game."

A scream pierced the air, shattering their divine moment of communion with Skogi. On his feet instantly, Aldewin reached for his broadsword and turned toward where the others had gathered around the fire.

Quickly counting heads, he saw that none of their party was missing. Imbica wound her hands, gathering Menaris energy for spell casting. Shel had already nocked an arrow, and Dio held a dagger in each hand. The three surrounded Yngvari, who did not appear helpless. A dagger in hand, Yngvari was prepared to defend herself from whatever they faced.

Aldewin and Omma quietly joined the others. They treaded carefully and searched the Ghost Wood for hints about who'd screamed—and why.

"Do you see anyone?" Aldewin whispered to Omma.

Her eyes squinting, she scanned the terrain. "Though I don't see anyone, I sense a presence here. Its intentions toward us are—uncertain."

Not comforting.

As they joined the pod, Aldewin asked, "Should we investigate? Or wait for whatever lurks in those shadows to show themselves?"

Dio and Imbica both said at once, "We wait."

Impatient as always and ready for a fight, Shel said, "Suda, what are we? Cowering drey waiting for a butcher's blade?" She tsked. "Wait. Fah."

Yngvari said, "They've been following us for leagues. But even when we hunt, we see no one."

"And they already left us a message. No, if we spread out into the wood, they will pick us off one by one. At least here, we stand a chance of a fair fight," Dio said.

"I agree with Dio," Imbica said. "Draw them to us, then we fight."

While they bickered, Nivi moved toward a rustle in the forest. He bared his teeth again and growled.

A young woman emerged from the Ghost Forest. Dressed in dark-brown leather armor adorned with fur, she stumbled into their camp, a crimson stain blooming on her right side. The woman clutched her abdomen and panted as she fell to her knees.

Her voice hoarse, she croaked, "They're coming."

CHAPTER 14

ALDEWIN

Shel ran to the young warrior who had emerged from the Ghost Forest and collapsed in their camp. "Who's coming?" she asked.

As healing was still new to him, Aldewin didn't know if he could help the dying woman. *But I must try.*

"Do what you can for her, Varskog," Omma said.

He had no time for lengthy meditation and visualization. Without formal training in the way of Doka, Aldewin relied on instinct as his guide.

He quickly centered himself and pulled in Menaris energy. Visualizing the feeling he'd had when in his trance, Aldewin thrust his hands toward the downed warrior's abdomen, trying his best to send threads of healing into her body. The energy of the Green—of root and vine—coursed through him. It felt like the alertness he got from chewing kabu stalk. This newfound power stimulated him, but Aldewin was unsure how to properly focus it.

The woman blinked and moaned. Omma lifted the woman's head into her lap and smoothed her sweat-soaked hair from her forehead. Placing her palm on the woman's wound, Omma stared at the horizon. Catching Aldewin's gaze, Omma shook her head.

The downed warrior must have seen what passed between them. "Thank you for trying, but you cannot save me. The cut is too deep."

Dio had come from behind. "Who are you?" he demanded of the dying woman. "Are you with the clan that left that totem in our camp?"

Omma ignored Dio's interrogation. In a soothing voice, she asked, "What is your name, brave one?"

The woman coughed, and Aldewin trickled water into her mouth from his water flask.

"They call me Løpeni." Trying to focus, her gaze found Aldewin. She pointed at him. "Searching for you." Løpeni coughed again, and bloody spittle tinged her lips.

Omma wiped Løpeni's mouth. "Be still. Skogi is with you. Think only on the Green and allow the roots to guide you."

Dio was on his knees now at Løpeni's side. "What clan are you with?"

Løpeni whispered, "Tradsmikor."

Aldewin sensed Omma's shudder. She had every reason to drop Løpeni, say no prayers for her soul, and let Vay'Nada take her. But to Omma's credit, she halted healing only an instant, then continued muttering soothing prayers to Skogi, Fréjoya, and the other gods and spirits of the wood.

Dio seemed satisfied that he had all the answers he needed. He returned to the group still gathered in a circle around the campfire.

Aldewin hated to interrogate a dying woman, but she'd singled him out. *What does she know of me? Omma has called me the Varskog and saw me in the Dreaming. Perhaps the wise women of Løpeni's clan did as well.*

Aldewin again gathered healing energy and sent it into Løpeni's wounded body. The crease on her forehead relaxed, and her mouth was less pinched.

Taking her bloody hand in his, Aldewin asked, "You know me, yet I've never seen you before. How do you know of me?"

She now breathed shallow but rapid breaths. *The death rattles are coming. We haven't much time to gather answers.* He cut to the chase.

"Did Tradsmikor leave the totem in this camp?"

She gave a single nod.

"Was it a warning?"

Again, a nod.

"But it was not a warning to stay away from your clan, was it?"

Løpeni shook her head.

"Who, then? Who's coming after us?"

She tried to speak, but her last breath was silent.

Omma pressed Løpeni's eyelids closed. "May the roots carry your burdened soul to rest with the Green." The Modra sighed. "More questions than answers, and another young person of the Vatnoyer cut down in their prime." Omma's face was careworn again. The vibrance she'd gathered from Aldewin's healing had vanished. "Why, Aldewin? What does that damned Dynasty offer to anyone worth the price our people pay?"

Aldewin had no answer for her. Even at the edge of death, Løpeni's essence filled the glen with vital life energy. The world shifted when she breathed no more, and a cool breeze tickled Aldewin's neck.

In the Shils where he'd grown up, they tossed their dead to the sea or buried them in mass graves outside of the city. He'd also spent time in Fen Menir. Like all the Mājas, Fen Menir interred their dead in an underground crypt.

Indrasi customs favored the funeral pyre. Indrasian people believed smoke carried the soul to the River Nixaya. There, gods and spirits guided souls to the Corner served in life.

Aldewin didn't know how Vatnoyer people cared for their dead. "Do we bury her or build a pyre?"

Omma gently laid Løpeni's body on the ground and rose. She stared down at the dead warrior's face and sighed. "Damn my old vengeful soul to Vay'Nada, but a part of me says let the scavengers take her. Her clan did nothing to honor our dead." Her tone had gone bitter. "They cut my people down, Aldewin. And for what? To help that filthy Dynasty that sits on a throne in a dungy palace atop a fetid pool of poison?"

"For a Myrskog person, you know much about Qülla."

"I have never been to Indrasi, or your Partha, for that matter. But I'm an old woman, Varskog. I've lived long enough to hear stories traded across the clans of the Myrskog, and the Dreaming brings the world to us

Modras. I know enough to understand the southern dynasty is trouble for Vatnoyer people."

Aldewin smoothed his beard as he considered what she said. "They're trouble for Indrasi folks too." *Though the exact trouble they are to Indrasi, I'm not sure I can fully articulate,* he thought. He turned his attention back to the dead woman. "She was trying to do the right thing by us, Omma. Should we not do right by her?"

Omma nodded. "With each passing day, I understand why the Dreaming sent you to us." She sighed. "You are right. We should bury her. That way, her clan can collect her body to return her to her family so they can grieve and say their rites. Or they might let her rot and feed the worms of this wood. But that is their business, not ours."

Aldewin approached Shel and Dio. "We must bury the dead woman. I don't think it's appropriate to ask Kāfe'vind to do it."

"Agreed," Shel said. She sent a glance toward Yngvari. "They suffered much at the hands of Tradsmikor Clan. It would be an insult to ask them to honor one of their dead."

Aldewin nodded. "That is Omma's sentiment."

"There are wolves at the gate, Aldewin," Dio said. "We must plan how we're going to protect ourselves against these heathen Tradsmikor. But you want to waste time burying a dead woman? A person who was our enemy?"

Dio is like lemon juice on an open wound. Aldewin took a deep breath and restrained himself from slugging Dio in the mouth, hoping to shut it permanently. "She was trying to show our group kindness, Dio, not issuing a threat. There is another party after us. In this instance, Tradsmikor clan is not the pod's enemy. Unless you're working for someone else?" He wasn't sure what made him ask that question, but it felt right.

Dio's look changed from petulant anger to acquiescence. "Fine. But let us be quick with it so we can eat and regroup."

Shel, Dio, and Aldewin buried Løpeni in a shallow grave at the southwestern edge of the clearing. Aldewin didn't know what sort of prayers Iska'kog clans folks said for their dead. He was tempted to pray to Sicara, the goddess of death worshipped by Fen Menir. Having said many prayers to the Dread Sister, the death rites came naturally to him. *But I doubt they are appropriate for the situation*, he thought.

Instead, he said the brief prayer he'd heard Dini say at the Nilva for Quen's father. The words had touched him, so he repeated them now, adjusted for the situation. "May Løpeni follow the eternal root and river to find peace within the waiting arms of the gods and spirits she prayed to in life."

Once he'd finished, Dio took his spade and returned to the fire without another word. Shel said, "Nice words. Maybe too good for her, but you're right. We didn't know Løpeni. Maybe she really was trying to help us."

Shel turned to go, but Aldewin caught her arm. "Wait. I want to talk to you."

"Uh oh. That's never a good way to begin a conversation. Am I in trouble?"

He shook his head. "Of course not. I want to know more about Dio. How did he come to be part of our rogue pod?"

"Why do you ask?"

"Do I need a reason?"

Shel looked back at Dio then returned her gaze to Aldewin. "I've got something to say, and you won't like it."

Aldewin crossed his arms. "Now, *that's* not a good start to a conversation."

Shel leaned on the latrine shovel she'd used, sucked her teeth, and said, "I don't trust Dio—"

That's what I was afraid of. Aldewin opened his mouth to speak, but Shel held up a hand.

"But I don't trust you either."

"Wow. That was… unexpected." *And stings more than I can show her.* Aldewin tried to maintain his face in a stiff and nonchalant mask.

Shel continued. "People rarely ask my opinion about things, but there you have it."

"You sound like Mishny."

"Well, maybe that's a good thing. Mishny is a sourpuss, but she survived a lot of bullshit. And not by being nice but by paying attention. I've paid attention to both Dio and you."

"Yeah? And what have you learned?" Aldewin asked.

Shel pulled kabu stalk from her pouch and sucked it between her teeth. "I've learned you both are so full of shite I need a bigger shovel to get through it." She kicked the latrine shovel she was leaning on. There wasn't a hint of joking or sarcasm in her voice.

Aldewin said, "Look, Druvna knew my background and mission but hid it from the pod."

Shel hissed and shook her head. "Don't you dare blame Druvna—"

Aldewin put up his hands. "No, gods no. I'm not. I was just going to say I can see how learning I'd been undercover for Archon Kine could lessen your trust. But I came clean to you and Imbica. You now know my background. And I've always had your back, haven't I?"

Shel narrowed her eyes, sucking on the kabu. "Maybe. But you told some pretty colossal lies, Aldewin. Then you try to brush it all away with, 'Sure, I tried to kidnap your best friend, but hey, she fell for me before I watched her become a dragon, so we're all good, right?' And you expect me to be okay with all you did? Not just with Quen but the life you had before." She spit out kabu juice. "Once a liar, always a liar."

Aldewin sighed. "Wow. Okay, so you don't believe in redemption."

Shel shrugged her shoulders. "Maybe. I guess I'm still waiting to decide if you've redeemed yourself."

"I've done nothing but protect Nivi, and now, you and the pod since that day…" He looked away, still not wanting to talk aloud about what happened in Volenex.

She offered him some kabu, and though he usually refused, he took it this time.

"Look, no offense to you," Shel said. "I know you're trying to do right by the pod. But Mishny didn't trust you, and it turns out she was right. You had an alternate agenda."

He sucked the stalk between his teeth. "I grant you that's true. But what did Mishny think of Dio?"

Shel pointed at Dio with her kabu stalk. "Mishny said, 'That one smells like the Northman.'" Shel pointed the kabu at Aldewin. "That means you."

Smells like me? "That's odd. What does that even mean?" Aldewin held Dio in low regard, so being compared to him hurt more than he'd admit.

She spoke through the kabu in her teeth and said, "Don't know what she meant by it exactly. Rhoji and Eira took to Dio right away. Dio has a way of cozying up, making himself seem like a best buddy. Doing things for people. But before we left to fetch you, Mishny took me aside. She said, 'Watch your back with Dio.' And I trust Mishny more than just about anyone except Eira. I know Mishny always has my back. But do you?"

Perhaps Shel hadn't intended to answer Aldewin's question about Dio, but in a roundabout way, she had. *I don't trust Dio either.* "You have every reason not to trust me. I get it. All I can say is I'll have your back, Shel. And I'll do everything I can to prove that my days of working in spinners' webs are over."

"Yeah? Well, why did you come with us? Who are you working for now?"

Aldewin wasn't sure he understood the question. He spit out kabu juice. *Gods, this stuff is nasty.* "Honestly, I'm not sure I work for anyone anymore." Aldewin disliked how that thought unsettled him. "And you? Who do you work for?"

Shel kicked the shovel, knocking clumps of dark soil off it. "Damned if I know." She laughed. "Gods, Aldewin. I'm just trying to discover the Dynasty's scheme so I can help protect Rhoji and Eira. And it'd be nice to find the dragon carrying my friend inside her 'cause I'd like to get Quen back. Especially before the Dynasty does something stupid with the Winter Dragon."

Aldewin put an arm around her shoulder and squeezed her to him. "Guess what? I want those things too. We *are* on the same team, Shel. I hope to prove to you that's true."

They returned to camp and joined Yngvari and Imbica as they tended a quick rabbit stew they'd thrown together with herbs Omma had gathered back in the Myrskog and tubers the Kāfe'vind had brought along.

"Wish we still had bread left to eat this with," Yngvari said.

Aldewin looked around the camp. "Where's Dio?"

"Not sure," Yngvari said.

Imbica ladled stew into a wooden bowl and passed it to Ivriga to give to Omma. "He returned from the burial, shovel still in hand, and went that direction." She pointed northeast with her head.

Aldewin exchanged a look with Shel, and her brows knitted.

Stomach growling at the whiff of food, Aldewin denied himself the comforts of a hot meal. He rose and said, "Damn his sorry hide. After what we saw today, I'd think he'd understand no one should head into this forest alone. I'll go look for him."

Shel rose and said, "I'll go with you."

Aldewin buckled his sword scabbard and put his weapon belt back on. He shook his head. "No, stay here with the others."

Her eyes ablaze, Shel stamped her foot. "You shite-eating piss-for-brains. You just said no one should go into the forest alone. If something happened to Dio, we're down a skilled guard. We can't lose you too."

He pushed aside the urge to show why he'd be okay alone in the forest. *Let's hope Shel never sees the worst I'm capable of.*

Without looking up from her ladling, Imbica said, "Take her with you, Aldewin. Do not forget what *I* can do."

Imbica had been reserved on the trip. He'd forgotten how she'd bested him more than once. *That mage snapped my favorite staff in two.*

"Fine. Come, then, Shel. Let us see what Dio has gotten himself into."

They tramped into the forest in the direction Imbica indicated and fanned out to search for his tracks. Aldewin was better in a fight, but Shel was a superior tracker. Her eyesight and sense of smell were keen, and she focused intensely on her surroundings. Before long, she whistled, calling Aldewin to her location.

Shel pointed to a copse of trees. "He went this way."

"How do you know?"

She picked up a bent twig and pointed to a footstep on the soft soil that Aldewin had missed. "Shall we?"

Aldewin followed her as she made her way into the thick brush. They found Dio kneeling by a tree. He jumped when he heard them approach from behind.

"What the—? Don't sneak up on a man like that." He clutched at his chest.

"What'ya doing out here?" Shel asked.

Dio lifted his shovel and tapped a mound of dirt he'd dug up then replaced. "What does it look like? I came for privacy to take a damned shit."

I've never felt more stupid in my life, Aldewin thought. Heat bloomed on Aldewin's neck and face. "We, eh— apologize. It's just that—"

"After what happened to Løpeni, we thought you shouldn't enter the forest alone," Shel said.

Dio swept by them. "I don't need anyone holding my hand while I take a crap, so…"

Feeling like two addled-brained drey calves, Aldewin and Shel returned to camp and settled for the dregs of the stewpot. They made up for the short rations by smoking a bowl of heja.

Omma refused the bowl and said, "Bed down early tonight. We'll rise at Big Brother's first light. We've got a tough climb ahead and need to travel a lesser trail to the west to avoid Eldisvat."

Yngvari said, "Eldisvat is the capital of the Tradsmikor Clan."

Murmurs rose from the Kāfe'vind Clan warriors traveling with the pod.

Dio asked, "Where are you taking us, Modra Omma? Shouldn't we head to Eldisvat to discover their dealings with the Dynasty? And perhaps glean news of any dragon sightings?"

A few people hissed, and murmurs rose. Aldewin heard someone say under their breath, "Dares to question our Modra." *Dio is not winning himself any friends tonight,* Aldewin thought.

Modra Omma regarded Dio. Her eyes squinted, but her lips smiled. "There are other clans in the Iska'kog besides the Tradsmikor Clan. Folks friendlier to Myrskog people. We cannot risk a confrontation with the Tradsmikor. Our last meeting didn't go well."

"And let us not forget Løpeni's warning," Ivriga said.

Dio let it go, but his jaw was set and twitching. He gave Omma a slight nod. "As you say, Modra."

"We'll strike camp and leave after first meal. So bed down early." Omma glanced at Yngvari and Shel. "That means everyone."

The day's events had exhausted the group, so Omma received no further argument. Everyone, including Shel and Yngvari, bedded down before Niyadi had set.

◆　　◆　　◆

Aldewin woke before Hiyadi's first light. With the small sun gone to rest, darkness shrouded the Ghost Forest in eerie silence. *I hear no night insects or birds.* Thick fog crept like a shadow, blanketing the ground. *An odd time of year for fog.* Aldewin blinked and rubbed his eyes. The air held a foul odor. *Not fog—smoke.*

On his feet instantly, Aldewin gently kicked Imbica's still-sleeping body and called out, "Fire!" He put two fingers between his teeth and let out a shrill whistle. "Fire in the Ghost Forest."

Already up when Aldewin rose, Dio had done nothing to rouse the others. *Was he going to allow the flames to overcome us?* Before he could question Dio, Omma tugged at Aldewin's sleeve.

Dark circles shadowed her tired eyes. "That smoke comes from the northeast. The direction of Eldisvat. Seat of Tradsmikor Clan."

Ivriga barked orders to her fellow Kāfe'vind while Imbica roused Shel. Striking camp before breaking their fast, the group was ready to move in half the usual time.

They had planned to veer off the Kinswood Trail and take an even smaller, less traveled path headed northwest rather than northeast. But as they set off for the day, Omma led them back onto Kinswood Road, which led to Eldisvat.

Kāfe'vind rarely questioned Omma's plans. But she was leading them toward the seat of the clan that had killed their parents and loved ones. Toward the clan that the people of the Myrskog called "skishatur" or "shite eaters." Some Kāfe'vind held back, clearly not keen on heading toward the skishatur.

Yngvari spoke up. "Modra Omma, I thought we were taking the western path to avoid Eldisvat?"

Another called, "Why are we headed *toward* the fire? Shouldn't we avoid it?"

"Because while Tradsmikor may be skishaturs, we are not," Omma said. "We might encounter injured folks who could use our help. Kāfe'vind will not turn our backs on suffering. That is not the way of the Green."

The group met her words with uncomfortable silence. They shifted packs and shuffled feet. While no one voiced agreement with Omma, they withheld arguing against her out of respect.

After a few moments, Ivriga said, "You heard our Modra. We're Kāfe'vind, and our vines are strong."

Ivriga's words roused the group from their hesitancy and solidified resolve. *Ivriga may not have Menaris skill, but I think she'll make one hell of a leader one day.*

They began the trudge up a steep rise, unsure what they'd find below. The farther up the hill they rose, the thicker the smoke. *Oh, for a keffla.* Imbica handed Shel and Aldewin head scarves like the ones worn by vignoisiers in the Vindaô province. Wrapping them around their faces to cover their noses and mouths kept at least some of the smoke from their lungs.

Dio, frequently hanging toward the back of the pack, walked at Omma's right elbow. *He's pretty eager to face a fiery town of skishaturs.* Aldewin checked his belt scabbard and fingered the ebony hilt of his Vandu blade. *I hope that slippery eel of a man doesn't make me use the Vandu before day's end.*

Once atop the rise, Omma halted, Dio and Ivriga on either side. They panted and scoured the valley below.

From the rear, Imbica hollered. "What do you see?"

After a few moments, Ivriga said, "Fire. Eldisvat is… no more."

Shel whispered to Aldewin, "Do you think it's dragon fire?"

He'd seen Vahgrin up close and hoped never again to see that beast open its maw and spew fire. The recollection of Solia, buildings and humans alike turned to ash, came to mind. "For the sake of anyone who lives in Eldisvat, let us hope they have not suffered a dragon attack."

Shel nodded and said, "Whatever set Eldisvat ablaze, we're marching right into it." Nocking an arrow, she said, "'Cause apparently, that's what Druvna's pod does. Charge headlong into the fire."

CHAPTER 15

ALDEWIN

The odor of smoke and sulfur assaulted Aldewin's senses. Black and grey flecks of burnt wood swirled in the air. Destroyed lives floating like newly fallen snow. Aldewin caught a fleck in his hand. The surreal beauty of the scene belied the devastation in the town below.

Eldisvat, home of the Tradsmikor clan, sat in a wide, shallow, and barren valley. The foothills of the Staket Mountains rose on the eastern edge, while tundra hugged the northern rise. To the west, the fringy pines of the Ghost Forest morphed into a taiga forest thick with towering conifers, birch, and other trees Aldewin didn't recognize.

From the rise where they stood, the valley below was a splotchy painting of teal blue, bright yellow, orange, and red. Ground fissures vented steam and smoke while geysers spouted. Rainbow colors rimmed shallow, steaming sulfurous pools.

At the valley's southeastern edge, at the bottom of the hill where they stood, Eldisvat burned. The fire had started at the edges and reduced the wood buildings to ashes. At the town's center, orange flames still licked upward, sending a column of grey smoke to the sky.

The hair on Nivi's back stood on end as he sniffed the air. His ears flat against his head and tail low, Nivi clearly didn't want to enter a fire zone.

Aldewin rested a hand on Nivi's back for reassurance. "I don't blame you for not wanting to go there." Aldewin inhaled more deeply and caught the odor of burnt flesh. *People down there need healers.* The concept of healing wounds rather than creating them was new to him. *But this is a chance to push myself toward helping rather than harming.*

Charging down the hill and toward the smoldering town, Aldewin said, "Let us see if there are survivors."

Dio called to the others, "Come and be ready for resistance."

With feet still planted on the hilltop, Shel said, "You two curd brains want us to run *to* the fire?"

Aldewin called back to her, "Jagaru do not ignore people in need of help."

"Suda! Don't you be quoting the Creed to me," Shel hollered. But she tromped down the hill, bow and arrow ready.

Aldewin ignored Dio's comment. *I'm going to Eldisvat to heal others, if I can. Not be a pawn in whatever game you're playing, Dio.*

The Kāfe'vind and Imbica followed. Heeding Dio's warning, everyone had weapons ready, and as they neared the edge of town, Aldewin pulled out his staff. He preferred the weapon's versatility in situations of unknown danger.

Aldewin saw no signs of Tradsmikor scouts on the slope, and they met no resistance as they crept into the still-smoldering outer edges of Eldisvat. Unlike Solia and other towns in Indrasi, Eldisvat had no walls or gate. A city at least twice the size of Solia during the spring, Eldisvat was eerily quiet save for the sizzling flames and crackling timbers.

Dio shouted orders to look for survivors, and the Kāfe'vind contingent fanned out to search. They stayed low and in the shadows as they moved through the town.

"A dragon attacked this town," Dio said.

Shel pulled her neckerchief down just enough to shout, "And you've seen many dragon attacks, have you?"

He glared over his shoulder at her. "It had to be a dragon. People of the Vatnoyer don't burn villages."

Omma said, "True enough. Even Tradsmikor did not burn Leivby Village during their raid."

Dio nodded. "Yes. It must be a dragon attack."

Aldewin stood among rubble in a smoldering building. He kicked the still-hot embers with his boot. Kneeling, he sifted through ash with a gloved hand. Pushing away debris, he uncovered a body and gasped. A woman's lifeless unblinking eyes stared up at him from the ash.

The fire had scorched her face and burned away her hair, but Aldewin could still discern her features. She'd been holding a war axe, and the weapon lay beside her. Fire had charred the still-intact wood handle, and the steel head was whole.

Reflecting on what he'd seen in Solia and Juinar, Aldewin said, "This was not a dragon attack."

Dio chortled and pointed to Aldewin. "Apparently, there's your expert, Shel. Mr. Knows-it-All." He glared at Aldewin, his once-veiled contempt becoming plain to see.

I don't know who pulled on his short hairs, but it wasn't me.

Aldewin gestured for Imbica and Shel to come see what he found. To Shel, he said, "You witnessed Solia and Juinar after Vahgrin set them ablaze. Dio says a dragon attacked Eldisvat. What do you think?"

Dio sidled over, as did several others of the group.

Shel knelt and examined the woman's face and weapon. After a moment, her eyes widened. "Definitely not a dragon attack."

Dio tasked. "Come on, Shel. Look around. Only dragons cause destruction on this scale. It would take dozens of men—maybe a hundred—to set an entire town ablaze. Yet where are they? And we saw no evidence of a large clan or army marching through here."

Shel said, "It couldn't have been a dragon, Dio. I saw two towns destroyed by dragon fire. If a dragon attacked Eldisvat, this poor woman wouldn't have a face."

Aldewin nodded. "That's right. In Solia, Vahgrin burned the bodies beyond recognition. His fire fused their skin to their skeletons."

Several people gasped, and Yngvari shuddered.

He continued. "Dragon fire is so hot, it turns sand into glass and melts steel. Why, I saw a smith's hands fused to his axe." He kicked at the dead woman's axe. "Fire burned this axe. But see? The fire didn't make steel molten like we saw in Solia and Juinar. And if Vahgrin had set fire to this town, it would burn hotter than it is. His fires infuse the very ground with heat."

Shel nodded. "And in both towns, we noticed that the fire was strategic. Vahgrin knows what he wants to burn. This fire is pure scorched earth. There's nothing strategic about it. The fire starter intended to destroy Eldisvat and kill everyone here."

"Like someone set fire to it, then ran off to let it burn," Imbica said.

Omma nodded. "Wise observations, Jagaru."

Dio's voice carried a pitchy edge, as if he was desperate for them to believe what he said. "Are you trying to make us believe that dragons have intelligence? That they're smart about how they destroy human settlements?" He tittered.

"How many dragons have you met, Dio?" Omma asked. He didn't answer. Omma continued. "It is true what you said about clan raids. Vatnoyer clans do not burn villages."

Dio crossed his arms. His smug look returned.

"But…" In a firm voice, Omma glared up at him and said, "Before Tradsmikor threw in with the skishatur Dynasty turds, no clans had sold away the Vatnoyer's magical resources, either."

Ivriga and others of Kāfe'vind edged closer and surrounded Dio. Weapons drawn, it looked like they were ready to filet the man.

Dio's smugness gave way to apprehension. His hand moved toward his weapons belt, but a voice calling from a nearby building took attention away from Dio.

"Help! Somebody? I'm pinned."

Everyone ran to the survivor, leaving Dio alone with the dead woman. Dodging still-smoldering embers and charred bodies, they found the person who had called out. Pinned under a fallen ceiling timber, a young man called again.

"Over here… help. Please."

Omma knelt at his side and took his shaky hand in hers. "Tell me your name."

"I'm… Jikurai." He screamed out as Shel, Aldewin, and two Kāfe'vind scouts shoved the timber off the man, revealing a gash so deep Jikurai's innards were visible.

Aldewin and Omma exchanged a look, and Aldewin shook his head. Omma released a long breath, closed her eyes briefly, then returned her attention to Jikurai. When she did, her face was a smooth mask.

"Now, Jikurai, Aldewin here is a healer. He'll do his best to tend to your wounds. It might be painful, so stay focused on me, Jikurai."

Jikurai nodded and gripped Omma's hand tighter. Tears streaked the grey ash covering his bronzed face.

Aldewin could do nothing for the lad. Even if he'd trained his entire life at Doka Pillar, Aldewin doubted he'd have the power to put a man's guts back together.

Imbica caught Aldewin's eye and whispered, "All we can do is provide comfort." She wound her hands and began mumbling an incantation in Soligian, the ancient language of the Pillars.

Aldewin closed his eyes, calling on the roots and vines to heal the man. The Green didn't respond to Aldewin like when in the clearing healing Omma. His mind raced, and his eyes and lungs burned, making it difficult to focus. After several attempts at refocusing, Aldewin finally sensed the threads of the Green. He wove a spell of root and vine around the man's middle.

Omma tried to keep Jikurai focused on her and away from his gaping wound. "How did this fire start?" she asked.

Jikurai panted, and Yngvari offered him water. He had difficulty swallowing, and what he got down, he immediately spat up. Jikurai pointed a shaky finger to his chest area and said, "Drag… on."

Now standing behind Imbica, Dio said, "A dragon?" With a satisfied smile, he said, "See, Aldewin. It was a dragon. Fire from above."

The dying man tried to shake his head but couldn't manage even that minimal movement. He tried to keep his eyes on Omma but had trouble focusing. Jikurai pointed to his chest again and repeated, "Dragon."

Imbica whispered, "By the gods, what have they done?"

Dio acted as though Imbica hadn't spoken. "A fire dragon's work, like I said."

Imbica glared at him with a look that could melt steel. "Stop with your dragon nonsense. This was no dragon attack, and you know it." All eyes were on her now. "This is the Dynasty's doing."

Several of the Kāfe'vind gasped, and Omma turned her attention to Imbica. "Why do you say this?"

Imbica took a deep breath and continued sending comforting energy into Jikurai. She hovered her hands over him as she spoke. "In recent months, Xa'Vatra has replaced the prior Dynasty sigil of the two brother suns. Now, the Dynasty symbol is a dragon against a background of one blazing sun—Hiyadi. This poor young man is trying to tell us that the Kovan Dynasty set his village ablaze, not a dragon."

Jikurai gave a single nod. He stared into Omma's warm green eyes, and Omma smiled down at him and nodded. She whispered, "To the River now, Jikurai. May you meet your gods and reunite with your loved ones."

The crease on Jikurai's forehead smoothed, and he smiled. His hand fell from Omma's.

Her face grim, Omma closed his eyes. "He's gone." Omma pushed up with a groan and slammed her walking stick into the ash-covered floor. "By Skogi and the spirits of the Green, this is the second damned person from Tradsmikor I've guided to the River in less than a full day." Omma shook her head. "For two years, we of the Kāfe'vind have sworn vengeance against Tradsmikor. But this trip north…" She pushed a hand through her ash-covered hair. "Perhaps our thirst for vengeance is better placed against the Kovan Dynasty."

Yngvari nodded and took Omma's hand in hers.

Shel put an arm around Aldewin's shoulders. "Jikurai was gone before we got here. You could do nothing for him."

Aldewin sighed. He appreciated Shel's comforting words, but they did little to ease his mind. No longer able to stomach the smell of the dead man's entrails, Aldewin headed back to the empty street. "I need air."

Most of the others joined Aldewin in leaving the scene of death. Omma remained for a few minutes and said a Nilva for Jikurai. Within a half hour, the party regrouped near the building where Jikurai died. They'd checked smoldering Eldisvat for survivors but found only a few in their last moments, like Jikurai. At Eldisvat's northeastern edge, Aldewin and Shel found people who died from knife wounds or arrows. But most people died from smoke inhalation or burns.

"A truly horrid way to die," Aldewin observed.

Shel only nodded in response.

"Such an odd burn pattern. It's like the blaze started at the outer edges all at once. And moved quickly—unnaturally quickly—toward the center." Aldewin looked over his shoulder and quieted his voice so only Shel could hear. "We know this wasn't a dragon attack. Imbica's probably right. This looks like the Kovan Dynasty's handiwork. But how did they do it?"

Shel sighed and pulled kabu stalk from her waist pouch. "Suda, Aldewin, I don't know." Her eyes were puffy and red from smoke and tears. "I need a drink, but even their alehouse is gone."

When they rejoined the others, Omma said, "Imbica, you say the Dynasty did this. If that's true, the bigger question is—why? Tradsmikor scouts for the Dynasty. They've killed for the Kovans and aided their quest to plunder magical naturfrandi from the Vatnoyer."

"The Tradsmikor and the Kovan Dynasty are allies?" Shel asked.

Yngvari and Omma nodded, and Omma added, "*Were* allies."

"They still are," Dio said. "Allies, I mean."

Everyone stared at him. Dio said, "Well, they must be. Because I stand by what I said. Aldewin is wrong, and you're all leaping to incorrect conclusions. This *was* a dragon attack."

Murmurs rose from the gathered. Shel tsked and shook her head. "What did you mix with your heja in the pipe you smoked last night?"

"Don't make light of this, Shel. It's a serious allegation against the Dynasty to accuse them of burning down an entire village. We've seen hints of hunters and Tradsmikor scouts in the forest for days, but have we seen a single sign of the Dynasty?" Dio asked.

Between the smoke in his lungs and the energy spent trying to heal Jikurai, Aldewin was too tired to argue with Dio. Speaking over each other, the others continued the argument.

Over the din, a woman called, "Give it up, Dio. They are correct. The Kovan Dynasty was here. And we did burn Eldisvat to the ground."

Chapter 16

Aldewin

A dozen soldiers armed in crimson leather armor flanked a tall, lithe woman marching toward them. Their chest plates bore the new sigil Imbica had described: a dragon against a blazing sun background.

The woman's voice was familiar, as was her gait. Full of confidence and swagger, her feet moving as if on glides, her short silvery-white hair shone in the morning light.

Imbica whispered, "It cannot be."

Aldewin squinted into the sun, trying to discern the woman's features. Nivi's keen sense of smell caught the woman's scent, and he bared his teeth and growled.

"Impossible," Aldewin said. He grabbed the hilt of his Vandu blade, and from the corner of his eye, he saw Imbica gathering Menaris energy.

"Who is this?" Shel whispered.

Aldewin had forgotten that Shel had never met her.

"This sounds crazy, but that woman is Pelagia, the Mistress of the Menagerie. You know—the woman Quen killed the night we escaped Qülla."

Pelagia brushed ash from her hair. "So lovely to see you again, Aldewin." Noticing Imbica at his side, she said, "I see you scraped Imbica off the floor where I left her. She's now stuck to the bottom of your shoe, isn't she? Like sticky drey dung."

Pelagia wore pale, mossy-green leather pants made from a marsh alligator's skin. Over those, she sported a long, open tunic made of spotted white fur. The laces of her undershirt partially undone, the opening revealed a vertical seam on her chest.

And from this wound grew scaly grey-brown bark.

Omma exhaled and whispered under her breath, "Skogi, preserve us. Vay'Nada's shadow touches her." Omma instinctively took a few steps back, distancing herself from Pelagia.

Pelagia's once pale grey-blue eyes were now a blue so deep and intense they were nearly black. Purple veins showed through papery pale skin at her temples and up her neck. She smiled, though mirth did not reach her eyes.

The Mistress pointed to Omma. "A Modra of the Myrskog, I presume?" She gave Omma a polite nod. "How you put up with this witless Pillar-trained fool, I'll never know." Pelagia pointed to Imbica.

Before the mage rebutted, Pelagia crooked her finger at Dio. "Come, my boy. Your work here is done."

Dio practically ran to Pelagia's side. He ducked away before Aldewin could jab his dagger into the skishatur's back.

"You thukna's nut sack," Shel said. "I'm going to put an arrow through that puny thing you call a heart." She steadied her bow, prepared to make good on her threat.

Pelagia rolled her eyes and waved her hand in the air. "You'll do no such thing."

Shel laughed, her arrow steady at her cheek and ready to fly. "Give me one damned reason not to end this putrid, double-dealing shite stain."

"Dio is a Dynasty asset. Killing Dio will displease the Exalted. To maintain my good standing, I must exact the ultimate price for your extreme indiscretion."

Pelagia's face morphed from smug to severe. "I am in no mood for games, Jagaru. If you kill Dio, I will finish you. *All* of you. Just as I ended the lives of every single gods-forsaken person in this gods-forsaken town. Do not test me, or you will all end up as charcoal briquets."

Though Pelagia's tone brooked no argument, Shel did not lower her weapon.

Yngvari put a pale hand on her arm and urged Shel to lower her bow. Yngvari whispered, "Live to fight another day, right? Isn't that what the Jagaru say?"

A tear glistened in the corner of Shel's eye. She lowered her bow and looked mighty unhappy about it.

Pelagia called, "Come, Nivi. It is time you were by my side again."

Nivi growled and leaped at Pelagia, his paws outstretched, claws out, and ready to shred her. The giant tiger yowled in pain in mid-jump and dropped to the ground.

Still wearing the gold ear bands Pelagia used as foci for her spells, Nivi was as subject to her control now as he'd been in the Menagerie. Looming over him, the Mistress of the Menagerie ordered, "Kneel, Nivi."

Nivi's eyes rolled, and his tongue lolled. Fighting against Pelagia's control, Nivi writhed in pain.

"Stop it!" Yngvari yelled. Tears streaked her face. "You're going to kill him."

Pelagia looked up from Nivi briefly, but it was long enough for her to take measure of Yngvari. "I thought I sold you to Māja Wix. How in the name of Sicara's blood did you end up with this rogue Jagaru pod?"

Yngvari stood tall and refused to answer.

Imbica pressed Yngvari behind her, and Shel blocked her in as well. Pulling on the abundant Menaris energy in the Vatnoyer without preparing for a spell, Imbica pulled a fiery magical blade from the fundament, its light shimmering. Imbica aimed the white-hot magical blade and hurled it toward the spot on Pelagia's chest where Quen had jabbed in a blade.

Aldewin had seen Quen kill Pelagia. The woman had fallen dead and lain as still as a stone. *She should be dead. Very dead*, Aldewin thought.

While maintaining control of Nivi, Pelagia deflected Imbica's projectile with a flick of her wrist. The fiery blade vaporized into the æther.

At the Menagerie, Aldewin had observed Pelagia's prodigious magical abilities. But he'd also seen her lose control over Nivi while battling Quen. *Whatever dark magic the Dynasty used to resurrect her also strengthened her*. It was a highly discomforting thought.

While Pelagia battled to force Nivi's obeisance and deflected Imbica's attacks, Aldewin lunged toward her, Vandu blade in hand. Pelagia nodded without flinching or letting up on Nivi, and a strong wind blew Aldewin onto his backside.

The blow knocked the wind out of him, but he was uninjured. Shel gave him a hand up. "Thank you for trying to end this Vay'Nada spawn."

Pelagia sighed and shook her head. "Now now, Jagaru. I am patient, but you push beyond my limit to forbear. Surely, you will not sacrifice your lives to avenge Tradsmikor. They had it coming, don't you agree? Kāfe'vind, the Tradsmikor killed your kin. Tradsmikor also reneged their agreements with the Dynasty, proving no one can trust them."

Standing tall, her arms crossed and chin out, Yngvari said, "*You* are the one who sold *me*. Kāfe'vind doesn't answer to you or your Exalted."

The clan murmured their agreement with what Yngvari said.

Omma put an arm out to hold Yngvari back. Not noticing Omma's move, several Kāfe'vind charged Pelagia. With swords and spears drawn, shields at the ready, the young and ill-trained would-be warriors made up for their lack of skill with conviction.

Omma cried out, "Halt, Kāfe'vind!" but it was too late. Their attack had begun.

They scuffled with the Dynasty soldiers flanking Pelagia. With the Dynasty surprised by the sudden attack, the Kāfe'vind landed lethal blows on a Dynasty soldier and sent another to the ground.

The Dynasty soldiers maintained a tight formation around Pelagia and Dio. Larger and with better swords and armor, the Kāfe'vind swordsmen bashed against wooden bucklers.

As if bored with the attack, Pelagia rolled her eyes and spread her arms outward. The Kāfe'vind soldiers fighting the Dynasty ignited instantly. Engulfed in flame, their bodies twisted as their blood-curdling screams sent chills up Aldewin's spine.

The remaining Kāfe'vind backed away from Pelagia while mumbling prayers to Skogi. Many cried out, and a few wailed from the emotional pain of watching their friends die such horrific deaths.

Imbica wound Enara spells and called the Waters. She sent quenching water balls toward the flaming Kāfe'vind, dousing the fires. Her face red, sweat dripped off her nose as Imbica sent volley after volley of white-hot weapons and tight, swirling balls of fire at Pelagia.

Even while managing both Nivi and the Kāfe'vind, Pelagia created a shield of Menaris energy around herself. The magical shield held, and none of Imbica's attacks hit their mark.

Frustrated, Shel drew her bow and fired an arrow at Pelagia. But Pelagia snapped the arrow in two with a nod of her head.

While Imbica looked exhausted, Pelagia hadn't even broken a sweat.

From the moment Imbica had pledged herself to Quen's cause, Aldewin had felt at least a modicum of security. Even at Val'Enara, he'd never seen a mage with such battle prowess without a yindril's aid. That Pelagia now bested Imbica so handily... *What chance do we have to prevent the Dynasty from getting their hands on whatever Pelagia came for? From pillaging the Myrskog of its magical naturfrandi or people? Or stopping the Dynasty from overpowering Bardivia and putting Rhoji to the sword?*

Aldewin and Yngvari tried to pull Nivi away. Pelagia tsked and waved a finger in a "no-no" fashion.

"Don't worry, Sea Singer. I will take good care of the kitten. And you."

This was too much for Shel. "By the Three, I will gut you and put that pretty head of yours on a pike."

Pelagia threw her head back and laughed. "You and what army?" She then glared at Shel with a withering gaze and said in a low, earnest voice, "Do not test me further, whelp, or I will freeze your blood and boil your innards." Pelagia ripped open her shirt even farther, revealing more of her bark-covered skin.

"See this? Can you guess what Prelate Vidar filled my chest with when he removed my damaged heart?" She turned her gaze on Aldewin. "The one your lady friend mangled with a blade so dull it couldn't even spread butter."

None of them answered.

Pelagia smiled a wide, unnerving smile. "Truly, I hold no ill will against Quen. After all, if she hadn't killed me, I would not be standing before you with the heart of a yindril."

Their entire group gasped collectively.

This made Pelagia smile even more broadly, her unnaturally dark-blue eyes alight with the fire of a zealot. She laughed, "It's poetic. Really, it is! You see, I'm the one who brought the yindril to the Dynasty. Captured one at the edge of Kāfe'vind territory and handed it to the Dynasty as a new specimen. That is how I became the Mistress of the Menagerie. Did you know that?"

Standing her ground in front of Yngvari, Imbica said, "So you clawed your way up. And not through skill but by exploiting a resource you stole."

"You can't steal what isn't owned," Dio said.

Pelagia continued as if neither had spoken. "I deserved that boon." Her voice now raised, she shouted, "And more! I *earned* every opportunity I got. And soon I will bring the Exalted a prize so powerful, she will reward me with a place on the Conclave." Pelagia pointed to Aldewin. "And you will lead me to something that not even the Exalted knows I can deliver."

Dio's eyebrows rose in surprise at revelations he apparently didn't know. But he didn't press her and stood behind Pelagia as if still afraid of the Jagaru but also perhaps of what Pelagia would do.

Pelagia's unwavering gaze froze Aldewin in place. His heartbeat throbbed in his neck. Slick sweat covered his face despite the chilly air. "I will not help you claw your sorry ass to more power," he said. "Not for the Dynasty. Not for anyone."

Pelagia laughed again. "Oh, you will."

Nivi, finally exhausted from the fight, gave in. He knelt at Pelagia's feet. "What a good kitty you are." She cooed and patted his head. Nivi glared at her but no longer growled or bared his shredding fangs.

Give in for now, Nivi. Otherwise, she might kill you. You may lose this battle, but I promise I will not give up trying to free you again.

"You see, Aldewin di Partha—or shall I call you Timonay?" She glanced at Dio, who stared at Aldewin, his arms crossed, his face plastered with the smuggest look Aldewin had ever witnessed.

"That's right. Dio is Fen Menir and knows all about Timonay. And how, technically, Fen Menir still holds your contract of indentureship. Shall I allow Dio to haul you to Fen Menir's gates? To do to you what they always do to a man who has escaped before fulfilling his contract of servitude?"

Aldewin recalled witnessing the slow, agonizing torture in the name of Fen Menir "justice," and it made his blood run cold. He felt like someone had opened a trapdoor beneath him, and he'd fallen into Vay'Nada's frozen realm.

Aldewin's fingers still on the hilt of his blade, he envisioned jabbing it into Dio's neck. Centuries of curing the blade with poison had imbued the green dagger with lethal toxicity. If he landed a cut, the ratling's blood would froth and foam before hitting the ground. *But if I kill Dio, someone she wants to protect, what will she do to Nivi? Or to Yngvari or the others?*

As if sensing Aldewin's hesitation to draw his blade, Pelagia moved closer and smiled. Now mere inches away, Aldewin caught her scent. She smelled of smoke—they all did—but also of wood and death. *She smells like a rotting tree.*

"Have no fear of me, Aldewin di Partha."

Aldewin scoffed. "Says the woman who is torturing an innocent animal while burning a half dozen young people alive."

She ignored his words. "I argued to the Exalted on your behalf. She spared you at my suggestion."

"How kind of you." Aldewin's voice dripped with sarcasm.

From behind Pelagia, Dio said, "Mind how you speak to the Mistress. I attended Xa'Vatra's court that day. You really must thank Pelagia for interceding when I asked to haul your sorry ass back to Partha for Fen Menir justice."

Inside, Aldewin shuddered at the thought. He couldn't erase the memory of a man whose name he never knew hung by his hands in the courtyard and flayed each day until he finally succumbed to his wounds.

On the outside, though, Aldewin didn't flinch. "I'd like to see you try to take me against my will."

Dio took the bait and lunged toward Aldewin, drawing both daggers as he launched. Aldewin drew his Vandu blade, prepared to end the double-crossing turd's life.

Shel swept her bow outward, knocking Dio's right dagger out of his hand. Aldewin's reach being longer, he grabbed Dio's right wrist while holding the edge of his poison dagger at Dio's neck.

Dio's face was red, his eyes wide, and his voice was a low growl. "Do it."

"If you kill Dio, I will withdraw the offer of aid I'm about to give. Help you desperately need to achieve the one desire your heart most holds dear," Pelagia said.

"I very much doubt you know anything about what a *human* heart desires," Aldewin said.

"Maybe not." Pelagia leaned closer and said quietly, "But I've been to the Dreaming too, Varskog."

Aldewin's heart beat faster. She had his attention, and she was right. He desperately wanted something, and now, he had to hear what she had to say.

Aldewin grunted and pushed Dio away. "Go cry under Pelagia's skirts."

Dio fell to the ground but picked himself up and brushed off the ash.

Aldewin stowed his blade and gestured to Pelagia. "Okay, you have our attention. Let us hear this magnificent offer that will undoubtedly require me to sell my soul. Again."

Pelagia continued, "When the Exalted learned you were a Vandu Assassin, and on the lam, no less, she allowed me to spare you. On one condition: You must serve the Dynasty."

Imbica snorted.

Shel sniggered and said, "Like he'd work for the Dynasty."

Pelagia continued. "The Exalted has extinguished the bounty on your head. Something she has never done before." She waved a thin hand at the people in his party. "She even repealed the arrest warrants for the granary-born mage and trigger-happy rogue. So long as you and your party serve Xa'Vatra's needs, the Exalted forgives all your transgressions against the Dynasty."

"That must pain you greatly to say," Imbica said. "But what makes you think Aldewin wouldn't rather die than commit himself to another indentured bond, and this time to the skeeving Dynasty?"

Pelagia turned her attention back to Aldewin. "Oh, he will. All of you will. And you will help me retrieve what I came to this gods-forsaken land for."

Aldewin was afraid to ask, but he had to. "And what *did* you come here for?"

Pelagia leaned in closer and whispered loud enough for Omma to hear too. "I know *all* about you, Varskog. And I know what you seek. I've seen you drink from the well of your deepest desire." She touched the amber pendant at his neck and stared unflinchingly into his eyes. "Help me retrieve the Heart of Menaris, and I will bring Quen back to you."

CHAPTER 17

ISHNA

Ishna's icy suture staved Docar's bleeding, but it would not hold his tough Dragos skin together long. The dragons had tried to avoid confrontation with Two-Leggeds when they entered Walker territory. But the coterie had set the forest ablaze and killed a dozen Two-Leggeds. Their arrival was secret no longer.

Resting a wing on Docar, Ishna called to Côzhili again. "Hurry, sa'gamlin. And bring Aurixia."

Within minutes, Ishna's dragonkin arrived. Seeing her friend Docar down and unresponsive, Rixi let out a mournful cry.

"Is he—?"

"Not dead," Ishna said. "Not yet, anyway. He took an elemental spear to the neck." She moved away from Docar to allow Rixi to get nearer. "A spear of Primal Ice."

"One of yours?" Côzhili asked.

Indignant, Ishna spat out, "Of course not," and glared at Côzhili.

With her head resting on Docar's chest, Aurixia had gone quiet. She wrapped a wing around him.

Ishna paced. "It was a Two-Legged attack. Hidden mages." She pointed to the still-smoking burned trees with her dew claw. The mage who had attacked Docar still lay on the ground, her eyes open wide but unblinking, her body frozen solid.

"I meant no offense, sa'gamlin." Côzhili dipped her head. "I did not know Two-Leggeds possessed command of elemental magic powerful enough to down Docar."

Ishna ceased pacing long enough to thump once and say, "Nor did I, sa'gamlin."

Aurixia's moss-green wings looked tiny compared to Docar's immense body. She did her best to envelop him in her wings anyway. Sniffing and inspecting his wound, she said, "A rather good healing tactic." She looked up at Ishna. "Freezing the gash, I mean."

"It was all I could do." *The gods created me to kill, not heal. Healing was — is — Veridia's domain*, Ishna thought.

Loxen had been a quiet observer. Like Ishna, the gods made him for battle. "I will patrol and ensure Two-Leggeds do not disturb Rixi's healing." Loxen put his forehead to Docar's and whispered, "It is not yet time for you to leave this realm, egg-brother." Loxen then took wing and circled the area, watching for Two-Leggeds or anything else that might disrupt Aurixia's healing efforts.

Aurixia kept her nose near Docar, her wings around him, and remained motionless. After several minutes, vines erupted from the scorched earth. Tendrils the color of spring's first growth wrapped loosely around Docar's body and encircled his neck.

As the vines wound around Docar, a sensation overcame Ishna. One she hadn't felt for centuries. Ishna moved her focus within and observed with her entire being.

A rhythmic thrum not unlike a heartbeat pulsed in the ground. At first, Ishna thought it was Docar's heartbeat. Though she felt the slow, steady beat of Docar's fiery dragon heart, there was a second, even more powerful thrum deep in Menauld.

This rhythm was so powerful that Aurixia's heart began beating in time with it. Soon, Côzhili's and even Ishna's heartbeats matched the deep rhythm thrumming beneath them.

I have not seen a Wood elemental dragon call the vine like this since… Not since my sister, Veridia. Is it Veridia's magic that fuels the vines? Or does Aurixia have the skill within her to create such powerful healing?

Côzhili gave voice to Ishna's thoughts. "Aurixia, I did not know you could call the vine."

Aurixia, deep in a healing trance, did not answer.

Now enveloped in a casing of bright-green vines, Docar looked like an enormous cocoon. Only his head remained uncovered.

The snow-covered forest was a silent specter in the frosty black of deep night. The only sound was the occasional slicing of air by Loxen's wings as he circled above.

For onlookers impatient with worry, minutes felt like days. Ishna continued pacing while Côzhili sat utterly still, her entire focus directed at Docar.

Rixi continued her healing endeavors throughout the darkest hours of the far-northern night. As dawn's first light arced on the horizon, Docar blinked and moved his head.

Rixi did not cease her healing endeavors, though. Her tone was flat and quiet. "Remain still."

Docar's moan rumbled through the glade. He flopped his head back down and snorted a steamy breath. His voice was raspy. "I could not move if I tried."

The tightness clamping Ishna's chest vanished. *Just like Docar to jest while we fear for his life.*

As quickly as the vines had grown from ash-covered soil, they released and withered. Once plump, green, and vibrant, the vines were now desiccated husks.

The gash on Docar's neck had closed. Where blood once poured from him, the skin knitted back together. Docar would undoubtedly have a sizeable scar, but Ishna knew her vôsh'lavi would wear it proudly, evidence of survival.

Aurixia at last removed her wings from Docar and took a step back. "I have done what I can."

Docar pushed up but teetered. Côzhili rushed forward and steadied him with her wing. With Côzhili's help, Docar soon righted himself.

"By the ancient rites of Ignati, you, young Dragos, have achieved a healing your egg-mother would be proud of," Docar said.

Both Ishna and Côzhili thumped in agreement. But Aurixia, ordinarily quick to devour praise, was quiet.

"What troubles you, Rixi?" Ishna asked.

Rixi paused before she answered. "The healing... It was not me. At least, not entirely."

"Of course it was," Docar said.

Rixi thumped twice and wore a solemn look.

Côzhili and Docar both looked to Ishna.

"I lent her no aid," Ishna said. *They should know I am no healer.*

Aurixia blurted out, "It was my egg-mother."

She had their full attention now. "Veridia. The Spring Dragon. She healed Docar."

When they said nothing in response, Aurixia asked, "Didn't you feel her?"

Docar and Côzhili thumped twice, but Ishna did not.

Of course, Ishna thought. *My Primal sister's life force flows through this land. That is the rhythm I sensed.*

Aurixia's voice rose. "Don't any of you believe me? If you don't believe the Spring Dragon lives, why did we come on this mission? Why did we face a danger that nearly cost Docar his life?"

Ishna wrapped a wing around the young dragon. "We believe you, Rixi. I felt her too."

Rixi's eyes grew wide. "You did?" She chuckled. "Of course you did. You are the Winter Dragon. And her sister." Excited, the young dragon hopped about. "If I sensed her, surely you did too."

"We are on the correct path. That much is clear," Ishna said. "The Spring Dragon remains hidden somewhere in these Two-Legged lands." Ishna brought her forehead to Rixi's, calming the young dragon and bringing her attention back to Ishna. "But Veridia did not heal Docar. You did, Rixi."

"I don't know about vine magic, though. How could it be me?"

"You allowed yourself to be guided by your instinct, Rixi." Ishna pulled her forehead from Aurixia's. Recalling an earlier conversation with Côzhili, Ishna caught her friend's eye. "You did what Veridia created you to do, Rixi. As Veridia's hatchling, so long as the Spring Dragon lives, you always have access to her power. The vines answered *your* call. And for saving the life of my vôsh'lavi, you have my eternal gratitude."

Côzhili laughed and blew out a whistling breath. "Since Ishna is practically immortal, that's a lot of gratitude. She must really like you, Docar."

He laughed too. Docar spread his wings and gave them a flap. "I am healed, thanks to my sa'gamlin, the youngest dragon."

Aurixia beamed at him.

"The healing leaves me feeling hollow inside, though," Docar said.

Mimicking what Côzhili had done for her after her injury on Kor Man'tol, Rixi shoved a carcass toward Docar. "You need to eat. It will build your strength."

Docar did as his healer suggested and crunched the icy flesh of the Two-Leggeds who had nearly killed him. Côzhili and Aurixia joined him.

After a time, Loxen swooped down, his wings creating a breeze. "My egg brother lives." He greeted Docar with a brief forehead rub.

"Thanks to our young friend," Docar said.

Eager for Loxen's report, Ishna asked, "What did you see?"

"The surrounding forest is quiet. Our battle frightened even night animals into their burrows and nests."

"But what of the Walkers?" Ishna asked.

"If any remain in the woods near here, they are exceedingly stealthy."

Still crunching a bone, Côzhili asked, "You observed nothing of import?"

"Northwest of here, the land glows," Loxen said.

"Fires?" Aurixia asked.

Loxen thumped twice. "A Walker settlement. And a sizeable one."

Rixi raised her snout from a Two-Legged's split-open chest where she ate. "To the north and west, you say?"

Loxen thumped once.

Abandoning her meal, Rixi settled on the charred ground and faced roughly the direction Loxen had described. Her belly resting on the soil, Rixi spread her wings so their sensitive undersides also touched the ground. She scooched this way and that, finally settling. Aurixia used her nose and forewing tip to point. "Is the Two-Legged settlement that direction?"

Loxen thumped once. "More or less. Why?"

"That is where we must go. To retrieve the Spring Dragon," Aurixia said.

I was afraid of that, Ishna thought. *Something—or someone—holds Veridia against her will. To retrieve Veridia, we must face a city of Two-Leggeds.*

The thought conjured memories of ancient battles. Images of cities ablaze and the screams of Two-Leggeds and Dragos alike flooded Ishna's mind.

Before her birth into human form, human screams never bothered Ishna. She was, after all, a war machine. *My early life did not include lessons in compassion*, she thought.

But years of unending war and experiencing life as a Two-Legged changed Ishna. Once, she would not have hesitated to demolish a Walker settlement and annihilate its inhabitants. But after living within Quen, being responsible for substantial loss of human life would weigh on her conscience.

With thoughts of war against Walkers filling her mind, Ishna expected Quen to make her presence known. But the human soul within was uncharacteristically quiet.

Ishna thought to Quen,

> What? No reproach for my mere thought of battling Two-Leggeds to retrieve Veridia?

But Quen did not vibrate Ishna's skull or otherwise make herself known.

> Why do you appear to me at the least opportune time yet ignore me when I address you directly?

A faint vibration tingled between Ishna's eyes. Ishna sighed with relief, and that surprised her. Though she wished to be rid of the parasitic soul, she did not wish for Quen to die.

> You must remain with me, Quen, for a while longer. My sister, Veridia, will help us. She may know how to sever our connection without killing you.

Distracted by her inner dialogue with Quen, Ishna did not know what the others were discussing. Côzhili raised her voice. "Is that not right, Ishna?"

Aurixia chuckled. "I did not know Primal dragons daydream too."

Côzhili narrowed her eyes at Ishna. "They don't."

Perhaps sensing an opportunity to ingratiate himself to the Winter Dragon, Loxen said, "We discussed that although we desire completing our mission immediately, Docar needs recovery time before facing Two-Leggeds again. And to succeed, we need Docar."

Ishna thumped once to show her agreement. She said, "I concur with all you said, Loxen."

Both Côzhili and Docar regarded Ishna with skepticism, as if they somehow knew she was hiding something. But neither raised a question.

"If you can fly, Docar, we should return to the rim. At least we have the high ground," Côzhili said.

They all thumped once then took wing. Docar's wing strokes were stiff initially but smoothed after a few minutes.

Once settled on the ledge at the mountain base, Côzhili offered to take first patrol while the others rested. Ishna didn't require rest like the others but didn't argue with Côzhili's offer. *Docar may need me.*

Ishna and Docar curled into each other to preserve warmth.

He whispered, "You are hiding something from us, vôsh'lavi."

At first, Ishna ignored him.

But Docar withdrew his wings from around her. His eyes narrowed, and his brow pinched. "I saw you wobble while flying, Ishna. I have known you since I hatched and have never seen you lose control in the air."

Ishna shook her head. "It was nothing."

Docar leaned to the side, exposing the now-healed gash in his neck. "This is nothing?"

"That is not what I meant."

His voice had risen, and his eyes blazed with anger. *He has never expressed anger toward me before*, Ishna thought.

"It is the human soul within you, isn't it?" Docar asked.

Ishna's heart raced, yet relief flooded her. She no longer had to hide the truth, at least not from Docar.

"You do not know what it is like. To have your thoughts interrupted, your mind usurped. Since my rebirth, I am Ishna but also something else. The Two-Legged soul within argues with me—pulls me from my thoughts. Interrupts my peace. Interferes with my actions."

"Then eradicate it," Docar said. "You are the Winter Dragon, Ishna. Your spirit is eternal and far stronger than any Two-Legged."

She had admitted that Quen had created turmoil within her, but Ishna was not ready to accept the whole truth. *That the Walker within me is far stronger than my dragonkin would believe.*

"Do not forget why I agreed to keep the Two-Legged soul alive and share consciousness with it," Ishna said. "The Rend, remember?"

Docar blew a puff of smoky breath. He rested his forehead on hers. "Vôsh, there must be another way. You cannot go on like this. What if...? Next time, we could lose someone."

He was right, and Ishna knew it. She'd had the same thoughts, of course.

Before the Dô'bedri—the long sleep—Ishna held herself aloof, even with Docar. In those days, she kept her innermost thoughts and feelings private.

Yet since the reawakening, she craved a deeper connection to dragonkin, especially Docar. Such a bond required vulnerability, and vulnerability required trust.

I trust in Docar wholly, Ishna thought.

"I am unsure if I can extinguish the Walker's soul even if I wanted to," she said.

"If you wanted to?" Docar's voice sounded incredulous.

"I do not expect you to understand this, Docar. Even I do not fully comprehend my feelings on the matter. But this Walker and I… we have shared something—unique."

Docar eyed her cautiously, perhaps trying to size up what she still left unsaid. At last, he said, "You are my vôsh'lavi." He touched his forehead to hers. "My heart's best friend—you know I support your choices and that my heart swells with love for you no matter what creature you share a mind with."

Ishna said nothing in return but nuzzled his neck.

Docar pulled away, his tone grave and sincere. "If we don't wrest the Two-Legged from you, you will have no choice but to press the human out of existence. You know that, don't you? Please promise that if that time comes—if you must choose between that Two-Legged and dragonkin—that you will choose Dragos."

He had put into words the exact thoughts Ishna had been having. *I cannot go on this way, and now, he knows it too.* Ishna hoped she could sever her connection with Quen while keeping Quen's soul whole.

But without hesitation, she said to Docar, "I promise you this, vôsh. I will not allow the Walker soul to put you or dragonkin at risk again." She nuzzled him again, and this time, he returned her affections.

"No matter what?" he whispered.

"No matter what," she replied.

PART III

Crowskir Song

When trees whispered ancient secrets,
And suns cast a rosy glow across new-fallen snow,
Crow spoke to Woman.

"The Great Barrow your people must protect,
And its contents you shall not harrow."

Woman answered, "You reveal not your true intent,
And without a boon, we shall not consent,
To perform Night Specter's will."

In answer, Crow shook,
And a lone ebony feather fell.
"Hark to me and heed me well.
Take this boon, it gifts you the sight,
To know your clan's strengths and when to fight."

Woman grasped the feather and devoured it whole.
Crow's sight now fused with her very soul.

With newfound knowledge of the here and now,
Woman guided her clan to worth and power.

And in Great Weaver's eyes,
Woman's clan possessed esteem.
As Keepers of the sacred barrow,
And Friends to the Unseen.

—from *Crowskir Songs of Sofan Drek*, memorialized
by Tinsalo of Māja Artifexa, Partha

Chapter 18

Aldewin

Pelagia's attack had killed four of the eight Kāfe'vind traveling with Aldewin's group. Two others were so severely burned they could travel no further, but neither could they return to Leivby Village.

Yngvari and Shel urged Omma to return the entire party to the Myrskog.

"Let us stay with the Veidmar Clan. There, among friends, our clan can heal. We can return home in a few weeks, perhaps a month," Yngvari said.

Shel agreed. "You can't seriously consider what that insane woman asks of you. We can't trust Pelagia. She smells of rot, which matches what we know was inside her all along."

Aldewin agreed with all Shel said. He knew Pelagia would always protect her own bark-scaled hide. *Web weavers sure have been busy spinning.* He didn't have to voice his feelings on the matter, though.

Omma leaned heavily on her walking stick, her lips a thin, grim line. "If we refuse this Vay'Nada spawn's bargain, she will simply kill us." The Modra glanced at Imbica.

The mage sat on a charred barrel, her back to them and her gaze far off. Perhaps sensing that they expected her guidance, Imbica sighed and turned her attention to them. "Never has vengeance boiled in me the way I burn to destroy that abomination."

"You refer to Pelagia?" Aldewin asked.

"The woman looks human enough to me," Yngvari said.

Imbica cackled. "Human? We shall assume Quen stabbed a human heart. Look at her, Yngvari. That woman is no longer human. The beast's heart has merged with her human spirit. Only Pelagia could twist such an innocent creature into something so foul."

Pelagia stood in the center of town with Nivi at her side. His brow furrowed, and he panted.

Nivi strains against Pelagia's control. The sight made Aldewin's gut roil. He wanted to draw the Vandu dagger and end the woman. *For good this time.*

Aldewin believed in his abilities but doubted he could accomplish a surprise attack on Pelagia. *If I attempt an ambush and fail, Pelagia will kill me. Then, who will guide Quen to her rebirth?*

With her arms outstretched, head and chest pointed skyward, Pelagia looked like a forest lily seeking sunlight. Her eyes closed and wearing a toothy grin, Pelagia resembled addle-brained people in the Shils who'd lost their senses.

Shel said, "She's—something. But at her core, Pelagia is still a skeeving, power-hungry climber. What did you call the Tradsmikor?"

"Skishatur?" Yngvari offered.

"Yeah. A real skishatur. And gods, Pelagia smells like something you scrape off your shoe after a thukna herd barrels through Solia," Shel said. "If we go with her, it will go sideways for us."

"It will go badly for us if we don't go with her." Aldewin sighed and scratched his beard. His hand came away grey from ash. "Imbica is among the most powerful mages I've seen. But even she cannot best Pelagia."

Imbica looked forlorn.

"Sorry, Imbica. I meant no offense," Aldewin said.

Imbica waved a hand. She sounded weary. "None taken, mageling. You are correct. I cannot best Pelagia now. It pains me to admit that, more than you know."

The mage's eyes were puffy and red, and unspent tears glistened. Imbica sucked in a deep breath and pushed off the sooty barrel. "You will not like this, Shel, but I agree with Omma and Aldewin. To survive, we must follow Pelagia's commands. At least for now."

Omma nodded. "Now is the time for faith."

In what? Aldewin wondered. *I've no more faith in gods or spirits. In what shall I place my trust, revered Modra?* He didn't ask the question, though. At the Pillar, he'd learned that masters never answer such questions. Instead, they reposed questions as riddles, deferring responsibility to the querent. *I have no patience for such games today.*

When none looked mollified by her admonition to keep the faith, Omma continued. "We cannot see the great Web that the Dreamers spin, but it is there. The Dreamers have already written our fates. We must follow the thread and trust that in the end—"

"We end up in the center of a giant spider's web, wrapped in silk, our life force drained until we're desiccated husks?" Aldewin asked.

Shel laughed. "Yeah, I'm with Aldewin on this one, Omma. I'm not one for blind faith. I make my own path." She cast a glance at Aldewin. "And *I* try to stay out of webs."

Aldewin nodded. "Couldn't say it better."

Omma remained calm in the face of their dissent. "Perhaps. But sometimes, the web reveals torn areas. Doors through which one can escape the web altogether."

Aldewin noted how Omma offered this idea with conviction, not as a long-shot opportunity. *She has spent considerable time in the Dreaming. Does she know something we don't?*

Aldewin adjusted his dagger belt. "So we're agreed? We're entering Pelagia's web and hoping we find one of those doors Omma mentioned?"

They all nodded, though their choice enthused no one.

Aldewin readjusted the pack and weapons on his back and marched toward Pelagia. "I'll go tell the spider we've agreed to go with her." *Let us hope her web spinning reveals a weakness somewhere along the way,* he thought.

❖   ❖   ❖

Though Pelagia seemed eager to depart, she insisted they remain in Eldisvat. She ordered the Dynasty soldiers and scouts to scavenge for supplies.

"You should have thought about resupply before you burned Eldisvat to the ground," Imbica said.

Aldewin admired Imbica's bravery. With only minimal effort, Pelagia could have turned Imbica into an ash pile.

But Pelagia didn't incinerate Imbica or punish her. *Has that yindril heart softened her? But that can't be right. She murdered an entire town and shows zero remorse for the deed. No, something else is at work here.*

Pelagia had spared the stabled horses and livestock, showing she wasn't a mindless killing monster. Aldewin was glad to have a break from walking, but he was especially relieved for Omma. She was the most physically capable elder he'd ever met. Though she demurred when asked her actual age, based on their talks, he figured she had to be at least ninety. But after their long journey from Leivby Village to Eldisvat, Omma offered no argument about accepting a horse to ride.

Dynasty scouts supplied the remaining Kāfe'vind clan with horses. To Aldewin's surprise, Pelagia allowed the injured and others of the Kāfe'vind Clan to head back to the Myrskog. *Another kindness that seems out of character for her.*

Aldewin whispered to Shel, "Why do you think she's letting them go?"

"No mystery there, Aldewin. She doesn't want sick or injured people slowing her down. 'Sides, the shite eater is nattered, and the worst kind of nuts too."

"How is that?" Yngvari asked.

"Sane one minute and as crazed as a spooked drey calf the next," Shel said.

"I'm not sure her being nattered is new. Quen's stories made it sound like Pelagia was off her nut before she got a beast heart put into her chest," Aldewin said.

"That's true. But she's worse now," Yngvari said. "Let us hope we discover a way to be free of her before her mind shatters."

Before she becomes completely nattered and, in a fit of rage, kills us all.

To everyone's surprise, Modra Omma ordered her assistant, Ivriga, to watch over the clan and see them safely return to Leivby Village.

Worry creased Ivriga's brow. "But Modra, who will tend you if I leave? You need me."

Omma took Ivriga's hands in hers and smiled warmly. "I need you, sweet child. But the Kāfe'vind need you more. You are a natural leader, Ivriga, and they listen to you. Without your guidance, I fear they will never return to Leivby."

Ivriga's look of fear dissipated. "But who will care for you?"

Modra Omma nodded toward Yngvari. "The Sea Singer will assist me, won't you?"

Yngvari nodded, happy for the honor of attending their Modra.

That Yngvari would take her place clearly displeased Ivriga. But she didn't argue against it.

Since most Kāfe'vind had never ridden a horse, Aldewin and Shel gave them lessons on how to saddle, unsaddle, and ride. The agile young scouts adapted well, and Ivriga led the Kāfe'vind out of Eldisvat. They headed back into the Ghost Forest, but this time, knowing Tradsmikor could not harm them.

A boon wrapped inside sadness, to be sure.

Their party was now down to Aldewin, Shel, and Imbica from their pod and Yngvari and Omma from the Kāfe'vind. Modra Omma appeared as determined as ever to see this trip through—to follow an unknown path to a future she'd observed in the Dreaming.

As they readied their mounts and finished packing, Shel asked, "And where exactly are we going?"

Hands on hips, Pelagia gazed to the northwest. "To the far reaches of the Iska'kog." She ordered the Dynasty scouts to hand out the warmer clothes they'd scavenged and some of their own. "You'll freeze without these."

Aldewin had spent six winters at Val'Enara. Tucked into the side of a mountain, Val'Enara Pillar remained frozen half of the year. He knew what it meant to be cold and appreciated the extra layers for the journey north. He donned the wool coat and leather gloves Finn had gifted him. Aldewin was glad for the mountain fox fur collar to counter the wool's itchiness.

Omma asked, "Which city are we headed for? Or do we travel to taiga forest wilds?"

Apparently not fond of horses, Pelagia opted to travel atop Nivi's back. For his part, Nivi wore a scowl, his brows pinched, his head down.

The poor fellow. By the gods, we must free him from her control. Somehow.

With silver hair flashing atop the snowy-white tiger, Pelagia led their column. "We head to Sofan Drek. Capital of the Spindel'vara Clan." She looked back and gave Omma an appraising look. "To the place where I was born."

Omma didn't respond to this news or show any emotion about it. Unfamiliar with the Vatnoyer's geography, Aldewin didn't know what they faced ahead.

"How far is it?" he asked.

Pelagia didn't immediately respond. Finally, she said, "Not far enough."

Aldewin and Shel exchanged glances. Shel handed him kabu, and he took it. *By the gods, this dank-tasting shite grows on you.*

With still-smoldering Eldisvat now a memory, Pelagia led them over harsh terrain once ruled by the Tradsmikor. They rode past spouting geysers and shallow, bubbling water pools smelling of rotten eggs.

Shel wrapped her face with the linen kerchief again, exposing only her eyes. "It's worse than the Phisma tar pit stench that Juka brings to Solia in the summer."

Aldewin had given his kerchief to Yngvari. *What I'd give for a keffla doused in huson pine oil.*

While the air smelled foul, the wide-open vistas revealed harsh beauty. The desolate landscape reminded him of the Sulmére. And thoughts of the Sulmére brought memories of Quen.

Quen. The amber pendant around his neck, barely any weight, felt like a powerful magnet tugging at him, pulling him into thoughts of his time with Quen. Aldewin revisited every tender moment they'd shared. *I wish I could do it all again. That night in Juinar… I shouldn't have pushed her away.* In hindsight, that he'd given up time with Quen for his duty to Kine… It alternately made him want to laugh or break something.

As was typical for men raised within the walls of the Fen Menir compound, his sexual experiences began in his early teen years, and he'd had several lovers in his youth. Though the Pillar valued celibacy to focus one's magical energy, few Rising at the Pillar followed the mandate. He'd been with dozens of people and even thought he loved someone once. But none had felt… right. Not like Quen.

Though he still had much to confess, Aldewin felt like Quen had *seen* him. She saw the real Aldewin—at least as much as he allowed. More than anyone else had, anyway.

And she did not run from me but professed love.

Aldewin pulled his fur collar closer to cover the pendant. Having it visible made him feel—exposed. *Who am I kidding? Even heartless Pelagia can see I'm willing to sell my soul for the chance to see Quen again.* And he hoped for much more. *I must know if what she professed to feel for me was real or only her desire to experience carnal truths before her Promena.*

The trek north was slow going. It gave Aldewin plenty of time to ponder these thoughts and more. After two days, the landscape morphed from rainbow-hued sulfurous pools and a barren landscape dotted with blunted trees to thick tundra.

They followed a trail cut through tangled brush, some nearly as tall as Aldewin. Purple-red heather and flowers of white, pink, and red bloomed at the edges of the spring-green trail, poking through what remained of winter snows. Occasionally, narrow paths wide enough for only one veered from the main road.

"Why bother to cut such a narrow path?" Shel asked.

Pelagia had ignored them since they left Eldisvat, but she chimed in. "A person did not cut those trails."

"Then who—or what—did?" Yngvari asked.

"Bears, mostly," Pelagia said. "Best be careful on those trails. Bears will smell you long before you see them. Most avoid humans, but some pursue encounters. Such meetings rarely end well for people."

Like in the Myrskog, the Iska'kog hummed with Spring's new life. Wildflowers and bright-green shoots brought beauty to the otherwise bleak land. But biting flies and mosquitos made the squishy trek through the tundra miserable.

On day five, another shift in scenery gladdened Aldewin. The tundra gave way to a mixed conifer forest as the mounts carried them up the mountain foothills.

Pelagia told them the mountains were called the Avlox mountains, and they effectively cut the Spindel'vara clan lands off from the clans of the southern Iska'kog. On their trip north, they'd spied the towering, craggy, glacier-covered peaks of the eastern Staket mountains for many leagues. By comparison, the Avlox mountains looked like a giant had pounded them down and rubbed them smooth.

They camped at a saddle known as Warrior's Rest. When they arrived after Hiyadi set, it was too dark to see clearly what lay beyond this northern slope.

As they'd done each night, Pelagia and the Dynasty soldiers and scouts she commanded made one camp while the pod made a separate, smaller camp. Pelagia ordered guards to accompany them hunting, but otherwise, the Dynasty left Aldewin and crew alone.

Typically, Pelagia escaped to her tent as soon as her scouts set it up. She then ignored everyone, including her own people. Shel and Yngvari joked perhaps Pelagia survived on air and sunshine now, like a plant or tree.

But this night, camping at Warrior's Rest, Pelagia joined them for the evening meal. When they noticed her approaching, Shel said under her breath, "Here comes the tree-devil."

Yngvari's face instantly darkened, and her previously jovial mood turned glum. Yngvari cowered, and Shel put an arm around her.

Though Yngvari's sea singing made her a formidable opponent on water, she was not a warrior or land-based battle mage. She clearly felt vulnerable around Pelagia.

"I won't let her take you." She crooked a finger under Yngvari's chin and kissed her softly.

Pelagia noted the closeness between the two as if cataloging it for later consideration. *I wish Shel would be more discreet in front of Pelagia. People like her exploit ties such as theirs.*

As soon as he thought it, Aldewin chortled within himself. *Gods, I should take my own advice.* While at Fen Menir, he'd once put someone he cared for in grave danger merely by acknowledging his feelings. *I should know better.*

Pelagia didn't ask for a plate of food, but Aldewin handed her one anyway. At first, Pelagia merely looked at the rabbit loin on her wooden plate as if eating was foreign to her. She then tore the roasted meat from the leg and tentatively put it in her mouth. Chewing slowly, she looked like she was tasting game for the first time.

After she swallowed the first bite, she picked the entire leg section up with her hands and devoured it. *Well, I guess that answers our question. She needs to eat and cannot live on air and sunlight alone.*

Having Pelagia in their camp thrilled no one. They were used to a nightly routine of hunting, cooking, cleaning, and then passing a pipe while sharing stories. They'd learned much about each other during their journey, but Aldewin figured none would share stories or intimate details with Pelagia.

Imbica, though, broke their silence toward Pelagia. "How many days left until we reach Sofan Drek?"

Still hovering over her rabbit leg, Pelagia regarded Imbica coolly. "Does the saddle callous your tender backside? You prefer wagons, if I recall correctly."

Undaunted, Imbica licked grease from her fingers and said, "Once, your taunts would have riled me, Pelagia. But now, your cutting words do not have the intended effect. Not since the night my master took your human life."

Pelagia raised an eyebrow. "Your Master? Do you mean the Doj'Anira?"

Imbica put her plate on the ground and smoothed the fabric covering her lap. "You mean Quen. And yes, I refer to Quen."

Pelagia let out a throaty laugh. "Master?" She laughed again. "You, one of Indrasi's greatest mages—your words, not mine—call a now-dead woman your master?" Pelagia tsked. "Poor, foolish Imbica. Stripped of rank and station by the Exalted, you are so desperate for acceptance that you'll bow to whoever will have you."

Imbica remained implacable, her face evincing neither insult nor anger. "Your words do not cut, Pelagia. You can speak ill of Quen, but she proved herself a bigger person than you."

Pelagia's eyes grew stormy.

Imbica continued. "And proved a better leader too. In fact, she earned my respect more than Xa'Vatra has."

As she rose to her feet, Pelagia's eyes grew wide, her nostrils flaring. "Careful with your words, mage."

Imbica remained unflappable. "Or what? As you said, Xa'Vatra cast me aside. Quen, though, had every reason to let me rot in that cell and succumb to my fate…" Imbica took a deep breath, regaining composure. "Quen showed compassion, though she did not have to."

And recognized your battle prowess, Aldewin thought. *Yes, she showed you compassion, Imbica. But cunning also fuels her choice.* The combination—compassion and cunning—had earned Aldewin's respect too. But he didn't intervene in their discussion.

Pelagia retorted, "You are not beyond the Dynasty's reach here, mage. Do not forget that."

"Maybe, but I know you won't harm me."

Pelagia chortled. "Do not be so sure of that. Xa'Vatra gifted you to me once, remember? By rights, I *own* you."

"I think that contract died when you did," Shel said.

"An excellent point," Aldewin said. "Plus, we're not on Indrasian soil here, Mistress. Indrasi's laws don't hold sway in the Vatnoyer."

Imbica remained unfazed by Pelagia's threat. She repeated, "You will not harm me."

Yngvari asked, "How can you be certain? You saw what Pelagia can do."

Imbica nodded. "True enough. The Mistress of the Menagerie has shown how she can light fires and control giant cats." Her voice dripped with disdain. "But she *needs* me. For what? I do not yet know." Imbica turned her dark eyes like two charred coals on Pelagia.

Rolling her eyes, Pelagia returned her focus to her plate. Her voice dripped with sarcasm. "Sure, Imbica. I need you." She laughed, though Aldewin detected a hint of nervousness in her laughter this time.

Whispering now to Yngvari, Imbica said, "She must need me. Otherwise, she would have set fire to me back in Eldisvat."

Perhaps Pelagia needed his entire party for some yet-unknown reason. The idea should have comforted Aldewin.

Yet the thought gave him no reassurance. Instead, a disturbing question bloomed, and he gave it voice. Aldewin whispered so only the pod could hear. "What is so formidable even Pelagia cannot best it?"

Chapter 19

Aldewin

In the new day's light, the view from Warrior's Rest revealed grassy plains stretching northward as far as Aldewin could see. An ambush was unlikely. Hiyadi bathed the green and yellow fields in soft light. With crisp morning air, the day promised to be a fair one for riding.

The morning also revealed Omma walking with a limp that hadn't been present the day prior. Before they saddled up, Aldewin offered healing comfort to Omma.

Typically stoic, Omma accepted his help. "I am feeling my age this morning." She stretched her arms overhead, and her joints creaked. "Thank you, Varskog, for your aid."

"I will do my best. Any advice?" Aldewin asked.

"Connect yourself to the spirit of the Green," she said.

Aldewin meditated. The morning's peace made finding the stillness he needed for spell work easier. Once he sensed Doka's energies answering his call, he asked Omma, "I've gathered Doka energy. What do I do with it?"

"Remember, you are a conduit for the spirit of the Green, Varskog. Use the Green to *see* the unseen. The Green reveals hidden ailments in a human body like it knows disease within a leaf, obstructions to roots, or even recognizes a tree's death."

Aldewin hovered his hands over Omma's body. In his mind's eye, golden vine tendrils swirled beneath his palms, and supple roots sprang from Menauld. These energetic cords of new-growth wood wrapped Modra Omma's lower body.

The energies pooled and resisted moving further at her left hip joint as if snagged on a hook. "Aha!" Aldewin said. His excitement broke the peace of the morning.

Omma laughed softly. "You see something exciting, Varskog?"

"I do *see*," he said. "By the gods, I see without seeing." He chortled again, thrilled with this new magical insight.

Pelagia sauntered over. Her arms crossed, she stared down at him. "Baby mage has found a new weave."

Baby? Towering over everyone in their group and nearly twice their shoulder width, Aldewin was no child. *Pelagia's diminutive taunt goads. Focus, Aldewin. Do not let the bark-covered skishatur get under your skin.* Aldewin focused instead on Omma. He called upon the roots to instill healing into her troublesome hip.

Pelagia cocked her head and studied his work as if she saw the energetic threads he wove. "Using only Doka?" She frowned. "That will provide only temporary relief."

She bit into a piece of dried fruit and continued inspecting his spell work.

"You're a healer now, are you?" Aldewin asked. "Okay, great all-knowing Mistress who never studied at a Pillar. What would you do?"

She spit out a pithy bit. Her face scrunched from the sour taste. "Your Pillars have a vital weakness that dooms them to fail at advancing magical knowledge in Indrasi."

"On this, I agree with her," Omma said.

"Doomed to fail? That's a dire prediction. Why, then, do you cast your lot with the Dynasty?" Aldewin asked.

She ignored his question and asked one of her own. "What feeds Doka? Hmm?"

Despite a general desire to ignore Pelagia, Aldewin couldn't resist seeds of magical learning. He thought about her question then answered, "Sunlight."

"You think literally. Use your imagination. Yes, the plants cannot survive without Hiyadi's light. But in Menaris, what element is sunlight?"

"Vatra."

Pelagia nodded and rolled her hand, urging him to continue his thought.

"Ah. Fire burns wood."

"And…"

He considered Qüira, earth energy. *Earth energies ground the Wood element.* That left Enara, and as soon as he thought it, he knew instinctively it was correct. *Why have I not seen it before?* "Water. Enara feeds Doka."

As if already bored with the lesson, Pelagia yawned. "When healing, weave Enara into a Doka spell to increase effectiveness."

Aldewin wove rings of swirling water. The elemental water wound around the twisting golden vines of Doka energy. The restriction he'd felt earlier eased as the energetic roots and vines welcomed the water spirit energy.

Omma moan in relief. "Ah, much better."

As he released the threads of elemental energy, his mood was brighter.

"I don't know what to say. Your advice worked and has advanced my training more than six years at Val'Enara. Where did you learn this?"

Her jaw set and lips thin, Pelagia said, "Once upon an Iska'kog time, I trained at the knee of a great Crowskir."

Omma stood, shook her left leg, and gave her hips a few swivels. "By the Green, Varskog, you performed a minor miracle today. My hip hasn't felt this spry in many years." She laughed and smiled up at him. "Many thanks to you." Without speaking further with Pelagia, Omma headed toward the horses to mount up for the day's ride.

Aldewin followed her but cast a glance over his shoulder toward Pelagia. He'd intended to thank her, but she was already heading toward the bushes, perhaps to take her morning relief before they set out for the day.

As if sensing Pelagia was no longer in earshot, Omma crooked her finger, beckoning Aldewin to get closer. Once he'd bent to hear, she said, "The Mistress reveals something crucial this morn."

"That she understands complex elemental weavings?"

"That I already knew," Omma said.

"I didn't. The Masters and Zeniths at the Pillars may know this magic, but they don't share the knowledge with lower ranks."

She shook her head and tsked. "More's the pity."

"What revelation do you refer to, then?" Aldewin asked.

"I know this Crowskir she trained under."

Aldewin helped Omma into her saddle and checked the girth to ensure it was secure. "And?"

More confident in the saddle than in the first days of riding, Omma took the reins. Aldewin's healing had lifted the fatigue from her face, and her eyes were bright. "The Crowskir is Thrud ag Isabré. She has been Spindel'vara Clan's matriarch for thirty years, but not because people love her. No, she wields formidable magic and is as harsh as she is talented."

Aldewin rubbed his beard. "Hmm, not promising to hear about the person who rules over the place we're headed."

"But there's more." She paused for effect, ensuring she had Aldewin's full attention. "Thrud had a granddaughter. One she trained to be her replacement when the time came."

Aldewin said, "You mean—"

"The Mistress of the Menagerie. This Pelagia is the granddaughter and heir to the Spindel'vara clan Leidship. I doubt Pelagia is her given name."

"Pelagia is a Parthinian name, to be sure. But isn't it odd that she'd leave a guaranteed seat of power to enter the fray in Qülla, eating up Xa'Vatra's scraps?"

"The spinners work mystery upon mystery into this weaving."

"That they do," Aldewin said. "And odd that the Dynasty sends Pelagia to her birthplace, a seat of power she recused herself from. What web are the weavers luring us into, Modra Omma?"

Omma sighed and shrugged her shoulders. "In all our Dreamings, we Modras never heard the term 'Heart of Menaris.' We felt its beat, though. A deep thrum that exists always and everywhere. I assumed it was the world's life force—the Green. But what if the Heart of Menaris is a physical thing? And connected to magic? Maybe even the source of magic."

Aldewin had felt the thrum, too, when he'd entered the Dreaming. A persistent beat, so low and slow, it was more felt than heard. Known but unseen, blending into the fabric of the dreamtime world. "You think it's truly possible that this 'Heart of Menaris' is something the Dynasty can seize for their purpose?"

"I don't know, Varskog. But Pelagia seems to think so. And my guess is that if she trained under Crowskir Thrud, that's how she knows about it. Thrud must have passed this knowledge to her, assuming she would be the next Spindel'vara Leid and a Crowskir someday."

Pelagia had already mounted Nivi. His forehead furrowed, and he held his tail low. She called out, "Mount up. We're heading out. We will be at Sofan Drek by Hiyadi's rest, but we'll make a stop along the way." She reached out to rub Nivi's head but pulled her hand back. "I have an errand first."

Astride a diminutive roan-colored horse, Shel whispered to Aldewin, "Now, what kind of errand can this bark-skinned shite eater have out in the middle of nowhere?"

Imbica, riding on the other side of Aldewin, answered. "Let us hope she's not planning to sacrifice one of us to shadow gods to win their favor." She might have meant it as a joke, but Imbica's demeanor was so serious no one laughed.

Pelagia led a column of twos with Dio at her side. With his chin thrust upward, Dio projected an imperious demeanor. He avoided Aldewin and the pod. *I notice he always rides on the side opposite of me. Concerned about a blade in the back, no doubt. He has cause for caution.*

The pod rode sandwiched between Pelagia at the front and the Dynasty soldiers at the rear. The Dynasty warriors behind subtly reminded that the pod wasn't free to leave.

After lunch, when the late-afternoon sleepiness was taking hold, Pelagia whistled and motioned for the others to follow her on a side path. Though not as narrow as the bear trails they'd seen earlier in the journey, this path was only wide enough for a single-file line of riders.

Perhaps fearful or deferential to Pelagia's leadership, no one asked for their destination. The path veered eastward off the main road.

"Sofan Drek lies northwest of here," Omma whispered to Aldewin. "What errand can she possibly have in this wilderness?"

After a few moments of consideration, Aldewin whispered, "I fear she intends to capture yet another magical creature for her menagerie."

The narrow path climbed steadily, slowing their progress. After nearly an hour of battling leg-eating brush and nettles, they came upon a small, oasis-like clearing. A fast-running stream poured down the northern hills, tumbled over large rocks and boulders, and created a natural pool. Reeds, tender grasses, and spring flowers surrounded the oasis, an ideal location to water their horses and refresh. *Quen would enjoy resting here with me.*

Pelagia dismounted, signaling that they were stopping. "Do not allow the horses to drink here," she called.

Gently stroking her brown horse's nose, Yngvari said, "It's cruel to not allow the horses a drink." She sang a soft, low note, holding it only long enough to curl a small water column upward. "These are fine, fresh waters."

Pelagia removed her riding gloves and stowed them at her belt. "This stream and spring are sacred to Spindel'vara. No clan can claim them. You may rest while I tend to my business, but do not stray. I won't be long."

Shel and the rest of their party began crossing a natural rock bridge across the stream to take up a spot on the northern bank. Most of the Dynasty soldiers headed toward the other end of the pool, leaving a half dozen near the pod as guards. Aldewin had followed his group, but Pelagia called to him.

"Aldewin." She waved him over. "I require you."

The pod was prepared to wait for him, but he shooed them away. "Go. Rest and enjoy the meadow. I can handle Pelagia." *A lie, but I don't want them to worry about me.*

Pelagia closed her eyes and stood like a statue for a moment. Opening her eyes, she waved a hand over Nivi's left ear as she mumbled an incantation in a language Aldewin didn't recognize.

Within a few minutes, the gold band that had dug into Nivi's ear released and fell into Pelagia's palm. The crease in Nivi's brow eased, and he rose, ready to bolt.

Pelagia whispered another spell, and he yowled in pain. "Patience, Nivi. If you want me to release the other one, you must cooperate."

"You're—freeing him?" *A far cry from what I had guessed her errand was.*

Pelagia's eyes were red and her lips drawn downward. "I am correcting a mistake made in my youth." Seeing Aldewin's incredulous look, she sighed. "Do not look so shocked. You may find this difficult to believe, but I truly love Nivi, even if he does not care for me."

"Honestly, that is hard to believe. That you love him, I mean."

Anger flared her nostrils.

Careful, Aldewin. Remember, the bark-covered she-beast is nattered. "So you're fond of animals, just not people?" Memories of Eldisvat's charred bodies came to mind.

"In truth? Most humans are detestable to me." Pelagia rubbed the grey-brown bark on her chest and looked annoyed. Impatience in her voice, she said, "None of that matters now. Sometimes, we must surrender the old to create space for the new."

Aldewin didn't grasp her meaning, but the implication sent a chill through him and made the hair on his arms stand on end. *I may regret asking this.* "What do you need me here for?"

"To say goodbye."

It was the last thing Aldewin expected. Pelagia seemed to enjoy "owning" creatures and even people, collecting them like prizes and symbols of her worth. He would have bet several Kovars that Pelagia would never voluntarily part with Nivi, let alone show Aldewin kindness. *Is she sincere? Or is this an odd ploy?* Pelagia's forlorn expression was convincing, but he'd learned not to trust outward appearances.

A murderer one minute but compassionate the next? Even more reason to exercise caution around her. People off their nut can be wildly unpredictable.

Since that fateful day at Volenex when Ishna destroyed Quen, Aldewin had assumed he and Nivi would be together for the foreseeable future. He tried to ruffle the tiger's mane as he'd done many times, but to his surprise, Nivi snarled.

"It's me, Nivi. Your friend Aldewin."

Realizing the hand was Aldewin's and not Pelagia's, Nivi relaxed and allowed Aldewin to stroke his fur.

"You and Nivi have grown fond of each other." She sighed. "Nivi was never as fond of me as I'd hoped he would grow to be."

"You cannot force someone to love you."

She didn't respond to that. "As soon as I release the other foci, Nivi will bolt. I will allow a brief goodbye."

"This is Nivi's home territory?"

Pelagia nodded. She gestured around them. "This glen is sacred, home to these special snow tigers known to the Spindel'vara Clan as Fros'vinspri."

"Frozen Water Spirit?"

"Yes." She nodded approvingly. "You're learning the language. Perhaps you've noticed. Nivi isn't a typical tiger."

Aldewin had noticed. Nivi seemed aware, as if he understood what humans said. Aldewin had assumed, though, that all animals from the Vatnoyer were special. After all, the area produced yindrils and flying mushrooms.

Pelagia seemed normal in these moments, away from others and alone with Aldewin. No spiteful comments or hurtful digs meant to lift herself above others. *It is like she is two people within that one bark-skinned body.*

"I used my formidable abilities and these foci I stole from our Crowskir to take this creature from his home." Her voice was small, placid, and remorseful. "It was a sin, Varskog. And I have paid the price." She put a finger to the bark covering her chest.

"Archon Kine once told me it's never too late to come to Vaya di Soli and live the Way. By purging ourselves of past wrongs and committing to the cannons, we can shed the taint of Vay'Nada's shadow that may have grown in our hearts."

Pelagia gave a wry laugh. "My heart wrapped in shadow is no more." She tapped her chest. "Yet Vay'Nada knows me still." Her look was dour. "Your Archons are not as wise—or forthcoming—as Pillar students believe."

Aldewin couldn't disagree with that statement. Archon Kine had lied to him—to everyone—about being a Nixan. She'd withheld valuable truths to manipulate Aldewin into doing her dirty work in the world while she remained secluded at Val'Enara.

Vaya di'Soli—the Way—taught acolytes to live a life of humility, compassion, and humanity. These teaching still felt right to Aldewin, even if he no longer trusted the masters and institutions they served.

Pelagia shielded her eyes and gazed at the sky. "We must arrive in Sofan Drek before full night and clouds approach from the west. Quickly, say your farewell so I can release him."

She stepped away, leaving Aldewin alone with the tiger, his only companion for nearly half a year.

Crimson blood beaded on Nivi's ear where the horrid gold foci had been. Aldewin wiped at it with his sleeve. He coughed to clear the painful tightness in his throat. "You'll have a scar, old friend." Without thinking about it, Aldewin intuitively called upon Doka and Enara and intertwined a healing weave. He hovered his palms over Nivi's wound and felt heat rise in the space between them. The bleeding stopped, and Aldewin rubbed away the dried blood.

Aldewin pressed his face closer to Nivi's ear and whispered, "I will see you again. I don't know how I know, but I do."

Nivi threw his head back and roared. He nuzzled his enormous head into Aldewin's shoulder.

Tears streamed down Aldewin's face, unbidden. "By the gods, I hadn't realized how attached to you I've become." He wiped a tear. "But you are home now, Nivi. Be at peace, my friend. And when I once again speak with Quen, I'll tell her you're safe and back where you belong."

Nivi rose, threw his head back, and sent a loud chirping call upstream.

Aldewin stepped back. "Release him now."

Pelagia repeated her spell, and the second gold foci released into her hand. As soon as the golden cuff fell, Nivi shot like an arrow. He ran at full speed, his mane flying in the breeze.

Within minutes, other tigers called back to him. Aldewin scanned the trees on the northeastern hills but saw neither tigers nor other animals.

"You will not see the Fros'vinspri unless they choose to be seen."

"Does he have family?"

Pelagia laughed. "Oh yes. Nivi is a grandfather, perhaps a great-grandsire now. Nivi's family will welcome him home."

"I hope so," Aldewin said. Though parting with Nivi saddened him, Aldewin couldn't help but smile at the thought that Nivi could live the rest of his years with loved ones rather than locked in Pelagia's menagerie.

Aldewin and Pelagia watched until they saw Nivi no more. His snowy fur blended into the scenery of the white-barked birch trees. Neither of them moved to join the others until someone screamed in pain.

Aldewin pulled the staff from his back and ran to the stream's banks where he'd left the pod. He quickly counted heads and noted that his party was still together, and none appeared injured.

Farther downstream, though, it was another story. The brook ran red with the blood of a Dynasty soldier, lying face up on the rocks, a spear sticking out of his chest.

Standing on the rocks above, at least two dozen archers stood with weapons ready. Scrambling over rocks and dashing, at least two dozen more people carrying spears and broadswords hooted and called.

Approaching from behind, Pelagia said, "Put away the staff. You're Fen Menir, aren't you? Draw that Vandu blade and cut them down."

"Who are they?" Aldewin asked.

"My dear family," Pelagia said.

CHAPTER 20

ALDEWIN

Screeching like wounded animals, warriors clad in leather armor poured from the southeastern hills. They leaped over rocks and thundered toward them with swords, spears, and war axes in hand. The spider web tattoos on their chins and necks made it clear they were from the Spindel'vara Clan.

Their archers took the high ground over the Dynasty soldiers. By the time a dozen Spindel'vara warriors descended to the riverbank, a second Dynasty soldier lay in the stream, an arrow protruding from his eye.

Several front-line Spindel'vara warriors wore helmets crafted from animal skulls and adorned with fur, feathers, wood, dried flowers, and herbs. Some headdresses covered the upper portion of their faces with skulls from animals and even humans. The masks made them appear like apparitions of the dead.

Pelagia had told Aldewin to pull his Vandu blade, but this was not a close-quarters fight. He stowed his staff, though, and opted for a broadsword as he ran toward his pod. *Anyone who intends harm to my sisters must go through me.*

Not that they needed him. Imbica stood on the northern bank in front of Yngvari and Omma. The mage already twirled her arms, gathering Menaris energy for spell casting.

Shel scrambled up a large rock and nocked an arrow, yelling to Yngvari and Omma. "Get behind us and hide as best you can." The two immediately did as Shel ordered and hunkered behind the mage and archer.

Aldewin glanced behind him, expecting to see Pelagia readying to blast the Spindel'vara attackers to Vay'Nada's cold shores. But she neither drew a weapon nor readied herself for spell casting. Pelagia stood like a stone effigy, her gaze aloof and unbothered. *She set fire to an entire town. Why doesn't she protect her soldiers—or us?*

The surprise attack took the Dynasty soldiers off guard, but they were on their feet and holding their own in the melee. Trained in the Orrokan arts by Pillar masters, the Dynasty soldiers drew true-edged steel and donned their shields. They quickly formed a circular formation with their shields out, well protected from rear and flanking attacks.

The remaining Dynasty warriors held their own against the rampaging Spindel'vara Clan. Iron met steel, and axes met the resistance of leather-plate armor and shields. Men yowled and shouted curses, and the southern stream bloomed crimson.

Shel pulled her bowstring taut, an arrow ready. "Do I shoot them or not?"

"I am uncertain of our part in this," Imbica said. "But the enemy of our enemy—"

"Could be our friend," Omma said.

Aldewin shifted his weight into a defensive position, his broadsword at the ready. "Or they are just a second enemy,"

Omma squinted at the warriors. "Perhaps. I know this, though. They are inexperienced. If Spindel'Vara's Crowskir sent them, she did not send her best warriors to this fight."

"How do you know?" Imbica held a tight ball of swirling fire between her hands, its heat radiating. The air around her shimmered.

Omma pointed to her chin. "Tattoos. Webs on their throats, some on their chins too. Experienced warriors bear webs and runes over their entire face and necks."

A group of Spindel'vara splintered off from the rest and made their way northward up the banks toward the pod. With their war axes held high and throaty war cries, Aldewin figured they weren't likely to have a chat and figure out who is friend and who is foe.

To Shel, he yelled, "Loose!"

She sent an arrow to the closest and largest of the half dozen advancing on them. It glanced off his spaulder crafted from leather and the skull of an animal.

"Dammit." Shel was already nocking another arrow.

The man Shel shot had been walking quickly before, but now, he rushed toward them, shouting a war cry. Seeing a hulking beastly man running toward him should have made Aldewin frightened. Instead, it fueled the bloodlust he had been holding back for weeks.

Aldewin screamed a holler of his own, taunting the Spindel'vara soldiers.

Shel shot another arrow. "Don't piss 'em off even more."

Mumbling an incantation in Soligian, Imbica turned the fireball she'd been holding aloft into a white-hot elemental spear. She hurled it at the man Shel had shot. The Vatra spear sizzled as it tore into the man's chest, searing through layers of leather and wool. The blow staggered the warrior but did not take him down.

That Vatra spear would have downed an Indrasian warrior. What magic is at work here? The thought ratcheted down Aldewin's bloodlust a notch. *If Imbica cannot fell them, we must rely on strategy and tactics.*

Imbica didn't wait to assess the damage she'd done. Immediately after her first volley, she crafted another projectile from elemental fire and sent it flying. Her second spear struck a woman warrior.

The woman put a hand to her right side and called out, "Healer!"

Imbica wasn't the only battle mage on the field. A woman with long white-gold braided hair wearing a half-human skull mask quickly approached the Spindel'vara warriors advancing on the pod. This healer pulled such tremendous amounts of Menaris energy that Aldewin saw it, like heat waves over dunes on a blistering hot day.

"Do you feel that?" Imbica asked. Her face was red and covered in sweat. She didn't let up her attacks, but crafting complex weapons like spears or swords from Menaris energy took greater effort. She now hurled fireballs instead.

Aldewin had felt the healer's magic, though he'd never experienced such a thing. He witnessed Imbica, Yngvari, and others frequently manipulate Menaris's energies, but he didn't feel their pull on Menaris. Not like he just had.

A second Spindel'vara mage positioned herself on a boulder high above the battle. This mage was clad in grey leathers and a wolf-skull headdress. She sent water spells to counteract Imbica's fire spells. The counterspells sent steam into the air, and soon, a misty fog rolled across the glen.

Yet a third mage took up position on an even higher vantage point. Apparently out of patience for Imbica's persistence, this mage lifted the water from the stream in a great wave. It crashed into Imbica and tumbled her to the ground. Soaked through and wobbly, Imbica pushed wet hair from her eyes and tried to push herself up, only to topple again.

Aldewin lent Imbica a hand up then twirled and sliced across the chest of a young warrior who had made it to them despite Shel's arrows and Imbica's fiery assault. Before the lad recovered from being staggered, Aldewin lunged and sank his sword into the young warrior's right side, just below the rib cage. Aldewin twisted his blade then quickly pulled it from the young man's belly. The Spindel'vara warrior fell to the once-peaceful pool, his crimson blood swirling into the water.

Yngvari still stood with Shel, Imbica, and Aldewin, forming a shield around her. She was not idle, though. Yngvari sang the waters and created a tide. It pressed their attackers back and staggered a few, sending them into the stream.

A cacophonous noise of clashing weapons and dying people broke the glen's sacred quality. When they had first arrived, the clear blue pool's surface had been like glass, the air smelling of damp earth and spring flowers. Now muddy and bloody, the pool was a quagmire. The odor of blood and sweat overpowered the sweet, inviting hint of spring.

Though the high clouds were not dark or pregnant with rain, thunder boomed. The ground shook. Soldiers on both sides of the melee wobbled, and several toppled. In mere seconds, high white clouds swirled into an angry dark mass as the air cracked with lightning.

Aldewin asked Yngvari, "Are you doing this, Sea Singer?"

She yelled back, "No!"

As lightning blazed across the sky and thunder rumbled, the ground quaked again, this time hard enough to knock Shel and the two Spindel'vara mages from their perches.

Above the din, Pelagia bellowed, "Enough!"

A powerful energy wave rippled across the glen. The force of it knocked everyone still standing to the ground, including Aldewin.

Pelagia strode toward the center of the clearing, her arms raised high. When they'd first seen her in Eldisvat, thin lines of purple-blue veins were visible under her skin on her temples and jawline. Now, those veins were more visible and throbbed. Additional veins created a purple mesh webbing across her face, arms, and hands.

"Do not make me destroy you!" Pelagia lowered her voice. "Or this sacred place."

The mage wearing the skull-face mask staggered out of the pool. Her grey leathers were drenched. She stumbled toward Pelagia, her lips pulled tight. With malice evident, she pointed a gloved finger at Pelagia. She said, "You dare enter this glen after your crimes against the Clan." She spread her arms out, and her voice sounded choked. "Against our beloved Fros'vinspri." The Spindel'vara mage hurtled orange-yellow fire at Pelagia.

Without emotional response, Pelagia thrust a hand and turned the mage's attack against her. The Spindel'vara mage's fire attack turned in midair and careened toward the mage.

Though the mage scrambled to avoid being hit, the fire caught her on the shoulder. Despite her soaking-wet leather, the fiery spell must have penetrated because the woman yowled.

The mage's attack didn't dissuade Pelagia. She marched toward the primary melee, undaunted. Arrows soared, but Pelagia shattered them in midair. Spears spiraled at her heart, but she flung them into the rocky riverbank. As the pod had experienced in Eldisvat, even two dozen Spindel'vara soldiers couldn't best Pelagia.

I again wonder what she could possibly need us for.

To the Dynasty soldiers, she called, "Dynasty—to me!"

Still holding a loose semicircular formation, the remaining Dynasty soldiers scrambled toward Pelagia. Aldewin counted eight plus Dio.

Blood dripped from a glancing slice to Dio's cheek. But with a dagger in each hand, both bloody from battle, Dio appeared uninjured and ready for more.

With Pelagia and the soldiers as shields, Aldewin and the pod moved close behind them. Shel still held her bow,

Imbica held a fireball aloft, and Yngvari, Omma, and Aldewin had weapons ready.

The Spindel'vara Clan gathered into a grouping as well. At the front stood one of the larger warriors. He was crowned with a large eagle-skull headdress trimmed in fur and feathers, and blood and mud matted his tightly woven plaits of white-gold hair. He wiped his sweaty forehead on his leather-clad shoulder and stepped forward, a war axe in each hand.

A Dynasty warrior lifted his bow to shoot the Spindel'vara man, but Pelagia told him to lower his weapon.

The eagle-skull man asked, "Is that—Ylfa?"

"Ylfa is dead." Pelagia tore open the lacings of her linen shirt, revealing a chest covered in silvery bark.

The approaching man stopped cold. His mouth agape, he stared at the line of scaly wood growing from Pelagia's chest. He halted and whispered, "By the gods…" The man called over his shoulder to his clan, "Stand down."

Pelagia continued walking toward him, the Dynasty and pod creeping with her.

The eagle-crested warrior took a few steps back, his arms up in a defensive position. The warrior's eyes widened. "Stay back from me, you—whatever you are."

The Mistress halted. In a soft voice, unusually tender for her, Pelagia said, "Brynjold. You are Brynjold, aren't you?"

He nodded but kept his weapons at the ready.

"We came to this sacred glen together in our youth." She pointed at the large stone upon which one of the Spindel'vara mages had stood. "We sat on that rock and shared fresh-picked berries while the Crowskirs—our grandmothers—conferred with the Fros'vinspri." She glanced at the rock then back at him. "Remember?"

His face softened slightly, and his voice was a whisper. "What have you become?"

With one hand on her bark-covered flesh and the other outstretched toward him, Pelagia pled. "Do not fear me. We were friends once. I intend you no harm—any of you…" She paused then said, "But the yindril in me—when it's frightened." Her arm dropped, and she looked away from him. "If threatened, I cannot control what I will do." Her body shook. Pelagia turned her gaze back to Brynjold. "My name is Pelagia. I am the woman your friend Ylfa became, and I do not want to kill you."

Brynjold gestured to the Dynasty soldiers flanking her. "No? Then why have you marched these shadow-spawn Dynasty fucks into our most sacred space? You already took the Fros'vinspri Sire. Did you come back for the Matriarch too?"

Pelagia shook her head. "You—"

Brynjold spat and interrupted. "You started it, you know. Now, these skishatur fuckers plunder our lands. Poaching our sacred Fros'vinspri." He looked around Pelagia and pointed to Omma and Yngvari. "We are not enemies with our Myrskog cousins. We know you've lost more than most Vatnoyer folks. Have they not taken your beloved naturfrandi? Even your people? Why in the name of the Green would you help her?"

Help her? More like sucked into her web and waiting for her to devour our souls.

"We won't allow you to claim more Fros'vinspri. This land's spirits belong to the Vatnoyer. They aren't yours to sell," Brynjold said.

From nearby, a snow tiger roared. Within a few seconds, Nivi sprang onto the highest rock overlooking the glen. Behind him, at least a dozen snow tigers approached. Several were nearly as large as Nivi, with snowy manes and glacial-blue eyes. The females were maneless but nearly as large as the males. At the back of the pack were youth, likely only a few years old.

As soon as the Spindel'vara saw Nivi, they knelt. Some mumbled phrases in an unknown language. Fearsome Spindel'vara warriors wept, their tears making trails down their mud-speckled and tattooed faces.

A female tiger sprang to the rock beside Nivi. She roared, and Brynjold stood but bowed his head to her. To Pelagia, he said, "You brought back the Fros'vinspri sire?"

Pelagia's voice was flat. "I did." She turned her attention to Nivi. "I was young when I left Sofan Drek. I'd intended to hurt the one who hurt me."

Though Pelagia may have intended them to take her words as an admission of wrongdoing, her flat tone did not sound remorseful. *She must have had an ulterior motive for releasing Nivi. There is no kindness in her bestial heart.*

Chest out and head high, Nivi stood tall atop the stone. He scanned the faces of the gathered and passed over Pelagia. Nivi's gaze landed on Aldewin, and he roared again. His eyes remained fixed on Aldewin, and he trilled. Nivi often made the sound when relaxed and content.

Though Brynjold's demeanor toward Pelagia softened, the skull-masked mage came forward, her face scrunched and angry. "You may be in a repentant mood, Ylfa, and maybe the Fros'vinspri will forgive you. But that doesn't mean we do." Her eyes were red and her voice choked. "You *abandoned* us." The woman took a breath, regained composure, and said through gritted teeth, "You broke the most sacred of Spindel'vara laws. That can't go unpunished."

Murmurs of agreement rose from the Spindel'vara. Several thumped their chests and shouted calls for justice.

Under his breath, one of the Dynasty soldiers standing in front of Aldewin said, "I'd like to see them try to punish her." The man next to him nodded and tittered.

Under her breath, Pelagia said, "I see Thrud poisoned my former clan against me. Very unfortunate for them."

To everyone's surprise, Pelagia stepped forward. She held her arms out and wrists up in a gesture of surrender. "You are right. I broke sacred laws and should face the Clan's justice."

Murmurs rose from both the Spindel'vara and the Dynasty soldiers. The Dynasty soldiers whispered among themselves and shifted nervously.

Shel whispered to Aldewin, "What is she playing at?"

Aldewin shook his head. "If only I knew."

Pelagia said, "I submit as your prisoner. Take me to your Crowskir. She will determine the punishment for my crimes against the Spindel'vara Clan—and the Fros'vinspri."

A hush fell over the crowd. The still air felt like the world held its breath, waiting to see if Pelagia's words were trick or truth.

Omma broke the silence with a whisper like a downy feather floating on a silent breeze. "The Dreaming threads all lead to this. Let us see what she weaves of it."

Chapter 21

Aldewin

To the surprise of every soul gathered in the sacred Fros'vinspri Glen, Pelagia allowed Spindel'vara to bind her hands. The skull-masked mage mumbled an incantation of binding, weaving an energetic cage intended to cut Pelagia's ties to Menaris. The air around Pelagia shimmered, a silvery swirl surrounding her.

In the Menagerie dungeon all those months ago, Aldewin had recognized Pelagia's magical binding around Imbica. It had been weak and easily undone. This weave, though, was far more intricate. *Not one I could undo, at least not easily.*

Stoic but with head held high, Pelagia acted like Spindel'vara Clan had bested her. For their part, the Spindel'vara acted like they'd gotten the better of Pelagia.

Do they not realize Pelagia has taken them prisoner rather than vice versa? Aldewin wondered.

Shel tsked. "Acting victorious though she surrendered without a fight. What a bunch of—"

"Cowards," Aldewin said.

"I was going to say shite-eating turds-for-brains. But yeah, cowards too," Shel said.

Despite the chest-pounding bravado of the Spindel'vara warriors, Pelagia's haughty and superior demeanor remained. She inspected the mage's attempts at magical binding and, for a moment, smirked.

Imbica gave voice to what Aldewin sensed. "That will not hold her if she doesn't allow it to."

"Agreed," Aldewin said. "Do you think we should advise the Spindel'vara?"

Imbica squinted at Pelagia, inspecting the shimmery air around her.

Aldewin had been asking Imbica, but Omma answered. "No." Her lips pulled in a grim line, and she frowned at the Spindel'vara clan. "Time provides clues to interpret much that we experience in the Dreaming. But sometimes, meaning is as clear as rain. Despite what Brynjold says, Spindel'vara are *not* our friends. Remember that, Jagaru. No matter what happens or how friendly Spindel'vara seem, they aren't friends of the Kāfe'vind. Or of any from the Myrskog."

"It sounds like there's bad blood between you," Imbica said.

Omma leaned heavily on her walking stick as she stared at the Spindel'vara Clan readying their prize prisoner. She sighed. "A tale for another time."

Pelagia urged the Spindel'vara to allow the Dynasty soldiers and Dio to return to Partha, but they denied her request. Her argument seemed half-hearted to Aldewin. *I suppose she can claim that she tried to act on their behalf.*

Pelagia then argued that the Jagaru and Myrskog folks should be free to go. "Surely, you cannot take them prisoner when they were *my* prisoners. They have not committed crimes against Spindel'vara."

Brynjold sounded as though he agreed with her, but the skull-masked mage said, "You *say* they were your prisoners. But we believe nothing you say. They could be Dynasty spies."

Shel laughed out loud, and Aldewin was ready to protest.

But Omma touched his arm and shook her head. "We are in the web, Varskog."

With great effort, Aldewin restrained his protest. *If I survive this damnable web, I'll find somewhere far from web spinners and power-hungry people.*

Brynjold relented. "Ketla is right. We will take you all to Sofan Drek. Leid Thrud will sort this out." He sent a pointed glare at Ketla, the skull-masked mage. "And Leid Thrud's word will be law, do you understand?"

Ketla glared at him but gave Brynjold a single nod.

Having settled their plan, the Spindel'vara surrounded their group, now only thirteen. Ketla wove magical bindings around all their group save for Shel. Aldewin had never experienced a magic binding spell used against him before. Ketla's binding irritated like an itch in an out-of-reach place. Aldewin tried to gather Menaris energy, but it was like trying to remember a name and being unable to recall it. Menaris was all around him, yet he could not gather it to himself.

Aldewin asked Imbica, "Can you free us of these magic shackles?"

Sweat beaded on Imbica's forehead as she tested Ketla's binding for a weakness. After several minutes, her face crimson and sweat-soaked, she sighed. "Her weaving is tight and made of at least three elements. I do not know how to undo an earth element weave. I'm sorry."

"No need to apologize," Aldewin said as he scratched at his neck. "Damned irritating."

"It helps if you try not to focus on it," Imbica said.

They marched out of the glen, leaving Nivi and his family behind, and traveled the same narrow trail they'd traversed earlier. Going downhill, it took less than an hour to return to the main road leading to Sofan Drek. As they marched north, Hiyadi kissed the horizon.

Unlike in the southerly places like Solia or Juinar, the Iska'kog sunset didn't blaze fiery orange and red. Instead, Hiyadi's dusk painted the sky violet and blue. Nearly at full and rising early, Lumine helped Niyadi illuminate the road enough to prevent them sinking knee-deep in large, muddy ruts.

It was too dark, though, to see beyond the road. Aldewin saw no fires or the warm glow of candlelight beaming from homes. Chilly air descended as soon as Hiyadi went to his rest. Insects and night birds sang night's song.

After nearly an hour, the road wound west. On the horizon, lights glowed.

"That must be Sofan Drek," Imbica said.

"It is," Omma said.

The warm glow of fire and hearth lit a wide swath of the northern horizon.

"Perhaps my eyes play tricks, but it appears nearly as large as Partha," Aldewin said.

"I do not know about that," Omma said. "As I have never set foot in Partha. But your eyes do not deceive you, Varskog. Sofan Drek is far larger than Leivby Village. Looks to have grown by bounds, too, since I last visited."

Yngvari asked, "How long has it been since you were here, Modra Omma?"

Omma chuckled. "Modras excel at many things, but keeping time is not one of them." She pondered the question momentarily. "I reckon it has been over thirty years. Much has changed." Omma sighed. "If only the changes had been for the better."

Still on the outskirts of Sofan Drek, additional Spindel'vara warriors popped from thickets to join their march. Some appeared young and bore the same web tattoos on their chins and necks as the people who they'd fought in the glen. But the closer they got to Sofan Drek, the warriors who joined grew broader. Many sported intricate webbings tattooed on their faces from forehead to chest. They now marched with a small army toward what seemed like the edge of the known world.

Unlike the cities of Partha, Qülla, and Bardivia, defensive walls did not surround Sofan Drek. The city had no parapets or catwalks for archers. There wasn't even a guard hut for sentries. *They don't seem concerned about protecting themselves from raids or invasions.* Sofan Drek's isolated location gave protection from attacks by land, and its icy coast protected it from invasions by sea. *And the army hidden in the bush along the road protects it from raids,* Aldewin thought. *Anyone trying to come here must pass through a well-hidden gauntlet.*

"It feels like they knew we were coming even before we did," Shel said.

"A network of able scouts, I suppose," Imbica said.

Omma tsked. "Pah, they've no need for scouts. Their Crowskir see all from the comfort of their fires."

"I thought you said they don't enter the Dreaming like Modra do," Aldewin said.

"They don't. We Modra explore futures the Weavers reveal. But Crowskir vision the here and now. I must admit, they are quite skilled at it."

If Aldewin could have either of the two skills, he'd have preferred the Crowskir sight. *I can handle foresight about now. But I don't know how to ready myself for multiple possible futures.*

They arrived by the main road at the southeastern outskirts of Sofan Drek. The tiny houses were built with stone foundations dug into the permafrost. Chimneys sprouted from sod-covered roofs, and smoke curled into the night sky. Some homes had stone pens for a family's personal livestock of chickens and northern wooly drey. Instead of glass windows, most had holes left in the stone covered by thin vellum sheets or oil paper. Lights within made the tiny cottages glow like night bugs against the town's cultivated fields, icy tundra, and sparse birch forests.

As they neared the central hub of Sofan Drek, the road widened and was paved in mottled grey and brown stone. People poured from their homes and stood alongside the road, eager perhaps to investigate the noisy procession of what was now close to a hundred marching warriors with their prized prisoners.

At the edges of Sofan Drek, the onlookers watched silently or quietly whispered with their neighbors. Now in the city proper, people hissed, booed, and shouted crude names at Pelagia.

Walking behind Pelagia and the Dynasty prisoners, Aldewin couldn't see Pelagia's expression. He imagined she stoically ignored—outwardly, anyway—the hate cast toward her from the onlookers.

The road curved westward, and they entered a wide boulevard covered in cobbled stones. Sea birds called, and waves lapped. The air smelled of briny ocean.

Stone buildings, most two stories high, lined the road on either side. People leaned out windows, perhaps hoping to glimpse what had raised such a commotion. Though the Spindel'vara warriors wore leather and fur from head to foot, these city dwellers opted for pale-grey silk or tan linen shirts or tunics over long pants made of grey, black, or brown wool. Both women and men bore face tattoos. Instead of complex web tattoos covering their entire faces, most had a single "thread" from the hairline ending in a lone spider between the eyes.

Brynjold led the group onto a side road that ascended a small hill away from the water's edge. Builders had dug a large round stone foundation into the earth and built a multi-tiered wooden structure atop it.

"That is the Leid's house. Since Spindel'vara Leids are almost always Crowskir, they call it Crowskir House," Omma said.

"Men are never Leids of this clan?" Aldewin asked.

"Not for the last three hundred years," Omma said. "We of the Myrskog believe men and women should share leadership of our people. Sometimes, the Leid is a man; other times, it is a woman. Our Eldurskir is a mix of people representing all types of folks within our clan."

"But Modras are always women," Yngvari added.

"Only because men—" Omma cast a glance toward Aldewin. "*Most* men cannot enter the Dreaming."

"In what way?" Imbica asked.

Omma laughed. "They inhale the vapors and see nothing but the insides of their eyelids."

They chuckled at this, but Yngvari added, "But there have been men who have seen. And afterward, their minds were like a spooked herd, running this way and that."

"They cannot handle the sideways slant of knowing what we see in the Dreaming," Omma said. "Of course, our Varskog here did just fine."

Aldewin didn't respond. *That remains to be seen*, he thought. *I'm not keen to do it again.*

When they reached the bottom of the small mount upon which the Crowskir House was built, Brynjold halted. He said to Ketla, "Take these Dynasty skishaturs to the holding pit to await Crowskir Thrud's decision."

Ketla smiled, and since she wore a half skull over her eyes and nose as a mask, she looked like a skull smiling. Ketla and a half dozen Spindel'vara warriors pushed and shoved at the Dynasty soldiers and Dio to separate them from the pack.

"I'm not with them," Dio said. With bound hands, Dio gestured to Pelagia with his head. "I'm with her."

"How precious. Ylfa has a pet." Using the handle of her war axe, Ketla shoved Dio hard in the back. "If you're her favorite, we'll make sure you get extra special treatment." Ketla sank her axe handle into Dio's gut, doubling him over. "Now, get going."

Dio rose, his face red and angry, but he walked as ordered. He called over his shoulder. "Tell them, Pelagia. I'm not with the Dynasty. I'm from Partha."

"From Partha, hey?" Ketla smacked Dio across the back with her axe handle. Even above the din of the large gathering, the crack across his back echoed.

"That's going to leave a mark," Shel said. Her matter-of-fact tone contained no empathy for Dio's plight.

Pelagia remained as stoic as ever, unmoved by Dio's desperate pleas. She said and did nothing to intercede on his behalf.

Shel tsked and whispered, "He expected her to be loyal to him? I doubt Pelagia is loyal to anyone but Pelagia."

Aldewin nodded and said, "That skishatur will probably meet the end he deserves."

"Let us hope so," Imbica said.

Aldewin wasted no more time on Dio. *The "holding pit" sounds unpleasant, but what if our fate is even worse?*

Brynjold pointed at Pelagia and Aldewin's party. "You lot—come with me. Leid Thrud will speak with you."

Brynjold led the group, flanked by a warrior and a battle mage. Pelagia walked with her head high, back straight. Magical bindings shimmered around them. Omma, Yngvari, Aldewin, and Shel walked just behind Pelagia.

They entered Crowskir House through a massive wooden double door. Carvings decorated the edges of the doors. The design began at the top with a forest spider whose webs created a rectangle pattern around the door.

The webs morphed from a crow's head to a wolf and finally a snake. The locking pattern repeated, creating a border. At the center, each door contained an inlay of polished whalebone, onyx, and white quartz depicting the Spindel'vara sigil—a crow's head against a spider's web.

From the exterior, Crowskir House looked airy inside, with a tall ceiling that matched the central roofline's three-story-high pitch. But once inside, minimal light from oil lamps and candlelight made the interior feel dark and squashed.

Hallways led away from the foyer to both left and right. The central area was open and contained multiple firepits around which benches had been dug into the earth and covered in the same grey and tan cobblestone as the streets outside. Pillows large enough for lounging and covered in fuzzy wool covers or colorful, intricately woven tapestries lined the bench seats. Several people lounged in this area, smoking pipes and drinking from large, earthenware mugs.

Upon a rounded dais at the farthest end of the hall, a thick-waisted elderly woman with long, unkempt black hair sat cross-legged on a wide, curved wooden seat. Incense smoke swirled around her, and colorful glass-mosaic oil lamps hung from the beams, providing a warm glow. The woman's eyes were cloudy and almost entirely white. *She likely sees only shapes and shadows.*

Two additional women sat on floor cushions on either side of the central woman. They, too, had hair as black as night, though they wore theirs plaited in a fishtail fashion, their braids pulled to the front and long enough to nearly reach their waists.

Brynjold approached the dais, bowed his head slightly, and with arms out to his sides, palms facing the dais, he bent his upper body forward. "Leid Thrud," he said. "Revered Crowskirs."

The women said together, "Rise, brother."

He did so and gestured behind him. "We found The Defiler at the sacred Fros'vinspri Glen, just as you said we would, Leid Thrud."

All the women collectively hissed. Leid Thrud, however, did not. She expressed no emotion, her face a mask of cold indifference.

"You have done well, Brynjold," Leid Thrud said. Given the length of her rule, age should have thinned her hair and voice, but neither was altered by time. Thrud's hair contained no grey, and her voice had a rich timbre. When she spoke, the Leid commanded the room.

Thrud rested her hands on a black walking stick so gnarled and smooth it looked like it had been carved from the world's first tree. She pounded it once on the wooden dais and called out, "You have earned your cheeks today, Brynjold."

Brynjold bowed again and said, "Thank you, Leid. Would you like me to advise you of—"

Thrud cut him off. "We do not need dry recitations, Brynjold. We have seen."

One of the Crowskir pulled a long, thin-handled pipe from her lips, blew out a smoke ring, and cackled. "We see."

The other women, their voices overlapping, repeated her words. "We see! We see! We see!"

Taking the hint, Brynjold bowed again and left, taking his warriors with him.

Brynjold was not leaving the Crowskir and Leid Thrud alone with the prisoners, though. In the shadows behind the dais, at least a dozen warriors with faces covered in tattooed webs stood with arms crossed. These men were as large as Aldewin, and some were even taller and with broader shoulders.

If they are as formidable as they look, I cannot defeat them without help. The thought was oddly thrilling. Aldewin had a latent hope that he could finally test his true mettle in battle rather than killing by stealth or against opponents with less skill and training. *To finally meet men of equal strength…*

The Leid and her Crowskir sisters probably didn't need the warriors for protection. Aldewin's time with Archon Kine, Mage Imbica, Enar'atori Yngvari, and Modra Omma had shown him that magic-wielding women were often more formidable than a burly man with an axe.

Discomforting silence filled the hall as Leid Thrud stared forward, her milky eyes likely seeing only dark shapes before her. Despite that, she finally said, "Step forward, Ylfa ag Thrud."

Yngvari gasped.

Shel whispered, "What? What is it?"

Whispering back, Yngvari said, "Ag Thrud. That means 'of Thrud.' That means Ylfa—Pelagia—is Leid Thrud's granddaughter."

As Modra Omma had suggested to me before. Omma was correct.

While Yngvari explained to Shel, Pelagia said, "Ylfa ag Thrud is dead."

Murmurs rose among the Spindel'vara people gathered in the room behind them.

Pelagia added, "I killed her." She spat the words out with venom to poison the listener.

Thrud didn't react. "We know what you did. We *see* you, Ylfa. Oh, you can try to hide the truth of who—what—you are. But *we* know."

"Enough games, old woman. I detested your attempts at wisdom when I lived under this roof. I have even less patience for your false power now."

Leid Thrud shifted slightly, and her mouth drew into a thin line. "Still as defiant as ever. And no more patience than when you were a pup. Worry not, Mistress of the Menagerie, we will get to you. But first, we sense a Modra. Can that be Omma of the Kāfe'vind?"

Omma pressed forward but didn't bow or show deference. *I am gladdened to see Modra Omma remains proud and does not easily bend the knee*, Aldewin thought.

"Thrud, it has been long. Your eyes show you have spent much time among the Weave. I wonder, though, if it has made you wise?"

Thrud's robust laugh filled the hall. "My duties as Leid chain me to this chair in Sofan Drek. Oh, how I have missed gatherings of the Crowskir and Modra. These young people don't know how to have fun anymore, do they, Omma?"

The other Crowskir chattered and laughed too. They acted as though the fate of five people didn't hang in the balance.

Omma didn't join their laughter, but she smiled warmly. "Simpler times, perhaps. Fewer complications from southern lands."

One of the Crowskir said, "Or from Partha, that fetid pool."

They all chittered and agreed with her.

Thrud pounded her cane again, and the hall quieted. "Perhaps we can enjoy a warm reunion later. My granddaughter boils with impatience. And what fool mage festooned you with that silly binding?" Thrud leaned her cane against a thigh and, hands free, gathered Menaris energy. She wound her hands, whispered an incantation, then thrust her hands outward toward Pelagia. The shimmery air surrounding Pelagia dissipated. "You came all this way, itching under that silly binding, rather than reveal it did not hold you?"

Pelagia remained quiet, though Aldewin sensed less tension from her now than before.

Imbica whispered to him, "They do itch. Gods, it's enough to drive a mage mad."

Thrud then released the bindings on Aldewin and the others. "Ketla does not have Crowskir sight. She did not know you were Ylfa's prisoners and not her allies."

Or that none of us can best Pelagia, and thus all of us are in her *command, not Spindel'vara's,* Aldewin thought.

Thrud leaned forward, again resting her hands on her cane. Though she still stared at the horizon, she spoke to Pelagia. "Tell me, granddaughter, what will it take to keep you from burning Sofan Drek to the ground?"

I did not expect that, Aldewin thought.

Apparently, no one else did either. The Crowskir mumbled among themselves, and the warriors behind them shifted nervously.

Pelagia got right to the point. "Exalted Xa'Vatra sent me to acquire the Heart of Menaris. I will leave with it, Thrud ag Isabré, and turn anyone who tries to stop me into cinders. If you love your people as you claim, you will deliver the Heart to me. Give me the Heart of Menaris, and I will leave Sofan Drek and its people unharmed."

I notice she makes no promise to leave Thrud alive.

The Crowskir hissed, and some laughed while the warriors stepped forward, their faces now out of the shadows. Leid Thrud raised a single hand, and the Spindel'vara warriors halted their movement forward. With her cane, she rapped the nearest Crowskir in the shoulders, hushing the assembled.

"I will not hand you the Heart of Menaris, Ylfa. And you will not take it either. Even if I was inclined to offer it, you are wildly mistaken about its nature." Leid Thrud sighed. "If only you had remained by my side, Ylfa. *You* would sit the Crowskir throne, not I. You would have learned *all* about the Heart of Menaris."

"I know plenty," Pelagia said.

Thrud laughed. She pointed her cane at Pelagia. "You learned just enough to make you dangerous. Acting on pride and youthful arrogance, you ran before I revealed the Heart's deep secrets." Thrud ran her hands along the smooth wood of her Leid's chair. "You could have owned this very seat. Become the Leid of the largest, most prosperous clan in the Vatnoyer. Instead, you sought status in the so-called 'civilized' world." Thrud's lips curled into a look of disgust. "What a banal thing to do. So beneath the blood of our line."

Pelagia didn't argue the point or show offense at Thrud's accusations. She pressed open her tunic's neckline and revealed the yindril-bark scar. "Pondering the past serves no purpose. I died, you see. A sorcerer made a bargain with Vay'Nada, no doubt to save his own precious ass. He offered a yindril's soul for mine." Pelagia thumped her chest. "I have the heart of a yindril."

The people and Crowskirs inside Crowskir House gasped. But Thrud showed no emotion upon hearing that her granddaughter now had a bestial heart.

"The yindril's magic is now my own. I don't need your blind eyes or beatings to see more than you ever will."

The Crowskir murmured again. A few looked aghast at Pelagia while others hissed again. They visibly recoiled from the woman they'd once known as Ylfa.

Leid Thrud, though, merely closed her eyes, shook her head, and sighed. "I failed you, Ylfa." Wetness played at her eyes, but she sucked in a breath, and the potential tears vanished.

"You failed both of us." Pelagia glared at Leid Thrud. "I saw her, you know. In death, I dreamed. And in that dream, she was there. Briefly, but I felt her warmth." Pelagia's voice shrieked, and her body quaked with anger. Spittle glistened on her lip. "I'm taking her too, you spiteful crow shite. You asked what it would take to save your shithole town? That's it. Give me the Heart, and release Jorfala."

These last words made Thrud shrink back and instantly altered her demeanor. After a moment, she said, "I cannot release Jorfala."

Pelagia laughed. "You *will* release her." Her voice rose in volume and pitch, her hands balled into fists at her side.

Though Thrud had destroyed the magical binding Ketla had woven around Pelagia, the air around Pelagia still shimmered. She crackled with skyfire energy and glowed white and purple.

Under her breath, Imbica said, "The old woman needs to be careful. Pelagia has little control of her moods or her magic." Imbica shifted to stand behind Aldewin so he shielded her from view. She wound her hands slowly and in a tight motion rather than her usual more sweeping arcs.

Perhaps hearing Imbica's warning or realizing how out of control she seemed, Pelagia took calming breaths before continuing. "You had me brought here to stand accused of crimes against the Fros'vinspri."

"Crimes against the Spindel'vara," one of the Crowskir shouted.

Voices of assent rose.

Pelagia ignored them. She pointed a thin finger at Thrud. "*You* have committed far worse crimes. And I will have *my* justice. My terms are simple. Release Jorfala and *give* me the Heart."

Thrud's eyes closed, and she sat momentarily as though listening for something. Her eyes still shut, she said, "So much raw power. Such a waste, really. You lack the patience to learn. And you know half what you think you do. You may have taken a yindril's heart but none of its wisdom." She leaned forward again. "You say you came for the Heart of Menaris. But do you know what it is? Have you seen it?"

"I don't need to see it. I have felt it. In here." Pelagia rapped her chest with a fist. "I *know* it's alive. Its beat lives now within me."

In a voice that seemed loud enough to carry to the Fros'vinspri Glen and back, Thrud yelled, "Its magic thrums within us all, Ylfa. That doesn't mean we own it."

"You hoard it here," Aldewin said. He immediately regretted opening his mouth. *Why in Sicara's name did I say that?* Sweat slicked his palms, and his stomach rumbled.

Aldewin coughed nervously. "Look, I hate Pelagia. To be honest, I'd like to see her dead. Again. But from what I've seen, all your people are like her. The Spindel'vara, the Tradsmikor—the Iska'kog have traded their natural heritage for gold, silver, and favor with the noble Houses."

Aldewin expected the Leid to order him thrown into the holding pit. Instead, she wore a bemused smile. "Ah, the Varskog speaks. Son of the Spindel'vara, raised outside the Vatnoyer. The man with no clan." When she saw his puzzled look, she continued. "Oh yes, your bodir was a member of Spindel'vara. Much like my granddaughter, left to seek fortune in a distant land, not realizing the treasure buried beneath his feet."

Aldewin's heart raced, his mouth dry. His voice came out as thin as dried reeds. "You knew my father?"

"You mean the man whose seed made you? Aye, that I did." Thrud sniffed the air. "Do not seek him, Varskog. The weavers cut his life thread from the Weave long ago."

In less time than it takes to blink an eye, Thrud dashed his hope to meet a father he'd never expected to know against the stony shore of this harsh place. His jaw twitched, and his chest felt tight from holding in the roiling emotions he kept inside.

"You may be born from Iska'kog seed, but you have been here less than a season. Yet you proclaim we Spindel'vara hoard the Heart of Menaris. You could not be further from the truth, Varskog."

Thrud turned her attention back to Pelagia. "I cannot give you what we do not own, Ylfa. And not even I possess the Heart of Menaris. We are merely its keepers, not its owners. For as long as our history remembers, we of the Spindel'vara have dutifully served our purpose."

"And what is that?" Imbica asked.

"To protect the Heart. To ensure no one disturbs it or tries what my woefully misguided granddaughter is attempting. We ensure the Heart of Menaris lives forever so that *all* people of Menauld have access to its gifts."

"But why?" Shel called out. "What the fuck is this thing?"

Leid Thrud sat back and said, "I will not tell you what it is. Only the Leid can know its true nature. But I will tell you why we protect it. The Heart is a wellspring, you see."

"No, I'm afraid I do not see," said Imbica.

Crowskir Thrud pointed her cane at Imbica. "Listen, mage. Not with your ears but with your animus. Your *soul*. What do you hear?"

Imbica paused, and as she sought the Still Point of Menaris, so did Aldewin. Soon, he felt it and knew Imbica did too. The faint but unmistakable thrum of what felt like a massive, powerful heart. But the thrum was more than a vessel for blood. Something else. Something Aldewin had difficulty naming but felt like he'd always known. The thrum of life he'd sensed ever since they landed on Vatnoyer shores.

"There," Leid Thrud whispered. "You *feel* it, don't you? That, Mage Imbica, is the source."

"Source of what?" Imbica asked.

"Of *all* human magic. That is the Heart of Menaris. And if we allow anyone to take it for themselves, magic as we humans know it would cease to exist. The Heart of Menaris is a gift from the gods, you see. Intended for all. No one can possess the Heart." Leid Thrud pointed her cane at Pelagia. "We will not let *you* plunder it."

From outside the hall, something screeched. Thunder rumbled and shook the rafters, sending the suspended oil lamps swinging.

Purple-white energy sizzled around Pelagia again, and she gave a wry laugh. "Your army is not large enough to stop me. No human army is." She said this with absolute confidence.

Thrud rose then, as did the Crowskir seated around her. Thrud sang a high-pitched note that reminded Aldewin of the horrid Rend sound he'd heard the Rajani dragomancers sing at Volenex. The other Crowskir repeated her Rend, and dragons answered with a low, rumbling yell.

"No *human* army can stop you, Ylfa. Fortunately, our dragons can."

CHAPTER 22

ISHNA

Though Aurixia's roots healed Docar's wound, the bleeding drained his strength. Unlike a Primal dragon, magic did not fuel his life. Though their mission to find Veridia pulled at Ishna, they could not risk pressing ahead before Docar regained vigor.

"We will hunt, rest, and recuperate here until the coterie is strong again," Ishna said.

Aurixia nursed Docar with zeal, bringing him fresh game to fuel his recovery. Côzhili and Loxen scouted together, flying high enough to avoid Two-Legged projectile weapons. On the third day, Ishna noticed they flew with their wing tips touching. *Earth and fire meet in that pairing. At long last, a new love has toppled the dam Côzhili built around her heart after she lost her last vôsh'lavi.*

Docar watched the pair as well. "I hope Loxen does not disappoint your sa'gamlin."

Ishna puffed an icy breath. "Look at them, Docar. Loxen does not flit from one lover's wing to the next. He has warmed to her as she has to him."

"Oh, I do not question his affection for her."

Ishna slapped his backside with her tail. "Spit it out, Docar. What worry should Côzhili have about him?"

Docar hopped backward, out of reach of her quick-flitting tail. "It is nothing personal to Côzhili. She is more than worthy of a love to last to the next age. But Loxen is Ignati faction through and through."

"And?"

"And… My egg-father will not be bound by dragomancers in the southern lands forever. And when he calls Ignati to his side, they will flock to him to do as he commands. If he says scatter to the winds, they will flee to this world's far corners to live solo as Vahgrin believes is best."

Ishna gazed skyward at the two dragons in silhouette against a pale-grey sky. Their wings still touching, they flew in unison. The sight warmed her ancient, icy heart. "Do you not think Loxen, after the closeness he has built with Côzhili, would instead choose to stay with her?"

Docar thumped twice.

"You are Vahgrin's hatchling, yet you have never lived solo for long like other Ignati faction Dragos. Cannot Loxen do the same?"

Puffing steam, Docar laughed. "I left Ignati faction not long after my hatching, remember? Century after century of solitary life and hierarchies never appealed to me."

"I wonder why. What makes you different?"

Docar breathed fire onto the freezing stone ledge, warming it to his liking. "Perhaps only Zedris has the wisdom to solve the puzzle. We could ask my egg-father, but he is currently unavailable. I can only guess that when Vahgrin made me, he fueled the egg with his most amiable essence."

Ishna didn't respond but pondered Docar's words. *It is perhaps a better guess than Docar realizes.* She was more than a thousand years older than Docar. Ishna knew Vahgrin in the days when Docar hatched. *During that era, Vahgrin basked in the warm wings of his one and only vôsh'lavi.*

After a time, Docar napped, and Ishna turned inward. She rarely allowed herself to spend time with the memories of her ancient past. Of the time before the Jik'Madar. But in the relative peace of the overcast morning, Ishna pondered what Docar had said.

Deep in the trance of meditating on her early memories, Quen's droning, insistent presence stole Ishna's peace.

What now, Quen?

Warm breath tickles my ear. Is my love near?

The winged one is my vôsh, not your Two-Legged love.

Not winged, but a Two-Legged. Amber at his neck and a poison blade at his thigh.

Do you sense Aldewin?

"I'm already caught in webs," he said. *"They might as well be yours."*

Once again he is trapped in a web, but not one of my making.

Aldewin is near?

Aldewin. And others. They chase the Heart.

Quiet now, Quen. Listen. We must focus.

With wingtips to the ground, Ishna sought the stillness of the deep quiet of a mind without internal chatter.

For many moments, Ishna meditated on emptiness. She tried to sense the connection she and Quen had with Aldewin.

There. Aldewin touches the source of magic. And he is near.

Ishna blinked and cleared the shroud of meditation from her mind. She called to Côzhili, Loxen, and Aurixia to return to their camp.

His movement languid, Docar blinked and roused himself from sleep. Perhaps fearing an attack by Two-Leggeds, Docar was on his feet instantly. "Do we face an enemy, vôsh?" He surveyed the valley below.

"Calm yourself. We are not in present danger. But we must cut our respite short."

Docar flapped his wings and stretched his once-wounded neck from side to side. "You know I loathe rest and was ready to soar days ago. But why the urgency, vôsh?"

She gazed past the taiga forest valley and northwest toward the ocean. "The water flows quickly now, Docar."

Côzhili and the others landed, and Ishna immediately told them they would leave for the region where Aurixia had sensed her egg-mother. The youngest dragon hopped excitedly. None opposed setting out at last for the final push to liberate Veridia.

"You did not answer my question. Why now?"

"My lost sister calls. Do you not feel her?"

Aurixia thumped once, but the others did not.

"No matter, for soon, you will." Ishna rose, and the others joined her in the air. "Our journey to find the Spring Dragon soon ends. Come. The tides of fate pull us into deep waters, sa'gamlin."

Soon, we will be reunited, my sister.

Chapter 23

Aldewin

Standing now in a small group just outside Crowskir house, the once briny sea air smelled of sulfurous fumes and charred hopes. Three dragons soared above, their massive flapping wings stirring up dust as they circled closer, obscuring Aldewin's vision. Enshrouded in dust, the three dragons were like specters, silhouettes of Aldewin's nightmares since Volenex.

Though typically unfazed by danger, Shel trembled. Aldewin shoved his three companions behind him, hoping his larger frame would provide at least some protection for them should the dragons unleash an attack. Aldewin expected Shel to call him a thukna's arse for this macho display of brotherly protection, but she didn't.

The Crowskir continued their discordant Rend. Dragons screeched and called to each other in the same language Aldewin had heard Ishna and Vahgrin speak. Behind Leid Thrud and the other Crowskir, the three black dragons landed. Hot dragon breath met evening's cool air creating wispy fog. With their heads and tails low, the dragons moved toward them.

Instinct told Aldewin to run. *Though not as large as Vahgrin or even Ishna, they could bite me into two, scald me to a cinder, or rip me to shreds with those razor-sharp talons.* Their talons made him think of Quen, and thoughts of her always made him aware of the amber pendant he hadn't removed in nearly eight months. *I must remain calm and do what I can to diffuse tensions here. I need Pelagia's power to restore Quen.*

Aldewin called on every ounce of training to calm his racing heart and the urge to flee. He reached for his Vandu blade, but it wasn't there. *I must get that back from Brynjold.* The poison-infused dagger had been his constant companion since he survived the Vandu trials. More than a mere dagger, the magical blade had a mind of its own. The Vandu protected Aldewin, and on cold nights, sang its bittersweet song of the Dread Sister. An odd but welcome comfort. Its absence panicked him.

Sweat beaded on Aldewin's forehead and his chest felt like a vise clamped it tightly. He closed his hand around the amber pendant and it warmed instantly beneath his touch. It had become his talisman and reminded him what he must fight for.

The largest of the three dragons crept toward Thrud with head down and eyes lowered. The dragon thrust his snout between her and the Crowskir next to her.

Leid Thrud stroked the dragon's black-skinned snout. "Meet Vingaska."

The dragon glared, and his nostrils flared. Vingaska permitted her touch but didn't look pleased about it.

Pelagia, still standing straight-backed and stoic, said nothing.

"Come now, Ylfa. You were always quick to speak your mind. Have you no thoughts on our dragon allies?"

The Mistress of the Menagerie remained silent.

Her silence is impressive. It's difficult to remain quiet when someone presses you to fight.

Thrud frowned, perhaps upset Pelagia refused to engage.

Omma said, "Where do these dragons hail from? And how did you take control of such powerful naturfrandi?"

Leid Thrud's look brightened. "About eight months ago, these three awakened. Clawed their way from their barrows just west of here. Fought to see the light of day once again."

Her eyes were wide and bright with joy. She again stroked Vingaska's nose. "They rose from sacred burial tombs, marked by our Spindel'vara ancestors. We watched. Protected. Waited. And we were there for the awakening. Ready to sing our song, the Rend. Taught to us by our mothers and our mothers' mothers."

"This Rend—it's what I witnessed the Rajani dragomancers do at Volenex. They use it to control Vahgrin, the Primal dragon of Vatra," Aldewin said.

Thrud pointed to Aldewin, modulated her voice into a series of clicks and chirps, then said, "Aldewin."

Vingaska lifted his head and stared at Aldewin with eyes the color of a Sulmére sunset. The stare discomfiting, Aldewin shifted.

"Yes, Vingaska, we know him. Touched by the Dragos, that one. But is he friend or foe to dragonkin?" Thrud shrugged her shoulders. "Remains to be seen."

Aldewin wasn't certain himself if he was a friend to dragons. *I must be, for now. At least until we somehow wrest Quen from Ishna. After that… well, Thrud is right. It remains to be seen.*

Finally, Pelagia spoke. "All my youth, you trained me to be Crowskir and someday to take your place as Leid. And yet you never mentioned dragon barrows or this song you call the Rend. Am I now to believe you knew a secret plan devised by our ancestors to control dragons if they arose?"

"As I said, there is much you did not learn. If only you hadn't run from your duties."

Her laugh shrill, Pelagia sounded near to losing her cool. Voice seething, she said, "I did not run from duty. I *escaped* your abuse."

Once again, purple-tinged skyfire crackled around Pelagia. She looked as though she had emerged from a thundercloud.

Vingaska lifted his head and opened his mouth. From his throat came a sound like a cauldron boiling.

Thrud put a hand to Vingaska as she sang her Rend again, trying to calm him.

Omma said, "Mistress, I suggest you stand down before Vingaska incinerates us."

Vingaska jerked his head back. His eyes rolled, and he screeched. He backed away from the Crowskir as if trying to escape their Rend.

The Crowskir did not let up. Their cries made everyone wince and furrow their brows in discomfort. After a few moments, Vingaska bent his head low again, his eyes once again downcast.

Tears in her eyes, Yngvari's voice quavered. "They're torturing the dragons."

Pelagia cast a glance back at Yngvari. "Where do you think I learned how to control animals? And people." She returned her attention to Thrud. "My grandmother is the master of commanding obedience. She taught me everything I know about using pain as a weapon. And how to wield it."

Like heat waves shimmering over the dunes in summer, the air around Pelagia flickered. Purple veins threaded her hands, balled into fists at her sides.

As though Pelagia had not hurled accusations of cruelty toward her, Thrud said, "We cannot abide an impasse. Say you will rejoin Spindel'vara. Stop being a workhorse for that child playing at being a queen. Return to your clan, Ylfa. To your family. If you return, I will teach you the Rend, and you, too, will have mastery over a dragon. You will have *true* power. That's what you really want, isn't it?"

Pelagia let out a pained cry. "I told you. Ylfa is dead!" The surrounding air lit up. Crackling lightning tore slits in Pelagia's pristine leather jacket and pants. Fighting an invisible battle within, Pelagia's voice was hoarse. "You know what I came for. Take me to her."

Thrud's expression softened, but she offered her granddaughter no aid.

Omma whispered to Aldewin. "Reach out to Pelagia, Varskog. Offer her any aid you can give."

He attempted to touch Pelagia—to determine what impaired her. But before his hand reached her, Pelagia shuddered, and bolts of skyfire pulsed from her. The mini lightning storm jolted Aldewin, sending him backward. Seeing this, the Spindel'vara guards surrounding her stepped back as well.

Pelagia's voice was strained. "You will take me to her. I will raze this city if you do not show her to me."

Thrud shook her head. "I told you. I cannot release Jorfala. She's—"

Menauld quaked beneath them. Pelagia's cry thundered as she sent a pulse of skyfire in a circle around her. "Show her to me!" she screamed.

Her unruly attack sent two of the Crowskir nearest to Pelagia to the ground. Their faces were singed and already turning black from burns. Their agonized screams could curdle blood. They pawed at their faces, trying to ease their pain.

Two Spindel'vara mages stepped forward and ushered the elderly women away. Now, down two Crowskir singing the Rend, the dragons whipped their heads and pranced, looking like they were trying to free themselves from Crowskir control.

Thrud shouted, "Crowskir and dragon handlers, take the dragons back to their pit. Chain them for now. We can't let this get out of hand."

The remaining Crowskir and Leid Thrud screeched their Rend. With the aid of a dozen warriors clad head to toe in thick leather plate armor and bearing cudgels, they finally chained the dragons and led them away.

Torturing these beasts with the Rend is despicable. But their Rend might be the only thing keeping the dragons from obliterating us.

Once the dragons were gone, Pelagia advanced on Thrud. Lightning bursts pulsed from her in violent waves.

Thrud's eyes widened, and she stumbled backward, away from Pelagia. She tried to speak, but her mouth had gone dry. Her voice warbled with fear.

"Pelagia is going to kill that woman," Shel said.

"I say good riddance," Yngvari said. "Such an awful person—to torture naturfrandi. She deserves to pay the ultimate price."

"I cannot disagree with you," Aldewin said. "But this Heart of Menaris—whatever it truly is—may be the key to separating Quen from her dragon host, Ishna."

Aldewin called to Pelagia. "You need her, Pelagia. She holds the key to the Heart. Only Leid Thrud knows how to access it."

Now in a frenzied state, Pelagia whipped her head like a wounded animal. Even the blood in her eyes pulsed with skyfire. She turned her glowing purple-white gaze on Aldewin.

Omma whispered, "The bargain made with the Shadow to bring her back to life has twisted the yindril's gentle nature. Its wholesome magic is now enmeshed with Vay'Nada's shadow."

"She is no longer human," Aldewin whispered back. "And highly unpredictable."

"Then we need to remember to approach her the way we approach a caged animal," Yngvari said.

"And how is that?" Shel asked.

"Slowly," Yngvari said. "And gently. At all times, we must show her we are no threat."

"Wise counsel," Aldewin said. *I only hope Leid Thrud understands this as well.*

Regaining some semblance of control, Pelagia halted her advance on Thrud. She panted, her voice ragged. "Only one thing will calm the yearning of my bestial soul. Take me to her."

Thrud shook her head, but before she could speak, Pelagia said through gritted teeth, "If you do not grant me this one kindness, I…" Tendrils of white-hot lightning pulsed from her, faster now. "I cannot control what the beast inside me will do."

Omma pled with Thrud. "Your granddaughter destroyed Tradsmikor, Thrud. You did not smell their burned flesh or see the remnants of their once-thriving village. The second-mightiest Iska'kog clan, reduced to ash and charred bone."

Thrud's eyes widened, and her lips trembled. "I—I did not know of this. How is it we Crowskir did not see the fate of Tradsmikor?"

"Because you see what I *want* you to see," Pelagia replied.

Pelagia continued to pulse with energy, but it calmed enough that Omma could get closer. "Do not surrender your people to the pitiable end Tradsmikor suffered. Let go your damnable pride, Thrud. Do as your granddaughter asks."

Tears pooled in Thrud's eyes. Her voice was soft and calm. "You do not understand. I'm protecting you, Ylfa. You say you have the heart of a yindril. But somewhere inside, you remain wee Ylfa. Jorfala's child. And I think neither the yindril nor the human in you will survive knowing what Jorfala has become."

Her voice wrenched with pain. Pelagia screamed, "None will survive if I do not!"

Thrud's head down, she exhaled. "So be it." She gazed up and met Omma's eyes. "The great unraveling begins."

Chapter 24

Aldewin

Thrud led Pelagia and the rest of their small group to a mounded ancient barrow outside the southwestern edge of Sofan Drek. Nearly two dozen Spindel'vara warriors accompanied them, keeping Pelagia, Aldewin, and the others in their party toward the group's center. Aldewin noticed Brynjold carried the Vandu blade he'd taken from Aldewin in a hip scabbard too large for the dagger. *It is a sin against Sicara to treat that blade with such carelessness.* As they trudged to the barrow, Aldewin mulled over various scenarios for retrieving the weapon.

After a half-hour hike up a steady rise, the group descended into a depression in the landscape. Scrub and spring grasses covered what looked like a symmetrical hillock. The stone lintel and moss-covered stone door frame offered the only evidence people had constructed the massive hill rather than being naturally occurring. Nature had done its best to reclaim the opening. Passers-by wouldn't notice the door if they weren't looking for it.

Once they arrived at the doorway, Thrud ordered her people to remain outside. When a burly warrior with a web-marked face protested, Thrud slammed her cane to the ground.

The larger sun was now fully set, and only Niyadi's pale light lit the night. Puffy bags under Thrud's eyes revealed her weariness. "Fréjoya and Skogi blast your iron hides to Vay'Nada's cruel shores." Gaining composure, her voice was once again commanding. "Your Leid has spoken. Stay here and watch over Modra Omma and the mage." She pointed her cane at Shel. "And make sure the trigger-happy archer does nothing stupid. The Sea Singer and Varskog will accompany me as I show Ylfa what she insists on seeing."

"I do not need these Fyrstua cousins with us," Pelagia said. The aura of skyfire energy around her had dissipated, but her face still shone purple from the pulsing veins under her skin.

At the doorway and gathering Menaris energy, Thrud gazed over her shoulder at them and said, "You may not need them, but *I* do."

Over the years, grass-covered soil had filled in the doorway opening. The entryway undisturbed, no one had entered—or exited—the crypt for centuries. *How can Pelagia's mother be in this ancient crypt? What could survive in such a place?*

Mumbling an incantation, Thrud moved her hands, palms facing the door, in a circular motion. As she did, the centuries-old-appearing earth blockage melted away. Within minutes, the ancient doorway no longer impeded their entry.

Leid Thrud took a torch and ordered two Spindel'vara guards to give their torches to Aldewin and Yngvari. "The wee sun's pale light will do us no good within. Stay close to one another."

Though she knew what they were stepping into, Leid Thrud looked anxious about it. She whispered a prayer to Skogi before entering. The builders had set the lintel so low even Thrud ducked to enter.

The doorway appeared like any other stone entry. But as soon as Aldewin stepped across the threshold, the world seemed… altered. Outside and only a few feet away, nearly two dozen people gathered. Their collected voices and movement filled the night with sound. Within the low, narrow stone passage, a magical ward dampened sound and cut them off from the outside world. They stood in a quiet so complete Aldewin heard the rush of blood in his ears and the beat of his heart.

But the sensation extended beyond absence of sound from outside the barrow. The feeling was familiar, like something Aldewin had experienced once before. The air smelled of skyfire and of the cold. Any lasting memory of joy drained from Aldewin like a hole cut in a bag of grain, the seed slowly pouring out as he moved through the winding passage as they moved farther down into the earth.

"Vay'Nada's shadow lives here," Aldewin said. He hadn't intended to speak the thought aloud but didn't regret it.

Yngvari reached for his hand. "Is that what I sense?"

Her thin fingers were like ice, and she trembled at his side.

Pelagia harrumphed. "Vay'Nada is a story intended to goad us into doing what those in power command." Venom dripped from her voice. "What you feel within these stony walls is the taint of an old woman's dark magic, nothing more."

Aldewin wanted to disagree with Pelagia. He had, after all, physically entered the Void, the Shadow realm from which some believed all evil arises. But he wasn't about to upset an unhinged person wielding untold power.

As they wound downward, musky dampness seeped through the plaster-covered earthen walls. Roots tried to reclaim the tunnel.

Time felt stretched, like they'd been traversing the downhill path for eons. Their torches still burned bright, so it was likely only minutes.

They arrived at the terminus, which opened into a circular room. Now deep within the crypt and cut off from the outside, the torches sputtered. Thrud thrust her arms out and spoke an incantation in an unknown language. Low braziers throughout the chamber flickered and burned with flame tinged green.

The chamber's stone floor looked like masons had set it yesterday. Nothing adorned the ceiling or walls. Except for the low, shallow bowls of green flame ringing the room, nothing existed within the chamber except a lone woman.

Covered only by the pale silvery hair flowing past her navel, the woman floated, suspended above the floor by an unseen magical force. Aldewin squinted, attempting to discern a magical weave of binding, but none was visible to him.

Aldewin had witnessed Zeniths suspend themselves during intense meditations, evidence that they had achieved a state of oneness with the gods and that their souls had left the mortal plane, at least for a time.

This was a different magic, though. The woman's body had withered, her skin like a raisin. Though she looked peaceful, lines pinched at the bridge of her nose, the only sign of discomfort.

Facing the woman, Pelagia fell to her knees. Her voice was as thin as a reed, and she cried, "Mama."

The hovering woman didn't respond. She showed no sign she heard them or knew they were there.

Yngvari gasped. "Is that—Jorfala? Pelagia's mother?"

Her shoulders hunched, hands on her cane, Thrud stood in the shadows. "It is."

Wetness played at the corners of Pelagia's eyes. Her voice came out thin and strained. "What did you do to her?"

Thrud stepped forward. Tear trails on her cheeks shimmered in the pale green light of the braziers. "This is what you traveled here for, Ylva. Your mama, Jorfala, *is* the Heart of Menaris."

Between choked sobs, Yngvari asked, "Is she… alive?"

"Yes, Sea Singer. My daughter lives. The tether that binds her also keeps her alive." Thrud paused a moment, collecting herself. "My mother was the Heart before your mother, Ylfa. That's why you never knew your grandmother."

"But what is—?" Aldewin shook his head. "I don't understand what's happening here. Why did you bind her to—?"

"*I* did not bind anyone," Thrud said, a testiness in her voice. "Jorfala volunteered to become the Heart. She serves not only Spindel'vara Clan but all humankind." Thrud brushed a weathered hand across her cheek. "So you see, Ylfa, I lost her too. My mother, my only daughter. You are not the only one to suffer for our duty—our Clan's duty—to the world."

Pelagia didn't acknowledge Thrud's words. She remained kneeling, staring into her mother's face, evincing no emotion about what she saw.

"What is she tethered to, Crowskir Thrud?" Yngvari asked.

Thrud gently rapped her cane on the stone floor. "Deep beneath Sofan Drek lies a well. A deep well of power. Of magical energy we call Menaris."

Aldewin chortled. "That's impossible. Val'Enara teaches Menaris does not dwell in one place but lives within everything and everywhere, all at once."

Thrud cast him a sideways glance. "A partial truth." She waved a hand in the air. "But we cannot fault them for not knowing what we never revealed. At least until now. There *is* a source for human magic. And we are standing atop it now."

Yngvari remained as skeptical as Aldewin. She shook her head, disbelieving. "The gods gifted us with Menaris. Skogi, Fréjoya, and the Green bless us with magic."

"A lie created to conceal the truth. And a lie told long enough becomes true." She pointed at suspended Jorfala and said, "*This* is the truth. Jorfala volunteered to be the conduit. She made an offering of herself to save someone she loved more than she loved life."

In a swift motion, Pelagia rose and rounded on Thrud. "Do not dare fill this chamber with your lies. There was no choice. No one living under your control ever had a choice."

Pelagia didn't cow Thrud. She met Pelagia's anger with ire of her own. "Do you think I wanted this? To see my dearest daughter taken from me as my mother was?" Her lip trembled. "*You* were supposed to be the one we committed to the Soul Rend. Every third generation, not two. That is how it has always been. Until now. Until you."

Both women shook, their faces twisted in anguish. They stood mere feet apart, each with both feet firmly entrenched in old hurts.

Finally, Pelagia spoke. "I do not care about tradition or duty or what generations before have done. I came for the Heart, and I *will* take it. Release her from this Soul Rend spell. Mama and I are leaving this place. Together."

Thrud shook her head. "You told me Ylfa is dead. Well, Jorfala died long ago. What you see suspended here—it is merely a husk. A vessel caught in time as her soul is consumed. That is the Soul Rend."

"Consumed by what?" Yngvari asked.

"By the Weavers? Vay'Nada? In truth, we Crowskirs no longer know—if we ever did."

"You agreed with an unknown force without knowing its true nature?" Aldewin asked.

Thrud glared at him. "I've seen the threads of the weave, Varskog. You have no standing to lay judgment at my doorstep."

She turned her attention back to Pelagia. "This pact is ancient. For countless generations, our foremothers made this sacrifice. Not solely for Spindel'vara's benefit but for *all* Menauld. Don't you see? We have a sacred honor, for without the Soul Rend, magic would not exist."

Thrud attempted to move closer to Pelagia and reached out to her. But Pelagia crackled again, and Thrud stepped away. "Ylfa, take comfort in this. Your mama's sacrifice brings the gift of Menaris to all the world. She is a hero," Thrud said.

The veins in Pelagia's neck pulsed, and lightning sparkled at her fingertips. "Comfort me?" Pelagia's laugh echoed off the stone walls. "Lies. Everything spilling from your mouth is a pile of beetle-infested dung." Cocking her head to the side, Pelagia stared blankly as if listening. She returned her attention to the Crowskir. "You don't feel it, do you?"

Pelagia's laughter sounded like the cackle Aldewin had heard from addle-brained wine sots who lived in the dark alleyways of the Shills. "The Soul Rend doesn't bring Menaris to the world. Oh no, dear grandmother. You sacrificed my mama for *your* power, as all Soul Rend victims have powered the Leids of Spindel'vara. Once her binding is severed, our magic will live on. But yours…"

Thrud shook her head vigorously. "That's—it's not true. My grandmother told me. The Soul Rend siphons Menaris from the well of magic, deep within Menauld."

The air around Pelagia burned white-hot now. Sweat poured down Aldewin's back.

Yngvari clasped Aldewin's hand again, and she held onto his arm for comfort. "Aldewin, what should we do? Pelagia is unstable. Her magic is pure chaos."

Dirt clumps fell from the ceiling. Timbers embedded in the earthen dome above groaned, threatening to give way.

Beneath the tumult, from deep below, Aldewin felt the thrum. The slow, persistent drumbeat of Menaris. *It is what Pelagia feels. And it is… familiar.*

Though they were on the precipice of chaos, Aldewin sought the Still Point of Menaris. In an instant, in his mind's eye, he hovered over that mirror-smooth pond, the energies of Enara and Doka feeding him. He followed the beat.

Tharump. Tharump. Tharump.

Down, down. Deep below. Something even more ancient than the dank crypt in which they stood.

Tharump. Tharump. Tharump.

It was more than an energetic pulse, like Pelagia's release of skyfire. No, it was an actual heart beating. An antediluvian vessel of life.

"Jorfala is not the Heart of Menaris," Aldewin whispered. He shook his head, clearing his mind of the trance.

Yngvari tugged at his sleeve. "What are you saying?"

He spoke louder, cutting through the rumbles and quakes. "The Heart of Menaris isn't a desiccated husk sacrificed to fuel a dark mage's magic." The amber pendant, warm against his chest, felt as though it thrummed too. He placed his hand around it. "The Heart of Menaris lives," he said. "And it is a dragon."

Chapter 25

Aldewin

Encased in a sphere of purple-white buzzing skyfire, Pelagia sent lightning energy around the suspended woman, severing the spell that had contained her. Pelagia cried, "She's alive!"

Released from the dark spell that held her, Jorfala fell to the ground. She lay in a heap, her long hair wound around her lifeless body.

Aldewin moved toward her, but Thrud pulled him back.

"There is nothing you can do. The Soul Rend infused life energy into her from the source. Pelagia severed the Soul Rend and cut Jorfala off from the life-giving source."

"Siphoning life from the dragon, you mean," Aldewin said.

Thrud nodded. "Just so. Whatever life remains within Jorfala will soon expire. I must comfort my daughter in her last moments."

Already on the spiral walkway leading upward, Yngvari waved to him. "Leave these Vay'Nada-touched curd brains to rot in this crypt. We need to find Shel, Omma, and Imbica."

At the bottom of the spiral walkway, Aldewin cast a glance back. Pelagia cradled her mother, Jorfala, in her arms. She murmured something and stroked her stringy hair.

Thrud rushed toward Jorfala. But before she reached her fallen daughter, Pelagia pulsed lightning energy at Thrud and toppled her. Her legs were wobbly, and Thrud used her cane to push up.

Pelagia screeched like a wounded animal and her face was purple from the skyfire rushing through her. Pelagia looked like a blood blister ready to pop. She thrust an arm toward her grandmother, and a shaft of lightning, pulled from the æther, skewered the elderly woman.

For a moment, Thrud stood like a statue, her eyes wide and mouth open in a silent O. She split into two halves, each falling like a toppled stone pillar.

Whatever happened next, Aldewin didn't know. He cast a ball of mage light ahead to illuminate the black passage, grabbed Yngvari's hand, and ran up the ramp as quickly as he could. When the Sea Singer fell behind, Aldewin pulled her along. He would have picked her up and carried her to safety, but he had to duck and barely fit as it was.

Magic tethered Jorfala to the dragon and siphoned magical energy to fuel the Crowskirs' power. Magical protection wards made the caverns feel like they existed separate from the outside world. Breaking the binding severed the warding spell. No longer magically protected from the outside world, sounds of chaos flooded the barrow.

"We left them in relative peace," Aldewin said. "What in Sicara's name is happening out there?"

When they'd entered the barrow, night had fallen dark. But now, as they entered the crypt's last spiral, the barrow glowed orange from fires raging outside. People screamed and yelled. Far off, the sound of clashing steel. Fires crackled, and the odor of burning grass and charred ground hit them as they neared the doorway.

Once at the threshold, Aldewin paused with Yngvari at his back. They were below the lip of the crater leading down to the cave's doorway. Above, the orange glow of fire lit the night sky.

"The dragons did this," Yngvari said. "Severing the binding on Jorfala weakened the Crowskir magic. The Crowskir's no longer control them."

Aldewin lead them up the steep incline. "I'm seeing a pattern."

"What pattern is that?" Yngvari asked.

"Humans meet a fiery end when they seek to control dragons."

When they'd entered the barrow, Omma, Imbica, and Shel had been just outside, guarded by a dozen Spindel'vara warriors and mages. But now, no one greeted them outside the barrow's door.

"Come. We must find our friends," Aldewin said.

When they reached the top of the crater's edge, Aldewin lent Yngvari a hand and pulled her up. They stood on the rise and scanned the area, seeking to make sense of the chaos.

Fires engulfed the western edge of Sofan Drek, the area closest to the barrow. Firelight illuminated the surrounding area. People scurried from Sofan Drek like rats escaping a sinking ship.

The three black dragons previously controlled by the Crowskir circled in the skies over Sofan Drek. They called to each other, and their plaintive songs reminded Aldewin of a yindril's mournful keening. The dragons had set Sofan Drek ablaze but now searched for something.

In the grassy valley below, chaos reigned. City dwellers and warriors scurried toward the southeastern hills.

"Do you think our friends escaped?" Tinged with fear, Yngvari's voice conveyed the unspoken worry that their friends had been victims of the dragon attack.

"Only one way to find out. Let's go."

Now in the grassy clearing between the barrow and Sofan Drek, Aldewin and Yngvari found their friends. It looked like Shel and the others had attempted to flee, but Spindel'vara warriors surrounded them. Brynjold and Ketla were trying to control Imbica and fight off Shel.

The ground still quaking, Imbica hurled a fiery spear at Brynjold. Ketla extinguished Imbica's spell with a burst of earth springing from the ground. Her Qüira spell swallowed Imbica's magical Vatra sword.

Ketla advanced on Imbica, her hands winding to unleash a spell. "I can do this all night."

Aldewin hunched and stepped lightly as they approached the remaining guards at the northern section of the clearing. He glanced back at Yngvari and put a finger to his lips, signaling her to tiptoe. Yngvari followed Aldewin's lead, stepping lightly and hunkered.

Fortunately, without Aldewin's weapon belts or armor, he wore nothing that clinked or clattered. Unfortunately, that meant he had no weapons. *Too bad we're not closer to shore. Yngvari could sing a wave to cast the Spindel'vara into the sea.*

Brynjold thwacked Shel across the head with the hilt of his sword as she scrapped with a guard. It spun her and likely rang her bell, but Shel remained standing.

Yngvari gasped but quickly covered her mouth to stifle her voice.

Aldewin whispered. "Shel is strong. She'll be okay." *I hope so, anyway*, he thought.

A quake shook so violently it felt like the tremors would split Menauld open. Nearly everyone toppled.

Aldewin planted himself and somehow remained standing. He took advantage of the brief upheaval and sped toward the nearest guard. The quake had disoriented the man, and Aldewin seized the advantage of surprise.

His years of Fen Menir training kicked in. Killing was instinctual. His only thoughts were of survival and protecting his pod.

Aldewin threw off the thick, fur-lined leather coat. While warm, it was too bulky for agile movement. Sneaking from behind, Aldewin grabbed the man's head in his powerful hands, twisted, and snapped the hapless fellow's neck. Aldewin caught the lifeless man in his arms, laid him to the ground, and snatched the man's spear and hunting knife.

Yngvari gasped at his cold, brutish killing. *I regret showing her this side of me.* The Sea Singer said nothing, though, and continued following Aldewin toward the remaining guards.

Aldewin and Yngvari continued moving low and stayed in the shadows as they circled wide. He again motioned for Yngvari to remain hidden, and she didn't argue.

Silently stalking, Aldewin came between the two from behind. With an upward thrust with the hunting knife, he struck the guard to his left in the neck. If he'd had his Vandu blade, the sharp dagger would have penetrated further, and the cut would have been quick and clean. The iron hunting knife, though, held an edge about as well as putty. Aldewin used brute force to shove the knife deeper and twisted. The man gasped, but his life's blood burbling in his throat extinguished his ability to scream.

Aldewin had intended a simultaneous kill. But as the warrior on his left fell, the guard to his right reached for a weapon.

Gripping the spear in both hands, Aldewin swung it upward and pierced under the man's chin. With brute force, he drove the spear through the man's skull. *It's not a technique either Fen Menir or the Pillars teach, but it works.* The man fell with a sickening thud, his legs jerking as his life ebbed.

Aldewin knelt and searched the guard for weapons they could use. He found another spear, a dull hunting knife, and dried meat and kabu stalk in a dead man's waist pouch. *The kabu will please Shel*, he thought. Aldewin stuffed the food and kabu stalk into a pocket.

Turning to pillage the guard he knifed in the neck, he found Yngvari doing just that. She handed Aldewin another spear, but he said, "Keep it and give it to Shel when we get to her. I think she could make use of it."

Noticing a dagger she'd found, Aldewin said, "I'll trade you a hunting knife for the dagger."

She handed him the dagger and continued searching the man's pockets. Yngvari shoved food and coin she'd found on the man into the small pouch at her waist. The Sea Singer moved swiftly and without a hint of disgust at picking a corpse of its valuables.

"You've done this before."

"I sailed for two years on a mercenary ship," she said. "You learn not to be squeamish about dead people. Besides, they no longer have any use for it, but we do." She kept the knife in hand as they readied to move closer to where Shel, Imbica, and Omma remained captives of Brynjold and Ketla.

Their actions had drawn attention. *No more surprise advantage,* he thought. Four men now rushed them.

"Stay behind and hidden as best you can," Aldewin said.

"Not a chance, Varskog. There are too many." Yngvari's voice revealed her worry.

Aldewin forced a wan smile and told her the truth. "I've got this."

One of the four, smaller than the others, had pulled ahead. Aldewin threw the dagger and struck the man between the eyes.

"Like the odds better now?" he asked.

Yngvari groaned. "Don't be an arse. Just come out of this alive."

He called over his shoulder, "I'll do my best." He charged the oncoming group and yelled, "Hika!"

The remaining three Spindel'vara warriors met his cry with a blood-curdling scream of their own.

Behind the approaching men, Imbica continued to fend off Ketla's attacks. But Shel stood behind Imbica, defenseless and cupping a hand to her ear. *Dammit, she's injured.*

The three men charging him were no longer people but obstacles to obliterate. Speed was his only advantage. They wore heavy leather plate armor, while Aldewin, without armor, moved more quickly. He darted past the downed man and grabbed the bloody dagger.

Fueled by worry for the safety of his friends and the still unfinished business of fulfilling his promise to Quen, Aldewin attacked with ferocity. He stowed the dagger at his waist and held the spear like a staff. They came at him with iron swords, shielding with leather bucklers.

He dodged and rolled, parried and feinted. Aldewin jabbed the spear into a soldier, sending him to the ground. As he contended with two others, he saw Yngvari inspecting a downed man's body.

"I asked you to stay hidden." Aldewin fended off a swordsman, slashing at him with the spear. He spun and stepped back, putting space between himself and his attackers.

"I'm searched for anything of use." A few moments later, she said, "Aha!"

Aldewin turned again, forcing the fight to shift so he could see what Yngvari was talking about.

Yngvari held a sword aloft like a sea maiden rising from the tide. She flung it into the air as she said, "Catch!"

While her instinct was perfection, her throwing arm needed work. She'd only sent it about five feet. Aldewin sped to where the iron sword lay in the muddy grass, scooped it up, took the buckler she held, and handed Yngvari his spear.

In relative safety at battle's edge, Yngvari held a spear in each hand, ready to defend herself. Armed with a shield and a better weapon, Aldewin spun and deflected a blow. He thrust the sword into the next opponent, dodged a spear, and ripped the sword from a man's belly. Like a charging thukna bull, Aldewin slashed his way through the remaining warriors.

Covered in the blood of men whose names he'd never know, Aldewin fell into an old habit. He whispered a prayer to Sicara as he felled each one. "Dread Sister, welcome them to the Well of Souls and the loving embrace of Night Everlasting."

Aldewin's mind reverted to a familiar rhythm. He slashed and tore through armor. Thrusting the hunting knife into a man's middle, he ripped until the steaming entrails covered his hand. Aldewin withdrew the blade, spun, and snapped the neck of a man approaching from behind. His bloodlust boiled hotter with each kill as he sang prayers to the Dread Sister.

"Sicara take you!"

More than a dozen men lay dead or dying in the field, and now, only Brynjold and Ketla remained to stop Aldewin's group from fleeing.

As Aldewin and Yngvari approached, Brynjold squared up and faced him. Ketla wound her hands, gathering Menaris.

Aldewin pointed the bloody sword at his Vandu dagger, still strapped into Brynjold's weapon belt. "You have something of mine. I intend to take it back."

Befitting his station as an upper-tier Spindel'vara warrior, Brynjold wielded a steel broadsword rather than a spear or iron weapon. The polished and finely honed blade glinted in the firelight. Brynjold glared at Aldewin. "Come and get it." He called over his shoulder to Ketla, "Leave this bitch's whelp to me. Guard the Modra and those other two."

Perhaps seeing the zeal to kill in Ketla's eyes, Brynjold added, "And don't kill them. Leid Thrud will want to pronounce her justice when she returns."

Aldewin laughed. *The world is burning down around him, yet he's still worried about "justice."*

Aldewin's mirth at the situation stoked Brynjold's ire. He shouted, "You think that's funny?"

"Look behind you, man. Your city burns, yet you're talking about justice?"

"Leid Thrud would not let Sofan Drek burn unless whatever is happening in that barrow is more important. She entrusted me with this. I'm going to do my job."

Aldewin laughed again. "Your Leid is dead, Brynjold. Dead and now buried beneath the rubble."

The expression on Brynjold's face turned from agitation to red-hot anger. He shouted, "I will kill you!"

Aldewin quickly stowed the sword and opted for the spear, holding it in both hands like a staff. He charged Brynjold and said, "Oh, I didn't kill her. But after what I saw in that cave, if Pelagia hadn't ended her, I would have."

Screaming out a throaty yell, Brynjold also charged. Aldewin swooped the spear low against Brynjold's lower legs, hoping to upend him.

Larger and more muscular than men Aldewin typically faced, Brynjold didn't topple. Aldewin rolled away, rose, and held his spear defensively to fend off Brynjold's downward slice.

Striking true and with anger-fueled power, Brynjold sliced Aldewin's spear in two. Aldewin dashed the useless weapon to the ground. He grabbed the sword in his right hand and the dagger with his left as he twirled away from Brynjold. Still a far cry from the dual-wield training of his youth, the iron dagger and crudely crafted sword felt more familiar than the spear-dagger combo.

The two men circled each other, Aldewin staying low to spring and Brynjold more upright, ready to exert force and power to win the fight. They sized each other up, and Aldewin sought weaknesses to exploit.

Brynjold quickly tired of the cat-and-mouse game. He sliced with the broadsword. Aldewin ducked and rolled, but Brynjold's sword caught him.

Fiery pain bloomed on his back. Aldewin popped up and backed away a few steps. The cut wasn't deep, but it burned. *Likely barely cutting through all the scar tissue on my back.* It should have caused him alarm, but instead, it urged him on. *Pain, you sweet old friend.*

Wearing a smile, Aldewin laughed as he again aimed low with the dagger. He stabbed Brynjold's thigh, and the dagger stuck there. Aldewin dodged to avoid another cut.

The dagger was still stuck in Brynjold's thigh, but the man was unfazed. He plucked the weapon from his flesh and chucked it away.

With Aldewin now down to a single dull-bladed iron sword, Brynjold held both the weapon and armor advantage. Aldewin wore only a linen tunic now and a leather jerkin.

Yngvari tossed a buckler to him, but Ketla set it ablaze in midair.

"Thanks for trying," Aldewin called.

"Wear him down," Shel yelled back.

He wanted to respond, "What do you think I'm doing?" Instead, he remained silent as he dodged and rolled, trying to tire Brynjold before he fatigued himself.

Aldewin landed a few cuts but not as many as Brynjold. Blood poured from a wound to his outer thigh and trickled from a slice to his shoulder. Brynjold continued his assault, though he'd finally slowed.

A low rumble thundered, and the ground quaked again. The most potent quake yet sent everyone tumbling. Brynjold pushed himself up, wiped the sweat from his eyes, and readied for another attack. Aldewin remained low and kneeling.

The *tharump, tharump* beat strong. Its pounding was so insistent it was like an uncomfortable second beat in Aldewin's chest. A sensation so like what he'd felt when near Ishna. *Could this dragon be a Primal dragon, like the Winter Dragon?* Whatever type of dragon it was, it was getting closer to busting out of its crypt.

The three fire dragons still circled over the barrow, calling and singing their dragon dirge. Menauld rumbled again, this time even louder. Brynjold's eyes widened, his mouth open in a silent "O." He stared at the hillock behind them, the one beyond which lay the dragon barrow.

Brynjold backed away, his face ashen. "Run!" he yelled to Ketla.

Aldewin didn't look behind to see what frightened Brynjold enough to flee a battle he was winning. All he thought about was retrieving his Vandu blade before he lost it forever.

He ran after Brynjold and flung himself toward him. Aldewin knocked the warrior to the ground.

As they tussled, Brynjold said, "What the fuck are you doing, curds for brains? The barrow is going to blow."

His hand finally on the hilt of the Vandu blade, Aldewin pulled it from the wonky scabbard. As Brynjold tried to push Aldewin away, the dagger tip nicked Brynjold's hand.

Only a glancing cut, normally, it would be only a nuisance. But Aldewin had "seasoned" the blade only a few days ago, awakening the deadly asperatu poison imbued in the blade over the centuries. Aldewin was only the most recent among many Vandu assassins to wield this blade.

Within a few moments, foam frothed from Brynjold's mouth. He rolled onto his back, his limbs already stiffening. He choked and tried to suck air, but inside, his lungs were hardening into a useless mass. Eyes still wide, he stared upward but breathed no more.

Aldewin stowed the blade in its scabbard, specially made to carry the deadly weapon safely. He disliked how relieved he felt to possess the dagger once again.

"Sorry, Brynjold. It was not a fitting death for a warrior such as you." Aldewin whispered his prayer to Sicara then grabbed the broadsword from Brynjold's already stiffening hands.

The fire sizzled, and he ducked, narrowly missing being set aflame by Ketla's attack. Shel held Yngvari's hand

and called to him, "Hurry!" while Imbica sent a white-hot Vatra spear at Ketla. Omma was already running toward the tree line, looking over her shoulder and calling to them to hurry.

Imbica's aim was true, and her magical weapon struck Ketla in the back. Ketla's leather armor took most of the damage, but the blow staggered her.

Val'Enara taught restraint. If Master Hrabke were here, he'd urge Aldewin to let Ketla live. Aldewin imagined him saying, "To strike a foe in the back is cowardly and is a blow born of fear. If your opponent runs, let them live another day with the shame of fleeing. That is a far worse outcome than death in an honorable fight."

Since leaving Val'Enara, Aldewin had often wondered if the Pillar's masters had ever fought in actual battle. *Honor on a battlefield? Death is death.*

Still reeling from Imbica's attack, when Ketla realized Aldewin was close enough to strike, she hadn't gathered enough Menaris energy to defend herself. Aldewin swung the broadsword with all his might. The blade was well crafted, and its edge was sharp. He landed the blow and sliced Ketla nearly in two at the waist.

The odor of her entrails assaulted him, but he didn't linger. Aldewin whispered the death prayer to Sicara as he ran to catch up with the others.

Waving him on, Imbica and Shel shouted, "Run!"

They didn't wait for him to catch up. The four women sprinted northeast toward the tree line as Menauld's fury quaked the ground.

Aldewin soon caught up as they fled the valley for the low hills. When they were nearly to the trees, the ground shuddered so hard the land was like a rug pulled from underneath them.

The fire dragons swooped, their screechy calls sending chills up Aldewin's spine. A fourth cry echoed. *The buried dragon is breaking free.*

Rock, snapped timbers, grass, and dirt from the barrow rained like a volcanic explosion.

Running a few steps ahead of Aldewin, Shel glanced back toward the exploding dragon crypt. She stopped, her mouth agape. "By the gods…"

Bathed in the glow of her skyfire armor, Pelagia trod across the valley, carrying Jorfala's desiccated body in her arms. Falling debris pinged off her magical shield as the Mistress of the Menagerie marched away from a giant crater in the ground where the mounded barrow used to be.

Above the crater rose a massive beast, its wingspan matching Vahgrin's and then some. The newly arisen dragon flapped its giant wings and hovered over the barrow. Sofan Drek still burned, and its firelight danced off the dragon's green scales.

In the distance, people screamed as they saw the dragon rise from the barrow. Aldewin and the pod did not. The four stood, struck mute and stilled by their awe at what they saw.

"The Heart of Menaris," Yngvari whispered.

Omma fell to her knees and wept. Her voice quavered with emotion. "Do you feel it?"

Shel, the only one among their group with no Menaris abilities, asked, "Feel what?" She turned to Aldewin. "What's gotten into them? We should run, no? Not pray to the damned Vay'Nada spawn."

She was right, of course. Aldewin had already come to the firm conclusion that humans and dragons together were a terrible combination. But this dragon… *This one feels different from the fire dragons,* he thought. Menaris energy pulsed from the creature.

"You don't feel that, Shel?" He couldn't help but smile. *I have never felt so—alive!*

The black dragons swooped and flew in a pattern resembling a dance in the air. They spoke Dragosi, and the verdant green dragon who'd just erupted from the grave spoke back to them. The four spiraled up and up, their wings catching dawn's first light.

Shel stamped a foot. "Dammit, tell me what's happening. Why aren't we running?" Her voice sounded panicked.

Yngvari, her cheeks wet, took Shel's hand. With the other, she pointed to the massive green dragon now circling the sky over Sofan Drek. "That dragon—she is the true Heart of Menaris. *Her* magic fuels mages—all magic—in the Vatnoyer."

"And maybe beyond," Imbica said. Her neck craned. She, too, eyed the dragons.

"I still don't get it," Shel said.

Aldewin chucked a sweaty, bloodstained arm around her shoulders and handed her the kabu he'd plucked from a man he'd cut down. "Here. Just suck on a stalk, and we'll try to figure it out later."

Pelagia had laid her mother's corpse on the ground, and she also watched the sky. But she stared to the east, not the west.

What is she looking at?

Aldewin followed the direction of her gaze. Over the eastern approach to Sofan Drek, something glimmered. Hiyadi's morning light shimmered off an iridescent white dragon, flying low.

Through the battle he'd just fought, Aldewin had remained relatively calm. Now, his heart pounded so hard he felt the blood pulsing through his neck. Sweat beaded on his forehead, and he felt like a bellows had sucked all the air from his lungs.

"What are you—" Shel stopped in midsentence and turned to see what he watched so intently. "By the gods. Is that—?"

He whispered. "Ishna."

Omma, Imbica, and Yngvari now also turned their attention to the eastern sky.

"What dragon is that?" Yngvari asked.

Aldewin's throat tight with emotion, he finally got out, "The Winter Dragon." Wiping at his eye, he said, "Quen."

CHAPTER 26

QUEN

Bird calls echo. Rocks behind and waves below.
Wake, Quen. Your vôsh'lavi awaits.
Black wings unfurl. Breath of fire. He is my love?
The black wings unfurl for me, Quen, not for you. You are thinking of Docar, my vôsh'lavi, not yours. Speak to me of your dearest one. He is a Walker. Tell me of Aldewin.
Warm breath tickles my ear. His lips so near.
Does he have arms to hold me? Or will wings enfold me?
Human arms will hold you. Tell me of your heart's desire.
Bathing in sun's last rays, shadows dance. Message sent.

Be here with me, Quen. Speak to me of your love.

Dreaming. Floating lotus. Poison roots.

Wake, dear Quen. Remember.

A Wolf amongst the Green. Running, I can't keep up. Is he still loving me?

The Varskog runs among the Green. He is your sol'dishi.

Sunlight fades. Night flowers bloom. Dreaming.

Your sol'dishi.

Memories fade like mists burned from the river by morning's first light. Does he think of me?

He strains to remember the sound of your laughter.

Dewdrops kiss morning blooms. Death gathers as edges unfurl. Does he still love me?

As Brother Suns rise to greet another day, he's still loving you.

Still loving me?

Your sol'dishi, Quen.

My soul's best friend?

With eyes like a winter sky and hair like goshi-berry blossoms in spring.

My love's eyes do not burn with flame?

Eyes alight only with the fires of love's sweet return. He wears your legacy 'round his neck.

Inside swells the rhythm of a heart I once held.

You hold it still. Below, your love awaits.

Once upon a meadow green, I received his kiss and sang his name.

Speak your lover's name.

Aldewin?

Still loving you.

Aldewin. And he still loves me?

Shall we greet your love with wings unfurled?

If only I had legs to run and lips to taste my sweet lover's wine.

There is one who knows the way. Awake, Quen, and you will love again.

Speak his name to me.

Aldewin.

Aldewin.

You still love me, Aldewin.

Chapter 27

Aldewin

Ishna's call rolled across the valley, rumbling deep in Aldewin's belly. She called a name in the Dragos language. An unfamiliar word not found in the common tongue, Aldewin was unsure what Ishna cried. But after several repetitions, Aldewin knew the name.

Veridia.

The dragons with Ishna called the name, too. Black-scaled, majestic dragons flew on either side of Ishna. Flying directly behind, a small golden-yellow dragon, flapping wildly to keep up with the larger ones. At the rear, yet another black-scaled dragon. This dragon reminded Aldewin of Vahgrin, though it didn't have a black beard as Vahgrin had.

The valley echoed with their dragon song, its notes sorrowful and exuberant at the same time. They called to the dragon who had erupted from the ancient barrow. The Dragon of Spring and Primal Wood. The dragon whose vital energy had fed human magic for over a thousand years, though people stole the magic rather than receive it as a gift freely given.

Humans called her the Heart of Menaris, but dragons knew her as Veridia.

Veridia landed in the clearing, the three black fire dragons at her sides. The Spring Dragon thrust her long neck up, her face to the sky. She shook and flung mud, dirt, and dust off her scales as she uttered a throaty cry. Her voice, scratchy and dusky from disuse, still rumbled across the valley as Ishna's had. Though she called in the dragon language, Aldewin discerned one word: Ishna.

Ishna and her companions still flew from the eastern end of Sofan Drek. As the dragons continued calling to one another, three Crowskir appeared at the southern knoll and ambled into the clearing. Soot covered their faces, and their clothes had been shredded to rags, but somehow, the three had survived the fire. They modulated their screechy voices up and down, trying to find the right pitch to Rend the dragons.

"They're going to Rend the dragons," Aldewin said. "To wear them down with pain so they can control them."

"By the Three, these Spindel'vara will torture them no longer." Imbica wound her hands, preparing to send a volley of Vatra attacks at the Crowskir women.

Omma put a hand on Imbica's shoulder. "Do not waste your energy, Mage Imbica. The Crowskir held only tenuous sway over the three young fire dragons, taking all the Crowskir and Thrud singing their Rend. These three alone cannot Rend the Heart of Menaris."

"And no need to call the dragons' attention our way," Shel added.

Imbica dropped her arms.

The largest of the three black dragons, the one Thrud had called Vingaska, opened his maw. Steam rolled from his mouth, and he drew back his head, ready to spew fire on the approaching Crowskir.

But the Spring Dragon lashed him with her tail, halting his attack.

"Why would she stop him from defending them against those horrid Crowskir?" Yngvari asked.

Before they could guess, spindly roots erupted from the ground around the three elderly women. Woody brown roots tangled their long hair and wrapped around their legs then dragged the women to where the dragons stood.

Panicked, the Crowskir screeched their Rend, the only defense against the dragons' power. Their voices were like broken bells flung into a well, clanging and catching as they tumbled.

The roots wound around them, tighter and tighter. Soon, a shroud of woody lattice encased and bound each Crowskir.

Veridia pulled the three cocooned women into her wings. Her neck still stretched upward, her face to the sky, Veridia held the encased Crowskir close to her chest. Their screams soon faded.

"Is she smothering them?" Shel asked.

Aldewin closed his eyes and concentrated on touching the Green—feeling the life force of plants and seeds yet to unfurl.

Nearby, life energy emanated from his companions. Omma's energy radiated exceptionally bright and active, throbbing in time with the subtle pulse of energy ever-present in the ground beneath them. *Omma touches the Green as well.*

"The dragon's attack on the Crowskir has a purpose, doesn't it, Varskog?" Omma said.

And she senses me touching the Green.

"I don't think dragons do anything without purpose," he said.

Aldewin opened his eyes and watched as Veridia unfolded her wings. The three woody casings that had bound the Crowskir toppled to the ground. They shattered open, the spindly roots turning to dust. Once the roots disintegrated, they revealed that nothing of the Crowskir remained save for withered husks shriveled inside their clothes.

"She fed on them," Aldewin said.

Though the millennias' grime still covered Veridia's body, her yellow-green eyes shone brighter. She called again to the dragons approaching from the east. Her deep, husky voice still lacked the strong timbre he'd heard from other dragons, but it was less scratchy now as she called, "Eeee-shh-naaaah!"

Aldewin stared, his attention rapt, as Ishna landed in the clearing. Her body had filled out since he'd last seen her, and she looked more robust and confident. His heartbeat picked up pace, and his palms got clammy.

He wrapped a hand around the pendant. It warmed to his touch as it always did, but it now pulsed. The sensation was subtle but undoubtedly there. *Somewhere within that enormous scaly body, Quen still exists. She lives, I know it.*

Without conscious intention, he began walking down the rise toward Ishna.

Shel grabbed at his arm, holding him back. "Suda, Aldewin. Stop! You'll get yourself killed. That giant green dragon may be the Heart of Menaris, but she's clearly famished and will suck your life, too, just like she did those Crowskir."

Maybe Shel was right. Within, he admitted to himself that his desire to rush to the dragons was irrational. All he could say, though, was, "Quen."

Shel's alarmed look gave way to a wan smile. "I know you want to push Pelagia to do what she promised. To see if that bark-scarred skishatur can really bring Quen back. But look around, man. There are eight fuckin' dragons in this valley, and they all look hungry."

His other three companions talked simultaneously, all on Shel's side. When he tried to speak, they'd cut him off, all trying to set him straight and convince him to abandon his plan to parlay with Ishna.

Over their chatter, a voice called to him. "Aldewin, do not think I have forgotten my promise," Pelagia said.

She strode toward them, her body outlined in the crackling purple-tinged skyfire aura that had become a permanent feature. Caked in mud and dirt, her hair sooty and ash covered, Pelagia looked like she'd been in the barrow nearly as long as Veridia.

Shel stepped in front of Yngvari. Reaching for her bow before remembering that the Spindel'vara had taken it, she pulled a knife from her belt and held it ready. "Slither under the rock you came from and leave us be."

With a slight flick of her wrist, Pelagia rolled her eyes and sent Shel's knife out of her hand. "That's the only warning I'll give you, girl. Pull a weapon on me again, and it will be the last thing you do." She continued marching up the hill toward them.

Shel whispered under her breath, "Suda, I want to get pished and forget about all this shite."

Aldewin couldn't agree more. *But I still have a job to do.* "Leave Shel and my companions be, and I will come with you."

Pelagia stopped, regarded him for a moment, and then laughed. "You all still think I'm interested in any of you? I came for the Heart of Menaris, not to be a Dynasty bounty hunter. Isn't that your line of work, Imbica?"

Imbica began speaking, and Pelagia's aura grew. Fiery tendrils pulsed off her. Behind him, Aldewin heard Shel stomp her foot onto Imbica's, a low "Oof," and Imbica went silent.

The desire to wipe the smirk from Pelagia's face was intense. *Not that I have the power to do that.* "You promised to help me restore Quen to human form." He pointed to Ishna, now by Veridia, their foreheads touching, standing like giant dragon statues. "There she is. Somewhere inside that white dragon, Quen still exists. So how can you create a human body *and* coax a soul from a dragon?"

"Oh, *I* will not create a human body." She pointed at Aldewin. "You will."

Imbica tittered. "Feh. Aldewin? Create a body? From what, Pelagia? Grass and air? No offense, Aldewin."

"None taken." Imbica had made all the points Aldewin was thinking. *Even after weeks of practice, I can barely touch the Green.* The more he thought about it, the more he realized the idea of magically creating a new body for

Quen—*and* somehow transferring her life essence into it—was… *Madness.*

Love can render one mad. Crazy enough to tread to the world's end, searching for a miracle.

Imbica added, "Even Zeniths at Val'Enara could not achieve this miracle you claim Aldewin can perform."

"You studied at two Pillars, Imbica, yet know little more than when you left the granary." Pelagia swept her arms, taking in the dragon reunion below. "This—this is miraculous, no? And it has nothing to do with your Pillar magic." She thumped her chest. "Nor does this. Yet I am here, and it was no intervention by so-called gods or a miracle."

"Vay'Nada touches the weave that brought you back from death," Omma said. "You practically reek with the stench of the Void." She touched a soft, warm hand to Aldewin's arm. "The lad does not want to dabble in shadow weaves."

How do you know? Aldewin thought.

As if seeing the doubt on his face, Pelagia's smirk became a smile. She gave him a nod. "Such a spell requires a sacrifice."

Aldewin tsked. "If you think I'm going to offer one of my friends—"

"I did not say it must be a human sacrifice."

"Well, I'm not sacrificing an animal either." Aldewin ran a hand through his dirty, ash-covered hair. "I didn't risk my life at sea, traipse halfway across the fuckin' world, fight my way through Spindel'vara warriors just to have some tea and a chat with you."

"Of course not." Pelagia's voice dripped sweetness like honeyed goshi-berry wine.

That he'd gone through all he had only to leave without the *only* thing he desired left Aldewin feeling exhausted and defeated. "Look, I've done—things. Horrid things. I admit to that." He sighed. "But having spent time, albeit brief, in the shadow's realm, I cannot live with the taint of Vay'Nada on my soul. I will leave this glen alone if that is what it takes."

Pelagia cackled. "You should have been a mummer, Aldewin. So melodramatic."

Quen said that to me once too. The thought might have been funny if his mood wasn't so far south as to be the butt-end of Volenex.

Pelagia's voice turned stern, now without false sweetness or sarcasm. "You *must* be the one to weave this spell, Aldewin, because you are the only one whom Quen trusts. She gifted you that piece of her." Pelagia pointed to the amber pendant. "It holds more magic within than you know."

His hand instinctively wrapped around it, guarding it from her dark gaze.

"Yes, that you must part with. And to it, you will add the sacrifice. If not a person, then an object that you hold dear." Her gaze pierced him as if she saw to his very soul. "There is something, isn't there? A thing which has been a part of you for so long, it's like an appendage?"

One hand still held the pendant, and the other grabbed the hilt of his prized dagger. His heart raced again, and sweat beaded on his upper lip.

"You wove yourself into the Dreaming, Varskog. You made your deepest desires known," Pelagia said.

"No one invited you to the Dreaming," Omma hissed.

Aldewin's head throbbed as he considered the ramifications of what Pelagia said. Ensnared in a sticky web—again. *Dammit, how can I escape these damnable spinners and their snares?*

Acting like she was bored now with the conversation, Pelagia picked mud from beneath a fingernail. "I go where I want." Her voice went pitchy and sounded urgent. "It's simple, Varskog. Sacrifice the damned blade." She spun and hastened to the clearing where the dragons gathered.

It should have been a straightforward decision. A blade for the return of his lover. For the restoration of Rhoji, Liodhan, and Zarate's sister. Aunt to wee Lumina and friend to Shel and others.

This should not be difficult. Why am I not running after her, offering the blade as a sacrifice?

But Aldewin knew why. Imbued with the essence of all assassins who'd ever wielded it, the Vandu gave Aldewin an uncanny edge in a fight. It guided his hand, and whispered the Dread Sister's prayer in his ear. *If I sacrifice the Vandu to bring Quen back into this life, will its magic transfer to her?*

"Don't trust Pelagia," Yngvari said. "Even before dark magic pulled her back from Vay'Nada's shadowed shores, Pelagia was a snake. She slithers and waits to strike as suits her purpose."

Shel added, "She literally wears snake skins, Aldewin. Listen to Yngvari. Even if Pelagia's magic works, she does not reveal the price she'll expect of you—"

"Or of Quen," Imbica added.

Shel nodded. "Exactly. Mark my words. Pelagia's help comes with strings attached."

Aldewin knew what they said was true. He'd lived within Fen Menir's shadowy walls for nearly half his life. Snakes? He'd been raised by them.

Taking Shel's hand, he asked, "If it was Eira—if that loony woman promised to restore him—would you not sell your soul to Vay'Nada for the chance to get him back?" His throat tight, he squeaked out, "It's Quen."

Shel said, "Suda, Aldewin." She wiped at her eye. "I would do it for someone I love." Shel gave Yngvari's hand a squeeze. "Well then, what are you waiting for?"

"He's waiting to decide if he can truly part with the piece of himself that holds him together," Imbica said.

"Varskog thinks it keeps him tethered," Omma added.

Aldewin's palm warmed the blade's onyx hilt. "We don't speak of the trials endured to claim the right to wield the Vandu dagger." Undoing the catch on the scabbard, he pulled out the blade and inspected it in the burgeoning morning light. "Such ugliness encased within an object of great beauty."

"Perhaps it is time to leave the ugliness behind," Imbica said.

In an instant that stretched to eternity and back, Aldewin's dark life flitted like a dream replayed. Of nights spent cold, alone, and naked. Retching and wishing for death that wouldn't come. Fiery tendrils of pain snaked through every sinew and fiber of his being, burning and etching him anew. A man nearly impervious to poisons and wielding a tool that would send many to the Dread Sister's open arms. He rarely knew their names or why the order had come for him to snuff out their candle. But he recalled each one. Details of clothing, a scent in the air, the glow of candles on the pale corpse were etched permanently in his mind.

Yngvari placed her thin hand on his shoulder. "You must release Timonay for good."

"Timonay?" Shel asked.

"I'll tell you later," Yngvari whispered.

"No one ever tells me anything." Shel also placed a hand on Aldewin's arm. "Whoever the shite Timonay is, let the fucker go if it helps you."

They all laughed, and Omma squeezed his hand gently in hers. "You can let Timonay go, Varskog. The wolf will remain. You can call on him whenever you need to, but you don't have to live his life anymore."

Her emerald-green eyes bored into him. Aldewin felt like he was in the Dreaming, though he knew he wasn't. Touched by the spirit of the Green, a golden aura surrounded Omma. Aldewin glanced down at her hand and realized he radiated golden too.

"It has always been there, Aldewin," she whispered.

"Don't ask me how I know this because I can't explain it. But I'll need your help—" Aldewin pointed to Omma, Imbica, and Yngvari. "All of you."

They each nodded.

To Shel, he said, "And I'll need you there for moral support."

Shel nodded and said, "Of course."

They sped down the hill and met up with Pelagia. She stood at the bottom of the rise but removed from the dragons.

Ishna and Veridia still stood like stone, their foreheads against each other, while the four dragons Ishna arrived with spoke in the dragon tongue with the three black fire dragons the Spindel'vara had held captive. There was much tail thumping, at times so vigorous that it shook the ground. Yet the two Primal dragons remained motionless, like they'd entered a realm where time stood still.

When they reached Pelagia, Aldewin said, "I am ready. Tell me what you have in mind."

Pelagia stared intently at the two Primal dragons. "You have a connection to the Winter Dragon. I suggest you be the first to approach. Hopefully, she will recognize you and not harm you."

An image of Ishna freezing Nevara solid in midair came to mind. *The Nixan dragomancer was a vile woman, but gods, seeing her splinter into a million frozen shards…*

In the Dreaming, he'd felt Quen. Knowing she still existed—somewhere—had motivated him to keep going. *Is she here now?*

Moving into stillness, he closed his eyes and sought the gentle pulse of Menauld and the thrumming lifeblood of the root, vine, and seed. Once attuned to it, he allowed the feeling of Menaris to take him.

Now, with the Spring Dragon nearby, finding the pulse of life was far easier. He listened… *there.* Thump… then a faint tharump. Thump… tharump. "She is here," he whispered.

Without speaking more with his friends or Pelagia, Aldewin slowly edged forward, approaching Ishna with caution. He stowed his dagger, not wanting the sight of it to alarm the dragons. Aldewin wrapped his hand around the amber pendant again and pictured Quen in his mind's eye, trying his best to form a mental image of her while feeling his heart racing with the urge to flee yet forcing himself forward.

Slowly, as if frozen in time now thawing, Ishna turned away from Veridia. Blinking her enormous eyes, one icy blue and the other amber-yellow, she finally said, "Ahlll-doooo-eeen."

Relief flooded Aldewin. *She recognizes me.*

He sped up and approached as she spoke to the dragons in their language. *Perhaps she's telling them not to burn me to a cinder or freeze me into an Aldewin-cicle.*

Once he was within a few feet of her, Ishna repeated his name and bent her long neck toward him. With a gentleness belying her great size, Ishna placed her forehead against his.

He did not hear her words in his mind or receive any form of communication from the dragon. But without leaving that clearing, he smelled the foggy meadow where he and Quen had lain together, heard the rush of water over a nearby waterfall, felt the cool ground beneath them, and tasted the sweetness of her lips on his.

"Quen," he whispered. "We believe we have a way to bring you back. To restore you to human form."

Ishna pulled her head away from his and gave him a single nod. She spoke then, and though she attempted to speak the human common tongue, it came out garbled.

She shifted and attempted to speak Soligian, the ancient tongue of the pillars. Perhaps more closely related to Dragosi, and with its emphasis on vowels, Soligian was more manageable for Ishna. But Aldewin's Soligian was amateur at best. *Languages are not my forte.*

He called to Imbica. "I need your help to translate."

Imbica approached slowly, her eyes never leaving Ishna's. "I do not speak Dragosi, Aldewin."

"No, but you are fluent in Soligian. Can you understand what Ishna is saying?"

Apparently understanding why he'd called Imbica over, Ishna repeated herself, slowly and with more emphasis this time.

With great concentration, Imbica listened intently. Finally, she said, "Some sounds are difficult for Ishna to pronounce. As best I can surmise, Ishna said, 'Quen is in love with seeing you.' Hmm, probably meant, 'Quen loves seeing you.'"

Quen is *still a presence within her*. He could barely breathe. "Is that it?"

"No, but be patient. I'm trying to piece it together. She also said, 'The Winter Dragon…' Hmm, what did she mean? I think she meant 'approves.' Yes, that must be it. She approves whatever that means to you."

"She means we can proceed with our plan. Tell her we need help from someone Quen won't approve of, but she has skills no one else has. Tell her not to attack this woman because we need her."

Pushing sweat-matted hair from her forehead, Imbica said, "That's a lot of words." She paused for a moment then began speaking.

It took several minutes for the exchange between them. Ishna had difficulty conveying her meaning in a foreign language she seldom used. Imbica asked for clarification several times, but finally, she said simply, "She understands."

"That was an awful lot of talking to end with two words for me."

Imbica shrugged. "Do you want me to leave this to you?"

He ignored the question and called to Pelagia and the others. "You can approach." Then he added, "But I'd do it slowly. And try to be as nonthreatening as possible."

"Not a simple task for Pelagia," Imbica whispered.

Though what Imbica said was true, Pelagia had experience dealing with wild beasts. Pelagia still glowed with an aura of skyfire and glided toward the dragons, her gait steady, measured, and controlled. She kept her head tilted down, her eyes averted from direct gaze, and her hands slightly away from her body, palms facing forward. Pelagia was the image of nonthreatening.

Images can deceive.

Though Pelagia had made no moves that should alarm the previously relaxed dragons, Veridia reared her head back, nostrils flaring. The three black fire dragons behind her did the same, their tails lashing.

"Imbica, ask Ishna to tell them not to harm Pelagia."

"Ask them to go against their instincts, you mean." Imbica glared back at Pelagia but spoke to Ishna again in Soligian.

Ishna must have understood well enough because she spoke now in the dragon tongue, her words full of long vowels, hard consonants, and clicks. Veridia said something back. Then, the largest of the three black dragons behind Veridia spoke. Veridia lashed him with her tail, and he stepped back, cowed.

I wish I knew what happened there.

Pelagia sauntered up and, to Aldewin's surprise, bowed first to Veridia, then to Ishna. To his even greater surprise, she spoke in the dragon language, or at least an attempt at it.

Whatever she said, it didn't appear to impress either dragon. They both stared at her and said nothing.

Pelagia rose from her bow, and her face fell. She had clearly expected to receive a favorable outcome from her attempt to parlay with the dragons in their language. She quickly recovered, however, and returned her demeanor to her typical haughty superiority.

"Since you have established a rapport with the Winter Dragon, perhaps, Imbica, you could translate?" Pelagia asked.

Asking for help from Imbica must be killing her inside.

"For you? No."

Pelagia began a protest, but Imbica held up a hand to stop her. "I *will* attempt to intermediate between you and the Winter Dragon, but only because it will aid Quen. Always remember, Mistress of the Menagerie, where my allegiance lies."

Imbica has proven her loyalty many times throughout this journey. I should question her allegiance no longer.

"Yes, yes. Allegiances." Pelagia waved a hand in the air. "Tell the Winter Dragon that Aldewin will perform the spell required to create a suitable body for Quen and that I will assist him in his endeavor."

Imbica began translating into Soligian, but Pelagia interrupted her. "But tell her, and this is important, Aldewin needs Veridia's help. He cannot do this without the Spring Dragon."

Rolling her eyes, Imbica called for her to halt. "Slow down. Allow me time to translate one bit before you barrage me with more."

Imbica began the tedious process of translating Pelagia's plan. She patiently waited for Ishna to repeat the words in the dragon tongue then painstakingly focused on Ishna's responses. Solidifying the plan with the dragons took nearly an hour, and Aldewin became increasingly anxious about whether it could work.

Finally, Imbica pronounced the dragons ready. To Aldewin, she said, "Veridia understands your intended outcome and agrees to aid you. She said something about it being like creating a dragon hatchling. Whatever that means. They seem quite confident that with the aid of the Primal dragons, you can actually create a human body."

The news bolstered Aldewin's confidence.

Imbica turned to Pelagia and said, "They also understand this plan hinges on Pelagia's abilities. Power linked to Vay'Nada. They are unhappy with this. There was much back and forth between Veridia and Ishna over it."

"But they agree to go forward?" Aldewin asked.

Imbica nodded. "They do." She hesitated. "You need to understand this. Working with the dragon subjects both the plan and Pelagia to risk."

"How so?" Pelagia asked.

"If Veridia senses a dark intent toward Quen, Ishna, or any dragon, the dragons will destroy you." Imbica turned to Aldewin. "Even if that means losing Quen."

"I see. Well, we knew the idea was risky." Aldewin fidgeted. "I wish I could speak to Quen. To know she consents to this. I mean, it's her existence at stake. Does Quen desire to live as a human again?" He chuckled and looked up at Ishna. "Living inside such a magnificent and powerful body—are we sure she wants to give that up? And potentially risk being lost entirely."

The thought of it was too much to bear, so he pushed it aside.

Imbica smiled warmly at him. "I asked those questions."

"You did? I mean, good. Then, hopefully, we have the answers."

"Quen most assuredly consents to this plan, Aldewin. At least that's what Ishna says." Imbica glanced up at the Winter Dragon. "I suppose she could be lying, but I don't believe she is." Imbica's face scrunched, and she bit her lip, clearly hesitating.

"What is it?" Aldewin asked.

"I hesitate to tell you this, as it might put a distraction in your path when you need full concentration—"

"Then do not speak it, Imbica," Pelagia said. "Aldewin needs every ounce of magical ability he possesses. This spell will require him to weave elemental threads like no mage has ever attempted. Why tell him something distracting now?"

"Suda, I can't *not* know it now." Aldewin waved his hand in a rolling motion. "Go ahead, Imbica. Spill it."

She sucked a deep breath and sighed. "Quen is with us. Of that, I am certain. But she is… fading."

"Fading?" Pelagia asked.

"What does that mean?" Aldewin asked.

"It means that Quen holds on to existence by the thinnest thread. And if this plan fails, we'll most assuredly lose her because she's barely there as it is."

Imbica wrung her hands, her eyes red and wet with unspent tears. She looked up at Aldewin, gazing directly into his eyes. "Pour every ounce of yourself into this weave, Aldewin. Quen's life depends on it."

Chapter 28

Aldewin

They wasted no time commencing the ritual to create a suitable body for Quen and transfer her vital essence from Ishna. All the humans present, including Pelagia, cleared the dead bodies from the center of the clearing.

"The stench of death lingers here," Omma observed.

Yngvari whispered to Shel, "Or is that just Pelagia?"

Ishna spoke to the dragons, and they formed a wide circle around the central area. With her back facing east, Veridia spread her wings and basked in her first sun in over a thousand years. Ishna stood opposite Veridia, her lips upturned into what looked like a smile. The majestic black dragon stood next to Ishna, their wings touching.

Aldewin sensed the two were intimate. Anger toward the black dragon rose in him, jealousy for the privilege of intimacy with the dragon that harbored Quen's soul. As soon as the emotion rose, he chided himself. *He is the dragon's lover, not Quen's.*

Pelagia stepped to the center of the circle of dragons and spoke words of power in a language Aldewin didn't recognize. *She does not speak Soligian, the language of the Pillars.* Nor was it the dragon language or the common tongue. Pelagia's crackling aura grew, and skyfire pulsed from her in gigantic waves.

Several of the dragons reared their heads, and a few stepped back. *I don't blame them,* Aldewin thought. Pelagia's ability to manipulate inherently chaotic lightning energy was unnatural and unnerving, even for magical beings or people.

Pelagia strode in a small circle then crisscrossed the area while chanting her incantation. After several minutes, the ground crackled like she did. A circle at the center of their gathering shone purple-white, and sparks of lightning sprang from the ground Pelagia had consecrated.

Once complete, Pelagia said, "Place the Vandu blade in the center. The gods will either accept your offering or reject it."

"How do I enter the circle without injury?" he asked.

Omma answered, "Weave a spell of protection around yourself. What counters skyfire?"

Aldewin should have known the answer immediately. It was the sort of thing the Masters of Val'Enara drilled into students. But his anxious mind felt like a crazed kopek in a dust storm.

Uncharacteristically free of superiority or judgment, Imbica said, "Qüira, Aldewin. Ground yourself with earth, and the skyfire will not singe you."

Of course. Aldewin nodded and concentrated on calling to himself the essential nature of earth. Of soil and rock and all things which form Menauld.

With Veridia's boost of Menaris energy flowing to him, Aldewin wove spells more quickly and with less effort than before. Those gifted with Menaris abilities could see the swirling grey, brown, white, and black bands of his protection weave flowing and swirling around him as he walked into the consecrated circle.

"Do I just lay it on the ground?" Aldewin asked.

"Yes, do it!" Pelagia said, her voice impatient.

"But is there an incantation I must speak or a special spell to weave?"

Her voice was thin and impatient, as if crafting human bodies from daggers and pendants was something mages did regularly. "Ask for blessings from the god or spirit whose favor you won to gain the blade."

Aldewin hastened to the center of the skyfire circle. He called upon the Dread Sister, and under his breath, he whispered. "Sicara, hear me. I offer you the object I have held most dear, gifted to me by passing your trials of death. This blade is imbued with the essence of the man I was but can no longer be. Take this boon for yourself and free me of its burden."

His hand shook as he placed the Vandu dagger in the center of Pelagia's consecrated ground. Aldewin stepped out of the circle and continued focusing on the offering, whispering prayers to the Dread Sister and waiting. Silence had descended despite the crowd of dragons and people gathered. The only sound was the crackling ground.

After several moments, the soil beneath the blade shifted. Dirt bubbled underneath the dagger, looking like a creature below had pushed dirt out of its hole. Soon, a small mound of earth encased the Vandu blade. After a few moments, the mound and dagger were gone. A small patch of disturbed soil was the only evidence of what had happened.

Pelagia's voice was ragged. "Hurry, Varskog. Your gods are with you and have accepted the offering. Place the pendant on the same spot where you put the dagger. The necklace will form the foundation to build the body anew."

Aldewin rushed back to the center of the circle. He untied the leather cord, singed from dragon fire in Solia. It likely still held oils from Santu, ground into the leather from years of wear. Aldewin's chest tightened, and he gripped the amber tightly. He held the key to Quen's life, both a burden and a blessing. He didn't want to let it go.

What if the pendant is the last I will know of her?

The talisman had seen him through these months from Volenex to now. A touchstone that guided him like the light that shone from Quen's eyes, urging him to follow Lumine's light the way no Master at Val'Enara had ever inspired him.

I have searched for a god or institution to place my faith in my whole life. Finally, I found it in you, Quen. If I lose you…

From behind, as if through a warbly bubble of water-speak, Pelagia called. "Place it now, Varskog. Before the moment is gone."

Aldewin kissed the amber then gently laid the pendant on the recently disturbed ground. He whispered his prayer. "Within this pendant lives the memory of Quen. Child of Santu Inzo Dakon di Sulmére and Suliam Vindiére di Vindaô. Sister of Liodhan and Rhoji, aunt to Lumina, and a friend to many. I call on the gods and spirits that dwell in this glen to bring forth a human vessel worthy of receiving the vital essence of Quen Tomo Santu di Sulmére, my sol'dishi and forever master of my heart."

He paused only momentarily then stepped away from the crackling circle again. As soon as he did, Pelagia called forth a new command.

"Weave now, Varskog, like you never have before. Pour yourself into the spell."

Aldewin released the protective spell he'd cast and called forth instead the energies of the Green. Veridia's heartbeat, the steady thrum of the Vatnoyer Province, rippled through the glen. The Spring Dragon's magical energy coursed through his body setting his hair on end, and energizing him. With his hands thrust toward the circle, Aldewin called upon the roots to create a cocoon to hold the work of the spell.

From the ground sprang tender shoots, supple roots of green and pale yellow. These new-growth roots wove themselves around and encased the amber pendant much as Veridia's roots had encased the cursed Crowskir women. But Aldewin's roots did not wither and desiccate but remained green and vibrant.

The Green had accepted the pendant and awaited his command, but Aldewin faltered. *I don't know what to do.*

Omma must have sensed that he flagged. "Commune with the Green, Varskog. As you did on our journey when you healed me. Skogi knows what to do. Listen to her."

While still unsure of his next steps, Aldewin did as Omma suggested. He sought the Still Waters of the glassy pond. In his mind's eye, he floated above water and rested on roots. At peace with the skog and naturfrandi, Aldewin wove a spell of water and root, of vine and life.

With closed eyes, he couldn't see what happened in the consecrated circle. But in this stated of heightened awareness, he didn't need eyes to see.

The world crackled with Menaris energy as if millions of fireflies lit everything from within. Roots beneath him connected to the roots encircling the pendant, and the encasement grew and swelled.

Within this small cocoon, waters of life swirled. The vision reminded him of Hooxaura's glistening orb. He quickly let the thought go lest it distract him from the focus required to continue the weave.

With all the feeling he could muster, Aldewin reached out to Ishna. He asked the Winter Dragon, carrier of the energies of Primal Water, to lend her power to the growing orb of Enara—the elixir of life.

She didn't speak aloud, but he felt her response. The pulse in the ground beneath them surged, and the swirling, watery orb grew.

Aldewin didn't think but relied on intuition and acted with feeling. He listened to the wisdom of the Green, and it told him to seek the help of Veridia, the Spring Dragon.

As he'd done with Ishna, Aldewin called to Veridia through the roots. In his mind's eye, Aldewin pictured what he intended and asked the Spring Dragon for aid.

And as it had been with Ishna, the roots pulsed again but more energetically. Aldewin was a conduit, a spoke through which Ishna and Veridia's vital energies flowed.

His pulse was rapid now, and sweat poured from him. Body shaking, he was unsure how long he could hold the weave. "It's so—powerful," he croaked.

From somewhere beyond the bubble of Menaris energies which contained him, someone shouted, "Help him!"

New energies flowed into him—buoyed him. Like a warm hug, he recognized Omma's loving touch. Her magic flowed through the roots easily, like an old friend they'd known for a long time. She healed the damage his body was taking from accepting the unbridled power from the dragons.

Now, a second flow. This one was riding a current woven of water, quenching the heat and tamping down the fires that raged in him. It was Yngvari, and he was grateful for the Sea Singer's help.

And now a third weave. The fiery passion for battle and life that was Vatra hit him like a jolt of potent kabu stalk. Imbica's deft magical weave lent him Vatra's robust stimulating energy without immolating him. Aldewin was thankful for the much-needed boost.

Having regained stamina, Aldewin continued weaving his creation spell. The pendant was like a seed within the cocoon, appearing dormant, as seeds often do. But fueled by Primal dragon magic, the pendant shattered and life burst forth from it. Germinating the initial life spark was the most intricate aspect of the weave.

From somewhere, someone shouted, "It's working!"

Time stretched unending, backward and forward. Water and earth. Fire and wood. All swirled in a bath of life. Pelagia continued feeding skyfire into the circle and fueled the spell. *From the chaos springs something new.*

Ready to sprout, Aldewin called upon the energies of the Spring Dragon. He asked the roots for renewal and rebirth. For growth like fresh shoots. For bone and blood, for skin and hair.

Again, as if warbling to him across the vacuum of Vay'Nada, a woman yelled, "It's growing!"

He'd kept his eyes closed to aid his concentration, but he opened them now.

The sight he beheld shocked him and nearly halted the process.

Before him, the circle held a swirling oblong of water like a giant egg of Enara energy, held aloft by a nest of intertwined roots and vines. The watery egg glowed from the purple-white skyfire Pelagia poured into it.

And within the watery wonder, a person curled into a ball like a babe sleeping. But this was no baby or even a wee child.

A fully grown human floated in the churning mass of magical energy. A woman. Long, dark hair twirling in the water partially obscured her body.

She looks so peaceful.

But something was missing. The body was there, but it was an empty vessel. Merely a sack of bones and flesh, missing what made a living thing alive.

"It is time," he heard someone say and realized he had spoken. His voice was thin and raspy.

Omma called to him again. "This part is for you alone, Aldewin. Reach out to Quen. Call her forth from the dragon. Your love will guide Quen back into this world."

As before, he didn't know what to do. He didn't speak the dragon language, so he could not talk directly to Ishna. *But you aren't speaking to the dragon, anyway.*

"Think on her," Imbica said.

I am. It's all I do.

He concentrated and refocused. Eyes closed again, easing himself away from the others. Leaving behind the world of flesh. Traveling the ways of the Green. Listening to the heart of Menauld. The gentle pulse of life buzzing ever and always and all around him.

Tharump… thump.

There you are!

Faint, like the sound of a butterfly's wings, he heard her.

"Remember," she said.

Every moment from when he first laid eyes on her to the instant she shattered and each second in between, Aldewin allowed himself to relive it all. The shape of her eyes, the tilt of her nose. The way she smelled of her father's tobacco and sunshine. Her laugh when Shel told a joke and her crinkled brow when Rhoji goaded her.

Quen.

How web-weaver Kine had sent him to retrieve Quen for a still unknown purpose. Aldewin wanted to kiss Quen's wine-stained lips. The pain of longing. The anguish of regret at pushing her away when he wanted only to enfold her in his arms. To take Quen far from palaces and pillars.

Far away, you and I.

"Quen."

Of the one blissful evening and morning spent in a meadow at a mountain's base. Of soft ground and welcoming kisses, of waterfalls and the spring's new grass.

Memories of the one time in his entire gods-forsaken life of death and following orders and being beholden to vows made to gods he never truly believed in out of fear and need and…

One moment among the many hoary, hairy nights filled with the ever-loving stench of self-loathing, among the countless days and nights alone.

A singular word spoken from her lips, sealing him into the only vow that would ever matter.

"Sol'dishi," she'd said.

My heart's dearest friend.

He whispered words, though whether he spoke them aloud or only in his mind, he'd never know. With every fiber of his being, Aldewin called to her. "Come back to me, Quen. Be with me again, my sol'dishi."

Menauld's pulse quickened. The drumbeat of his heart raced like the thunder of a herd galloping to water's sweet promise.

Aldewin's head felt like a vise was squashing it. He heard the Winter Dragon now, and though they didn't speak the same language, he understood her thoughts.

You must leave my body now, Quen.

I don't know how.

Follow your feelings. Aldewin... he awaits you.

My body... I don't have one of my own, remember?

By his love and with the aid of your sa'gamlin, they created one. You, Quen, are made anew.

Both the dragon and Quen went silent. Aldewin's body convulsed, and he sensed Ishna's agony as Quen's soul vibrated with the intense desire to be free of its caged existence inside the body of another.

Goodbye, Quen Tomo Santu. Go to him and rejoice. Today is your birthday.

Then, both outside himself and inside his mind, silence. The moment stretched like honey taffy, pulled taut to the point of breaking…

Pop!

The beat of her heart. The thump that had beckoned and soothed. Gone.

His eyes still closed, afraid to look…

Gasps.

Water soaking his feet.

A shriek and Shel's voice. "Quen?"

A deep breath. *Open your eyes.*

Curled into a ball, back to him, a woman. Still and lying inside a singed circle that once crackled with skyfire.

Seconds before, exhausted and nearly collapsed, now, he ran to her. Still and unmoving. *Please, gods, if any there be. Don't let all this be for naught. Do not let her be lost.*

Arms beneath her, Aldewin scooped the woman from the sodden ground. At first, he feared she was dead if she had, in fact, ever harbored the spark of life.

But she turned toward him, and her eyes blinked.

She stared up at him, searching, her eyes still bleary, as if waking from an overly long sleep. Eyes not bicolored as

Quen's had been but brown. As morning's glow lit her face, Aldewin felt like he was staring into Rhoji's eyes.

"Quen?" he asked.

Her voice was weak, but she said, "Aldewin."

Quen's voice. The one he'd dreamed of and longed to hear.

Aldewin cradled Quen close and planted a light kiss on her wet forehead. "Sol'dishi," he said.

Chapter 29

Ishna

Searing pain between her eyes brought Ishna to the ground. The thrum in her skull, present since the day of her rebirth at Volenex, shook her now so violently that Ishna feared her head would erupt. Quen, the human soul enmeshed with her own, quaked and shrieked for release.

Docar screamed for the Two-Legged woman the humans called Pelagia to end the ritual, but Ishna lashed him with her tail.

"It is… working," she said.

At the center of their dragon circle, a watery orb floated. Inside, an empty shell awaited a soul. *It is an egg awaiting vital essence,* Ishna thought.

Ishna's body quaked as the ground beneath them did. Her vision was bleary, and she saw as if through murky water. Ishna's ears buzzed as if infested by a million insects.

Ishna feared she would, after more than three thousand years, meet her ultimate end.

Finally… peace.

Silence, so fervently desired, descended on the entire glen. The ever-present vibration of the human soul she had carried ceased. The phantom thump of a second heartbeat… gone.

Pain no longer bent Ishna low. She rose, straightened, and held her head high. Her mind had not been this clear since before she was reborn at Volenex.

The human dwells in me no more, Ishna thought to her sister, Veridia. *But will she live?*

After several moments, Veridia thought back to her. *Her Two-Legged friend weaves a tight spell, and with the aid of the other Walkers, he is an apt conduit for receiving my magic. He will survive, and she is reborn.*

Aldewin dashed to the form inside the watery egg. Docar, who had been at Ishna's side through the entire ritual, wrapped a wing around Ishna. Côzhili nuzzled her head into Ishna's neck, and they pressed their foreheads together. Loxen cheered. And Aurixia, at Veridia's wingtip, flapped and hopped excitedly.

The joy of her dragonkin was not for the rebirth of the human known as Quen but for Ishna's release from the burden of housing the human soul. Though Ishna had told only Docar of the difficulty Quen had created for her, Côzhili and Loxen had flown into enough battles with Ishna to know that she had not been her old self.

Aldewin scooped Quen into his arms. Relief flooded Ishna when she saw Quen's eyes open.

He recognizes her, and she knows him, Ishna thought. *All is well, then. Quen will once again know the love of her vôsh and reunite with the sa'gamlin who support her.*

Aldewin carried the wet and still-limp body of the newly reborn Quen to the Two-Leggeds who had gathered. They wrapped her in warm skins Walkers wore to protect their fragile bodies. The one Quen had called Pelagia—the woman who harnessed skyfire—was not with the other humans.

Perhaps the energy she harvested consumed her. All the better. Vay'Nada touches that one, and good never comes from Two-Leggeds dancing with the Shadow.

The larger sun was now well up in the eastern sky, and the morning dawned crisp. Sunlight had already vaporized the night's fog and dew. *A new day dawns, too, for dragonkin.*

Eager to greet her sister again, Ishna ran toward Veridia.

When she was halfway across the circle, near where Quen had been reborn, the skies above them grew dark. Thunder rumbled the glen, and skyfire scorched the ground. It looked like bolts of purple-white fire came from the sky above and the ground below.

Only moments before, Ishna had enjoyed the much-longed-for peace of a clear mind. Now, her skull again vibrated. Voices warbled, and through bleary eyes, she saw Veridia calling to her, but she could not discern what her sister said.

Fiery tendrils of white-hot flame licked through her from snout to tail. Skyfire blazed in her blood.

Agony again sent her reeling. Ishna screeched, unable to even form words. Her head thrashed, and her body convulsed.

Veridia ran to her from the east as Docar moved toward her from the west. But before either reached Ishna, Pelagia appeared in the circle. Her arms outstretched toward Ishna, she spoke in an approximation of Dragosi.

"Do not interfere, Dragos, or I will call down my skyfire and destroy every dragon here," Pelagia said.

Sounds warbled as if Ishna was underwater. Movement from behind. *Is that Docar priming his weapon?* She tried to call out to him—to plead for him to heed the woman's warning. Her throat was dry and made raw by the skyfire coursing through her, and Ishna's voice came out merely as a scratchy screech.

Pelagia thrust an arm toward Moxprai, the smallest of the three Ignati faction dragons the Crowskir women had held captive. Purple-white skyfire energy rose from the ground beneath Moxprai while a bolt of blue-white lightning shot down from above and speared the fire dragon.

Moxprai writhed, his eyes wide and rolling. But the Dragos, strong as his egg-father Vahgrin created him to be, pushed up and stood on trembling legs, defiant.

Still immobilizing Ishna with her torture, Pelagia called another jolt of lightning from above. This second bolt, even brighter and broader than the last, again pierced into Moxprai, sending him to the ground.

Her head whipped from side to side from the pain of Pelagia's attack, and the scene in the glen flashed before Ishna. Docar, Côzhili, Aurixia, and the rest of her dragonkin screeched and called. Veridia rushed to Moxprai's side while Docar and Loxen ran toward Ishna.

Aldewin, still cradling Quen in his arms, screamed at Pelagia to cease her attack. Quen, her hair still wet and partially obstructing her face, trembled, her cheeks wet with tears. Quen's friend, Shel, nocked an arrow and shot it at Pelagia, but the yindril-fueled dark mage shielded herself. Shel's arrows burst into flames when they met Pelagia's shield.

Pelagia brought yet another bolt of skyfire into Moxprai. "I can do this all day and to every dragon here," Pelagia called out in Dragosi. She repeated the phrase in the language of the Two-Leggeds.

Despite her warning, Loxen and Docar unleashed their fiery attack. Fire blazed toward Pelagia from two directions, and the dragonkin did not hold back. Docar and Loxen assailed the Two-Legged woman with everything they had. Their barrage of fire would normally incinerate a human immediately and burn the ground so hot it would melt rock and make sand into glass.

But the mage's shield held firm and repelled their attack. Safely ensconced within her energetic cage of protection, Pelagia's lips curled into an ugly sneer.

Though she remained unharmed, Pelagia punished the dragons for not heeding her warning. She raised one thin, pale arm high then brought it down with a swift stroke. A massive jolt of lightning speared Moxprai, splitting him nearly in two.

His body, now lifeless, sizzled and steamed as his warm innards met the cool morning air.

Pelagia, eyes wide and wild, screamed out to Ishna. "Tell your dragon friends to back off, Ishna, or each of them will meet the same end as Moxprai."

Fiery tendrils still threaded their way through every fiber of Ishna's body. She tried to fly, but her wings were useless, dead appendages, and her magic was dampened by Pelagia's torture.

Though her throat remained dry and raw, Ishna attempted to hurl an icy spear at Pelagia. But the skyfire coursing through Ishna evaporated her frozen breath before it could escape her mouth. All she managed was a steamy breath.

By what magic does this mere human overpower me? She does not sing the Rend, nor does her spirit possess me. Yet somehow, this Two-Legged has a hold on my Primal soul.

Ishna finally spoke aloud one word. "How?"

Still enshrouded in a protective cage, Pelagia held out a hand. She opened her hand, revealing two small golden cuffs. "Remember these? Your friend Quen once wore a pair like them."

Quen screamed out, "No!" But in her anguish, Ishna could not discern whether the cry was a memory from their shared past or one of the first words uttered by the newly reborn Quen.

The bark-scarred woman bent nearer, the smell of her rot assaulting Ishna's sensitive senses. "I never released that binding, you see. But the foci I used live now within you, Ishna. And the spell still answers to me."

Ishna tried to concentrate—to remember all that had happened to Quen while at the Menagerie and, later, at Volenex. Living as a sequestered spirit within Quen, Ishna only had fleeting glimpses of what Quen lived through.

And Pelagia's magic-fueled torture further sundered Ishna's ability to recall. Her memories were like splinters of shattered glass.

But she focused as best she could, recalling the moment at Volenex when she came forth into her new dragon body. To remember the day of her second birth.

When Ishna sprang forth from Quen's body, she devoured Quen. The nourishment fueled her reentry into the world. All that Quen had been subsumed into Ishna and remained with her now.

As if sensing the realization dawning on Ishna, Pelagia moved closer and spoke in a low voice only Ishna could hear. "That's right, Ishna. With the magic of a yindril's heart fueling my power, even the mighty Winter Dragon cannot resist me. Command your friends and kin to yield. I am only interested in you. The rest can fly away if they leave you to me."

Surrender was not in the nature of Ignati faction dragonkin like Loxen. And Ishna knew Docar would rather die fighting than voluntarily leave his vôsh'lavi in the hands of a Two-Legged.

Ishna croaked, "Goes against our nature."

Her vision growing dark, sounds warbled as if coming through a tunnel. Ishna felt like she was again leaving the living plane of existence. She had spent a third of her soul's life in the cold void of Vay'Nada.

Not again…

She closed her eyes and pulled within herself to marshal her last reserves. Ishna screamed, "Stop!"

Though she spoke the word in Dragosi, the Two-Leggeds seemed to understand. Save for the crackle of skyfire energy emanating from Pelagia, the glen was once again quiet.

Her head now resting on the cold ground, her eyes landed on Moxprai's lifeless face. *I cannot abide another death among my dragonkin today. Not when we, at long last, have Veridia back and the chance for a new Urixos. Veridia is the lifeblood of dragonkin. She is more critical than I am to the survival of dragonkin.*

Ishna tried to mind-speak these ideas to Veridia but was unsure if her sister received her thoughts. Ishna gathered strength once again and called out in Dragosi. "Do not attack this Two-Legged, sa'gamlin. I will go with her."

Docar yelled, "No!" and again spewed flames at Pelagia. But the yindril-fueled shield held and repelled Docar's assault.

The other dragonkin also screeched and hollered their disapproval.

But Veridia thumped the ground hard enough to shake the glen. She bellowed, "Cease, dragonkin." Once they settled, the Spring Dragon said, "Your leader has commanded you, sa'gamlin. Remember the words of Zedris. Respect or perish."

Ishna sighed with relief. *Veridia will guide them. My dragonkin and my vôsh'lavi will survive to fly another day.*

For over two thousand years, Ishna had fended off attempts to control her by both Walkers and Rajani who wielded the Rend. Not since the Jik'Madar and the wars of the old world had Ishna been debased by a Two-Legged sitting astride her shoulders, using her as a mount. *Except for Aldewin, but I allowed that.*

But now, her head bent low, her neck on the ground in supplication, Ishna signaled her defeat. Like a black ocean of tar bubbling in the Phisma pits, memories of debasement washed over her.

Pelagia grabbed a handful of Ishna's snowy-white hair and hoisted herself onto the Winter Dragon's shoulders. Ishna had never desired to devour a Two-Legged the way she longed to rip Pelagia apart, limb by limb, to draw out the woman's suffering.

Someday, I shall savor the sweet tang of her blood and the satisfying crunch of her bones.

After months of Quen's reproaches at Ishna's plans for violence against Walkers, the silence within her was odd. She had longed to finally be alone in her own mind but now wished for a companion as she stepped into a daunting unknown.

Now that Ishna had offered herself in supplication, Pelagia eased up on her torture. Though the searing pain throughout her body ceased, the insistent and mind-numbing thrum once again pained her head. Thoughts entered her mind, unbidden and unwanted, intrusive, persistent, and nagging thoughts.

Against her will, Ishna rose on trembling legs.

"Good," Pelagia whispered in Dragosi to Ishna. Pelagia said to the gathered dragonkin and humans, "Even the mighty Winter Dragon heeds my command. Remember what you witnessed here today. Soon, all Indrasi will bow as the Winter Dragon has."

Veridia spoke to Ishna's mind. *"Do not despair, sa'gamlin. Her defilement is a temporary setback. She will meet the end of all Two-Leggeds who seek to harness the power of dragonkin. As we ended the Two-Legged reign over us in the Drowned World, so shall we end this vile woman."*

Veridia's thoughts comforted Ishna's mind, but her soul, perhaps imprinted with Quen's echo, shuddered at the implication. After all, to end Walker tyranny over dragons, Zedris had to break the old world.

For the sake of Quen and her human kin, I hope we find another way this time.

"To wing," Pelagia commanded Ishna in Dragosi.

Now that Pelagia had eased her torture, Ishna pulled on the power of water and ice energy from the world around her and recharged. Ishna still trembled and felt weak, but she rose into the sky.

Ishna thought to Veridia, *"Tell Docar not to do anything rash and to not worry about me. This Two-Legged needs me, so she will not kill me."*

Veridia thought back to her, *"We will break the chains that bind you, sa'gamlin. We must find a way."*

"Free Vahgrin. And seek Zedris. You will need the united power of Spring, Summer, and Autumn to overpower the Two-Legged who commands the will of the Winter Dragon."

"Yes, my sister," Veridia thought to her.

"To liberate me from this vile Walker, dragonkin may need assistance from Two-Leggeds. You can trust Quen, Aldewin, and their sa'gamlin."

Veridia was silent. Ishna feared that after what the vile Walkers had done to her, Veridia could never trust Two-Leggeds again.

"You must trust me, Veridia. Quen and Aldewin will not help other Walkers imprison or control us. Please assure me that if you need help only a Walker can give, you will seek them out."

Finally, Veridia thought back to her, *"You have my Dragos vow, sister."*

Ishna hovered over the scorched circle from which Quen rose anew. Soaring above the land where she lost control of her life again.

Festering wounds of ancient conflicts made Ishna want to shout the dragon battle cry so that it thundered across the Two-Leggeds' lands below. But Pelagia understood Dragosi, so Ishna instead repeated the wisdom of her brother Zedris, the Autumn Dragon.

Ishna said, "To exist is to remain, sa'gamlin. For eternity, my vôsh'lavi."

Pelagia jolted Ishna with skyfire, a painful prod and a reminder that the Two-Legged had control of her. "To Indrasi," Pelagia shouted.

The End of Book Two

GLOSSARY

asperatu—(*as-per-AH-too*): A poison used on the grooves carved into Vandu daggers.

Aurixia—(*aur-IHX-ee-ah*): A hatchling of the Primal Wood dragon. She is golden-scaled with green eyes. She is the youngest dragon, born only a decade before the Dø'bedri (see below).

Avlox Mountains—(*AV-lahx*): The mountain pass between the two highest peaks in the Staket mountain range on the continent of Tinox.

Bardivia—(*bar-DIHV-ee-ah*): The capital of the Vindaô Province in Indrasi. City where Quen and Rhoji were born and where their father, Santu, was the Consular (chief administrator).

bodir—(*BOH-deer*): Word for birth father in the Vatnoyer. Bodir specifically means genetic or birth father. The word "father" refers to the man or men who raised you, and could be someone other than biological father.

Brynjold—(*BRIN-yohld*): A warrior for the Spindel'vara Clan.

Cantiva Faction—(*can-TEEV-ah*): A dragon faction formed by Veridia, Primal Wood dragon. Cantiva translates loosely as "Heart of the Dragon." This is the largest and most social dragon faction.

Coterie (of dragons)—(*KOH-tuh-ree*): A small group of dragons, especially in the context of battle or a war party.

Crowskir—(CROH-skeer): "Crow Mother." Crowskir are the shamans, wise women, and seers of the northern clans of the Vatnoyer Province on the continent of Tinox. Crowskir and Modra (see below) are nearly identical in their duties, though Crowskir, as the name implies, have the crow as their animal guide and do not use the flygesroom for visions. Crowskir are seers of the now, while Modras are seers of possible futures.

Dô'bedri—(doh-BEHD-ree): A Dragos word that roughly translates as "long sleep" in the common tongue. It refers to the nearly thousand-year hibernation of all dragon kin after Ishna was killed by Indrasian at the dawn of the Kovan Dynasty.

Docar—(doh-CAR): A hatchling of Vahgrin, the Primal Fire dragon. Docar's scales are red-tinged black, and his skin black. His eyes are orange. Though he is a fire dragon, he's social and belongs to Cantiva faction. Ishna's lover and very loyal to her.

Doj'Enara Bay—(dohzh-ehn-AIR-ah): "Blessed Waters" Bay. A large, crescent-shaped bay south of Bardivia. The primary trading port, Mourigi, sits at the mouth of the bay.

Doma di Consular (aka "The Doma")—(DOH-mah dee CAHN-soo-lar): The Consular's home in Bardivia. The city-state of Bardivia owns the compound, and thus, technically, the Bardivian people own the Doma. It is solely occupied by the Consular, his family, and a small cadre of administrative assistants. Though the Doma is a stately walled compound with a sprawling villa-style home and lush gardens, it's not as palatial as the Palace di Soli in Qülla.

Dragosi—(drag-OH-see): The dragon language.

Dragos Teplo—(DRAG-ohs TEHP-loh): The Age of Dragons.

The Dreaming*:* What the Modra call their time experiencing visions and seeing possible futures. Most Modra can attain a Dreaming without the aid of flygesroom vapors, but such visions are shorter and not as layered with meaning. When Modras use the flygesroom, especially when they enter the Dreaming collectively, the visions are powerful and more fully formed, like entering a vivid dream. They see possible futures of the Myrskog clans.

Enar'atori—*(ehn-ar-ah-TOR-ee):* Soligian (language used by the Pillars) word for "Sea Singer." Mages from Tinox, usually women, who command the sea and, to some extent, the skies (i.e. call storms and lightning). Yngvari (see below) is one of the most powerful Enar'atori.

Engarda—*(ehn-GUARD-ah):* Navy; military or police sailors.

Eldurskir—*(EHL-dur-skeer):* "Elder Council." The name for the elder council that each clan of the Myrskog have. Each Eldurskir has the Modra of that clan as their spiritual leader and guide. The rest of the Eldurskir is composed of men and women of the clan, generally people who are in their middle years or older and nominated by the clan. They meet as needed to discuss the business of the clan or are called to special meetings if something significant happens. They are like the lawmakers, judges, and enforcers, though the "laws" are few and "punishment" generally unnecessary. The Myrskog is a land of abundance, and its people live in harmony with the natural world, seen as a gift from their patron deity, Skogi. The Eldurskir mediate disagreements between neighbors, merchants and customers, or even amongst families or bonded couples.

Eldisvat—*(EHL-dihz-vaht):* "Fire Waters." A town in the Iska'kog that is the hub for the Tradsmikor Clan.

Fen Menir—*(fehn- MEN-eer):* The house of assassins in spies in Partha. One of the seven Mājas (noble houses/consortiums) in Partha.

flygesroom—*(FLIHG-ehs-room):* "Flying mushroom." In appearance, similar to a chanterelle mushroom, with a floppy, golden cap and underside gills tapering to the stem. Flygesroom are highly toxic to eat, but Modras distill the mushroom's liquid and simmer it to produce a powerful neurotropic that is used to achieve a state known as The Dreaming.

Like yindrils, some flygesroom can uproot themselves at will. They flap their cap and take to the air. They will land on animals or people passing by and hitch a ride. Seeing flygesroom fly *en masse* is a wondrous sight, but rare.

Fréjoya—*(fray-JOY-ah):* In the Vatnoyer (both Myrskog and Iska'kog), Fréjoya is the patron goddess of water and ice and ruler of the water element. This contrasts with people of Indrasi who follow Vaya di Soli who believe that Lumine, the moon, is the goddess of Enara (water element).

Fros'vinspri—*(FRAHS-vihn-spree):* Embodied by the giant snow tigers of the region, what the clans of the Iska'kog (the northern Vatnoyer Province) call the spirit of the mountains and of snow and ice.

Fyrstua—*(feer-STOO-ah):* Translates as "First People." Refers to all people native to the Vatnoyer Province in Tinox.

goshi berry wine—*(GOH-shee):* A sweet wine made from goshi berries, a fruit that grows wild in the forests of the Myrskog region in the Vatnoyer Province. The berries look similar to the raspberry/strawberry/blackberry family. Goshi taste like a combination of blackberry and raspberry. The fruity wine is smooth and clean tasting, lacking the yeasty or brioche notes of Earth wines made from grapes.

Green: In the Myrskog, the "Green" encompasses a religion, philosophy, and a way of life. Presided over by the patron deity Skogi (see below), people who follow the "Way of the Green" revere all life, and believe it is their moral duty to protect the "naturfrandi," or plants and creatures of the Myrskog.

helja—*(hehl-YAH):* An exclamation. A combination of the words "hell" and "yes," and is an exclamation of approval.

Hepeilgur—*(HEP-eel-ghur):* A member of the Tradsmikor Clan.

hustaig tree—*(HUE-stayg):* Giant trees in the Myrskog in which people make their dwellings by carving wide holes in the trunk of the tree's spongy interior.

Ignati Faction—*(ihg-NOT-ee):* Translates loosely as "Fiery." An ancient Dragos faction formed by Vahgrin. Originally a war battalion, most members scattered after the Jik'Madar (see below). After Jik'Madar, Ignati faction is now a loose association of solitary dragons. Ignati faction gathers infrequently.

Iska'kog—*(IHSKA-kahg):* The region and peoples of the northern Vatnoyer Province (from north of the Ghost Forest to the northern coast of Tinox).

Iska'van Faction—*(IHSKAH-van):* A dragon cohort created by Ishna. Iska is the root word for "ice" and "van" is water. Thus, this is the "icy water" faction. Like Ignati Faction, originally formed as a battle battalion. However, after Jik'Madar, Iska'van Faction did not disband and remained a social faction of mostly Water elemental dragons.

Jik'Madar—(ZHIHK-mah-dar): A Dragosi word that translates as "the Breaking." Refers to the time of cataclysm in the Old World, aka the "Drowned World," where dragons originated.

Jorfala—(jor-FAH-lah): Pelagia's mother and Thrud ag Isabré's daughter.

Kāfe'vind Clan—(kayfah-VIHND): The "Choke-Vine Clan." A clan in the Myrskog region of the Vatnoyer Province. Once the largest clans in the Myrskog, two years ago this clan was raided by the Dynasty with the help of the Tradsmikor Clan. Though their numbers have dwindled, they are still leaders in the Myrskog region and protect the southern coastal area of the Vatnoyer.

Kinswood Road: The main "road" cutting north and south through the Vatnoyer. Less a road and more a wide trail.

Kor Man'tol—(KOR man-TOHL): The Dragosi word for the westernmost island in the Xathi Tol'galen island chain to the east of Tinox.

Kovatha—(koh-VAH-thah): Agents of the Kovan Dynasty. Originally palace guards and tax collectors, in the last decade, the Dynasty has recruited Pillar-trained mages into the Kovatha ranks and sent them out across Indrasi to become an extended arm of the Dynasty. Kovathas are now replacing the former duties of Jagaru as peacekeepers, roving judges, and legal enforcers. Their increasingly coercive measures have sowed unrest across the continent, especially in the Vindaô Province.

Leid—(LEED): Leaders in the Vatnoyer. Similar to a Mayor.

Lievby Village—*(LEHV-bee):* Settlement of the Kāfe'vind Clan and largest settlement in the Myrskog.

Linjeera—*(lihn-JEER-ah):* A junior member of the *Sicara's Bane* crew. She mans one of the crow's nests.

Lít Council—*(LEET):* In dragon culture, a small advisory council within Nao Faction.

Menaris—*(mehn-AIR-ihs):* Human magic.

mizan bark—*(MEYE-zan):* Smooth bark from the mizan tree. With the medicinal property of killing bacteria, people chew the bark in the morning to freshen their breath. Can also be brewed into a tea and used for stomach problems caused by "infestations."

modir—*(MOH-deer):* A term used in the Vatnoyer Province. Like bodir, modir connotes the woman from whose womb a child is born. Mother is a more general term and can refer to a woman who raised a child but is not their birth mother, or to women that are mother figures.

Modra—*(MOH-drah):* "Moth Mother." Modra are the shamans, wise women, healers, and seers of the Myrskog clans. Each clan has a Modra. Like Bruxia's of the Sulmére, Modra's pass their wisdom from woman to woman in an unbroken chain. The Modra are more magical, though, than Bruxia, and have powerful visions both with and without the help of the flygesroom vapors. No man has ever been a Modra, or "touched by the moth." Men can, however, be healers via herbal lore and such. But men lack the "sight" that Modra have and are considered lacking the patience for wisdom to come as it does to Modra—in its own good time.

Mourigi—(MOHR-ee-ghee): A seedy, coastal town on the southern outskirts of Bardivia. A center of sailing on the western coast of Indrasi.

Moxprai—(MAHX-pray): The smallest and youngest of the three fire dragons controlled by the Crowskir at Sofan Drek.

Mundaré Province—(muhn-DAR-ay): A province in Tinox, east of the Staket Mountains, south of Nacostis Province, and north of Bacio di Mar Province. The second largest province by area (after the Vatnoyer). Mundaré is known for its agriculture and mostly grows grains and rice, though the southernmost region also grows fruits. While Bardivia and the Vindaô Province supply Menauld with olives, grapes, wine, nuts, honey, dates, figs, and other warm-weather goods and foods, Mundaré is the "bread basket" of Menauld.

Myrskog—(MEER-skahg): The region and peoples of the lower (southern) Vatnoyer Province, including the coastal region, marshes, and boreal forests west of the Staket mountains and south and east of the taiga forests.

Nacostis Province—(nah-COHST-ihs): The northeastern most province in Tinox. The region east of the Staket Mountains, and north of Mundaré Province. Sparsely populated, dry, and cold. Mostly known for mining ores necessary to forge steel, copper, brass. Most of the ores in Partha and Indrasi come from this region.

Nalija—(nah–LEE–ah): Yngvari's younger sister. Also an Enar'atori (Sea Singer). A member of the Kāfe'vind clan of the Fyrstua people in the Myrskog region of the Vatnoyer Province.

Nao Faction—(NOW): An ancient dragon faction created by Zedris, the Autumn and Primal Earth dragon. The Dragosi word "Nao" translates roughly as "wisdom." A faction dedicated to maintaining dragon history and the philosophers and thinkers of dragon culture.

naturfrandi—*(nat-uhr-FROND-ee):* A word in the Myrskog region that translates as "nature friends," and refers to all living things. Myrskog people do not view their rights to live as being superior to the rights of naturfrandi.

Nox'Kili!—*(nox-kihl-EE):* A dragon war cry. Translates loosely as "show no mercy."

Orju Crest—*(OR-zhoo):* The hill in Bardivia that is the nobility district. The Consular's home, Doma di Consular, sits atop this hill. It's the highest point in Bardivia and has a commanding view west to the Orju Sea.

sa'gamlin—*(sah-GAM-lihn):* A Dragosi word that roughly translates as "dearest friend."

Shills: In the city of Partha, the seedy area near the docks were the poor live.

shock *(of dragons):* A large group of dragons, particularly in battle. Smaller than a battalion, but larger than a squadron or coterie.

Sicara—(sih-KAR-ah): Also known as the "Dread Sister," the goddess of death to the people of Partha. Sicara is the patron god of Fen Menir, the house of assassins and spies in Partha.

skishatur—*(skish-AH-tur):* A derogatory word used in the Vatnoyer region. Translates roughly as "shit eater."

skog—*(SKAHG):* root word for "wood" or more generally plants and all living things other than animals. On Earth, the term we might use is the Latin 'flora,' as opposed to 'fauna.' For people of the Myrskog region, though, its meaning is more than a label. For the Clans of the Myrskog, 'skog' is life itself, and revered.

Skogi—*(SKAH-ghee):* The patron deity of the Myrskog people and goddess of the wood or the Green as some call it. Though they recognize several gods, goddesses, and spirits in the region, for people of the Myrskog, Skogi is the main deity they revere.

Sofan Drek—*(soh-FAHN drehk):* A large settlement in the northwestern portion of the Iska'kog lands in the Vatnoyer Province, Tinox, and largest city in the region. Hub for the Spindel'vara Clan.

Spindel'vara Clan—*(spihn-dl VAIR-ah):* Translates as "Web Weaver's Clan." This large and historically prosperous clan is the northernmost clan in the Vatnoyer Province. They are also one of the oldest continuously operating clan units in the world. Spindel'vara's hub is the town of Sofan Drek on the northwestern coast of Vatnoyer Province. Pelagia, aka Mistress of the Menagerie, is originally from Spindel'vara, and her grandmother, Thrud, is the current matriarch of the clan.

Staket Mountains—*(sta-KEHT):* The mountain chain in Tinox that separates the eastern portion from the west. Most of the northern portion of these mountains are above the treeline, while the southern portion is lower and covered in alpine forests. Much geothermal activity on the western side, with geysers, hot-springs, and sulfuric pools. This mountain chain is part of the ridge that goes from southern Indrasi all the way to the polar regions.

tanxia—*(tan-ZHEE-ah):* A bitter tea made from bark. A morning pick-me-up, similar to coffee.

Thrud ag Isabré—*(THROOD-ag-ihs-AH-bray)*: Pelagia's grandmother (and mother to Jorfala). A Crowskir and Leid of the Spindel'vara Clan. She lives in and governs from Sofan Drek.

Tinsalo—*(tihn-SAH-loh)*: A noted scholar from Partha, with Maja Artifexa. He is known for his work cataloging history, lineages, and information about the Vatnoyer Province.

Tradsmikor—*(TRADZ-mih-kor)*: A clan in the Iska'kog region of the Vatnoyer Province. Translates as "Angry Earth." As guides and warriors, this clan has helped Māja Wix (in Partha) and the Kovan Dynasty to plunder magical resources from the Vatnoyer, all while making plenty of enemies among both Myrskog clans and Iska'kog clans.

Two-Legged: How dragons refer to humans. They also refer to humans as 'walkers.'

Urixos—*(yur-ihx-OHS)*: A Dragosi word. Translates as "Golden Time." Refers to the time after the Jik'Madar (the Breaking) when dragons lived without control by Rajani or humans.

Varskog—*(VAR-skahg)*: "Wolf in the Wood." Omma, the Modra of Kāfe'vind Clan, calls Aldewin "Varskog," and refers to him as the Wolf. The term 'wolf' is metaphorical, not literal. Aldewin doesn't turn into a wolf. 'Varskog' instead encompasses Aldewin's two opposing aspects—one is the assassin/predator, and the other is the healer.

Vatnoyer—*(vat-NOY-yur)*: Western province in Tinox. Stretches from the western side of the Staket mountains to the western archipelago. Divided roughly north to south by the Ghost Forest, with the southern region known as the Myrskog, and the northern region as the Iska'kog. As a derogatory term, people in Partha refer to the Vatnoyer Province as the "Vats."

Veidmar Clan—*(VEYED-mar):* A clan in the Myrskog region of Vatnoyer Province, Tinox.

Vingaska—*(vihn-GAH-skah):* The largest of the three fire dragons controlled by the Crowskir at Sofan Drek in Spindel'vara territory.

vôsh'lavi—*(vohsh-LAH-vee):* In Dragosi, a term of endearment that roughly translates to "soul friend that ignites passion for the hunt in my heart." This is reserved for intimate relationships, as opposed to friends or egg-kin (the term for which is sa'gamlin).

Walker—What dragons call humans (also known as Two-Legged).

Warrior's Rest—A saddle in the Avlox Mountains.

Xathi Tol'galen—*(ZA-thee TOHL-gahl-ehn):* The Dragosi name for the group of subarctic islands that humans in Tinox refer to as the Bídean Archipelago.

Yngvari—*(ihng-VAR-ee):* A Sea Singer (Enar'atori) from the Myrskog region of the Vatnoyer Province, Tinox.

Zedris—*(ZEHD-rihs):* The Autumn Dragon and dragon of Primal earth.

Acknowledgments

Thank you first and foremost to readers and fans of the Dragos Primeri series. Your generous support inspires me to continue writing this epic saga. Writing from the dragon point of view proved more challenging than I imagined! But once I found the "voice" of Ishna, writing from her perspective became a joy. And when the writing got tough, interactions with readers helped me push through. Thank you readers!

Thank you Red Adept Editing, including beta reader Rashida and proof reading by Kim.

Thank you Braken for the beautiful cover art and for the "secret" cover painting, and to Streetlight Graphics for cover design.

Thank you to Jo of Bookish.by.jo for design and execution of the sprayed edges, and to Leraynne and Kate for the character portraits for the overlays. A huge thanks to Rian at Aesoterik for creating the amazing maps.

Thank you to Tessa at StarCandy.co for creating the gorgeous portrait pin of Veridia, the Spring Dragon, and to Tanya at Castle Door Wax Melts for creating the signature scent for *The Spring Dragon*.

Thank you to Robyn Dabney, my sa'gamlin, for your support. Thank you Jennifer and Donnie Ivan for the generous use of your home for my private writing retreat. And as always, thank you to Felix, my muse and raison d'écrire.

To my vôsh'lavi, JRF, you are not only my soul's mate, but my alpha reader and plot designing buddy. I truly cannot write this series without you, sol'dishi.

About the Author

You will find author Natalie Wright ensconced in her dark academia writing den, crafting the next installment of her epic Dragos Primeri series. Her debut epic fantasy, *Season of the Dragon*, was named a Top 10 Indie Epic Fantasy by Bookshop.org and Ingram. She's eager to reveal more of  Dragos Primeri's expansive world and characters to readers.

Natalie's intricate worldbuilding and unique characters stem from her lifelong love of fantastical fiction. When she's not writing, she's likely immersed in a sci-fi or fantasy book, movie, series, or open-world RPG. She lives in Arizona with her husband and two cats, and frequently visits her son in NYC.

A regular at Sci-Fi & Fantasy conventions, book festivals, and signing events, you can find Natalie's tour schedule and order special editions of her books at www.NatalieWrightAuthor.com.